I0675515

This is a work of fiction. Names, characters, places, and incidents are products of the author's imagination or are used fictitiously and are not to be construed as real. Any resemblance to actual events, locales, organizations or persons, living or dead, is entirely coincidental.

©2013 Tuundu Publishers

Brampton, Ontario

www.tuundupublishers.com

ISBN 978-0-9918487-0-6

DEDICATION

In memory of Mum Bernadette
and
Grandma Janet

ACKNOWLEDGEMENTS

I wish to thank my editor, Elizabeth Phinney, for the dedication and the many hours of hard work she put into this book; my wife, Sarah, for the moral support and for preparing the daily bag lunch; my children, Jesse, Stephanie, and Jerry, for their patience as I spent hours away from them to write this story; and a special thank-you to my father, Edward, who expressed his joy when he learned that this book was in progress—his dream of writing has been fulfilled through me.

CHAPTER ONE
Toronto, Canada, June 2012

As he waited in line to order his lunch, Makula Musoke overheard a conversation between three women who had a copy of the *Toronto Star* spread out on their table. They were talking about the story of renowned financial adviser and TV personality Pietro Monterissi who had, two days earlier, filed for bankruptcy.

"Isn't this an example of a doctor who prescribes medication to his patients but fails to take his own dose for the same ailment?" one of the women said, causing all three to break out in laughter.

"I couldn't have put it better myself," thought Makula, who was hearing about Monterissi's bankruptcy for the first time. "This man advised me just months ago to put my finances in order, yet he was in the same situation as I was."

"Next," the young man behind the counter said, but Makula, lost in thought, did not respond.

The man who was standing behind him in the line said, "Excuse me, but it's your turn to order."

Makula quickly ordered his favourite combo—a Double Whopper, large fries, and a soft drink. When it was ready, he carried his tray to the condiments station to get mustard and ketchup, and then sat down at an empty table. He had just started to eat his burger when his phone rang. "Hey, Mak, how are you doing?" his friend Nicholas Wabudi asked.

"I could be better, Nick. Right now everything seems to be going wrong in my life," Makula answered.

"Have you seen today's *Informed Pages*?" Wabudi asked.

"Informed pages? No. What's that?" Makula replied.

"You don't know what *Informed Pages* is?" Wabudi asked. "It's John Kabenge's tabloid."

"No, I don't know it," Makula said. "Is it online?"

"Yes, it's online but they have a paper version in Kampala," Wabudi told him.

"Is there something in it that you wanted me to read?" Makula asked. His heart began to pound as he wondered what John Kabenge was up to now.

"Yes," Wabudi said. "There's a story about people who abandon their well-paid jobs in Africa for menial jobs in the developed world."

"Oh," Makula said, his heart pounding even faster.

"Unfortunately, he used a picture of you at work to illustrate the story," Wabudi told him.

"What? What kind of picture?" Makula asked.

"It appears that you were carrying a big box that you were about to load into the trunk of a car for a customer," Wabudi said. "You can Google informedpages.com. You will see both the story and the picture.

Makula accessed informedpages.com on his iPhone and found the photo. He remembered that occasion, just three weeks earlier. He had carried a boxed flat-screen TV for a friendly female customer across the street, and then loaded it into the trunk of her car. The woman had given him a ten-dollar bill as a tip. The picture showed him carrying a big box as he walked behind a very well dressed woman.

As he looked at the picture, Makula regretted not disguising himself or at least wearing a hat to conceal his face before he had helped her with the box. But he hadn't known that somebody was going to take a picture of him. Makula then began to wonder if the whole scenario had been planned. He remembered wondering at the time why the customer had not parked in the store's free parking lot but had instead parked across the street in the pay-to-park lot.

He put his phone back into his pocket and finished his burger and fries. His phone rang again. It was his friend Chris Luku.

"Hey, Mak. Nick just called me to tell me about your picture in *Informed Pages*. Have you seen it?" Luku asked.

"Yes, Chris," Makula said. "I've seen it, but I don't want to get too upset about it. Let them write whatever they want; they can't bring me down."

"Isn't it so annoying, though?" Luku said. "I love technology. I love phone cameras and their many benefits. But then there's their ugly side. These days I think we should always be aware that somebody could be photographing or filming us wherever we are. It's pretty scary. Are you at home?"

"No, I'm at the Burger King," Makula said.

"Oh great, I'm actually on my way there. If you want to wait for me, we could have a chat," Luku said eagerly. The fast food restaurant was a favourite place for the two to meet to share a bite and talk.

"Yeah, I'll wait for you," Makula said, and ended the call.

Makula's phone rang yet again. It was Wabudi. "Mak, where are you? We could meet if you have time."

"I'm at the Burger King. I just had lunch and I'm waiting for Chris to get here," Makula said.

"Well, sit tight. I'll join you both in half an hour," Wabudi said.

Makula got up and got a free refill of his soda to drink while he waited for his two buddies to arrive. He pondered the story about financial advisor Pietro Monterissi that was in the *Toronto Star*. He was amazed that Monterissi had advised others when his own finances were in a mess. He didn't believe that Monterissi had had bad intentions toward him, though.

He remembered the first session that he and his wife had had with Monterissi. He had asked them to bring all their bills to the consultation. Makula's wife had gathered their large pile of unpaid bills. She was worried about the money she had spent outsourcing all of her housework. Makula was worried about the undocumented amounts that he had sent to Kasaka on a monthly basis to "help out with worthy causes."

"Do you know how much you owe?" Monterissi had asked them when they had met in his office. Makula had looked down, unable to come up with a response. "We don't know the exact amount but we know it's a lot," his wife had answered. "In order to dig yourselves out of the hole, you have to know exactly how much you owe," Mr. Monterissi had added.

As he sat thinking about their sessions with Monterissi, Makula's phone rang. It was his friend Paul Mugisha, calling from Kampala, to tell Makula that a friend had woken him to inform him about Makula's picture in *Informed Pages*. When Makula told him that he had already seen it, Mugisha said that he had talked to John Kabenge and had blasted him about the photo. "Actually, Kabenge apologized, and asked for your phone number. He wants to apologize to you personally," Mugisha said.

"No," responded Makula. "I don't want to talk to him."

"He also told me that there is something very important that he would like to share with you," Mugisha said.

After ending his call with Mugisha, Makula's thoughts again drifted back to Monterissi. He remembered one session in particular in which Monterissi had given them a detailed plan to get out of debt.

"You've got to put away or even cut up and throw away your credit cards. Learn to use cash, and get receipts to keep track of your spending," Monterissi had said. Makula had decided to cut up all of his credit cards except one, but his wife had refused to heed Monterissi's advice. She had kept all of her credit cards even though most of them were maxed out.

"Next," Monterissi had continued, "you've got to make a budget. You need to know how much money you are making, and how much and where you are spending it. This also means eliminating all unessential items."

Makula remembered how he and his wife had immediately begun accusing each other of spending money on "useless stuff." He had railed at her for spending money on designer clothes, some of which she never wore, and she had accused him of wasting money on ungrateful relatives. Monterissi had halted the argument by telling them that the purpose of the consultation was not to apportion blame but to help them sort out their financial mess.

"There are other ways that you can save a lot of money," Monterissi had said. "For instance, stop paying somebody else to do things like washing your car or cutting your lawn. Learn to do simple maintenance work on your home, or team up with friends to do the bigger jobs. All this will help you save money." Makula had found this advice very useful. He had asked Luku and Wabudi to help them repaint their house, saving them thousands of dollars.

Makula's wife, however, had not liked the final piece of advice—to use coupons and other discounts to save money, especially in grocery stores. She refused to do anything that she believed made her look poor.

Monterissi had ruled out the refinancing of the couple's two-million-dollar home to deal with their debt load. As they had already refinanced their mortgage twice, he told them that they had treated their home like an ATM from which they withdrew money to fund their lavish lifestyle. This comment had annoyed Makula's wife so much that she had almost walked out of Monterissi's office. However, even now there was one question Monterissi had asked that Makula did not know how to answer: "How did your situation change from your making $500,000 a year to your now being almost penniless, hardly making ends meet on a minimum wage, all in a period of two years?"

Makula looked up to see Luku walking toward him. And as soon as Luku sat down, Wabudi called Makula to ask them to meet him at a new restaurant called Uncle Lee's where they could eat ribs or wings. Makula was about to remind him that he had just eaten, but when he glanced at the clock on the wall, he realized that he had been in the Burger King for close to three hours.

Makula Googled the address of Uncle Lee's and saw that it was a twenty-minute drive. He and Luku left the Burger King and got into Luku's Toyota Corolla. Luku was excited about getting to the restaurant that Wabudi had said served some of the best ribs and wings in Toronto. After they were seated at their table in the busy, upscale restaurant, Makula told his friends that he wasn't hungry. Wabudi, however, argued that the food was terrific and offered to buy his dinner, so Makula agreed to order half a rack of ribs. Wabudi and Luku settled for "all you can eat" chicken wings.

While they enjoyed their food and beer, the three friends talked about the article in *Informed Pages*. "People are free to live and work wherever they choose. I just don't see what's wrong with someone quitting a so-called lucrative job in Africa to take up a so-called menial job in a developed country," Luku said.

Makula agreed with Luku. "Yes, and after all, statistics now show that the money that Ugandans abroad send home is the number one source of income for the country."

Wabudi pulled his chair closer to the table and said, "That's true, but don't you think the guys that we left back home are better off than we are? In fact…"

"It's sad that Kabenge chose to publish Makula's picture," Luku interrupted, steering the conversation away from Wabudi's favourite topic—comparing the economic situation of Ugandans working overseas with those who resided in Uganda.

"The Kabenges, both Tom and John, have always been a problem for Makula, and we know why. I don't think it's shocking to any-one who knows their history that John chose to print that photo," Wabudi said.

"But that all happened more than twenty years ago. What's in it for John to disturb Makula's peace now?" Luku asked.

"By the way, Mugisha called while I was waiting for you at the Burger King," Makula told them. "He said that Kabenge wanted to call me to apologize. I told him to let Kabenge know that I didn't want to talk to him."

"Don't talk to him if you don't want to," Luku said. "I guess he knew before he printed that picture that what he was doing was wrong."

"Yes, I have enough problems to deal with right now," Makula said as he pulled a few business cards out of his shirt pocket.

"How's the job search going?" Wabudi asked.

"I've been out walking the streets but no luck yet," Makula responded with obvious disappointment.

"Walking the streets? Why would you do that?" Wabudi asked.

"To drop off résumés of course. And to meet with potential employers," Luku retorted.

"Do you still need to walk to drop off résumés in this day and age?" Wabudi asked, unconvinced.

"Well, I have e-mailed hundreds of résumés without getting

even a single interview. That's why I decided to drop them off personally, but that doesn't seem to be working either," Makula said sadly.

"How about your life coach? Can't he help you out?" Wabudi asked.

"I've been consulting him, but this time it doesn't seem to be working," Makula told him.

Makula sat back in his chair and looked at the business cards he had collected that day. His mind drifted from his friends' chat as he struggled to remember each of the conversations he had had with the potential employers who had given him the cards. "It's tough to look for a job when you are over fifty," he thought to himself.

"Don't lose hope. Everything will be all right," Luku said as he patted Makula on the shoulder.

"Did you get anything done on your recent visit to Kasaka? You went to see your house, right?" Wabudi asked.

Makula had hoped that the conversation would not turn to his investments in Kasaka because these always turned into long arguments. Wabudi thought that Makula was spending way too much money trying to develop the village and that it was not his responsibility to do so.

"No, I went to give Senfuka a piece of my mind. He seems to be hatching a plan to encroach on my property," Makula said bitterly.

"Encroaching on your property? Why would he? He's now very rich, isn't he, and owns a lot of property himself?" Wabudi asked.

"Well," Makula said, "he convinced my father to let him donate some doors and windows to help complete my house…"

"Why would he donate doors and windows to help you with your house? He's not your friend!" Wabudi exclaimed.

"Now you understand why I had to rush over there to deal with him," Makula said.

"So, how do you feel after that visit? Do you still want to go back to settle in that little village?" Wabudi asked.

Luku asked, "Do you think the journey was worth the expense?"

"I was kind of disappointed, to be honest. Even though I explained why I was there, a lot of people wanted me to give them money to solve their problems," Makula said.

"You see? It would be better for you to concentrate on what you are trying to do here for now. And who knows? Things might improve so you can continue with your work in Kasaka," Luku said.

"Mak, I think you made a very costly mistake in thinking that you could singlehandedly develop that village," Wabudi said.

"Like I've told you, the people in Kasaka are counting on me to help them out. I do what I can. And right now, as I'm going through this difficult phase in my life, many of them are going through the same. When I am well, they are well; when I suffer, they suffer…"

"Are you their king or something?" Wabudi asked.

Makula ignored Wabudi's taunt. He continued, "I have been paying tuition for three university students in Kampala who are doing very well in their studies. Because I no longer have the money to pay for their education, they are likely to drop out. Isn't that sad?"

"It's sad, but for now, they've got to look for other means until you sort yourself out," Wabudi said.

"That's right, but it's still unfortunate that they may have to drop out because of my failure," Makula said.

"You've done what you could. Wouldn't they understand if you told them that you can no longer pay for them?" Luku asked.

"They would, but for now, I've got to find some way to help them," Makula said, rising from his seat. He told his friends, "I've got to go now."

During his ride home on the subway, Makula thought about a new project that he would start in Kasaka if he had the money. During his recent visit to the village, one of his friends had told him that a tourist resort would be a money-maker in Kasaka. Makula had laughed at the idea at first, because he didn't think there was anything in Kasaka for a tourist to see. However, on his long flight from Dubai to Toronto, he had changed his mind. "That's not such a crazy idea after all. If people can construct luxurious resorts in the desert, what would stop me from building one in Kasaka?" he had thought. "And with my experience in marketing, I could create a buzz around it in the international media. People would surely go on all-inclusive vacations there. Kasaka could eventually become another Cancun."

Just thinking about this project made Makula feel good for the first time that day. He felt energized by his thoughts of a luxury resort in Kasaka, unlike the effect the rest of the day's news had had on him—that of Pietro Monterissi's bankruptcy and his picture being printed in *Informed Pages*.

However, this good feeling did not last for long. As the subway hurtled along, Makula thought of all that would stop him from making his dream a reality. "This project would require a minimum of five million US dollars to take off. Where would I get that kind of money?" He also thought about what Wabudi, his most passionate but well-meaning critic, would say: "Another investment in Kasaka? Where would you get the money? Assuming you found a bank that was interested enough to look at your proposal, could you prepare one that would even go beyond the feasibility stage? Is this another scheme intended to provide employment for your many relatives?"

These thoughts had dampened Makula's optimism a little as he gave up his seat to an elderly woman. He looked out at the platform and realized that he was two stations south of where he should have exited. He squeezed himself through the closing, chiming doors, climbed the stairs, and then crossed the station to take the northbound subway train.

When he arrived home, Makula said to his wife, "Honey, I have two pieces of news. One is ironic; the other is annoying. Which would you like to hear first?"

CHAPTER TWO
Kasaka, Uganda, February 1971

"Young man, this is the third time this week that I've seen you peeping in that window. That is a classroom. What do you want?" asked Mr. Kasaato, who stood a few metres away in the schoolyard.

When he heard these words, Makula walked slowly over the dusty ground toward Mr. Kasaato.

"Why were you peeping in the window?" Mr. Kasaato asked again.

"I wanted to listen to what the children were saying," Makula replied.

"Oh, do you mean what they are learning? But that is a kindergarten class. Of what use would what the children are learning be to you, an older boy?" Mr. Kasaato asked.

"I would like to learn," Makula said humbly.

"To learn? In the kindergarten? Don't you go to school? Who are you?" Mr. Kasaato asked with some disbelief.

"My name is Makula Musoke," Makula replied.
"I don't go to school."

Mr. Kasaato continued to question him. "Why don't you go to school?

You are of school-going age. How old are you?"

"I am eleven years old. I don't go to school because my father
does not have the money to pay the school fees. But I would like
to be in school and learn like the other children,"
Makula explained.

"Who is your father?" Mr. Kasaato asked.

"My father is Filipo Musoke," Makula answered, a little
frightened by the headmaster's tone.

"Listen. I don't want to see you here again. Make sure you don't
interrupt my classes," Mr. Kasaato said sternly.

When he realized that the headmaster did not want him at the school,
Makula ran away.

Despite his gruffness, the headmaster was touched by this brief exchange.
This was not the first time in his five years as headmaster of Kasaka
Primary School, a school with a total of seventy students, that he had
witnessed a vagabond child at the school compound. He had seen, many
times before, boys grazing cattle nearby, girls carrying baskets on their
heads with merchandise for sale, even boys engaged in fist fights on the
school playground. But this particular boy had really caught his attention
with his boldness. Mr. Kasaato thought about their conversation for
much of the evening and concluded that, due to a certain intensity and
brightness he had seen in his eyes, this boy might be quite brilliant. He
wondered if he would ever see him again.

Makula was so excited by his conversation with the headmaster that
he forgot that his mother had asked him to go the market. Because the
headmaster had taken the time to listen to him, Makula thought that
he could approach him again about enrolling in the school. He ran
home and, almost out of breath, struggled to tell his mother about his
encounter with the school's headmaster.

Kabejja waited for a few moments to let her son recover from his run
and then asked, "Makula, is that why it took you longer than usual to
return from the market?"

Makula began, "Mother, I wanted to try my luck…"

"What do you mean?" Kabejja asked.

"I wanted to ask the headmaster to let me join his school,"
Makula said.

"And what did he say?" Kabejja asked impatiently.

"He told me never to go near the classroom again," Makula answered.

"Can I see the items you bought from the market?" Kabejja asked, although it was obvious to her that he had purchased nothing.

Makula stared blankly at the ground. He was afraid to tell his mother that he had forgotten to go to the bi-monthly market.

Kabejja lost her temper. She had sent her son to the market to buy salt, soap and paraffin. He had instead stopped at the school, stood by the window to listen to what the children were learning, talked to the headmaster, got excited, and abandoned the errand. "That market is not open every day, Makula!" she said.

"Mother, I was going to the market but Toofa asked me to go with him to the school," Makula said, in an attempt to place the blame on his cousin.

Kabejja asked, "What do you want from the school? You have to go back to the market now!"

Kabejja ordered Makula to walk the three kilometres back to the market. Despite the fact that he did not know how to count, she trusted his ability to buy small household items. Makula walked briskly and resisted the urge to return to the school to talk to the headmaster. Perhaps if he could clearly explain his situation, the headmaster might allow him to join the school. He did not waste his time at the market. He bought a bar of soap, a packet of salt, and two litres of paraffin and walked right back home. When he arrived, he asked his mother if he could go back to the school to talk to the headmaster. His mother told him that as she had not given him permission to go to the school when he first did so, it was up to him.

The following morning, Makula walked back to the school. He was determined to talk to the headmaster about the possibility of his joining the school. But luck was not on his side. He waited at a safe distance from the kindergarten class for three hours but did not see the headmaster. He decided to return to the school the following morning, but again he did not see the headmaster. He went to the school every morning for the rest of the week without seeing him. He thought of asking one of the teachers about the headmaster's whereabouts but feared that they would only send him on his way.

Twenty-five-year-old Kabejja was worried about her son's future. She thought about the circumstances surrounding his birth. At fourteen years of age, she had still been struggling to learn how to count. She was frustrated in school and was therefore very happy when she met Filipo Musoke, who sold charcoal and fruit near her school. From that time onward, Kabejja would leave to go to school but would end up in Filipo's one-bedroom rented house. When she conceived a child, her father was so angry with her that he sent her away from his home. She went to Filipo, who was forced by her father to marry her, and who decided to start a new life with her in Kasaka, his birthplace. When their son was born, they named him after his paternal grandfather, Makula Musoke. When Makula turned five, Filipo Musoke decided to move in search of work, as he was unable to make a living in Kasaka. He then found a job as a supervisor at a sugar cane plantation.

Kabejja did not see her father again until he summoned her to his deathbed so that he could "forgive her for her wrongdoing." Although her mother was still alive, Kabejja rarely saw her. When she thought about her past, Kabejja hoped that an education could help her son escape poverty.

Kasaka was a village about 56 kilometres from Kayunga, the nearest town. There was a dirt road that connected this quiet village to Kayunga. In fact, on a journey along the dirt road, one was struck by the beauty of the plains and the regular pattern of hills covered by lush green trees. Whenever he talked about his birthplace, Filipo Musoke informed his listeners that Kasaka would make a very good tourist attraction as it was endowed with picture-perfect landscapes. However, despite its physical beauty, the land in Kasaka was not very fertile. Although its residents depended on farming to support them, the major crop was a variety of green plantain that was best suited for making beer. This variety did not fetch a good price, unlike *matooke* (the more common variety of plantain grown in Uganda). However, this did not stop the people of Kasaka from growing a lot of it to make beer. Kasaka was well-known for its homemade brew, and on an average day, one could see about thirty men riding bicycles loaded with big plastic containers of it along the main dirt road, for sale in Kayunga.

Filipo and Kabejja, Makula's parents, owned a small two-bedroom house in Kasaka that Filipo had singlehandedly built when he and Kabejja had married. There were coffee trees and a few banana trees on both sides of the front yard. About twenty metres from the back door was a large tree on which passion fruit grew twice a year. When it was ripe, Kabejja would carry half a sack to the market to sell. This earned her a few shillings to buy necessities. There were also two jackfruit trees nearby where Makula and some of his friends and cousins spent entire days eating fruit and telling stories during the hot months. The latrine and a makeshift bathroom were about twelve metres from the back of the house.

Filipo had been raised by his elder brother, Lameka. Lameka was a large man who always spoke at the top of his voice. In his youth, Lameka had worked in a market in Kayunga. Whenever he returned to Kasaka, people would gather around him as he humorously shared the latest news from far and near. This earned him the nickname "Radio Uganda."

In Kasaka, Lameka was considered a rich man. He owned a large expanse of land that he had inherited from his father. He had twenty-four children whom he raised in addition to many other relatives who lived in his home. This large family provided labour for Lameka's coffee and plantain plantations where the harvest, particularly of green plantain, was very plentiful. Lameka's home was full of activity, especially during the time when his workers brewed beer.

When Filipo had been forced to marry Kabejja, he turned to his brother. Lameka gave him four acres of land, right in front of his own home, on which to build. When Makula was born, he was raised together with his many cousins.

Makula, like many of his friends and cousins, enjoyed playing in the village until late in the evening but he did not like to bathe. Whenever his mother asked him why he did not want to, he would say that the water was too cold or that he feared doing so alone when it was dark. When she insisted, he would take a plastic basin, fill it with water, and then carry it outside. However, many times he did not bathe; instead, he would wash his feet, wet his hair, and thoroughly wash his hands and face. He would then make some loud noises with the water as he splashed it all over the place so that his mother would think he was actually bathing. The only time Makula truly took a bath was when his father was at home and ordered him to do so before sunset. His father would check his body after the bath to make sure he was clean.

***

When he was enrolled, Makula very much enjoyed his new life as a student at Kasaka Primary School. Although he was about five years older than most of his classmates in the kindergarten, they loved him because of the stories that he told them. The story that made the children laugh the most was about his Uncle Lameka's cow, which had kicked Makula one morning as he tried to milk it. The children would laugh whenever he told them this story. Makula would often laugh with them, although he reminded them that it had not been a laughing matter when it had happened. His uncle's response had been that the kick should serve as a lesson to Makula and other boys like him who didn't know how to milk cows to never come near his. Makula's teacher liked him because he was a quick learner who helped organize the rest of the children.

By the end of his first month in kindergarten, Makula had memorized the alphabet. He woke early each morning to do his work at home before walking briskly to the school. Filipo, his father, was at work on a sugar cane plantation about 110 kilometres away and only came home about four times a year on special occasions. Although his father lived away from home, Makula did not look forward to his father's homecomings. Thirty-year-old Filipo was a happy man who used to enjoy the company of the other men in the village but was very tough on his son. Although he said that he lacked the means to send his son to a good school in the nearby town of Kayunga, he still expected Makula to be "productive."

When he returned home at the end of that month, Filipo listened attentively as Kabejja told him how Makula had convinced the headmaster to enroll him at the school. "He told him that he wanted to study because that would enable him to become an important person in the country," Kabejja said.

"Oh," Filipo said.

"Yes. And he told him that when he grows up, he will work hard to develop this village," Kabejja said.

"Interesting," Filipo said.

"The headmaster came here and personally delivered this letter that he wrote to us. He said that this is the admission letter," Kabejja said as she handed the handwritten letter to Filipo.

Filipo looked intently at it but did not understand a thing, because he, like his wife, could not read English. However, they could give the letter to their friend Othieno, a former teacher, who could both read and write English. Othieno would soon be visiting, so Filipo put the letter in his hip pocket.

"Makula!" Filipo called out at the top of his voice.

"Yes, sir," Makula responded, while staring with a little fear at his father. He thought that this might turn out to be one of those times that the "old man" scolded him after taking a little too much drink.

"I am glad to know that you are in school. This is a good thing. You are our hope. I knew it, yes, I knew all along that you would do us proud," Filipo said as he raised his arms in the air in a drunken manner that made his wife laugh. But Makula did not join in; he never knew when he would rub his father the wrong way.

"Poor boy, he has just started school. How sure are we that he will do us proud?" Kabejja said, almost to herself.

"Makula!" Filipo shouted loudly again.

"Yes, sir," Makula replied.

"Bring me a chair," Filipo said.

"Right away," Makula said, as he went in the house and brought out a chair. He placed the wooden chair in front of his father.

"Take it over there," Filipo said, "in front of the entrance to the kitchen! See, I am talking to your mother. Do you expect me to sit this far away when the person I am talking to is in the kitchen?"

Makula did not respond. He would never talk back to his father. He took the chair, placed it in front of the entrance to the kitchen, and walked quietly back to the house. It was beginning to get dark. Filipo placed his bottle of gin on the ground next to the chair and sat down.

"So what did the headmaster say?" Filipo asked.

"The headmaster came here one evening after school. He told me that he had had a conversation with our son and had concluded that Makula was a bright child whose future we needed to seriously consider by enrolling him in school," Kabejja said.

"Wait a minute. Did he want to tell us what to do with our own child?" Filipo asked in an angry tone.

"I don't think that is what he intended to do," Kabejja said soothingly.

"But that is exactly what he did," Filipo insisted.

"Just a few minutes ago you seemed to be happy with the fact that Makula is now in school," Kabejja answered.

"Sorry," said Filipo. "I will let you go on."

"The headmaster said that he was surprised to see that we had never thought of enrolling our child in school. He said that since Makula is a bright child, giving him an education would help him have a better future. I agreed with him and told him that you have been trying for the last few years to enroll him in a big school but that you were still looking for money," Kabejja said as she tried to sound as if she had defended her husband.

"What is the headmaster's name?" Filipo asked.

"Kasaato," replied Kabejja, who was relieved to see that Filipo had not taken offense at the fact that, year after year, he had not sent his only child to the village school on the pretext that he was looking for money to enroll him in a good school.

"I don't know him. I don't think he grew up in this area. I have never heard of him before," Filipo said.

"I have been hearing about him for a few years, especially since he started transforming that little school into a better one," Kabejja told him. "Right now he is constructing a four-classroom block. Anyway, no one would blame you for not knowing him since you don't live here anymore. He too didn't know us before he came here, but he knows your brother, Lameka."

"Everyone knows Lameka," Filipo said, as he got up to go to his brother's home to drink.

***

Makula's life changed when he started going to school. In addition to attending class, he had to help his mother with housework. Early in the morning, he would work in the garden for about forty-five minutes, then go twice to the well to fetch water in a twenty-litre can that he carried on his head. He didn't have time to sit down to have breakfast. Every evening after dinner his mother would wrap a few pieces of cassava or sweet potato in banana leaves, which Makula would take with him to eat at school. But in the morning before he left, Makula would pick up a big piece of cooked cassava that he munched on as he walked, barefooted, the three kilometres to school. About half a kilometre from his home, he would usually meet a group of schoolmates that came from the neighbouring village of Nanziba. The children would then all run to get to school on time. If they arrived late, they would be punished.

Kasaka Primary School was small, consisting of only four classrooms. Each of the four was divided into two by a papyrus wall to accommodate all the classes. There was a doorway in each of these rooms that allowed access to the others. Only one of the four classrooms had a permanent roof, doors, and windows. This is the one that also housed the head-master's office—a desk, and a space for the seven teachers. The rest of the classrooms had papyrus roofs, and whenever it rained, and it often rained hard in Kasaka, all the students and teachers would be crammed into the classroom with the permanent roof. To reduce the amount of dust in the classrooms, the students would resurface the dirt floor with a mixture of mud and cow dung at least once every two months. This mixture smelled awful when it was fresh, but Mr. Kasaato would be happy that the students did not fall sick due to the dust.

There were eight students in Makula's kindergarten class. The class was completely bare except for a small desk for the teacher. The children sat on the floor and wrote on little slates with chalk that they wiped clean over and over again as they learned to write. At the end of each school day, the children would sing:

Twajja tuli mbuzi
Kati tugunjuse
Bakadde mwebale
Okutuwelera

("We were as ignorant as goats when we first came to school. But now we are enlightened. Thanks, dear parents, for paying for our education.")

They would then take their slates to the headmaster's office for safe custody.

When he had completed the first year of kindergarten, Makula was interviewed. Based on his answers in the oral interview and the assessment that both his teacher and the headmaster made, and given his age, he was asked to skip Primary 1. He would try Primary 2 the following year. The Primary 1 and the Primary 2 teachers discussed Makula's case and agreed to support him in different ways to enable him to bridge the gap. Mr. Kasaato asked Makula to work very hard both in school and at home in order to catch up with the other students in his Primary 2 class.

The following year, Makula was very happy to study in Primary 2. He did his work diligently, although many times he did not have enough exercise books to write in. Whenever he needed a new exercise book and his mother could not buy one from the market, he would take some exercise books that belonged to his cousins Makko and Lukka, who had dropped out of school a few years earlier, and erase their work in order to write in his.

When Makula's classes ended at three o'clock, he would return home, take the goats to graze, then fetch water from the well twice, as he did each morning. He would then go to his Uncle Lameka's home where he would join his cousins at play. There were ten boys in total, all between the ages of ten and seventeen. The boys would usually walk along a narrow path that separated Lameka's land from his neighbour's. They would walk all the way to the edge of the valley that separated Kasaka from Nanziba, the next village. At the very end of Lameka's land, there was a long line of fruit trees that included jackfruit, mango, orange, and avocado. When he was younger, Makula's mother Kabejja told him that she had heard that his grandfather had planted those trees in the 1940s and that, although Makula's grandfather had planted them, people in Kasaka and Nanziba considered them to be no man's property. It was therefore very common for children from both villages to meet there to fight over the fruit. Jackfruit was the most prized, and these fights came to be known as the "jackfruit battles." Makula and his cousins would fight with the boys from Nanziba over the jackfruit, and the group that won the fight would take the bulk of the fruit home to eat, or share it there and then to annoy the losing group.

One year later, when he started Primary 3, classwork became harder for Makula. The number of subjects increased, and since the school had few teachers, one teacher was responsible for as many as three subjects. Miss Namata taught geography, mathematics, and music. She would teach geography, take a short break, and then come back to start teaching math. She would ask the students to copy the homework from the blackboard into their exercise books. She would then rub off part of the board to add more work. The students would sometimes stand to move closer to the board in order to see as they copied their homework. This would annoy Miss Namata, who would yell at them to sit down. They would then respond in unison, "Excuse me madam, I can't see." Miss Namata would relent for a minute, and then ask them again to sit down.

Geography was Makula's favourite subject. In Primary 3 he learned about several countries, including Kenya, Nigeria, India, Holland, the United

Kingdom, and Canada. In the Primary 3 textbook, World Geography, a child from each of these countries would talk about life in their country including life in the cities, the economy, and the people. Makula was very fascinated by life in Canada. A Canadian girl named Mary talked about wheat farming, combine harvesters, the lumber industry, snow, and frozen lakes. Miss Namata made the lessons so enjoyable that whenever they ended Makula felt a little sad; he never wanted them to stop.

Makula and his classmates found Primary 3 hard as the students had to complete their homework every night or Miss Namata would beat them for not completing it. When he was in Primary 3 Makula played less with his cousins because he had to do his homework before sunset. His cousins did not go to school; they therefore repeatedly told him that he was missing out on the fun. Kabejja was aware of this and never missed an opportunity to tell her son that despite the hardship he was facing, he was lucky to be in school. She watched her son every evening as he worked hard to complete his homework.

One Thursday evening Makula still had not finished his homework by sunset, so she lit the lantern and put it beside him as he bent down on the floor to write. The family did not own a table. Makula had so much work that he could not sit down to eat his dinner. He held a piece of cassava in one hand as he wrote with the other.

"Why don't you eat first, then do your homework later?" Kabejja asked.

"Mother, I have a lot of work this evening. If I sat down to eat, I would not finish it all. It's cassava anyway; I can eat it in any way I want," Makula answered.

"True, it is cassava, but cassava is food. My son, learn to appreciate whatever little we have. We have this cassava today but we may not have it tomorrow," Kabejja said.

"I appreciate what we have, Mother, but I have to finish this homework. Miss Namata will punish me if I don't complete it," Makula explained.

"Go on, my son. You will be rewarded for your effort," Kabejja said as she sat down on a mat beside Makula to watch him work.

The following day Makula was let out early from school. While walking home, he felt a great urge to eat some jackfruit. When he found that his mother was not home, he did not bother to eat anything. He walked to his uncle's house where he and his cousin Toofa decided to go to the valley to look for jackfruit. The boys usually went to the valley in a group of at least seven but Toofa's older brothers Makko and Lukka had recently left home to look for employment in Kampala. Makula and Toofa therefore took a risk in going all by themselves. Makula convinced Toofa that since it was early in the afternoon, the "gang" from Nanziba would not be there.

When they reached the trees, Makula climbed the jackfruit tree that bore the biggest fruit as Toofa waited below to watch for anyone coming. Makula started tapping the big fruit, one by one, with his open palm. By doing so, he could tell from the sound on their rough skin which fruit were ripe. Whenever Makula tapped a fruit, Toofa would ask, "Is that it?" and Makula would answer, "No. Be patient." Makula finally tapped one huge fruit that revealed its ripeness from the sound of its skin and its smell.

"So, are you ready? Here it comes!" Makula shouted.

Toofa did not respond. Makula dropped the huge fruit and a voice he did not recognize said, "That's a good one."

When he looked down, Makula saw a group of about seven boys from Nanziba. Toofa was standing there, speechless. The leader of the boys from Nanziba, Simeon Senfuka, a big, tall boy and a notorious bully, asked Makula to find more ripe fruit before coming down from the tree. Makula dropped two more of the juicy fruit, then begged for mercy as he came down.

"We are not going to hit you," Senfuka assured him. "How could we hit you when you have dropped such juicy fruit for us?"

Makula came down from the tree, and Senfuka asked him and Toofa to carry a fruit each on their heads and lead the way to Nanziba. When they neared Senfuka's parents' home, Senfuka handed a machete to Makula and asked him to chop the fruit. Senfuka and his companions then enjoyed it as Makula and Toofa looked on helplessly, both hungry and angry. They were then told to return home but not until they had declared out loud that "the boys from Nanziba are stronger than we are."

CHAPTER THREE
Kasaka, Uganda, May 1974

Makula was so clever and hard-working that he quickly became one of the best students at Kasaka Primary School. The headmaster, Mr. Kasaato, was very pleased with his progress and glad that he had enrolled him. Mr. Kasaato was only too aware, however, of the low standard of education that was offered in his rural school as compared to the schools in the more affluent areas of the district. And he was certain that, given his achievements, Makula would do even better in a bigger school.

In Primary 4, fourteen-year-old Makula joined the school choir. His voice was now beginning to deepen and the other students teased him about it, saying that he crowed like a cock. Gentle by nature, Makula did not turn on his young schoolmates; he just laughed.

That year, for the first time, Kasaka Primary School was given the opportunity to participate in the zonal school singing competition. In this prestigious competition, the winning schools would move on to compete at the district level and ultimately at the national level in Kampala. Miss Namata worked hard to train her students in singing and drama. She and the students put in extra hours and felt prepared for the competition that would take place in Kayunga.

On the day of the competition, the students who were taking part were very excited about the fifty-six-kilometre journey to Kayunga. Although they were to start their journey from the school at eight o'clock in the morning, most of the students arrived over an hour and a half early. They waited impatiently for the truck, which did not arrive until half past eight. Makula could not believe his eyes when he saw the truck reversing into the small school compound. This was going to be his very first ride in a motor vehicle. Miss Namata read each of the students' names out loud to make certain all were present, and the journey finally began at nine. The students sang and shouted with joy all the way to Kayunga.

There were seven schools participating in the singing competition. The first four schools performed the set piece "Good News, The Chariot Is Coming" and impressed everyone, including the judges. Each group had an average of twelve singers; some sang soprano while others sang alto.

When it was time for the students of Kasaka Primary School to perform, a total of twenty-two singers stepped onto the stage. However, they did not know anything about the set piece. And even before they began to sing, the audience was amused by the poorly dressed, barefooted group. They began singing "*Ensejjele kawomera*," a story about some delicious white ants, which, by the time the farmer goes to catch them in the morning, have flown out of the anthill and into the jungle. The audience burst out laughing so loudly that the group could not continue singing.

The students were very embarrassed and walked off the stage one by one. Outside, Makula joined his teachers in consoling the young crying girls. The day had turned out to be a sad one for the students of Kasaka Primary School. They quietly ate their snacks of cassava and avocado in the shade of a tree while the students from the other schools ate samosas stuffed with rice or beans, licked ice cream cones, and drank soda.

After the lunch break, the schools had to sing a song in the category of traditional folklore. The demoralized students of Kasaka Primary School kicked off this section of the competition. Makula sang a folklore song, "*Namudaale*," about a brave hunter who kills a warthog after a serious battle with the animal. Three girls danced to the drums as Makula sang and dragged a log that was entangled in a net to represent the fierce animal. Makula's performance was so good that the audience clapped and cheered. When all of the schools had sung, the judges declared Kasaka Primary School the winner in the traditional folklore category. The guest of honour, the Bugerere County chief, himself a former performer of traditional drama and music, was also very impressed with Makula's performance. Because of this, Makula was one of three students selected to be interviewed for an article about the singing competition. Although the other two students answered the questions in English, Makula decided to speak Luganda because that was the language in which he could best express himself. He had not yet mastered enough vocabulary to carry on a conversation in English. The county chief, though, was impressed by Makula's ease of speech and knowledge of local music.

On the journey back to Kasaka, the students sang and celebrated the winning performance of Makula's group. However, the singing was not as loud as it had been during the trip to Kayunga. The students were quite upset that they hadn't known how to perform the set piece.

The following morning, Miss Namata addressed the students and encouraged them not to give up. "Don't be discouraged," she said. "We know now what to do. Next year, we will start preparations early."

***

Makula liked his studies and was eager to learn. His only problem was that he was unaccustomed to the beatings that the students received from the teachers. One could get as many as three strokes of the cane for failing an exercise in class. Although he was very good at the other subjects, Makula performed poorly in math.

A few months after the school music contest, the headmaster, Mr. Kasaato, met with the Bugerere County chief. During their meeting, the chief asked about Makula. Mr. Kasaato informed him that Makula had started school late and this was why he was older than the other students. He also said that Makula was quite a brilliant student who was likely to succeed in his educational endeavours, given his level of interest. He also told him that Makula, like all of the students in the school, faced the hurdle of extreme poverty. The county chief offered to help Makula with his education if his parents were interested.

Mr. Kasaato was very pleased to hear this. Upon his return to Kasaka, he went to see Kabejja and told her what the county chief had said about helping Makula. Kabejja told him that she would be very glad to accept any assistance the chief could offer to her son.

The headmaster shared Kabejja's positive response with the county chief, and the chief agreed to pay the school fees so that Makula could complete his primary education in a better school. Thus, the following year, as a fifteen-year-old Primary 5 student, Makula enrolled in Kayunga Primary School.

The headmaster of Kayunga Primary School was Mr. Kasule, an old friend of Mr. Kasaato. Makula was enrolled in the boarding section of the school, and Mr. Kasaato accompanied him to his new school two days before the school term began to acquaint him with the new environment. Mr. Kasaato told Makula how fortunate he was to have this opportunity. Many children in Kasaka wished for it but could not have it. "You are our ambassador," he said. "We are proud of you and would like to see you succeed. Know that you are lucky and make the best of this opportunity."

As it was getting dark, the headmaster's wife, Mrs. Kasule, showed Makula into one of the bedrooms of their home where he would be sleeping that night. As Makula set down his metallic suitcase, he gasped with surprise at the brightness that suddenly engulfed the room as Mrs. Kasule switched on the overhead fluorescent light. Makula was amazed by his first sight of electric lighting, which he had heard about for so long. After Mrs. Kasule left him, he stared intently at the glowing fluorescent tube. He grew even more excited about the new life that was before him.

CHAPTER FOUR
Kayunga, Uganda, February 1975

Makula found the environment at Kayunga Primary School to be very different from that of the school in Kasaka. The school itself was bigger and there were far more students. And even though the school compound was large, Makula felt that his freedom was now greatly restricted. Here, he could no longer roam the village to look for jackfruit or mangoes. He also missed his mother. Sometimes he wondered if he would have been better off remaining in Kasaka. And instead of having to carry cans of water from the well, he need only fill a can of water from the tap next to the dormitory to bathe; there were not many chores for him to do.

Makula still found the study of mathematics to be very challenging. His difficulty became an even bigger problem for him because the subject was taught by Mr. Kasule himself, the headmaster. Makula learned that Mr. Kasule was a no-nonsense man from the students in Primary 7, who were in their final year before moving on to high school.

When he addressed Makula's class on the first day of school, Mr. Kasule informed them that work would begin promptly the following day. "Newcomer, expect to be surprised. We work hard here," he told Makula. "Ask the older students in case you need clarification, okay?"

Makula did not understand what Mr. Kasule meant by "clarification." The following day, however, he learned that Mr. Kasule never took the time to repeat what he had said. A cane on the back would do.

Makula had his math class first thing each morning. The students would sit quietly with their exercise books open and pens ready as they waited for Mr. Kasule to enter. When he arrived at the door, he would announce, "Mental work. Question number one…" The students would answer ten questions and those who answered fewer than five correctly would receive a whack of the cane on the behind for each incorrect answer. Makula rarely had more than five out of ten correct but he would at times escape a beating whenever he got a chance to copy answers from his new friend Paul Mugisha. Mugisha was a naughty but very clever boy who, like the majority of his classmates, was five years younger than Makula.

Headmaster Kasule was not the most feared teacher in the school. That was Mr. Mubiru, whom the students had nicknamed "*Pili Pili*" (hot pepper) because his temper was as hot and he would not tolerate any lack of discipline. Pili Pili would be laughing with his students one minute and caning them the next. He taught Primary 3 and 4 math and science, but he seemed to spend most of his time enforcing discipline and making sure the school compound was clean. Each week, there was a teacher in charge of the general administration at the school. These duties ranged from timekeeping to addressing the school assembly. The weeks when Pili Pili was in charge were very difficult for the students. Pili Pili's motto was "Be at the right place at the right time." A student would be punished for arriving even two minutes late for lunch. Some of the students skipped lunch as they were routinely served beans with cassava or beans with "*posho*," a meal made from corn. However, during Pili Pili's week, everyone was present for the lunch hour roll call.

The students in the boarding section of Kayunga Primary School were given a Sunday afternoon off every fortnight. Those whose homes were nearby would visit their families for a change of diet. And those whose families were far away, like Makula, were often invited to the homes of their friends.

Kayunga was a small town of about two thousand people. Shops lined each of the two streets and sold household essentials such as paraffin, sugar, soap, tea, and dried foodstuffs. However, one shop sold and repaired radios.

One Sunday afternoon, Makula went into Kayunga with his friend Paul Mugisha to tour the town. This was Makula's first visit, and he enjoyed himself a lot. They went into the shop that sold radios and listened to the music that was being played. When Mugisha informed the shop-keeper that this was Makula's first visit to Kayunga, the shopkeeper was glad to show them all the latest makes of radios that he had on display. Makula was very excited when he saw a radio cassette player. He told the shopkeeper that when he completed school, he would like to own one of the biggest radios. "Great dream, young man. When I was in school like you, I thought of far smaller things, like beer parties," the shopkeeper said.

When they left the radio shop, the boys peeped through the window of a bar. They saw a few people drinking beer and listening to Congolese music that was playing on the jukebox. Makula was amazed by the jukebox, as it automatically glided to select records.

Makula thought the town of Kayunga was beautiful. To him, it seemed huge. Mugisha took Makula to his mother's house. Although his mother was not home, Mugisha picked up the key from under a brick next to a flower pot where his mother had left it for him. There was more than enough food for the two boys. They enjoyed a hot meal of matooke and fish stew and drank orange juice.

The two boys enjoyed themselves so much that they lost track of time. When they left his mother's house, Mugisha asked a shopkeeper what time it was, and he told him it was six o'clock. The boys were supposed to have been back at the school by five. They knew that they were in big trouble because Pili Pili was on duty this week. They ran as fast as they could to the school. When they were about twenty metres away from the school compound, they saw Pili Pili standing at the door to their dormitory with a stick in his hands. He was muttering loudly and was obviously annoyed, and it was apparent that he had just hit a student or two for being late. Mugisha suggested that their best option was to hide in the nearby shrub until nightfall, when they could sneak into the dormitory—Pili Pili could not stand there all night. Mugisha took three steps backward toward the shrub.

"Don't even think about it!" Pili Pili yelled to the boys. "Come right here and lie down flat!"

"But, sir…" Makula said.

"Quiet!" Pili Pili commanded. "Say one more word and I will double the number of strokes."

"Mugisha took me to the town…" Makula said.

"Quiet! Come right here and lie down flat!" Pili Pili repeated. Mugisha remained silent, knowing that any pleas for mercy would have no effect.

Pili Pili struck each of the boys three times and told them never to be late again. "The punishment will be more severe next time," he warned them. "Now, get into your dormitory."

This was not the only time that Makula and Mugisha got into trouble with Pili Pili that week.

The students enjoyed making fun of the way Pili Pili pronounced some words. For example, he could not pronounce the word "three"; he pronounced it as "siree." He also said "zat" instead of "that." On Wednesday afternoon as he was crisscrossing the school compound to check on its cleanliness, Pili Pili passed close to Makula's classroom. One of the students said, "One, two, siree," and the whole class burst out laughing. Pili Pili continued on his way, and the students assumed that he had not heard them. But no sooner had the laughter died down than he appeared in the doorway.

"Now tell me. Who made fun of me?" Pili Pili asked. The class was quiet.

He asked again, "Who made fun of me?" and started to swing a stick in the air. "I know it was one of you boys. If you do not tell me who did it, I will punish all of you, including the girls."

The class remained silent. Then after about a minute, two boys started accusing each other. Because no one confessed, Pili Pili decided to punish everyone. The boys each got three strokes and the girls, two.

Makula found Kayunga Primary School to be a good school but the beatings made him think about quitting and going home. His other source of trouble at the school was with speaking in the vernacular. The school required all of the students to speak English at all times. Each morning, the head prefect would hand out cards to those who spoke any language other than English. And those who were handed cards would be punished that evening or at the end of the week. Because he had attended a poor rural school, even though he was in Primary 5, Makula still had trouble expressing himself in English. So whenever he had to explain something, he reverted to Luganda. One day he ended up with three cards in his pocket because he had been caught speaking Luganda three times that day.

Although he himself had a lot of trouble expressing himself in English, Pili Pili was always quick to cane any students who were caught speaking any other language. Actually, the students often joked that Pili Pili was so dense that if he were asked to re-sit the Primary Leaving Examinations (PLE), he would not pass. When Makula received three cards on one day, he knew Pili Pili would be ready to administer nine strokes of the cane, three for each time that Makula had been caught speaking Luganda.

Makula thought about the conversation that he would have with Pili Pili. He imagined Pili Pili asking him whether he wanted to receive the strokes all at once or on three different occasions, three at a time. Makula then imagined himself asking angrily, "Why should I be beaten for speaking Luganda when it is my mother tongue?" He imagined Pili Pili answering, "I think you are right. One should not be punished for speaking their mother tongue." Makula felt good when he imagined this conversation but he was aware that it was merely wishful thinking.

When Makula went to see Pili Pili at the end of the school day about his punishment for vernacular speaking, the teacher told him that he would see him later. "Come to the staff room tomorrow morning after the morning assembly. I will see what to do with you," Pili Pili said. When Makula left, he was relieved to note that Pili Pili had been calm.

Makula went to see Pili Pili in the staff room the following morning, and one of the other teachers told him that Pili Pili had lost a relative and had left for the burial. He would return the following week. Makula did not go back to see Pili Pili the following week. That case of the three cards ended there. And in subsequent weeks, the students were delighted to see that Pili Pili had lost some of his zeal for punishing vernacular speakers.

The Parent Teacher Association (PTA) met in April and its primary concern was the high level of absenteeism that the headmaster had reported in the previous two months. The parents attending the meeting wanted to know why there was such a persistent problem with absenteeism. The new deputy chairman of the PTA told everyone present that they didn't need to look far to find the cause of the problem. He said that the students were being beaten on a regular basis, even for very flimsy reasons. In his opinion, this made many of them hate going to school. Many of the parents disagreed with his point of view.

The chairman himself, however, said that behaviour in the school was exemplary as compared to the other schools in Kayunga.

Not to be silenced, the deputy chairman asked the headmaster, Mr.

Kasule, what kind of punishments Mr. Mubiru dealt out to the students.

The headmaster replied, "He gets them to clean the compound; he also strikes them once in a while when there is need to do so. Actually, all of us do that. I think you too must have received these kinds of punishments when you were in school."

"With all due respect, Mr. Kasule, Mr. Mubiru (Pili Pili) does not strike these students only once in a while; he flogs them daily. I was told that he beat the entire Primary 5 class last week and frogmarched each of them," the deputy chairman responded.

"Frogmarched them? What are you talking about?" the headmaster asked.

"See? You don't know what's happening in the school. He frogmarched them while the rest of the students laughed at them. Because of this kind of treatment, some students leave home to come to school but never arrive. Instead, they choose to stop on the way to eat mangoes. Some students have actually told me…"

"You talk to the students? Is that allowed? Why would you talk to the students about discipline?" one parent asked angrily. "They are only children. They are there to be corrected whenever they go wrong. The chairman should see that his deputy needs to be disciplined."

The deputy chairman was asked to leave the room so that the parents could discuss his actions. After a few minutes, he was called back in and the chairman informed him that he had been relieved of his duties as deputy chairman of the PTA.

One of the teachers who attended the meeting told Pili Pili what had happened in the PTA meeting. Pili Pili was happy to learn that he had the full support of the parents as far as the enforcement of discipline was concerned. Thus, armed with the knowledge that the parents supported the way he "corrected" the students, Pili Pili roamed the school compound hitting any student he thought was doing something wrong. He gave instant punishments to vernacular speakers, caned those who dropped rubbish on the school compound, and rebuked those that did not run immediately to wherever they were supposed to go when the bell rang. That month, Pili Pili's punishments were so severe that two female student-teachers said he was crazy. Makula overheard the comment but he did not know what "crazy" meant.

Despite the water tap just outside his dormitory, Makula did not overcome his dislike of bathing while at the school. In fact, he found out that many of the boys in his dormitory did not bathe regularly. The bathrooms were outside, about ten metres from the dormitory, and the water tap was next to the bathrooms. There was no hot water. Some of the boys had towels, but Makula did not. The boys would go into the bathrooms in groups of three or four, wash their feet, hair, and face, and then those with towels would wrap them around their bodies to appear to have bathed. During the hot, sunny season, the boys would pour water into their plastic basins at around three o'clock, then set them out in the sun to warm. They would then bathe completely as the water was warm. However, the boys had to watch their basins as some malicious students would sometimes empty them of water and hide them, and they were never to be seen again.

The students enjoyed the nights when, well beyond the administration's control, there was neither electricity nor running water at the school. On such evenings the teachers would ask them to go to a well in the nearby village of Kisa to fetch water so that the students could bathe and the kitchen staff could prepare breakfast. The students would walk quietly away from the school compound, but when they reached the well, they would yell and shout. They would also run onto sugar cane or banana plantations and take whatever they laid their hands on. This ransacking angered the farmers. They would report these incidents to the school, but since entire classes were involved, there was no way of catching the culprits.

Pili Pili, however, devised a way to catch the wrongdoers. On those nights when there was no water and students were sent to fetch it, he would disguise himself as a villager and then follow them and watch what they did. The guilty students were shocked the next morning when he called out the names of those that had made too much noise or stole sugar cane from the farmers. And they were even more shocked when he told each one what he had done before caning him.

He told the group of boys, "Crimes committed in the village will not be forgiven. Some of you may ask why, but the reason is simply that some of you will become tomorrow's village chiefs. When you steal, what kind of example do you think you would be setting for those under your care?" He then asked the students to bend over until they touched their toes with their fingers. They had to remain in that position until he had given each of them three or four strokes of the cane. With this kind of punishment, the students eventually gave up terrorizing the village.

As he grew more comfortable at Kayunga Primary School, Makula joined both the school choir and the school athletics team. His good performance in athletics sometimes helped him escape Pili Pili's punishments.

CHAPTER FIVE
Kayunga, Uganda, January 1977

Makula returned to Kayunga for his final year of primary school. Unlike the previous two years when the students had been given at least a day to settle in, this year the headmaster, Mr. Kasule, came to the first math class with his mental workbook already open.

"Good morning, candidate class," he greeted them. "Mental work. Question number one…"

In shock, the students pulled out their notebooks to begin calculating the answers. Mr. Kasule then asked them to exchange books to mark each other's work. The performance of many, except for a few individuals like Mugisha, was below standard.

Mr. Kasule announced that he was giving them a little gift; he would not be caning anyone for getting fewer than five out of ten questions right because the exercise had just been a warm-up. He did, however, tell them to begin working hard right away. "The final year is going to be tough for all of you. You will be 'pumped with material' to ensure your results are excellent at the end of the year. Is that clear?"

"Yes, sir," they responded in unison.

Mr. Kasule completed the math lesson, then asked the students to make note of their homework. "I hope you have your textbooks. You are to do all the exercises in Essential Mathematics, pages 1 to 10. Please hand in your work first thing tomorrow morning." As he turned to leave the classroom, he said, "Makula, come see me in my office."

When Makula entered the headmaster's office, he was happy to see a large parcel from the county chief. "Lucky man," the headmaster said. "You now have everything you need for school from the chief himself. You will have no excuse to perform poorly. Now, get out of my office. Go open your parcel in your dormitory."

Makula carried the big parcel on his head. A few female classmates who were standing outside the classroom laughed at him but he ignored them. On his small bed in the dormitory, he ripped open the package and was happy to see the contents. There was a pair of khaki shorts and two blue cotton shirts—the school uniform. And there were six textbooks—*Nile English Course, Common Mistakes in English, Essentials of Mathematics, The World Atlas, The Geography of East Africa, and an Oxford Learner's Dictionary.*

Also tucked into the parcel was a short handwritten note from the county chief: "Dear Makula, I hope you are still doing a good job at school. Remember, many people in your village have hope in you. Please work even harder. Don't disappoint them."

The next morning Makula woke up early and walked to class in his new school uniform, barefooted like the rest of his classmates. Makula had no backpack. Instead, he curled his right arm around his text and exercise books. There were so many that he bent a little awkwardly to the left to balance himself. He, like many of the students in Primary 7, did not mind carrying around huge piles of books, even those that he never read—it made him appear to be very serious about his academic work.

In Primary 7, Makula studied the geography of Canada in a little more detail than previously. He learned about various cities in Canada, including the port and city of Montreal. The geography teacher, Miss Mabel, and the students pronounced it as "Montirio." They also learned about wheat farming on the prairies. All these things fascinated Makula, and he imagined that life was very good and easy for those who lived there.

Encouraged by the parents' approval of his discipline during the PTA meeting, Pili Pili continued the crackdown on vernacular speakers in Makula's final year of primary school. And yet, Luganda was also taught as a subject. Mr. Sebina, the Luganda teacher, hated it when the students mixed Luganda and English during his lessons and insisted that they read at least one chapter of the textbook every day.

Mr. Sebina liked Makula because he could read Luganda very well, and Makula was often called upon to do the readings in the local Anglican church on Sundays. Many of the other students had trouble reading Luganda, but Mr. Sebina required each of them to stand before the class to read. He would position himself behind the reader with a cane in his hand, peering over to monitor the text as they were reading and annoying the students with his breath that often smelled of alcohol.

"Raise your voice so that those at the back of the room can hear you," he would say to those who had trouble reading Luganda. And the students would shake as they fumbled to read. Whoever did not read well enough to meet Mr. Sebina's standards had to attend an extra class on Friday evenings to improve their skill.

Although Mr. Sebina always came to class with a cane in his hand, unlike the other teachers, he did not hit his students. Because of this, as the year progressed, the students began to like him. And he was also the only teacher with whom they could joke. When Mr. Sebina told the Primary 7 class that he wanted to see some improvement in their performance in Luganda, Makula retorted that the students could hardly be expected to improve their performance in Luganda when they were not allowed to speak the language at school. "That's not my problem," Mr. Sebina said as he chuckled. "All I want to see are better results. How you do it is not my concern."

One Sunday morning, the bishop was expected to visit the school. Mr. Sebina chose Makula and another student to do the readings in the church as he was proud of their ability to read Luganda. When Mr. Sebina sat down at the beginning of the service, the headmaster told him that the school wished to honour him for his contribution to the development of Luganda by seating him next to the bishop. Mr. Sebina was terrified. He ran to Kayunga to buy chewing gum. He put three pieces of gum in his mouth and ran back to the school. When he arrived, sweating profusely, the bishop had already taken his seat. The other teachers urged Mr. Sebina to go sit next to the bishop. However, he refused to budge as he was sweaty and, despite the chewing gum, smelled of alcohol.

***

The Primary 7 students had almost no free time. Their school day began at seven o'clock with the math lesson. Mr. Kasule would give them an exercise in mental work, followed by the correction of the previous day's homework. Although it was rare for the students not to have completed their homework, those who had not were punished. The students would continue their class studies until seven o'clock in the evening when the local students would head for home. They were expected to complete their homework despite having to walk long distances and complete chores at home. The boarding students would go to the dining hall for dinner. The boarders would then return to class at eight o'clock to complete their homework, usually finishing at around midnight. Makula was always surprised by how clever his friend Mugisha and a girl named Bukirwa were—they were the brightest students in Primary 7. These two often scored over 90 percent on their tests. To encourage the students to work hard, Mr. Kasule would sometimes reward the best performing student and it was expected that either Mugisha or Bukirwa would receive the reward. However, in one English language test that they wrote toward the end of the year, the reward—a geometry set—went to Makula. Bukirwa became so angry at this that she stopped talking to Makula. She said that he had cheated on the test.

As the school year neared its end, the students in Primary 7 spent even more time studying, getting up at five o'clock to begin reading. To fight sleep early in the morning, they would dip their feet in plastic basins half full of cold water. They called this a "winter session." They also drank lots of coffee. The students were allowed to work independently: they spent less time in class and more doing revision. This freedom caused some of the students to feel that they were now grown up. They began to treat their teachers in a demeaning fashion and openly refused to be punished.

At the end of the year, Makula and the rest of the students in Primary 7 sat for the national Primary Leaving Examinations (PLE), which included tests in English, Mathematics, and General Paper (the latter encompassed geography, history, and science). Makula found the examinations quite easy and was certain that he had done well.

On the last evening of the exams, a party was organized to honour and congratulate the students on having completed their primary education. The merry-making lasted until seven o'clock. Some of the teachers remained in the main hall to chat while a few returned home. Pili Pili, however, went to Kayunga to drink more.

When he was returning to the teachers' quarters at a quarter to midnight, some people stopped Pili Pili at the shrub near the school, in a poorly lit area. They beat him so badly that he cried out loudly in pain. Two members of the kitchen staff heard his wailing and went to his rescue.

With their flashlights, they established that he had been badly beaten and his clothes were covered in blood. One of the men ran to the school to inform the headmaster and the other teachers about the incident while the other hurried to get his bicycle to take Pili Pili to the hospital, which was about two kilometres away.

At the hospital, Pili Pili's numerous wounds were stitched. When the headmaster arrived at the hospital, he asked Pili Pili whether he had recognized any of his assailants. "No, I didn't recognize any of them," Pili Pili told him. "I couldn't even tell what kind of people they were because they beat me in total silence."

"They didn't say even a single word?" Mr. Kasule asked.

"No. They pounced on me in total silence," he said.

"We will report this matter to the police right away," Mr. Kasule said.

***

The following morning, as Makula packed his books and clothes into his suitcase in preparation for his return home, a teacher came to the dormitory and asked him to report to the headmaster's office. Makula wondered why. The door to the headmaster's office was wide open when he arrived but he knocked because all of the students had been taught to do so. Makula was very surprised to see both his parents seated inside. After he had greeted them, the headmaster told Makula that he would be leaving his belongings behind at Miss Mabel's home because he was going on a journey with his parents. Makula wondered where, but he did not dare question his father. Filipo talked to the headmaster for a few more minutes as Kabejja went out with her son to thank his teachers.

When he joined them outside, Filipo told Makula that they were going to the home of the county chief to thank him for having paid for Makula's education in Kayunga Primary School. This was a very exciting moment for Makula because it was the first time ever that he would be going anywhere with his parents.

As they walked to the market in Kayunga, Makula dared to ask his father, "Wouldn't it have been better if we had let the chief know that we would be paying him a visit?"

"I went to see him last month and told him that we would be going to see him the day after you completed your examinations. What he has done for us is a great thing; we need to thank him in a respectful way," Filipo answered.

They went to the market and bought a large bunch of matooke and a cock as gifts for the chief. Filipo paid a few shillings to a man who carried the matooke on his head up to the bus. The fact that Filipo had not asked him to carry the matooke made Makula to feel important and grown up.

When they arrived at the chief's home in Bikajjo, about twenty kilometres from Kayunga, he was waiting for them, seated on a chair under a big tree that stood close to the front yard. There were two other chairs beside him and a mat. When he saw them get off the bus, the chief walked toward them with his hands stretched out to hug Makula. Two of his sons came running after him to take the bunch of matooke and the cock that the "conductor"—the driver's assistant who collected the fares—had placed on the ground. After the chief had hugged and greeted the three visitors, he led them back to the seating area by the tree. Makula felt even more important when he was asked to sit on one of the chairs next to his father while Kabejja sat on the mat. Then the long greetings began. There were about twenty people that lived in the chief's home, and after each of them had greeted the visitors, they were served with a pot of tea and roasted corn. As they drank the tea, Filipo thanked the chief for having paid for Makula's education.

"It was my pleasure to help, but above all, it was a very wise thing to do," he told Filipo. Then turning to Makula, he said, "I have received reports from both the headmaster and your teachers that you are an excellent student."

"Thank you very much for saying so," Kabejja responded. "We know that he will not let us down; he is a good child."

"Makula, remember that my home is open to you. Pay us a visit whenever you are in the area," the chief said.

The visit to the chief ended late in the afternoon after Makula and his parents had enjoyed a big meal that included the cock that they had brought as a gift.

CHAPTER SIX
Kasaka, Uganda, December 1977

Makula returned to his home in Kasaka to await the results of the Primary Leaving Examinations, which would be released in two months. He found he did not like village life anymore; the people were boring and the water tasted bad. He was no longer used to the dark of night after having had electric lighting, and his mother, Kabejja, insisted that they have dinner at sunset to save the paraffin in the one lantern they owned.

Soon after Makula's return, Luyima, a friend of Makula's cousin Makko, came to the village. Although he was considered rich, Luyima did not have a job—he earned his living as a trader in illegal commodities, such as coffee beans, that he and his friends smuggled across Lake Victoria. However, the people in Kasaka did not know anything about Luyima's source of income other than the fact that he was a trader; no one had the courage to ask him directly what he did for a living.

Luyima also had very little formal education. He saw it as a waste of time; he had managed to make a lot of money without going to school. When Makko argued about the need for education when attending international business meetings, Luyima said that he could marry an educated woman because he had money. His wife could help him with any business transactions that required more sophisticated knowledge than he had.

When Luyima came to the village, he was wearing brown bell-bottom pants, brown platform shoes, dark glasses, and an expensive watch, and all the children in the area gathered around as he talked to the adults about his many journeys and the exciting encounters he and his moneyed friends had. He told them the story of how they had gone to a bar and found twelve people drinking. Luyima had asked the tallest man in the bar to stand up. The man was about 6 foot 4. He then asked for crates of beer to be stacked one on top of the other until they were as high as the man's head. Luyima paid for the beer and told the patrons in the bar to drink it, free of charge. He and his friends then left the bar.

Luyima also bragged that he took pity on poor people, especially women. He said that one day he had gone to the market in Kayunga, to the stalls where women sold oranges, onions, or tomatoes, paid for all their merchandise, and asked them to go home. "I asked them how they expected to get rich when all they sell are a few kilos of tomatoes or oranges," he said. He added that those who happened to be around enjoyed the freebies.

Although he was almost certain that his future depended on education, Makula was attracted to Luyima's lifestyle. He wished he had a new Honda motorbike like Luyima's. Also, because they had a rich son, Luyima's parents enjoyed a better life than the rest of the people in the village. They could afford to buy sugar in the market and owned one of the two radio sets in the village. The other, much smaller radio belonged to Makula's Uncle Lameka. Some of the village men gathered every evening at Luyima's parents' home to listen to the news and then went to Lameka's house to drink. There was a rumour in Kasaka that Luyima did not live in Kampala as he claimed but in a rented room in Kayunga. However, there was no way to verify this. Because he admired Luyima's wealth, Makula asked Othieno, the former teacher who lived in his village, whether he should perhaps follow in Luyima's footsteps.

"My friend, don't be fooled by outside appearances. Who knows what he does to earn that money?" Othieno asked.

"I heard him say that he is a trader," Makula replied.

"And just what does he deal in?" Othieno asked.

"I have no idea," Makula said.

"I don't blame you, though, for thinking of quitting school," Othieno said. "I am quite educated, but look at me. What kind of life am I leading? Here I am languishing in the village. You are our only hope. You should not quit school because, in the future, your education might help you to get a stable, respectable job."

Makula decided to pursue further education. However, as he waited for the results of his Primary Leaving Examinations, he pondered what he would do if he failed them. He could become a tailor in Kayunga. He could set up a small restaurant in Kayunga, or join his cousins Lukka and Makko in Kampala. Then he remembered Lukka's troubles as a dealer in raw food in Owino market, the largest market in Kampala. One day, Lukka had hired a pickup truck to transport cassava to the market in hopes of making a profit. When he arrived, he saw that the loading area was full of trucks carrying cassava. Lukka had tried to convince the buyers to pay him enough to at least cover the cost of transport but failed. When he realized that he would need to borrow money to pay the driver of the pickup truck, Lukka had simply vanished, leaving the driver stranded with the load of cassava.

Makko was not doing any better. During the day, he sold banana juice in a market in Kampala, and in the evenings, he helped pack traders' wares into storage at the end of the business day. Makko's banana juice sold well during the dry season but demand halted during the rainy season. Lukka and Makko lived together in a rented room in a cheap neighbourhood in Kampala. Thinking of this, Makula understood why he was "the hope of Kasaka."

***

During the days before Christmas, the people of Kasaka cleared the village paths. Some put a fresh coat of mud on their huts while others prepared their homes for visiting relatives. Makula's father, Filipo, returned four days before Christmas to join his family in the festivities. On Christmas Eve, as he had done for several years, Lameka slaughtered a bull. Two of his sons carefully wrapped the meat in banana leaves and secured the packs with banana fibre. Makula and his cousin Toofa then loaded the packs of meat in handwoven baskets and gave one as a present to each of the homes in the village. The thankful neighbours in return sent the boys back to Lameka's with yet more meat, rice, or sugar.

Kabejja joined Lameka's two wives in preparing a feast for their two families. Along with three of Lameka's teenage daughters, they peeled the matooke on Christmas Eve and divided it into two piles. They then carefully wrapped the piles in banana leaves and tied them firmly with banana fibre. They put water in two big saucepans, placed the matooke in the pans, and then covered it with yet more banana leaves to preserve the heat. The boys roasted plenty of beef and chicken on the bonfire in the front yard while Lameka and Filipo sat on wooden chairs to watch all the activity. The house and yard were full of festive aromas. The younger children played soccer with footballs made of banana fibre while the older boys served the roasted meat.

"So which school will Makula join when he gets his results?" Lameka asked.

"It will depend on his performance, but he would really like to study at Musasa High School," Filipo replied. "He applied for admission there shortly before he sat for his examinations."

"That is a fine school. Good choice," Lameka said.

"There is one problem, though. It is certainly not cheap to educate a child in that school," Filipo said.

"I know, but it would be a great opportunity for him and for us if he got a place there," Lameka said.

"You are right, but can I afford to pay the fees? I don't think so," Filipo added.

"How about Buweela High School? That is another great school," Lameka said.

"Buweela High School is a great school, but it is for girls only."

"It does not admit boys?" Lameka asked.

"No," Filipo told him. "I am working hard to save money for his education. Two years ago, I opened a bank account in Kayunga for that purpose."

"That's very good planning. By saving money now, if he gets admitted to Musasa, there will be less pressure on you to pay the exorbitant fees. I am very proud of you, my brother," Lameka said.

The women woke up very early in the morning on Christmas Day to start preparing the food. They made a fire using wood that had been chopped and thoroughly dried months before and soon the flames were licking away at the bottom of the big sauce pans. They also cooked beef and chicken. At eight o'clock they mashed the cooked matooke, wrapped it again in banana leaves, and put it back into the saucepans to simmer until lunchtime.

At one o'clock, as Lameka, Filipo, and their sons were beginning to eat in the shade of a mango tree in the front yard, Othieno arrived with his wife Auma and their three children. "Come on, my friends," Lameka said. "We were not expecting you, but you are welcome."

"You were not expecting us, and we had not planned to come here. Unfortunately, when we returned home from church this afternoon, we found our food gone," Othieno said.

"What do you mean your food was gone? Did it grow legs?" Lameka asked in his usual humorous way.

"There is no lock on the door to our kitchen, so some hungry man must have broken in and helped himself to our meal," Auma said angrily.

"It could have been a woman," Lameka said jokingly.

"Yes, but such thieves are usually men," Auma responded.

"That's unfortunate, but you are welcome to join us for lunch. There is more than enough food for all of us," Lameka said. And they carried on with their lunch.

About ten minutes later, Senjo, a young man who was just a couple of years older than Makula and who had no fixed place of abode, arrived. "Come on, my friend," Lameka said. "We were not expecting you, but you are welcome."

"You were not expecting me, but I have some bad news," Senjo said.

One of the boys gave Senjo a small wooden stool to sit on. He declined Lameka's offer of food but did accept a mug of beer.

"What kind of bad news are you bringing, my friend?" Lameka asked.

"We have just received news that Luyima has not been seen for close to a month. One of his friends came by this afternoon to tell his father just as the family was about to have lunch," Senjo replied.

"Well, that's pretty bad news. Do they know where he could be?" Lameka asked.

"Nobody knows where he is. We are very worried about him," Senjo said.

After lunch the women came outside to join the men in conversation. They discussed Luyima's case for a while, then talked about the bountiful harvest. Senjo irritated Auma as he laughed incessantly, even when there was no apparent reason to.

On the way home, Auma told her husband that she was convinced that Senjo had stolen their food.

"Why do you think so?" Othieno asked.

"It is obvious—what would have stopped Senjo from having lunch at Lameka's house except for the fact that he was already full? We know that he does not cook; where did he get the food to eat? Besides, his teeth had millet stuck on them. Where did he get the millet from? We are the only family that eats millet around here."

"You are right. Whenever he laughed, his teeth showed the millet stuck on them. It's very sad to see such a young man waste his life that way," Othieno said.

Makula and his cousins, including Lukka and Makko who had returned from Kampala to celebrate Christmas with the family, went out to enjoy the evening. They joined about two hundred others from Kasaka and the neighbouring villages who had gathered at a temporary enclosure that had been constructed in the school playground. There, they watched a group of dancers and drummers from Kayunga. Makula felt like he was the star of the evening—he grabbed the attention of all the girls and he heard several of them gossiping about how he had completed primary school and was going to attend the prestigious Musasa High School. He did feel the pressure of this, though. "What if I don't make it to Musasa? What will people say?" he thought. "I wonder how people know that I want to go to Musasa High School. Did my mother, in her excitement, tell the entire village?"

CHAPTER SEVEN
Musasa, Uganda, February 1978

One afternoon, while resting under the mango tree in front of Uncle Lameka's house after working in the cassava garden, Makula looked up to see Othieno running toward him. Breathless and smiling, Othieno told Makula that the Primary Leaving Examination results had been released and that many of the students of Kayunga Primary School had passed in Grade A. Othieno had heard the news from some villagers who had arrived home on the bus from Kayunga. Makula felt both happy and anxious. When he shared the news with his uncle, Lameka promised to tune in to the evening newscast on the radio for more information on the best performing schools and students, which would be broadcast over the next few days.

Makula, Kabejja, and many of the members of Lameka's household gathered in the front yard to listen to the news that same evening; the radio's reception was better outside than inside. The broadcast confirmed that the schools had received the results. Othieno offered to go to Kayunga with Makula to find out how he had performed on the exams. Because Kabejja did not have the money to pay Makula's bus fare, Othieno agreed to lend her the money; after all, Makula was "the hope of the village." Early the next morning, they walked the three kilometres to the bus stop to find more than ten people already waiting for the daily bus.

Makula received very good news at Kayunga Primary School: he had done well on the examinations. As expected, his friend Paul Mugisha and Bukirwa had achieved the highest grades. The news of Bukirwa's achievement was received with mixed reaction by the teachers because they had been informed that very morning that the fifteen-year-old girl was pregnant and would not be continuing with her education.

Given his results, Makula was now certain that he would be admitted to Musasa High School, the school of his dreams. Makula shared the news with Kabejja once he had arrived back in Kasaka. She was so pleased to learn that her son had passed his examinations that she went from house to house proclaiming the news until sunset. She returned home exhausted. While resting, it dawned on her that, although her husband had been saving money, he still could not afford to pay the fees and buy all the items required by Musasa High School. Saddened, she cried a few tears. Othieno, who had not left Makula's side since their return from the school, assured her that they would find a way.

***

Musasa High School was a boys' boarding school and one of the most popular in the country. It was known as the school for rich men's sons, and attendance there was generally considered to be a passport to success and future prosperity. Makula was thrilled when he received the letter admitting him to Musasa High School. However, he also knew that life at the school was going to be very different and therefore very challenging.

For Filipo, Makula's admission offered a challenge of a different sort. He had hoped that he had saved enough to pay Makula's tuition for a full year. Instead, he learned that the sum he had would pay for only one term. He could not disappoint his son by asking him to attend a less expensive school, and he would have to work much harder to come up with enough money to ensure that Makula would be able to continue his education at this prestigious school.

The school was located thirty kilometres north of the city of Kampala. To get there, Makula would need to board the bus to Kayunga. Once there, he would need to travel on a second bus that would take him to Kampala. He would then board a third bus, which, unfortunately, did not go directly to the school. He would need to get off the bus on a main road and then walk four kilometres along a dirt road to reach the school.

On his first day, he and Kabejja boarded the bus in Kasaka to Kayunga, then the bus to Kampala, which was Makula's first visit to the capital city.

After getting off the third and final bus early in the afternoon, Makula and his mother Kabejja were the only people walking on the dusty road that led to the school. The other parents and students stared as they passed them in their cars. Makula carried his metallic suitcase on his head while his mother carried his small mattress and a handwoven bag filled with yams and roasted nuts that Makula could snack on. By the time they reached the school, they were covered in dust from the road.

Kabejja sat patiently in the corner of the room where three of the teachers were registering the Senior 1 students. When processing Makula, the teacher mentioned to Kabejja that her son did not have many of the items required for school. Although he had a few textbooks and a school uniform, he had brought only two pairs of shorts and no shoes. Kabejja informed the teacher that they could only afford the basic necessities, items that were essential for his study. This was not the first time the teacher had heard this, and he didn't pursue the matter any further.

Kabejja accompanied her son to the dormitory and helped him set up his bedding on the lower deck of a bunk bed. Before leaving, Kabejja said, "My son, do not squander this opportunity to study in this great school. Many would love to study here, but don't have the chance. You are here to study, nothing more, and nothing less. Don't be bothered by what the other students have that you don't have. Whatever you desire you will get in the future if you work hard now. Your father and I are determined to support you all the way. You are our only hope. Don't disappoint your mother." She hugged him, bade him goodbye, and cried as she began her journey back home.

Makula felt lost. He walked outside the dormitory to search for his friend Paul Mugisha, whose name he had seen on the admissions list at the school's administration building. But Mugisha was nowhere to be seen.

Makula's first night in Musasa High School was a very noisy one as the students settled into their dormitories. Although he was usually a quiet person, Makula talked a lot that evening. He was obviously the oldest student in Camp Hope dormitory, even though there were students in Senior 2, 3, and 4 that would reside there. A large group gathered around Makula's bed, both to behold his unkempt look and to hear his stories about his visit to Kampala on the way to the school. He told them how impressed he had been by the tall buildings, such as the Bank of Uganda and the International Hotel, the one-way streets, fast cars, and the big shops, among many other things.

Among the students listening to Makula was a Senior 2 student named Tom Kabenge. Kabenge was the son of James Kabenge, the managing director of the East African Bank of Commerce, and was known to be one of the most notorious bullies in the school.

"Did you see the train? Were the streets in Kampala clean? Would you like to climb one of those tall buildings?" Kabenge teased Makula. Excited, Makula tried to answer Kabenge's questions as the other students laughed.

The next morning, as he prepared to go out for breakfast, Makula noticed that much of his food had been stolen. As he was the last to leave the dormitory, he looked around and for the first time became aware of how truly poor he was in comparison to the other students in the dormitory. He did not have a bath towel; he was the only one that did not have shoes; his mattress, donated by Othieno, was the smallest and oldest; his blanket, given to him by Uncle Lameka, was the most worn. Makula felt ashamed as he realized that his younger schoolmates had really only been making fun of him the previous evening by listening to his stories—many of them must come from wealthy homes in and around Kampala.

Makula was one of only a few students who went to the dining room for breakfast. The majority of the students did not go as they had brought better food from home. Other students, with money given to them by their wealthy parents at the beginning of the term, bought food from the school canteen. Makula sat quietly alone at a table eating his warm, sugarless porridge until another student, Ben Kasede, came over and introduced himself. From his appearance, Makula guessed that Kasede might be even poorer than he was. Kasede told him that he was also in Senior 1 and that he already found the school environment hard to cope with.

"What kind of difficulties have you had so far?" Makula asked.

"No difficulties yet, but I don't have most of the required items," Kasede told him.

"I don't either. Do you have exercise and workbooks?" Makula asked.

"Yes, I do," Kasede replied.

"I guess you are good to go. Don't worry, we are in a similar situation; we will look out for each other. What dormitory are you in?" Makula asked.

"I am in Fort Larry," Kasede said.

"Good," Makula said. "I am in Camp Hope. Our dormitories are close to each other."

After breakfast, the school's 1,223 students lined up according to their classes in front of the administration building for the first assembly. Makula looked around him and saw that he and Kasede were the only ones without shoes on their feet. Makula was impressed by the size and cleanliness of the school but also slightly overwhelmed. The headmaster, Mr. Atiku, addressed the assembly for over fifteen minutes in the presence of all the teachers and other members of the support staff. And after listening to Mr. Atiku, Makula concluded that he was an eloquent man who did not mince words.

"Musasa High School is not a conduit for failures," Mr. Atiku told them. "Here, academic dwarfism is not an option. You either perform or face the 'guillotine' at the end of the year."

This was the first time that many of the Senior 1 students had heard the word "guillotine." In Musasa High School, it meant the automatic expulsion of a student from the school if he failed to score an overall average of 50 percent.

As he walked to his class, Makula heard Paul Mugisha's familiar voice calling out his name. Mugisha told Makula that he had just arrived that morning and had settled in Camp Hope. They were overjoyed to know that they would both be living in the same dormitory.

***

One evening, a month before the end of the school term, Kabejja packed a bag full of steamed cassava, corn, and yams, and some roasted dried corn to take to Makula at Musasa High School. Early the next morning, she happily walked to board the bus to Kayunga. Others soon joined her at the bus stop, and everyone seemed to be in a good mood, talking and laughing, once they were on their way. Kabejja had to board another bus for Kampala and found everyone on it to also to be in good spirits. Kabejja sat quietly as she thought about how Makula would react to her visit. An elderly woman soon started up a friendly conversation with her. Kabejja told the woman that she had a son at Musasa High School and that she was going to see him there. The woman told her that she had a grandson at the school and that her husband had gone to visit him the previous week.

The woman cautioned Kabejja, "They have specific visitation days. If I am not mistaken, it's only allowed once a month and only on a Sunday. Since this is Wednesday, I wonder whether they will allow you to go in, let alone see him. Didn't you read about it in the admission letter?"

"No, I didn't see that detail. At least, I don't remember reading about it," Kabejja said. She was sorry to be lying but she was too ashamed to tell the woman that she could not read English.

Kabejja felt a bit discouraged by this news, but decided to continue on her way. When she reached the school, the gatekeeper asked if he could help her. She told him that she was there to see her son.

"You want to see your son? Visitation Sunday was last week," he said.

"I was not aware of that," Kabejja replied.

"Mum, the regulations are clear, and you must have read about this in your son's admission letter," he said.

"Sir, have pity on me," she said. "I come from very far away. I can't go back home without seeing my son. I have walked for an hour and a half to get here from the main road. I found it hard to walk fast on the dirt road in this heat. Surely you wouldn't let me go without seeing him."

Kabejja was speaking loudly, and the gatekeeper asked her to calm down. He said that he would talk to the deputy headmaster to see whether he could at least give her son the food she had brought. He also told her that he was only trying, as it was unlikely that the deputy headmaster would allow this other than on a scheduled visitation day.

When he returned, the gatekeeper asked Kabejja for a proper identity card. Kabejja told him that she did not have one. The gatekeeper said that, in that case, he could not help her. Kabejja threatened to sleep there if she was not allowed to see her son. The gatekeeper decided to ignore her and went about his duties. After about half an hour, Kabejja realized that the man was not going to give in to her demands. She started pleading with him again to let her see her son, even for five minutes. The gatekeeper refused and warned Kabejja never to come to the school again except on a designated visitation day. He then asked her to hand over the bag of food for Makula. Kabejja gave him the bag and went on her way.

After Kabejja had left, the gatekeeper went to the Senior 1 class and asked a few of the boys if they knew Makula. No one seemed to know him and he had decided to give up when he saw a boy walking toward him.

"Are you Makula?" the gatekeeper asked.

"No, I am not Makula, but I know him," the boy replied.

"Can you please ask him to come see me right away?" the gatekeeper said.

"No problem," the boy said, as he ran to find Makula and tell him to go talk to the gatekeeper.

Makula stood near the gate and waited for the gatekeeper to finish talking to another student. He felt anxious and wondered if there were a problem. The gatekeeper noticed his worried look. When he had finished speaking to the other student, he called Makula over. "Are you Makula?" he asked.

"Yes, I am Makula," Makula answered in a worried tone.

"Don't worry. You are not in any kind of trouble," the gatekeeper said as he led Makula into the duty station.

The gatekeeper then pointed to the bag that Makula knew belonged to his mother. "How did it get here?" he wondered.

"Do you recognize that bag? Open it and tell me if you recognize anything in it," said the gatekeeper in a low tone of voice.

"Yes, I recognize it. I don't need to open it. It belongs to my mother," Makula said.

"The woman who left it looked too young to be your mother. Are you sure it is her bag?" the gatekeeper asked.

"Yes, it is my mother's. I am her only child," Makula answered.

"Well, your mother was here and she wanted to see you, but she can't do so in the middle of the week. She can only visit on proper visitation days," the gatekeeper said.

Ashamed of his mother's unauthorized visit, Makula said, "I guess I did not let her know that—I didn't expect her to come to see me here."

The gatekeeper told Makula, "I will let you have the food she left but you can only take a little at a time. You can come for some every day, but I can't let you take it to the dormitory all at once. It could cost me my job. Do you understand?"

"Yes," Makula said.

"Now, have a look at what is in the bag. I wouldn't want you to accuse me of stealing your food! After you've seen what is there, take a little of it, beginning with the perishable items. And please make sure that you don't cause a commotion in the dormitory. Have I made myself clear?" the gatekeeper said.

"Yes. I will be discreet," Makula said.

"I can see that you are old enough to know the possible consequences of the risk that I am taking. Can I trust you?" the gatekeeper asked.

"Yes. Trust me," Makula said. The gatekeeper let Makula take three big pieces of cassava and two pieces of yam.

In the following days, Makula picked up only a little of his food at a time until he and his friends Mugisha and Kasede had eaten all of it.

***

Despite his hardships, Makula did well at his studies during the first term. When it had ended and he was on his way back to Kasaka, he once again stopped by the county chief's home in Bikajjo. The chief, who had just retired from public service, was happy to see Makula and to hear that he was doing well at Musasa High School.

When he returned home, Makula talked to Kabejja about her trip to the school on a day that was not designated as a visitation day. "Mother, why did you do that? The school is very far," Makula said.

"Weren't you happy that I brought you some food? By the way, did that man give you your food?" she asked.

"Yes, he gave me all the food. Thank you," Makula said.

"I was very angry with him for not letting me see you. How could he do that?" she asked.

"Mother, the school is strict on that matter. I didn't let you know about it because it never occurred to me that you would come to see me," Makula said.

"Well, I did it out of love. I thought that it would be nice to surprise you," she said.

"Weren't you worn out by the time you walked back to the main road?" Makula asked.

"No. I didn't walk back. When I left the school, I had only walked for about five minutes when a car stopped to give me a lift…" Kabejja told him.

"Are you sure?" Makula asked.

"Yes, a very beautiful black car. The gentleman who was driving it told me that the gatekeeper, who happened to be his acquaintance, had asked him to drop me off at the main road," she said. "So I sat in the back seat and off we went. He was a very well mannered man. He introduced himself to me. He told me his name was James Kabenge and that he has two sons in the school."

"Yes, I know Mr. Kabenge. His son Tom is one class ahead of me and his son John is in my class. Mother, you got a ride in James Kabenge's car?" Makula asked incredulously.

"Yes I did. It was very comfortable," Kabejja replied.

Makula told her, "You are very lucky. You enjoyed a ride in a Mercedes Benz."

"That was a Mercedes Benz?" Kabejja asked.

"Yes. I saw Mr. Kabenge's car at the school one Sunday. It is a black Mercedes Benz. Did he drop you off at the main road?" Makula asked.

"No, he drove me all the way to the bus park in Kampala, and so I was able to arrive in Kayunga just before dark. When I arrived at your former school, I thought they would let me stay there until morning. However, Mr. Kasule kindly let me spend the night in his house," Kabejja told him.

"But why was Mr. Kabenge allowed into the school and not you?" Makula asked angrily.

"No," Kabejja said, "he was not there to see his sons. He told me that he had come to attend a meeting. He said that he heads the committee that governs your school."

"Oh, I see," Makula said. "He is the chairman of the school's Board of Governors."

"Whatever you call it. He had come to a meeting," Kabejja said again.

Othieno visited Makula and asked him about the school and his studies. Makula said that everything was okay. "I have something to show you," Othieno said.

Makula followed Othieno into the backyard. "Luyima is in jail in Kayunga," Othieno said.

"Is that so? His family must be relieved to at least know where he is," Makula said.

"About a month after you left for school, we received word that he was in jail," Othieno continued. "His father asked me to go to see him, so I went, and we talked for some time. He gave me this note to take to one of his girlfriends, a teacher at your former school."

"What?" Makula exclaimed, as he took the note from Othieno's hand, and read:

> "*Deer Mebo*
> *I am doing big wak but I come back soon. dot no wory*
> > > *Big boss*"

"What does it mean?" Makula asked.

"What, you don't get it?" Othieno said. "He is telling his girl-friend not to worry because he is busy doing some important work, but he will be returning soon. He told me that the girl is a teacher in your former school. Her name is Mabel."

"What? I can't believe it. Miss Mabel is Luyima's girlfriend?" asked Makula.

"Yes, Miss Mabel is Luyima's girlfriend," Othieno replied.

"I can't believe she would have that man for a boyfriend," Makula said with some disgust.

"Why not? He has money, or should I say, he had money. Now that he is locked up, I don't think he will have any money left by the time he gets out of there." Othieno chuckled and said, "Isn't it funny that he signed off as 'Big boss'? I found that really hilarious."

***

At the end of his first year in Musasa, Makula convinced Kabejja to talk to his father about how difficult it was to walk around the school barefooted while everyone else wore shoes. When she brought up the subject with Filipo, he immediately called for Makula and said to him, "Because of your performance in school, you have earned your shoes. I will give you the money to buy them before you return to school next year."

Kabejja suggested that the shoes be bought in Kayunga on Makula's journey back to school. But Makula's cousin Makko, who was visiting from Kampala, said that there was more variety in Kampala and that the prices were lower. Makko offered to wait for him at the bus park in Kampala and they could then go together to buy the shoes. Makula did not agree to this—he was excited at the thought of touring the city alone while he shopped for his first pair of shoes.

And so it happened that, on the first day of school, following the morning assembly, Makula was given permission by the deputy headmaster to go to Kampala to buy his shoes. He was given a note that allowed him to board the school truck that was going into Kampala to purchase school supplies.

When he stepped off the school truck at the City Square, Makula was slightly daunted by the task before him. He had no idea where he needed to go, because he did not know where the shops were. He hadn't asked any of his classmates, as he did not want them to think he knew nothing about the city. However, he decided not to ask for directions from anyone—at least, not yet. He waited five minutes until he got the chance to follow two young men who were crossing the busy Kampala Road. Once across, he walked down another busy street. He was overwhelmed by the number of people walking in all directions, and he was jostled and shoved as he walked slowly down the street.

Luckily, Makula happened upon a shop with many shoes on display in its glass window. He went inside to look at the shoes but wasn't sure what to do next. He stood close to the entrance. "Should I call a salesperson over?" he thought to himself. He then went out of the shop to figure out what he should do. He looked at the big sign in front of the shop, which read "Bata." He knew that many of the boys at his school wore Bata shoes. As he pondered what to do next, a smiling middle-aged man came up to him and said, "Hello, brother. Are you going to buy shoes today?"

"Yes," Makula replied.

"I am also going to buy shoes," said the friendly stranger.
"Do you know what type of shoes and what size you need?"

Before Makula responded, another man came over to them and addressed the stranger. "Toto, are you two buying shoes?"

"Yes," Toto replied.

"Don't you know that this shop is expensive?" he asked. "There are better bargains just down the street. If you wish, I could take you two there."

Toto asked Makula if he would go with them to purchase his shoes. Makula followed the two men down the busy street to another shop. He and Toto stood outside while Toto's friend went inside. He came back out and asked Toto to go inside the shop to "see for himself." Toto handed a stuffed envelope to his friend, explaining to Makula that it's never a good idea to go into these shops with bulging pockets, because if you did, they would guess that you had a lot of money and hike up the prices. Toto went inside and came back, telling them that he was very impressed by the wide selection of shoes. His friend then handed him back his envelope. Then it was Makula's turn to go inside. As Makula started to enter the shop, Toto's friend reminded him that it wasn't wise to go into the shop with his money. So Makula pulled out all the money from his pocket and handed it over to Toto's friend. He then proceeded into the shop. He looked all around but did not see any men's shoes. There were only a few pairs of women's shoes on display. He quickly left the shop to question Toto and his friend. However, when he looked around, the two men had vanished. Makula was not aware that he had been duped; he stood outside the shop for close to an hour waiting for the men to return. He did not want to believe that the men had stolen his money.

Having seen all three of the men outside the shop and now seeing Makula still waiting, one of the salesmen went out and asked Makula what had happened. Makula anxiously told him what had occurred. And when the salesman told him that he had just received an undesirable "welcome to Kampala," Makula broke down and cried.

The man took pity on him and asked him if he had any money left to board the bus back to school. Makula said that he did not have any money at all, and that he was very hungry.

The man led him into the shop and repeated Makula's story to everyone. Makula was very embarrassed. Two teenage girls had just purchased lingerie, and they laughed as they went out of the store. Makula felt even more hurt. Then one kind shopper gave him some money for the bus. And the shop's manager gave him a snack at the back of the shop and asked the salesman who had brought Makula in to take him to the bus park.

Makula silently wept as he travelled on the bus back to school. He had so looked forward to owning and wearing his first pair of shoes, but this was not to be. He was very angry at himself for having listened to the two strangers in the first place. And what was he going to tell his father? Lost in thought, he looked up to see that the bus had almost passed the dirt road that led to his school. He had to shout to the driver to stop the bus. He cried a little as his feet swept the dust and the small pebbles pricked him as he slowly walked up the first hill. He couldn't stop thinking about his predicament. When he reached the school, he went to Fort Larry dormitory to talk to Kasede. His friend told him to take heart, because everything happens for a reason.

"Yes, everything happens for a reason," Makula agreed.
"But what is the reason in this case?"

"I don't know," Kasede replied.

"I don't want to go to Kampala ever again," said Makula, shaking his head.

"Come on, Makula," Kasede said. "Kampala is not full of thieves. There are lots of good people too. Like the people who helped you after the incident. This is just a lesson for us to be cautious wherever we go."

"You are right, Ben," Makula said, "but how will I explain this to my father?"

"Well, you will tell him everything just as it happened. He will understand," Kasede advised.

"Oh, I hope so," Makula said.

In the end, Makula would not be the one to tell his father that he had been conned out of the money he had been given to buy his first pair of shoes.

CHAPTER EIGHT
Musasa, Uganda, January 1979

Although he still did not have shoes, Makula's second year in Musasa High School was a little easier than the first, as both the environment and his fellow students were now familiar to him. His second year was also very eventful. He and Kasede grew so close that they became almost inseparable. Although they did not live in the same dormitory, Makula and Kasede still shared what little they had. They were among the poorest students in the school and were well aware of this fact. The two never missed a meal in the dining room, as this was their only source of sustenance. If one of them could not make it to the dining room, the other kept his portion of food, even if it meant hiding it in a dormitory.

At Musasa High School, the headmaster, Mr. Atiku, encouraged each student to discover his talents and to find ways to use these talents to develop both himself and the school. Therefore, in Senior 2, Makula joined the school's athletics team. He was a very good runner, especially in the two-hundred- and four-hundred-metre races. By the end of his second year, he was the fastest runner in the school.

Because he was very physically active, Makula's appetite had greatly increased. Luckily, the prefect in charge of the kitchen had noticed Kasede's organizational capabilities and strictness as a volunteer and had appointed him as overseer of the dining room—a student whose duty it was to make certain that all students were served their meals. This was good news for Makula as Kasede ensured that they both got extra portions at every meal.

As his performance as an athlete improved, Makula became popular with the other boys in the school, who came to cheer him on at the running track. His popularity also offered other advantages—although he did not have the money to buy deep-fried cassava or pancakes at the canteen, he always returned from the mid-morning break with a full stomach as the others boys gave some to him. Makula also became friendly with Namala, the woman who managed the school canteen with her two sons. She too sometimes gave him free food.

In his Senior 2 year, Makula met a young teacher who he would re-member for a long time. His name was Mr. Thadeus Byamukama. He taught geography and math. Mr. Byamukama was very popular. He knew almost all of the students that he taught by name and was very friendly toward many of them.

When he first came to Makula's class, he introduced himself. "Good morning gentlemen. My name is Thadeus Byamukama but I am mostly addressed by my initials, T.B." The students laughed. He continued, "I know my name sounds like that horrible disease but I'm not at all horrible. I will be teaching you geography and maths. I hope to get to know each of you as we go along."

Mr. T.B. taught mathematics in a calm, systematic manner and explained the concepts until all the students understood them. Mr. T.B.'s method of teaching math helped Makula to grasp and improve his mastery of the subject.

Mr. T.B. often talked with the students after class. He would tell them that whatever they were being taught in the school would benefit them in the future. "Will you remember me when you enjoy your buttered bread?" he would ask jokingly.

Makula especially enjoyed Mr. T.B.'s geography classes. He would speak with him afterward, and they would discuss various issues at length. Mr. T.B. liked Makula because he found him to be mature and hard-working.

One Friday afternoon, Makula and a group of Senior 2, 3 and 4 students sat on some benches in the shade and discussed economic growth and development with Mr. T.B. Tom Kabenge said that although urban areas such as Kampala and Jinja seemed to have the potential for quick development, rural areas such as Musasa would lag behind. In his opinion, people in rural areas would continue to face economic difficulties for many years to come. He used Namala as an example, the canteen manager and her sons who had very little formal education, and wondered how long it would take such uneducated people to develop economically.

"Development will catch up with them one way or the other," Mr. T.B. responded rather sarcastically.

"What do you mean by that?" Kabenge asked.

"As the country develops, people in rural areas will also benefit eventually. This is especially true with the likes of Namala, who owns land near the capital city," Mr. T.B. replied.

"That seems to be somewhat of a simplistic answer to me," another student, Pius Bitaro, said.

"Listen boys," Mr. T.B. said. "In life, many questions are answered by seemingly simplistic answers. Wait and see, the future will prove me right."

"Okay, development will catch up with them. But when will that be?" Kabenge asked.

"Well, it may not be in Namala's lifetime, given that she is now an old woman, but certainly her two sons will make money, especially the younger one, who seems to be both hard-working and enterprising," Mr. T.B. responded.

"He may be hard-working, but considering the line of business they are in, it would take them a very long time to get rich," Kabenge said.

"Boys, hard work pays. Don't forget that. Now and in the future," Mr. T.B. said.

Makula had been listening attentively to the conversation. His interest peaked when it turned into a discussion about the importance of hard work, and he said, "Two years ago, my cousin Toofa and I thought we could earn money by making and selling charcoal. Well, if there are hard-working people, charcoal makers are definitely among them. We cut the trees, chopped them into short pieces, piled them, and then covered them with elephant grass and wet earth. These were thorny trees, because they make the best charcoal, so our hands were all sore. We did all this work within ten days. When everything was ready, in the evening we lit the fire and started smoking the wood and the whole pile was smoldering in a few hours. In the middle of the night we agreed that we would sleep in turns, one hour at a time, to keep an eye on the charcoal. But because we were so tired after all those days of hard work, we both fell into a deep sleep not far from the pile of smoldering wood. I was awakened early in the morning by the extreme heat from the wood. I woke up my cousin and we realized that air had penetrated the pile, thereby causing a gaping hole that led to a massive fire. We tried to stop the fire by adding wet earth, but we could not put it out. We saw all our hard work and dreams of making some money go up in smoke. Literally."

Kabenge and Makula's other schoolmates laughed at Makula's story, making him feel uneasy and wondering if he had been wise to share it.

***

Because Makula was so absorbed in extracurricular activities, his academic performance declined. He was shocked at his poor report card at the end of the first term of Senior 2, especially when he saw that he had fallen below average in history and agriculture, two subjects that he really liked. In his comments on Makula's report, the headmaster, Mr. Atiku, had written, "You need to pull up your socks; otherwise, this performance will not see you through at the end of the year." Kasede's report card was not any better. He had spent most of his time minding the students' welfare in the dining room instead of studying.

On the last day of the term, Makula and Kasede left their few belongings in the care of Miss Namala, the canteen manager. To avoid the embarrassment of being seen walking along the road, they woke up early and began their trek before the parents of the other students started coming to pick up their sons. Their early departure did not prevent them from being seen, however. James Kabenge had already driven to the school to pick up his sons, Tom and John, and take them home. James Kabenge wondered aloud who the boys were up ahead on the road. If they were students at Musasa High School, why were they walking? His son Tom said, "Come on daddy, not everyone has a car."

"Things have really changed," James Kabenge explained. "When I was studying in Musasa you wouldn't see anyone walking home. All of our fathers drove cars, and remember, this was in the 1950s when there were very few of them. I think they first looked at a parent's bank account before they admitted their child as a student."

"Come on, daddy, that was then. The general economic situation in the country is different now," Tom said as the Kabenges sped away from the walking boys.

Upon his arrival back home in Kasaka, Makula was surprised when his mother did not ask about his new shoes, even though he had returned home barefooted. He certainly did not want to talk about them and wasn't going to raise the subject. And he did not talk much about his studies because he had done so poorly. Whenever Kabejja asked about his grades, Makula would switch the topic to his athletic performance; since she could not read his report card, Kabejja did not pursue the matter any further.

Two days after Makula had returned from school, his father came home from his work at the sugar cane plantation. Makula was surprised at how happy his father was to see him. For the first time, Makula and his father actually sat together and had a conversation. And this was also the first time that Filipo hugged his son. Early that evening, Filipo asked to see Makula's report card. When Makula gave it to him, his father looked at it intently as if he understood it. Then he put it in his pocket, saying that he would wait for Othieno to read it for him. No sooner had Filipo said this than Othieno appeared, happy to see both Makula and Filipo. After an exchange of pleasantries, Filipo asked him to read the report card. Othieno read Makula's grades in each subject while interjecting, "Math is hard," and "Geography is tricky" in an effort to defend Makula's poor performance. When he had finished, Filipo thanked him and then handed the report card back to Makula without comment.

After Othieno had left to go home, Filipo asked Makula whether he had bought the shoes that he had given him the money to buy. Makula was shaking with shame and fear as he explained that he had been conned out of the money. Filipo cut the story short by saying that they already knew about it. Makula wondered how but did not have the courage to directly ask his father. To Makula's surprise, Filipo did not chastise him. He said only that Makula needed to be very cautious whenever he was carrying money anywhere in this world and told him, "Son, money can get you killed."

Filipo told Makula that he would perform better in his studies if he had more of the things that he needed. To that end, they would go together before the next school term began to buy shoes for Makula in Kayunga. Makula was very happy that he was finally going to get his first pair of shoes.

When Filipo had left to go drink at Lameka's, Makula approached

Kabejja and shyly asked how they had learned about the theft of the money he had been given to buy shoes. Kabejja shocked him by telling him that, on the very day his money had been stolen, his cousin Makko had gone to the very same shop to pick up their merchandise for overnight storage. The salesmen had been talking and laughing about what had happened to the poor "student from Musasa." Knowing that his cousin had planned to buy shoes, Makko had asked for a description of the "student." There was no doubt that it had been his cousin Makula who had been conned out of his money. Makko had informed Kabejja about the incident as soon as he could.

***

Toward the end of the year, the campaigns began for the election of the head prefect and his deputy. The head prefect would be elected from the Senior 5 class; his deputy, from Senior 3. Voting was by secret ballot. Popular Tom Kabenge was a candidate for the position of deputy head prefect. He started by campaigning in his dormitory, Camp Hope. As all the residents had promised to vote for him, he concentrated his energy on the other dormitories. Kabenge was the richest of all the candidates, and the students therefore sought to identify with him.

In addition to his wealthy background, Kabenge was also popular because of his physical appearance and way with words. Tall and handsome and always well groomed, he commanded respect and admiration both from fellow students and his teachers. As he addressed the students, Kabenge would tilt his head slightly to the left, put one hand in his pocket, and then speak eloquently as he gently moved his heels up and down as if his shoes had some sort of springs. His demeanour captivated his potential supporters who looked forward to his speeches and followed him wherever he went to address the various classes. Kabenge's use of uncommon English words in his speeches also impressed the students and made them think that he was very bright and would boldly represent them before the teachers.

> "Gentlemen, at this hypersensitive stage of our lives, it is imperative for us to elect people of character and acumen who will be able to articulate our concerns," he told them. "The fact that we have to elect people that will serve our interests is a no-brainer."

When the election results were released, Kabenge had handily won the position of deputy head prefect. This entitled him to special privileges, including his own cubicle in his dormitory.

***

In addition to his outstanding performances as an athlete, another skill helped increase Makula's popularity in school—his excellent handwriting. When the boys discovered this, some of them asked him to write out their love letters to their girlfriends, many of whom were students in other high schools. All Makula required was a draft of their letters and a promise to pay in the form of food at the canteen during break time. Makula enjoyed himself as he copied the flowery language. Two letters stood out, and whenever he remembered their wording, he would laugh to himself or share it with his friends Mugisha and Kasede.

In one letter, Tom Kabenge wrote to his girlfriend Pam:

> *"Sweetheart Pam, I can't believe I am writing this but I would like to let you know that I am both flabbergasted and frustrated in that however much I try, I can't flush your beautiful face out of my mind. Oh my goodness, you are so cute."*

The other letter was from Pius Bitaro to his girlfriend Brenda:

> *"Hi dear,*
> *are you enjoying the atmospheric pressure those ends?*
> *I wish I could be there with you to float with you on this beautiful cloud called LOVE.*
>
> > *I love and adore you immensely."*

Since he spent a lot of his nights handwriting letters, Makula was often deprived of sleep. Sometimes during the day when there was no teacher in class, Makula would sit quietly at his desk to read but would doze off. His younger classmates enjoyed seeing this and would make fun of him. John Kabenge would quietly turn a few pages of the book that Makula was supposed to be reading. When he was once again alert, Makula would continue reading without noticing that he was on a new page. This would make the boys laugh at him. Makula thought that the boys were only being naughty and would not bother to find out why they were laughing. Being older than the other students, he had grown used to this behaviour.

***

In a school where students from rich families often talked about their comfortable lifestyles, those whose families were poor were sometimes tempted to lie about the economic status of their families. Chris Luku was one such student. He told the other students that his father was the managing director of Argon, a new import and export company, and that on several occasions he had accompanied his father on business trips overseas. Although his possessions at school did not support his claims, some of his classmates believed his stories. He would join in as the rich students talked about the soccer matches they had attended, or the films they had watched, or the places they had visited. Luku was able to pull this off for three years.

One Saturday, the Senior 4 class went to a social evening at Buweela High School. Roll call was usually lax after such events and the students would normally head straight to their dormitories. Knowing this, on the return trip to Musasa, Luku and two of his friends jumped off the school truck as it slowed down at a pothole on the dirt road and headed to an all-night disco in Kampala. Since the following day was a visitation Sunday, they planned to return to the school unnoticed among the visiting parents.

On this particular occasion, however, when the school truck returned, Mr. Atiku was waiting at the administration building. He asked Mr. T.B., the teacher in charge, to do a roll call of the returning students. Mr. T.B. panicked when it was discovered that three of the students were missing. When they realized that the next step would be informing the police about the missing boys, the returning students told Mr. Atiku that the three boys had stayed behind to dance.

The three students returned around noon the following day, and as planned, they attempted to enter through the school gate as the gate-keeper was talking with a visiting parent. The other gatekeeper, who was watching from a distance and who Mr. Atiku had assigned the task of nabbing the three students, stopped them and took them straight to the headmaster's office. Makula and his friend Kasede who were watching some visiting parents enjoy homemade lunches with their children and hoping to get some leftover food, laughed as the three boys were marched past them. Makula had no idea that his laughter would earn him a long-time enemy.

The headmaster suspended the delinquent students for three days. When they returned to school on Thursday, the three students were greeted by the presence of their fathers at the front of the school assembly. Chris Luku's father was the most furious, and as soon as the three students were asked to step forward, he pointed menacingly at his son and ranted, "I am a poor man. I sacrifice everything to make sure that this brat completes school. Look. What does he decide to do in return?

Go to the disco. Hopeless," he said in Luganda. The students burst out laughing. An embarrassed Luku covered his face with both his hands.

When his father realized that many of the students did not speak Luganda and therefore had not understood him, he switched to English: "I work very hard driving a taxi to pay fees this old school. I have many childrens but this one is lucky I pay him here. But he does what? He steals himself and go to dance disco. Stupid donkey."

The students laughed and shouted but Luku's father was not finished. He walked up to his son and slapped him hard on the shoulder. The headmaster came over to restrain him if he attempted to strike him again. However, Luku's father did not hit him. Instead, he pulled a ten-shilling note from his pocket and handed it to his son, saying, "As usual, your ten shillings," and walked briskly away.

One would think that this public display would have stopped Luku from lying about his socio-economic status, but it did not. When he returned to his dormitory, his schoolmates made a lot of fun of him.

"I have many childrens but this one is lucky," one boy said aloud. "As usual, your ten shillings," another said. "Stupid donkey," said yet another. The boys laughed even louder.

Luku was not a fellow who could be shaken by the boys' tormenting. With his hands in the pockets of his shorts, and in his usual boastful way, he approached a handful of boys who were willing to listen to him and told them that the man was actually not his father. He said that the man was his father's driver. "That man has worked so long for dad that he thinks he has authority over us," he said.

After saying this, Luku went and sat on his bed. He was silent and appeared to be lost in thought.

After a few minutes, Tom Kabenge walked over to him, tapped him on the shoulder and said, "You resemble your dad's driver a lot."

The following morning as he walked to class, Makula saw Pius Bitaro, another of the students who had been suspended, walking straight toward him. As with Tom Kabenge, the students admired Bitaro because he was one of the best students in the school. He was also chairman of the school's debating club. However, Bitaro was notorious for his perpetually bad temper. When he accosted Makula, Bitaro accused him of being a snitch and reporting the missing students to the headmaster.

Makula defended himself by telling Bitaro that he had not been on the truck nor was he part of the class that had gone out that day. He told Bitaro that he was simply using him as a scapegoat; he knew nothing about their escapade.

"If you didn't know about it," Bitaro retorted, "how come you stood there to watch and laughed at us as that stupid gatekeeper led us to the headmaster's office?"

"Who are you to tell me when to laugh and when not to laugh?" Makula asked.

Although Bitaro was younger than Makula, he shoved him as he told him to mind his own business. Then he walked away.

The three boys were the talk of the school. Some students continued to laugh at Chris Luku while others felt bad for him. Despite the incident of the previous day, many students loved Luku for his lively nature that uplifted others. He was always cheerful and ready to talk to anyone, including the students in the lower classes. Luku only remained sad until that weekend; by the following week, he was back to his old self.

***

Makula worked hard to improve his grades, and he escaped the "guillotine" at the end of the year. Unfortunately, Kasede did not. When he heard that his friend had been expelled from the school, Makula shed a tear. How would he be able to continue without him?

"Well, this is a tough result for me," Kasede said sadly.

"Too bad, my friend," Makula said as he held back more tears.

"Let's write to each other," Kasede said, "and I hope we'll meet again whenever you are in Kampala."

"I know you will make it, Ben. This is not the end of the world," Makula said as he hugged his friend.

The two boys walked the dusty road toward home very early the next day with their few belongings on their heads. Unlike previous occasions when they had walked together, they did not talk much as each thought about his own future. Makula missed his friend already. He had found Kasede to be both intelligent and mature for his age. He had also found him to be a loyal friend.

***

Makula's third year in Musasa High School was less eventful than the first two, and it passed very quickly.

To help him live among the many rich students in Musasa High School, Makula took on an odd job. Every Saturday morning, he would wake up early to hand wash clothes for some of the rich students who felt that this chore was too hard for them. Among these was the deputy head prefect Tom Kabenge. Makula would go to Kabenge's cubicle very early to pick up the plastic basin piled with Kabenge's laundry. Makula would then go outside the dormitory to hand wash a big pile of clothes until noon, when he would go to have lunch. Kabenge and the other students whose clothes he washed paid Makula a few shillings or bought him deep-fried cassava at the school canteen.

Knowing that he had barely survived the "guillotine," Makula concentrated more on his studies this year than on anything else. His major highlight outside of school was stopping by the home of the county chief while on his way to Kasaka for the holidays. The chief had a letter written by Filipo permitting Makula to sleep over for the weekend. Makula renewed his love for music during those two days as he and the chief entertained the many people that lived there with a few songs and drums.

In Senior 4, the following year, Makula again learned about Canada in his geography class. He read in more detail about the wheat farming on the prairies. The name "Saskatchewan" was difficult for the students to pronounce. They also learned about the St. Lawrence Seaway and Hudson Bay. At the end of that year, Makula wrote another round of national examinations that would usher him into his final two years of high school. When the results of the examinations were released, he had performed well, especially in history, geography, and agriculture.

During the final break in his last year of high school, Makula went home and was greeted by a pleasant sight: he was thrilled to see a bulge in his mother's stomach. However, as a child, especially a grown one, there was no way he could ask her about it. He had always felt lonely as an only child, and it was clear to him that his mother was going to have another. As usual, one of the first places that he went to whenever he returned from school was to his Uncle Lameka's home. Lameka was his usual, jovial, humorous self and reminisced for a while about the birth of Filipo. Makula thought how perfectly the nickname "Radio Uganda" suited his uncle. Lameka told him the year, the month, and the day when Filipo was born. He even mentioned that it had been a rainy day during a very sunny dry spell. People had interpreted the rain to mean that the child was going to be a very blessed one. Lameka said that Filipo's blessings were now manifesting through Makula.

Makula was worried when he returned to school after the break because his father had not returned home, and Makula was not able to pay the fees for his final examinations. Two months later, as the students were preparing for the examinations, Mr. Atiku reminded all those who had not paid their fees to do so now, before the tests began. On Friday of that week, hoping that his father would be home, Makula asked for permission from the deputy headmaster to board the school truck as it went to Kampala. There, he would ask his cousins Makko and Lukka for the bus fare to Kayunga and then to Kasaka. When he met with Lukka in Kampala, though, Lukka told him that he had been in Kasaka the previous week and Kabejja had not mentioned when Filipo would be home. Lukka also shared some joyous news: his mother had given birth to a girl, Manjeri, named after Kabejja's own mother.

However, Makula's joy at this news quickly turned to worry as he wondered whether his father would be home to give him the money for the fees. He travelled to Kasaka and was very glad to see his baby sister but was troubled at learning that his father was not expected until the following week. Makula decided to wait at least two days, until Monday. But on Monday, Filipo still had not come home. That evening, Makula started to panic—the examinations were scheduled to start on Wednesday. Kabejja didn't know where to turn for help. She asked Lameka for the money but he could only give her half the sum.

The following morning, despite having a fever, Othieno came to see Makula and to comfort him. "It is hard to imagine that this little sum of 800 shillings could mess up your life. Yet this is exactly what happened to me more than ten years ago," Othieno told him.

"What do you mean?" asked Makula, interested in hearing more about Othieno's life.

"I was not born here in Kasaka and did not grow up here…" Othieno began.

"I know that," Makula said.

"Like you," Othieno continued, "in high school I always had trouble paying my school fees. As the national examinations were approaching, just as they are for you, I decided to come here to Kasaka to ask my uncle for some money. He used to own a little house in the same spot where mine now stands. Unfortunately my uncle didn't have any money to spare. So he asked me to join him at his work, which was digging on plantations to earn wages. As I didn't have even the few shillings I needed to take me back home and to school, I obliged. We worked for months, though, without ever raising the amount I needed. Months turned into years, but I kept hoping that one day I would be able to return to school. Unfortunately my uncle passed away, and I inherited his land, his little house, and his few belongings. That was when I took up the job of teaching in Kasaka. That's my story, my friend."

Makula was very touched by Othieno's story. But Othieno, ever helpful, said that this was no time to lament over the past—they had to do something now to make sure Makula could return to school.

Othieno immediately came up with a plan. He had three mature bunches of matooke in his garden, which they could cut down and push along the road to Kayunga on his bicycle. Surely they would not fail to get a buyer, and the money might well be enough to pay the examination fees and Makula's bus fare back to school. When Kabejja heard about the plan, she was concerned about Othieno's health since he still had a fever. She suggested that Makula wait one more day for his father to come. Othieno, however, insisted that everything would be okay—and Makula needed to get back to school this very day to be on time to write his final examinations. Othieno's plan seemed to be impractical to Makula, but given his lack of options, he agreed to it.

Othieno and Makula therefore cut down the matooke, tied it to Othieno's bicycle, and began pushing it down the road toward Kayunga. They pushed the bicycle for about an hour, each taking a turn as the other walked along. Makula was wearing his full school uniform as no student was allowed to return to school wearing any other clothing. Then, the bicycle broke down, and they had to untie the matooke so that Othieno could find and fix the problem.

It took a full hour to fix the bicycle, and by this time Makula was panicking. He knew now that he might not be able to make it to the school by evening in time for his first examination the following day. He knew that there was no bus at this time of day to take him to Kayunga, and eventually to Musasa. By the time they reached the main road to Kayunga, it was already two o'clock. As they considered what to do next, they spotted a pickup truck coming in the distance toward them. When it neared, Othieno jumped into the middle of the road and raised both his hands so that the driver would not fail to stop. Makula remarked that it was a fish transportation truck, but Othieno said that there was no problem as long as the driver of the truck agreed to two things: one, to buy all three bunches of matooke at a price high enough to pay Makula's examination fees; and, two, to take Makula to Kayunga.

The driver of the pickup stopped and Makula and Othieno saw that it was full of raw fish. Two men were seated at the back on top of the pile of fish, and two women sat breastfeeding their babies in the front seat next to the driver. Before even asking why Othieno had stopped him, the driver mentioned the beautiful bunches of matooke. Othieno told the driver that he would like him to buy all three bunches. The driver said that he would buy only one. Othieno suggested that the driver buy all three and give some to his friends. The driver declined. Othieno turned to the two women inside the truck to ask them if they would buy the remaining matooke. The women looked at him with disgust as they didn't understand Luganda and did not wish to be disturbed. Othieno then told the driver that the future of the young man before him depended on this one transaction—they needed money to pay for his national examinations. The driver agreed to pack all the matooke onto the truck and told Makula to board as well. He said that he could not promise anything, but that he was willing to assist in any way possible. The two men who were seated at the back of the truck made space on the tarpaulin for Makula to sit.

***

When he had finished writing his examinations, Makula set out for home in Kasaka. And as he had done several times during his six years as a student at Musasa High School, he stopped by the former county chief's home in Bikajjo for a visit. As soon as the bus stopped, Makula saw a large, somber crowd of people gathered in the former chief's front yard and he heard a woman saying, "That's a tragic story."

When he was off the bus and waiting for the "conductor" to bring his suitcase down from the bus' roof, one of the former chief's sons came up to him and asked, "Makula, have you heard the terrible news?"

"What news?" Makula asked the weeping young man.

"The news of my father's death," the man said.

"No, I wasn't aware of it," Makula told him. "I was just stopping in to see him on my way home from school." Makula too started to weep.

"He died in his sleep two days ago. We are now preparing for the burial that will take place in the next hour," the chief's son told Makula.

Makula wept so much at the loss of the former chief that some of those present wondered whether he too was one of the chief's sons.

After the burial, Makula stayed for two days at the chief's house before returning home.

***

Makula returned to Kasaka determined to apply the knowledge he had acquired in his agricultural classes. He asked his father to lend him some land. Filipo told Makula that he could use as much land as he wanted in the part of Kasaka that was close to the main road. Lameka had given this land to Filipo a few years after Makula was born, as his inheritance. When he thought of who he could recruit to join him on his farming project, Makula decided to talk to Luyima, the former moneyed man who had spent the last few years in Kasaka living as a pauper. Luyima seemed to live in the past and despised all work, but he hesitantly accepted Makula's offer. Makula also convinced Othieno and Senjo, who was still jobless, to join him in clearing three acres of land to plant matooke. He said that if all went well and according to plan, in two years they would have an abundant supply of food, both for their families and for sale.

Othieno was the most excited of the three. On a recent visit to Kampala, he had heard that the prospects for farmers throughout the country were good as there was a growing demand for fresh food in markets abroad. He thought that this was a chance for them all to make a lot of money.

The people who heard about Makula's plan predicted failure, because they foresaw two problems. One, Kasaka was not an area suitable for growing matooke; the major crop was green plantain to make beer. Two, they thought that neither Luyima nor Senjo could be trusted to do any meaningful work on anything. Makula simply responded to his critics with "Wait and see."

The four men cleared shrub and toiled from dawn to dusk for two months until they had planted the matooke. Makula's Uncle Lameka was so proud of his nephew's efforts that he donated most of the plantain suckers that they needed to plant. All four worked hard to ensure the project thrived.

When he was not working on the farm, Makula spoke with many children who were sent to him by their parents for tips on how to work hard in school and how "to make it in life."

Othieno was put in charge of the farm as Makula was planning to go on to the university in the near future.

CHAPTER NINE
Kampala, Uganda, October 1984

Like all high school students in Uganda who sought further education, Makula's ultimate goal was to be accepted at Makerere University. When the results of the national examinations were released, Makula saw that he had not performed as well as he had hoped. Still, his grades were high enough to admit him to the university where he would study history, economics, and political science. Makula was the first student ever from Kasaka to complete high school. And like all the other students at the university, Makula had received a full government scholarship that included accommodation on the university campus.

Students in Makerere University referred to courses such as Makula's as "flat courses," because most of them did not lead to any particular professional qualification. Students in medicine and law felt superior to those in the "flat courses." Still, Makula was very happy to be at the university and to see that there were students from all over the country. He and his friend Paul Mugisha, who had been admitted to the course in medicine, shared a room. And some of their former schoolmates from Musasa High School had joined them at the university; Chris Luku was in his third year of medicine and lived in the same hall of residence as Makula and Mugisha.

Registering at the university was a long process. Among the things Makula and Mugisha were required to do was undergo a medical examination at a hospital—Makula's first visit to one.

The traditional Freshers' Ball was planned to welcome the new students. Although there was a lot of excitement as the students prepared for the dance, Makula and Mugisha decided not to go. Instead, they stayed in their room. As a medical student, Mugisha felt that he had no time to waste on frivolity, even this early in the year. So while Makula stretched out on his bed to read the newspaper, Mugisha sat at their table to review his notes. Then there was an unexpected knock on their door. "Come in," Makula called out, and a young man that he had seen a few times before on their floor walked in.

"Hey guys, how are you doing? Listen, my roommate has dustbinned me…" the student began.

"What?" Mugisha asked, not understanding what may have happened to the young man.

"My roommate dustbinned me…" the young student said again.

"What do you mean?" Mugisha repeated.

"Are you guys freshers?" asked the young man, a second-year student, puzzled as to why they were inside their room at this time of the evening, reading.

"Yes, we are," Mugisha said.

"Well, anyway, my roommate's girlfriend is spending the night with him in our room tonight. Naturally, I have to keep away. I'll be dancing the night away at the Freshers' Ball, so I was wondering whether I can leave my clothes here, sleep here for a little while in the morning, and then change…" the young student explained.

"No man, I don't think it will work that way," Mugisha said.

"Come on!" the student exclaimed. "That's not the kind of spirit we want in this university. Well, you are freshers. How did you get this room in the first place?"

"What do you mean?" Mugisha asked testily.

"Don't get mad. All I'm saying is that on this floor we share everything. Radios, cups, fans, clothes, even food. So when a guy is dustbinned just as I am, all chip in to help," he explained. "By the way, I'm Tim."

"Hello, Tim," Makula said. Unlike Mugisha, Makula was pleased to learn that there would be opportunities for him to share things with the other students. Being poor, he could use a few borrowed items. Tim left his clothes in a plastic bag next to Makula's bed and said, "See you in the morning."

***

Makula realized that, just as at Musasa High School, his poverty had followed him to Makerere University. His mattress was thin, his blanket was old, and all his clothes were second-hand. Emboldened by what Tim had told them about how the students shared, one morning he decided to knock on the door of the room next to his to borrow an iron. The occupant of the room, Ahmed Jingo, allowed him to borrow the iron. Two days later, Makula had to borrow the iron again. This second time, he apologized to Jingo for being a nuisance. "Come on, don't be shy," said Jingo. "Just blend in. This is Makerere. There's no discrimination here. All you need to do when you need anything from here is knock, come in, pick what you want, go use it, then return it to its place."

"Thanks, man. I appreciate it," said Makula, as he closed the door behind him. Jingo's kindness and that of the other students on his floor made Makula feel more at ease at the university. The students borrowed everything from each other, from bed covers to stereos, to empty wine bottles meant to impress female visitors.

Makula appreciated the freedom he enjoyed at the university. No bells rang to signal the beginning or end of a lecture; no one insisted that a student attend every lecture. Each morning, he jogged around the campus in the company of other freshmen, who jogged apart from the other students for fear of being teased. It did not take long, however, for the older students to identify them. They would yell at them through the open windows, "Suffer, freshers!" The freshmen would simply continue jogging without responding. After about a month, when the freshmen were more used to university life and were more confident, they would respond to anyone who teased them. "Suffer, elders!" they would say.

After a few weeks of study, Makula realized that his success or failure at the university depended solely upon him. Although he continued to go back to Kasaka twice a month to oversee his farming project, he used his time on campus to study seriously. He and Mugisha didn't go out dancing or drinking like many of the students in their hall of residence. Mugisha studied mostly at the university library while Makula read in their room.

Makula's largest class, with 147 students, was economics. The lecturer spoke into a microphone and Makula found him hard to follow. Fortunately, there were smaller tutorial groups where the students discussed the lecture and asked questions. And, thankfully, by the end of the first term, Makula was feeling comfortable in his studies.

Soon after enrolling at the university, Makula had joined the Makerere University Bugerere Students Association, an association formed to unite the students who hailed from the county. At the first meeting of the association he attended, Makula was very surprised to see that the chairman was none other than Simeon Senfuka, a young man from Nanziba whom he had encountered many times during the "jackfruit battles" years earlier. Makula remembered Senfuka well because he had bullied him and his cousins. Makula noticed that Senfuka had grown into a man of impressive physical stature and seemed to be quite well off. At the end of the meeting, Makula approached the towering Senfuka, who, though surprised to see him, for some reason gave him a rather cold reception. Senfuka told him that he had thought he was the only student in the university who hailed from one of those two villages. Makula told him that he was perhaps right, as he had just joined the university while Senfuka was in his second year. Senfuka then turned away to talk to the other students who had been at the meeting.

Toward the end of Makula's first year at the university, elections were held for the position of president of the Students' Guild. Makula was pleased that Senfuka was standing as a candidate, and when Senfuka asked him to be a part of his campaign team, he accepted readily. When he learned that Tom Kabenge was among the other candidates, however, Makula knew that Senfuka faced an uphill battle to win the position. "How can a relatively unknown young man from a rural village compete with the popular, rich, and well-spoken Tom Kabenge?" he thought to himself.

On the fourth day of the campaign, Senfuka and his team visited a hall of residence that housed female students just after Kabenge had addressed a rally there. Some of the students seemed to be disdainful of Senfuka's attire and showed their disinterest in him by walking out of the room. However, many stayed to listen.

"Makerere *oyee*!" Senfuka yelled, with his fist raised in the air.

"*Oyee*!" a few voices responded.

"Morale where? Makerere *oyee*!" he repeated.

"*Oyee*!" a few more voices responded.

"Fellow students, I am Simeon Senfuka. I am in my second year in Agriculture. Without further ado, I would like to unveil my action plan to you. As someone who is well informed about farming and nutrition, I find our food here at the university to be very pathetic. If elected, I would like, among other things, to improve our welfare, especially our diet…"

"Senfuka *oyee!*" the students yelled in unison.

Senfuka felt energized. He continued, "And, if elected, I plan to take drastic measures in order to implement my program. During the two years that I have spent at this great university, I have realized that there are many poorly allocated resources. A good example is the swimming pool. Tell me, why should students be subjected to poor unbalanced meals when a resource such as the swimming pool is going to waste?"

"Senfuka *oyee!*" the students yelled again.

Makula wondered why Senfuka had said that about the swimming pool. He did not wait long for an explanation.

"If I am elected, as someone with an enterprising mind, I will turn the swimming pool into a fish pond…" Senfuka told them.

The students laughed and booed so loudly that Senfuka could not continue with his speech. Embarrassed, Makula and his fellow campaign team members started sneaking out of the room one by one.

In the following week Senfuka was forced to call off his campaign. He had become an object of ridicule at the university and was now widely known as the "Fish Farmer." Senfuka felt humiliated by his failed campaign, and he unjustly blamed its failure on his campaign team. He was especially disappointed with Makula whom he accused of leaving the rally instead of trying to convince the female students to listen to what he had to say. At the end of the four-week campaign, Tom Kabenge was declared the new president of the Students' Guild.

Makula returned to his home in Kasaka at the end of his first year of university, where he delighted in the company of his little sister. She adored him and loved it when he carried her. He bought her some clothes and two used pairs of shoes in the market in Kayunga. Kabejja was grateful to see her son taking care of his little sister. She realized that when Makula was born, Filipo had been much younger than Makula was now.

Makula told his mother about Senfuka, the student from Nanziba whom he had met at Makerere University.

"Oh, that is good. I didn't know that we had other fine young men in our area. This will be good for our future. What is his name?" Kabejja asked.

"His name is Simeon Senfuka," Makula answered.

"Senfuka?" Kabejja said in a surprised tone.

"You seem to be surprised. Do you know him?" Makula asked.

Kabejja tilted her head slightly and asked him, "Did you introduce yourself to him and tell him who your parents are?"

"Yes. Why?" Makula responded.

"How did he react when you told him who you were?" Kabejja asked.

"Mother, am I missing something here? This is someone I grew up with. Why are you so concerned about him?" Makula asked.

"The Senfukas have a long history of enmity with your family," Kabejja said. "That is partly why you and your cousins fought with those boys over the fruits along the valley during your child-hood. I don't know whether your father would like you to know these things, but I will tell you since you are now a grown man."

Makula was keen to hear what his mother had to tell him. He was also surprised to learn that she knew about the "jackfruit battles."

Kabejja said, "Senfuka's grandfather was your grandfather's faithful servant. It is said that Senfuka, the grandfather to your contemporary, worked so diligently that your grandfather gave him part of his land. However, when your grandfather passed away, your Uncle Lameka repossessed the land, and when your father was old enough, Lameka gave it to him. That is the land where you and your friends have your farm now."

"Why didn't father build his house on that land? It's closer to the main road," Makula said.

Kabejja explained, "As you see, even up to now there are no people living in that area. At that time most people preferred to build their houses on hilltops. Your father wanted us to live here next to his brother."

Makula said, "I didn't know all that."

Kabejja continued, "You couldn't know because your father should have been the person to tell you, but he is not good at conversation. The enmity that persists to this day between your family and the Senfukas was caused by land wrangles."

"That explains it. When Senfuka first saw me in the university, he wasn't at all welcoming," Makula said. He wondered if Senfuka had deliberately sought an opportunity to prolong the enmity between the two families when he had asked Makula to join his campaign team.

***

In his second year at university, Makula majored in economics. He studied hard because he liked and enjoyed all the courses that he took. One afternoon, Makula decided to take a break from his studies and walk around the large campus. He stopped by the tennis court where several students were watching a match between two female students. Makula joined the spectators and was not only impressed by the girls' skill at the game but was stunned by one of the players. She was tall, well groomed, and very beautiful. Makula was so captivated by the girl's beauty that he stayed until the end of the match simply to watch her. He thought about her all that evening.

Two weeks later, Makula saw the same girl walking out of the chapel after Sunday service. He hurried toward her to take a closer look. As she walked past him, he looked straight at her. He thought he saw her smile a little. From that day onward, Makula could not stop thinking about her. One afternoon as he was walking to the library, he saw her walking down the hall to a lecture room. He decided to follow at a safe distance to see where she was going. He discovered that she was about to attend an economics lecture in a second-year class. "Why haven't I seen her before now?" he thought to himself. From that time on, Makula came just to catch a glimpse of her leaving that particular lecture room. He also went back to the tennis court several times but did not see her play again. It seemed that she did not play tennis often. Despite his popularity among the girls in Kasaka, the shy and somewhat introverted Makula had not yet had a girlfriend and the thought of even being friends with this beautiful girl gave him much joy. There was one problem, though. From her appearance, it was obvious that this girl came from a rich urban family. And he was from a very poor rural one. Despite this, Makula did not lose hope, and luck was soon on his side.

Two months after first seeing her, Makula saw the girl again at the chapel. He began to go there, and whenever he could, he would sit in a place that gave him a clear view of her. One morning, he approached her and said, "Hello." She responded with "Hello" and a smile. Makula was excited that he had had the courage to talk to her and that she had responded so nicely. That was all he thought about that day, that evening, and for the next few days. He also continued to follow her at a distance as she went to and from her lectures.

This went on for months. Makula, wondering how much longer he could continue like this, finally mustered up the courage to talk to her. As she was walking alone back to her hall of residence after church service, Makula followed her. And when he was close enough, he remarked, "Isn't this a bright day?"

"Oh, yes, it is," she replied.

"It would be a great day for an outdoor party or a good game," Makula said.

"Yes, that's exactly what I was thinking about," she said. "An outdoor game."

"Do you mean tennis?" Makula asked.

"Yes," she replied. "How did you guess that?"

"I saw you playing tennis a few months ago," he confessed.

"Oh." The girl said nothing further as they continued on their walk.

Makula said, "By the way, I am Makula."

"It was nice to see you, Makula. I am Pam," she said coolly, seeming to suggest that she no longer wanted to talk to him.

"It was nice talking to you, Pam. Have a good day," Makula said.

"You too," she said.

Makula turned down another path and congratulated himself on his accomplishment. He was so happy that he had spoken with her that he went to the canteen to buy a bottle of soda to celebrate. He had found the girl to be very easy to talk to and now he knew her name, Pam.

When he returned to his room, Makula told Mugisha about his conversation with Pam. Mugisha said that her taking the time to talk with him was a good sign and it seemed she was a well-mannered girl.

"You know these university girls are very conceited. At least, that is my opinion. The girls at the medical school seem to think that they are on top of the world. A girl talks to you as if she were doing you a favour."

"Yes, I got a very good impression of her. The problem is, she seems to be a rich man's daughter," Makula said.

"That's no problem. Every journey starts somewhere. What do you intend to do next?" Mugisha asked.

"Well, I guess I will look for another opportunity to talk to her," Makula replied.

Makula saw Pam two weeks later, toward the end of the academic year. She was walking out of a lecture room with another girl. He looked at her and smiled, but to his disappointment, Pam merely glanced at him and looked away, continuing her conversation with the other girl.

Makula felt very discouraged. He felt rebuffed and hurt by her lack of interest in him. And unlike the happiness he had felt after their conversation, Makula did not share his disappointment with Mugisha.

The school year ended and Makula returned home to Kasaka. He thought that if he were to impress Pam, he would need to make himself more presentable. He would have to wear better clothes and be better groomed. This would take money, and he worked hard on his farm to have plenty of matooke to sell.

As the partners began to harvest the matooke, Othieno noticed that, each morning, some bunches had disappeared. This continued over a period of several days, and it became obvious that someone was stealing their produce. Because the theft was taking place at night, the partners took turns lying quietly in the plantation overnight for a week but the thief did not appear. They stopped guarding the matooke, and two days later, the thief struck again. For the next two nights, they again guarded the crop, but again the thief did not appear. Suspicious, Makula and Othieno decided to wait among the matooke for one more night without telling Senjo or Luyima. That night, just when they were ready to give up on the thief appearing, they saw the dim light of a flashlight approaching. Walking cautiously on the dry leaves on the ground, the thief approached the area where the mature bunches were more abundant. He cut one bunch and then another, and then whistled as if to signal an accomplice. Before the thief was joined by another person, Othieno jumped onto his back as Makula snatched the machete from his hand. They pushed the thief onto the ground and shone the flashlight straight into the face of their friend and partner Senjo.

Senjo was very embarrassed. Makula and Othieno made him promise not to steal again; in return, they agreed not to tell anyone else about the incident.

The harvest was good but not only for Makula and his partners. All the other farmers also had large crops of matooke to sell, which drove down the price. Still, with his portion of the profits, he was able to purchase three used shirts and two used pairs of trousers at Owino market in Kampala before returning to university.

***

Makula resumed his pursuit of Pam when the university reopened for his third and final year. "I have to strike while the iron is still hot," he thought to himself. The next time he spoke with her, she told him that she knew him to be an excellent athlete. Makula felt very good about this.

One afternoon Pam accepted Makula's invitation to join him for a soda at the university canteen. He did not want to ask her any personal questions and appear to be too eager to get close to her. He kept the conversation impersonal and light, and they spoke about their studies. After this date, Makula began to feel hopeful about having a relationship with Pam, but he was acutely aware of his poverty. He was extremely self-conscious about his appearance and feared that his clothes were too old and worn out. However, he was happy with the way things unfolded. After getting to know each other better over the next two months, Pam told Makula that she would not mind if he paid her a visit at her room. That Saturday, Makula visited Pam and enjoyed a cup of tea. He was impressed by the neatness of the room, which she shared with another girl. Its tasteful decor and the quality of the items in the room confirmed what Makula had thought all along—Pam was a rich man's daughter. She even had a television.

Makula's pleasure in the growing closeness of their relationship did not last long. On Monday afternoon, on his way to the library after lunch, he was shocked to see Pam having what appeared to be an intimate conversation with Tom Kabenge. "Pam. Oh my goodness. Pam. That was the name in Tom's love letter!" he thought. Makula laughed when he remembered how Tom had expressed himself in the letter that he had copied for him at Musasa High School: "Sweetheart Pam, I am both flabbergasted and frustrated in that however much I try, I can't flush your beautiful face out of my mind…" With the realization that this was Tom's "Pam," Makula's keen disappointment led him back to his room. He almost felt cheated, although he had really not formed any intimate ties with Pam. "How stupid I have been! What on earth was I thinking?" he thought to himself.

Makula felt so bad because he had had such high hopes for his relationship with Pam. And when he compared himself to Tom Kabenge, he knew he was far too poor to ever convince Pam to love him, let alone marry him. He was now a grown man and he had thought it would be good for him to get married and start a family soon after completing his university studies. His hope for himself and Pam had grown quickly because, for him, she had seemed to be "the one."

When Mugisha returned to their room that evening after his classes, Makula told him about his troubles. "Hey, Paul, can I tell you what happened to me this afternoon?"

"Sure. Tell me what happened. Are you okay?" Mugisha asked.

"I was on my way to the library this afternoon when I saw Pam with Tom Kabenge," Makula confessed.

"What? Tom Kabenge?" Mugisha asked, surprised.

"Yes," Makula replied.

"What were they doing?" Mugisha asked.

"They were seated at one of the tables at the canteen and were sharing a soda as they talked. I watched them for a moment and they seemed to be on very intimate terms," Makula said.

"Oh dear," said Mugisha. "That's not going to be good—Tom Kabenge of all people. Those rich guys get every beautiful girl."

"She is the very same Pam that I helped him write letters to. I am certain of it," Makula said.

"Chris can help us find out more," Mugisha reassured him.

Chris Luku had always been a trusted source of social information, even at Musasa High School. He attended all social gatherings including seminars, weddings, parties, dances, and reunions, both at, and outside, the university, whether he was invited or not. Thus, he knew many of the girls whom his former schoolmates had befriended at the university. Luku lived one floor below Makula and Mugisha in the same hall of residence. When they asked him about Pam, Luku confirmed that she was the one that Tom Kabenge used to write to when they were in Musasa. "But don't worry, Makula," he said. "That girl does not love him. I think when you saw them he was trying to convince her to commit herself to him, but I don't think he will succeed."

"Why not?" Mugisha asked. "He has money. I mean, he is rich."

"He has money, but that's a rich man's daughter, my friend. I don't think money alone would lure her. Besides, that guy is a nut," Luku assured him. "I don't see how he would be able to convince any sensible girl to love him."

"Whose daughter is she?" Makula asked.

"Do you know of Dr. Sempaka of the White Nile Clinic?" Luku asked. "Well, he is her father."

"I have heard that he is one of the best surgeons in East Africa," Makula said.

"One of the best? He is the best!" Luku exclaimed.

"That is good," Mugisha said. "She is from a respectable family."

"I know her roommate, Peggy. I'll get more information from her. Don't worry, I will get back to you within forty-eight hours," Luku said confidently.

Although Luku had told him that Pam did not love Kabenge, Makula was not fully convinced that this was true. He decided to avoid Pam at all costs, hoping that by not seeing her, he would soon forget her. He was wrong. The more he stayed away from her, the more he longed to be with her.

That weekend, Makula talked with Nicholas Wabudi, one of Tom Kabenge's former classmates at Musasa about his chances if he pursued a relationship with Pam. Makula regretted bringing the subject up because, instead of reassuring him, Wabudi praised Kabenge and his prowess. "That guy is both handsome and rich," Wabudi said. "What girl wouldn't like him to be her boyfriend?"

"Well, I didn't think I would have any luck with her, but when I talked to her, she seemed to be perhaps open to the idea," said Makula.

"What idea? Of befriending a poor man's son? Forget it," Wabudi told him. "Let's face it, we sons of poor men are at a disadvantage. To get any of these beautiful girls, we will have to work hard and get rich first. That might take years, though. In the meantime, let these rich kids enjoy each other. I am sorry to tell you this, but that's how it goes, my friend."

"So, what you mean is that there is no hope for me?" Makula asked.

"Well, who knows?" Wabudi said. "There may be hope but what other plans do you have in case things don't work out for you? Chris may have told you that the girl does not love Tom, but both you and I know how cunning Tom is. You may seem to be winning but then he can outsmart you. You know the Luganda saying, 'When you chase a fellow man, you must reserve enough energy for your retreat.' What will you do if she rejects you and chooses him instead?" When he realized that Wabudi was far from encouraging about his pursuit of Pam, Makula changed the subject to their progress with their studies.

Despite his promise that he would have information about Pam's relationship with Tom within two days, two weeks had passed before Luku came to Makula's room one evening and told him that he had some information from Peggy, Pam's roommate. It was as Luku had suspected—Pam did not love Kabenge.

"But what about those love letters that he used to write to her?" Makula asked.

"He wrote them. She could not stop him from writing to her, but I doubt whether she responded to any of them," Luku told him.

"But why wouldn't she love him?" Makula asked.

"He has lots of other girls," Luku said. "And he is proud. You know how proud he is. And now that he is studying law, and is a top student at that, he feels he is better than everybody else. One thing I discovered, though, is that Peggy seems to be in love with him. She was vigorous in dispelling any connection between him and Pam." Luku did not confess that he himself was pursuing Peggy and had welcomed the opportunity to visit her in her and Pam's room.

"All right. I will remain positive," Makula said.

"Don't be discouraged," Luku said, as he patted Makula on the shoulder. "I wish you success. That girl is really beautiful. I too admire her a lot, but I'm not saying that I will interfere with your plans."

The following day, as Makula was going to the library, he saw Pam and

Peggy. Although he knew that they had seen him too, he quickly looked the other way. Makula continued on his way to the library, where he remained until six o'clock. Although he had spent more than three hours at the library, he was not really studying. He could not stop thinking about Pam. Seeing her that afternoon had reawakened all of his feelings for her. She seemed even more beautiful than he had first thought. He felt frustrated and jealous.

As he was leaving the library, Makula was very surprised to see Pam standing calmly by the railing.

"Hi, Pam. Are you waiting for someone?" he asked.

"Yes," Pam said. "I am waiting for you."

"For me?" Makula asked.

"Yes. Is that okay with you?" Pam asked.

"Yes, indeed," Makula responded. "I am glad to hear that."

"Why have you been avoiding me?" Pam asked him in an annoyed tone.

"I am not avoiding you," Makula told her. "Why would I?"

"That's exactly what I would like to know," Pam said.

"I am not avoiding you," Makula assured her. "I have been so busy these days. That's why you have not seen me lately."

"Oh. That explains it. Well, have a good night," said Pam as she turned to leave. Before she could do so, Makula grabbed her hand, and they walked slowly back to her room.

When Luku had asked Peggy about the relationship between Tom Kabenge and Pam, Peggy had asked him why he wanted to know. Luku had told her that he was asking on behalf of Makula, who was trying to befriend Pam. Peggy had been happy to hear about this. It was the ammunition she needed to fire at Kabenge to make him abandon his plans to pursue Pam. When she next saw him, Peggy eagerly told Kabenge that Pam was seeing Makula.

"Are you talking about the Makula I know?" Kabenge asked her.

"Yes. He is an older guy. He is also an athlete," Peggy told him.

"I know him," Kabenge said. "He was one class behind me at Musasa High School. This can't be."

"Believe me, it's true," Peggy said.

"How do you know it's true?" Kabenge asked.

"Someone told me, but I will not tell you who it was. But you know what's interesting? I think you two guys resemble each other a little," Peggy said.

"Who do I resemble?" Kabenge asked.

"Makula," Peggy said.

"Come on!" Kabenge told her. "I don't resemble that son of a peasant. I know you said it just to be funny, but it's not funny," Tom said.

"I am quite serious," Peggy said.

***

Makula's old friend Ben Kasede came to pay him a visit at the university. When Kasede walked into his room, Makula was very surprised to see how his friend had changed: he looked old for his age and his clothes looked old and worn.

"Hey, man, long time no see. How are you doing?"
asked Makula as he smiled and shook his friend's hand.

"Mak, life is not good," Kasede confessed. "You know after I was expelled from Musasa, I joined Heaton High School in Kampala. However, I had to drop out of school early due to lack of money. My uncle later loaned me a bit, and I am now running a small business in Owino market. But business is not good."

"That's sad my friend, but don't lose hope. What are you dealing in?" Makula asked.

"Fruits, but their prices dwindle a lot depending on the season. Right now I am frustrated," Kasede said.

"Don't lose hope Ben, things will improve," Makula said encouragingly.

While they were talking, there was a knock on the door. "Come in," Makula said. It was Tom Kabenge. Makula suspected that Kabenge was angry with him. He asked him to sit down, but Kabenge refused. Instead, he asked whether Makula had a moment to speak with him privately. Makula said that they could talk later, since he had a visitor now. Kabenge looked at Kasede as if to ask, "Who is this to stop you from talking with me now?" Kasede remembered Tom Kabenge well from their days at Musasa High School but he doubted if Kabenge remembered him. Kasede said that he could leave to allow Makula to talk to Kabenge. And before Makula could say anything, Kabenge was thanking Kasede and handing him two thousand shillings that he had pulled from his pocket. Kasede was very happy to accept the money. He thanked Kabenge, bade farewell to Makula, and left the room.

Kabenge turned to Makula and said, "I have been informed that you are trying to befriend my girlfriend." Makula did not deny it. "Man, leave my girl alone," Kabenge said angrily.

"No," Makula shot back. "She is not your girl. She does not love you."

"Listen, if you want, I will pay you to back off. Just tell me here and now how much money you want," Kabenge said.

"No, you can't buy me," Makula told him.

"Shut up!" Kabenge shouted. "Tell me how much you want. I have paid you before to wash my clothes, so you can trust me to keep my word. How much do you want?"

"I will let you know," Makula said, so that Kabenge would leave. Kabenge walked out of the room without saying another word.

Makula did not talk to Kabenge again.

That Saturday afternoon, Pam surprised Makula by coming to visit him at his room. Makula was lying down on his bed while reading a novel when she knocked on the door. He said, "Come in if you are beautiful," a common response to a knock at the door among the male students. When Pam entered, Makula was embarrassed to see that it was she. To conceal his embarrassment, he bravely said, "Yes, come in. You are certainly beautiful."

Makula offered Pam a soda or a cup of tea. Pam asked for tea. While he waited for the water to boil, Makula went quickly downstairs to the hall canteen and bought two eggs and a bun. Pam told him that she did not really want anything to eat. Makula insisted, so he fried the eggs nicely and made a sandwich. Pam enjoyed her tea as they chatted, but she took only one bite of the sandwich. When she was done with her tea, Makula asked her why she had not eaten the sandwich. She said that she was not hungry but had taken a bite simply because he had insisted she do so. Makula carefully wrapped the sandwich in a paper bag and tossed it into the dustbin.

When it was time for Pam to leave, Makula said, "I will give you a push," meaning, "I will escort you out," and he walked her through the hall's compound and out to the street. Pam told him that she was going home to see her parents, so Makula said goodbye and returned to his room.

When he had closed the door, he lifted the paper bag out of the dustbin and put the sandwich on the table. He then picked up his book, and began to read. After a couple of minutes, Makula got up, washed his hands, and began to eat the sandwich. As soon as he had started eating, there was a loud knock on the door, like that of Chris Luku whenever he had "breaking news" for the guys. "Come in," Makula said. But it was Pam who opened the door. She had forgotten her umbrella under the chair.

She stopped when she saw Makula eating the sandwich that he had thrown into the dustbin. Makula was so embarrassed that he lowered his eyes and covered his mouth with his hand. Pam reached for his other hand. "Don't worry about it, dear," Pam said soothingly. "I didn't know that you were hungry. Come, let's go have a snack downtown. I care for you." And she threw the unfinished sandwich back into the dustbin.

Makula changed his shirt, and went out with Pam. When he returned to his room that evening, he told Mugisha that he was deeply in love with Pam and that his feelings for her "had grown by leaps and bounds." He didn't tell him why.

CHAPTER TEN
Kampala, Uganda, March 1987

Makula and Pam grew closer, and they enjoyed each other's company. Three months before they finished their studies at the university, Makula invited Pam out to dinner at the trendy Smart Diner restaurant. Pam was pleased to see that Makula was now "raising standards," as the girls termed it in Makerere-speak.

When they had finished their dinner, Makula popped the question: "Pam, will you marry me?"

Pam was quiet for a moment. Makula was also quiet as she thought it over. She then said, "Mak, I don't have an answer to that right now. You need to meet my family first. My answer will depend on their opinion of you."

Makula was happy that Pam had not rejected him outright. However, he was unhappy to hear that he would have to meet her family before she would consider marrying him. Here he was, the son of a poor rural man, proposing to the daughter of the most celebrated surgeon in the land. He wondered whether they would even let him near their home. "Okay, I would be pleased to meet your family," Makula said. "I am ready to do anything for you, my dear Pam."

"Good. I will arrange a date," Pam said. "I will let you know. Can we leave now?"

As they left the table, Makula asked, "So what kind of reception should I expect from your family?"

"No worries," Pam told him. "My parents are warm and welcoming."

Outside of the restaurant, Makula asked, "Do you think all will go well for me?"

"Yes, all should go well. Expect a lot of questions, though," Pam warned him.

"Oh. What kind of questions?" Makula asked.

"I don't know. I can't read their minds," Pam said, laughing.

Makula waited for what seemed an eternity for an opportunity to meet Pam's parents. And while he waited, he did not even get to see Pam. He waited impatiently for her to tell him that a visit had been arranged, but he did not inform any of his friends of his proposal other than his only confidant, Mugisha, for fear of hearing negative or discouraging words.

Two weeks after their date at the Smart Diner restaurant, Pam finally visited Makula in his room and informed him that her parents were ready to meet him in yet another two weeks' time. She asked Makula to show her what he was planning to wear for the occasion. Makula showed her a pair of brownish, tight-fitting corduroy trousers and a plain light-green shirt.

"You can't meet my father dressed like that!" Pam exclaimed. "Well, you can, but you certainly won't impress him."

"What should I wear?" asked Makula as he opened his suitcase full of not-so-new clothes. Pam went through each item one by one, beginning with his shirts, saying "Not this one." She did the same with all of his pairs of trousers and asked, "You don't have suits? You have to wear a suit."

"No. I am not that rich, you know. But I can get a suit, at the latest, by tomorrow," Makula promised.

"That's all right, then," Pam said. "I'll come to check it out."

When Pam left, Makula went next door to see Ahmed Jingo and asked if he could borrow a suit from him for one day.

"What's up, man? Are you going on a date? Is she beautiful?" Jingo asked.

"Yes, she is beautiful, but I'm not going to a date with her. I am going to meet her parents," Makula replied.

"Great! That's important. Check over there in the closet. There must be three or four dry-cleaned suits in there," said Jingo, waving his hand in a boastful manner. "Try them all on to see which one you will take."

Makula tried on three suits and finally chose a brown one. He also chose a matching shirt and a tie. "Thanks man," he told Jingo. "I guess this will do it."

When she returned the following morning, Pam asked to see the suit. "Can you put it on?" she asked.

Makula modelled the suit for Pam, who said that the shirt and the tie matched well with the suit but the jacket's sleeves were too long. When she took a closer look, she noticed that Makula had merely folded the hem of the pants to fit. "Mak, you can't do that!" she chastised him. "Where would you go dressed like that?" she asked in a bewildered tone. "Did you actually buy that suit?"

"No. I borrowed it from a friend," Makula confessed.

"What?" Pam said, and then burst into laughter. "Is history about to repeat itself?"

"Why? What do you mean?" Makula asked, perplexed.

"History is about to repeat itself. Second dates and borrowed suits," Pam said, laughing.

"What do you mean?" Makula asked again.

"My parents met in Vancouver where they were both students. My brother and I were actually born in Vancouver," Pam said.

"Oh, in Canada. That's great," Makula said.

"Anyway, to make a long story short, on their second date, my dad borrowed a suit from his elder brother, who was also living and working in Vancouver at the time. As the two lovers enjoyed their meal in a corner restaurant, my uncle saw them and went in to meet his brother's future fiancée. Unfortunately, my uncle was with his five-year-old daughter, my cousin Esther. Now here is the funny part, and my mother still laughs a lot when she tells this story: after she had hugged her uncle, Esther asked him loudly, 'Uncle, why are you wearing my dad's clothes?'"

"Uh oh," Makula said, laughing uneasily.

"Listen, Mak," Pam said. "My brother knows a good tailor. Let's go over there and get him to make a nicely fitting suit for you."

"Right now?" Makula asked.

"Yes, right now," Pam insisted. "Two weeks is not a long time, you know. I think you will also need a good pair of shoes and a visit to the dentist."

"Why would I need to visit a dentist? I don't have a tooth ache," Makula asked.

"Listen, Mak, we don't visit the dentist only when we have a tooth ache. I think you'll need a good cleaning. I am not implying that you have bad teeth," Pam said, "but first impressions matter, you know."

Makula wanted to tell Pam that he had never been to a dentist before but he decided to keep that to himself. Instead he said, "Listen, Pam. Buying a new suit and shoes for this occasion would be a brilliant idea, but I am not ready to do it. We are talking about thousands of shillings here and…"

"Don't worry," Pam told him. "I'll pay for it all for you."

"What? Why would you do that?" Makula asked.

"Because you are worth it," Pam replied.

"I'm worth it?" Makula asked.

"Yes. You didn't think so?" Pam asked him in turn.

"Well, I may be worth it, but I didn't in a million years expect it. Thank you," he said effusively, trying to show how grateful he was.

They went directly to the tailor's, who took Makula's measurements, and Pam chose a very nice navy blue material for the suit. She also purchased a black pair of shoes, a pair of socks, a striped tie, and a light cream shirt.

The Saturday arrived when Makula was to meet Pam's parents. Makula woke up early, took a shower, and drank only a cup of coffee. He was dressed in his new suit by nine o'clock and nervously paced around his room as he waited for half past ten. He could then go to Pam's room. At exactly eleven o'clock, a driver arrived to take Makula and Pam to her parents' home. When Makula and Pam entered the car, the driver greeted them and then was silent for the rest of the trip. The journey took only twenty minutes.

Makula felt even more nervous when he saw the height of the perimeter wall around the house. The driver honked, and a gatekeeper immediately opened the gate. Makula was now feeling so anxious that he wanted to tell Pam to give up on the idea of his meeting her parents. The lawn was immaculately trimmed. Patio benches had been placed under each of the trees. The multi-storey house was the largest Makula had ever seen. The car stopped at the steps in front of the house, and Dr. Sempaka himself was there, waiting. He opened the car's doors, first for Pam, then for Makula, and welcomed them both with a wide smile and hugs. Pam had told him, "My parents are welcoming people," and Makula could see that this was true.

Dr. Sempaka led the way into the house, which was expensively furnished. He and Makula walked through the living room, which held a piano and two matching leather sofas. They then entered the well-lit family room, where numerous photographs of Pam and her brother filled the walls. Doctor Sempaka motioned to Makula to sit down. This was only the third home Makula had visited. The first was Mr. Kasule's home in Kayunga at the beginning of his studies at Kayunga Primary School. The second was the home of the late county chief. Makula pictured his parents' incomplete two-bedroom house in Kasaka, and he panicked. "Can I really pull this off?" he thought, not seeing Dr. Sempaka's outstretched hand for a moment.

"It is nice to see you," said Dr. Sempaka, shaking his hand. "What is your name?"

Makula replied, "My name is Makula Musoke."

"I am John Sempaka," he said. "You are welcome here, Makula. Please feel at home."

"Thank you," Makula responded nervously.

Pam then came into the room along with her mother. Pam said, "This is my mother, Paula. Mum, this is my friend Makula."

"Nice to meet you, Makula," said Mrs. Sempaka.

"Nice to meet you…" Makula said, unsure of how to properly address Pam's mother. He stood up to greet her, smiling as he glanced first at her and then at Pam. Pam smiled back, happy with Makula's gesture of confidence.

"Would you like a glass of orange juice, Makula? Lunch will be served shortly," Mrs. Sempaka said.

"Yes, I would like some juice," Makula said, sitting back down.

Pam and her mother left the room and Pam returned with a tray holding two glasses of juice. She gave one to her father and one to Makula. She then said, "Will you please excuse me?" and returned to the kitchen to help her mother prepare lunch.

At that moment a teenaged girl walked into the room to greet Makula. "Hi. How are you? I am Linda," she said, smiling.

"Hello, I am Makula," Makula replied.

"Linda, meet Makula, Pam's special friend. Makula, meet Linda, Pam's cousin," Doctor Sempaka said.

"Nice to see you, Makula," Linda said as she walked out of the room. Makula did not see her again during his visit.

Soon after, a middle-aged couple entered. The woman placed a mat on the floor and sat down to greet Makula. The man sat on a chair and also greeted Makula.

"Folks, meet Makula, Pam's special friend. We will get to know more about him when we talk to him after lunch. Makula, meet Mr. Kamoga and his wife," Dr. Sempaka said. The couple exchanged pleasantries with Makula and then excused themselves.

When they were alone in the living room, Dr. Sempaka made his visitor feel at ease by engaging him in small talk about his former school, Musasa High School. Dr. Sempaka said that he himself had been very lucky to study in Musasa as this had contributed to his current success in his career. "You can't substitute a good education with anything," he said. "Actually many of my contemporaries are doing well, such as James Kabenge…" When he heard the name "Kabenge," Makula thought about Tom. He wondered whether Dr. Sempaka knew about Pam and Tom, and he missed his mention of other former schoolmates.

Pam then came into the room to announce that lunch was ready. Dr. Sempaka asked Makula to please follow him to the table in the dining room. A starter of fresh salad was served. Makula enjoyed the salad, although he was a little nervous as Pam sat across the table from him and their eyes met quite often. Makula knew that this was only the beginning and that tough questions were coming. After they had eaten the salad, Pam cleared the dishes while her mother put another set of clean plates and cutlery on the table. At that moment, Pam's brother, Patrick, came in.

"Hello, Pat," Dr. Sempaka said. "Meet Makula."

"Hello, Makula. I have heard a lot of good things about you. How are you doing?" Patrick asked.

"Hello, Patrick. I am doing well, thank you," Makula replied.

"Do you mind joining us for lunch?" Dr. Sempaka asked his son.

"I wouldn't mind having lunch, Dad," Patrick said, seating himself in the empty chair next to Makula.

"Makula, meet my son, Patrick. He has just completed his first degree in Engineering in the U.K.," Dr. Sempaka said proudly.

"Not easy stuff, though," Patrick said jokingly and then laughed.

"Pat, we are about to learn more about Makula," Dr. Sempaka said. "He is your sister's special friend."

"Oh, I see. Of course," Patrick said.

After lunch, Makula, Pam, and Patrick stayed at the dining table and chatted lightly about education and jobs. Dr. Sempaka then came back and asked to speak with Makula alone. Makula followed him into the living room where they sat face to face, and Dr. Sempaka began firing questions at Makula.

"So, Makula, where do you come from?" Dr. Sempaka asked.

"You mean where was I born?" Makula asked.

"Yes," Dr. Sempaka confirmed.

"I am from Kasaka in Bugerere County," Makula replied.

"I have never heard of that town. Is it a town?" Dr. Sempaka asked.

"No, it's a small village," Makula told him.

"Whose son are you?" Dr. Sempaka asked.

"My father is Filipo Musoke," Makula said.

"Oh, I don't know him. He didn't go to school?" Dr. Sempaka asked.

"No. Unfortunately not," Makula replied.

When Dr. Sempaka asked, "He didn't go to school?" in reference to

Makula's father, he was not really asking whether Makula's father had gone to school or not, but whether he had attended Musasa High School. To the "Old Boys" of Musasa High School, one was not considered to have gone to school if one did not study at Musasa. But Makula was not aware of this.

"So, what does your father do?" Dr. Sempaka asked.

"He is a supervisor at a sugar cane plantation," Makula replied.

"Oh, that's interesting," Dr. Sempaka said. "How does he like it?"

"I guess he likes it. He's been working there for years," Makula answered.

"Pam tells me that you are studying economics. What do you intend to do when you graduate?" Dr. Sempaka asked.

"I have actually already started work at what I want to do," Makula told him. "I would like to develop and promote farming, first in Bugerere County and then in this country as a whole."

"Interesting. How do you intend to do that?" Dr. Sempaka asked.

"By promoting the use of cheap and easy-to-use methods of farming to help our farmers increase production," Makula responded. "We are using farmyard manure to grow matooke on a large scale. I know you will say that this has been done for years. But I am not going to stop at that. I am going to develop the marketing mechanisms as well, and this will serve not only to boost the farmers' incomes but also to improve their livelihoods that are currently in a poor state. I, together with some friends, am planning to start a farm market."

"That's a bright idea," Dr. Sempaka said. "And where does my daughter fit in?"

"If it's acceptable to you, I would like to marry her, settle down, and start a family," Makula said nervously.

"Right away?" Dr. Sempaka asked.

"Well, not right away. I would like to marry her after we've graduated," Makula said.

At that moment, Pam's mother came in and sat beside Dr. Sempaka on the sofa. Her husband then excused himself and left the room. And then Mrs. Sempaka started on Makula with her own battery of questions. "So Makula, how do you like your visit so far?" she asked.

"I have enjoyed myself very much. Thank you very much for your hospitality," Makula replied.

"You are welcome," Mrs. Sempaka said. "How do you find Pam?"

"Pam is a very good person. You brought her up very well. She is very respectful and kind to me," Makula told her.

"I am glad to hear that," Mrs. Sempaka said. "However, I must add that, just as she treats you that way, you should treat her in the same way. Women deserve respect, you know. My husband loves and respects me, and that is what has kept my marriage strong for close to thirty years."

"Yes, I get that, and I am committed to loving and respecting her. You have my word on that," Makula assured her.

"Good. What is your next step?" Mrs. Sempaka asked.

"I would like, if it's agreeable to you, to marry her and settle down," Makula replied.

"Good!" Mrs. Sempaka said, laughing. "Times have really changed. Just a few years ago one would never have imagined having this kind of conversation with one's future mother-in-law."

Makula was pleased that Mrs. Sempaka had referred to herself as his future mother-in-law. Mrs. Sempaka wished both Makula and Pam well and told him that she would be glad to see him again. Dr. Sempaka, on the other hand, had not expressed an opinion to Makula, and this left Makula wondering whether his wife was more impressed with him.

At the end of his visit, Makula thanked the Sempakas for their hospitality. He complimented them on their beautiful home, and said that he hoped to see them again. Dr. Sempaka said that he was happy that Makula had visited and asked his son, Patrick, to drive him back to the university. Pam did not return with Makula but stood at the gate and waved to him with a wide smile on her face as he and Patrick drove away.

When Makula arrived at his room, Mugisha was waiting to hear about his visit. "So how did it go with her parents? How was the visit?" he asked.

"Everything seemed to work out fine. Man, those are very rich people. You can't imagine the size and the beauty of their house," Makula told him.

"Wealth aside, do you think you will be accepted?" Mugisha asked.

"I hope so," Makula replied. "Pam's mother seemed particularly enthusiastic, although she cautioned me about not respecting her daughter."

"That's a good sign," Mugisha said. "What about her father?"

"He asked me a number of tough questions, like what I planned to do after university and what plans I had for a possible future with his daughter," Makula told him.

"I hope you didn't tell him about your crazy ideas of developing rural areas," Mugisha said.

"Why do you find those ideas crazy?" Makula asked. "For your information, the good doctor seemed impressed with my proposed action plan."

"Well, good luck, friend," Mugisha said sincerely. "Did Pam say when she would give you some feedback?"

"No, not really," Makula said, "but I think she should be here first thing tomorrow morning. I can't begin to tell you how excited and anxious I am."

"Oh, I can see that!" Mugisha said.

The following morning, Makula waited anxiously for a knock on the door to his room. He was expecting Pam to be bringing good news; he thought that his meeting with the Sempakas had gone very well. Makula did not go anywhere that day except to the dining room. When he went out, he left a note pinned to the door to let Pam know where he was and that he would be returning shortly. He picked up his lunch and took it back to his room, but, to his disappointment, the note was still pinned to the door when he arrived back. He pulled it off and went inside to wait. When Mugisha returned that evening, he asked Makula whether he had heard from Pam. "No, not yet," Makula said anxiously.

"Be patient," Mugisha said. "Sometimes these things take time, even though we often want a quick answer." Makula did not respond.

Makula did not hear from Pam for two weeks. Although he kept telling himself that he had not gone to university to find a wife, he found it hard to concentrate on his studies. After the first few days of not hearing from her, he went to her room at her hall of residence. She was not in, but her roommate Peggy assured him that Pam was well. She wanted to know why he was asking how Pam was, but he was too ashamed to tell her. "She seems fine to me," Peggy said.

Makula even walked past Pam's lecture rooms in hopes of running into her but he did not see her. He was angry and disgusted with her behaviour and complained to his friend Chris Luku. He asked Luku, "Why did she decide to introduce me to her parents if she knew she was not interested in me?"

"Her parents may have influenced her decision," Luku said. "But if you want, I can try to find out more."

"Go right ahead, Chris, so long as she does not find out about it," Makula said.

"Good. I will start asking right away. You will get some answers soon," Luku said, ever confident.

At the end of Makula's second week of waiting to hear from Pam, Luku brought him some shocking news. Pam had been seen walking around the university on several occasions with Tom Kabenge. Makula felt sick to his stomach. "This can't be true," he groaned. "Why would she do that when she assured me that she wanted nothing at all to do with Tom?"

"I don't know," Luku said.

"Chris, do you trust the source of this information? You and I know that Tom has finished his course in law. He's no longer at the university," Makula said.

"Yes, I double-checked everything. That's why I didn't get back to you for a few days—I wanted to be sure," Luku said. "Tom comes to the campus every once in a while. Do you know that he is already driving a sleek new car? Still, that guy is a nut. I don't trust him."

"I give up," Makula said sadly, and collapsed onto his bed.

"No, don't lose hope. At times things turn out positively in the end," Luku said as he poured some water in the kettle. "Would you like a cup of coffee?" he asked Makula.

"No. I'm feeling really bad," Makula answered.

"Take heart, man. Everything will be okay," Luku told him.

Luku stayed with Makula until he had finished his coffee. After Makula had assured him that he would be all right, he left to go downstairs to his room.

Just minutes after Luku had left, Makula heard a familiar knock on the door. "Come in," he said, suddenly excited.

It was Pam. Makula wanted to tell her to get out of his room, but he could not do it. And as if she had intended to hurt him even more, Pam now had a different hairstyle from when he had last seen her. She looked stunningly beautiful in a tight-fitting yellow skirt and a cream top. Before he could stop himself, Makula said, "Sit down, my love." Pam normally sat on Makula's bed when she visited but not this time. She chose to sit on a chair that was next to the door.

"So, tell me, Pam. What's happening with you? Where have you been?" Makula asked somewhat angrily.

"I'm sorry I didn't come to see you sooner, Mak," she said.
"I had a number of things to sort out."

"Concerning me?" Makula asked.

"Not really," Pam replied.

"Okay. Tell me more. Do you have any news for me?"
Makula asked, dreading her answer.

"Mak, I am sorry, but why don't we just be friends?" Pam asked.

Makula was stunned by this and quickly covered his face with his hands. Pam said, "Sorry dear, but I think that's what we have to do."

"This is so cruel of you!" Makula said. "What went wrong? Did your dad or mum dissuade you?"

"No, it has nothing to do with my parents," Pam said.
"By the way, I think they liked you a lot."

Makula begged Pam, "What's the problem, then?"

"Let's just be friends, Mak," she said calmly.
"Can we leave it at that?"

"Does this have something to do with Tom? You want to leave me for Tom?" Makula asked.

"Tom who?" Pam said.

"You know who I'm talking about. Don't pretend you don't. Tom Kabenge, the rich man," Makula said.

"Come on, be serious, Mak. I have already told you that I don't love Tom. Believe me," Pam said convincingly.

"Then what's the problem?" Makula asked again.
"Please tell me."

"I have nothing to add. Let me leave now. Bye, Mak," Pam said as she stood up to leave. For a moment, Makula looked at Pam's shapely figure. He felt jealous.

He put on his sandals to walk her out. In the hallway, they met Mugisha, who was just returning from his lectures. "Hello, Pam. Nice to see you," Mugisha said as he shook Pam's hand.

"Hello, Paul. Nice to see you as well. How are you?" Pam asked.

"I am well, thank you," Mugisha said, aiming a quick wink at Makula before going into their room.

Pam and Makula walked down the stairs, outside the hall's main gate, and onto a dark path where Makula placed his hand across Pam's waist. It felt so good! Pam touched his arm gently with her smooth hands. Makula's emotions overflowed. "Please don't leave me, Pam. I love you. I would be lost without you," Makula said.

They talked as they walked slowly to Pam's hall of residence. Makula did his best to persuade Pam to commit to marrying him. Pam, however, resisted, continuing to insist that they remain only friends. Makula returned to his own room feeling much better simply for having been with her, even though Pam had not truly explained her change of heart. Pam meant everything to him now; even more than his studies.

Despite their meeting of that evening, Pam remained elusive. And Makula finally noticed that he was spending so much time thinking about her that he was giving hardly any time to his studies. He knew that if he did not work hard to complete his course on time and also ended up without Pam, he would have lost on two fronts. He therefore decided to give up his pursuit of Pam and concentrate on his studies. To his surprise, Makula found that the more he concentrated on his studies, the less he thought about Pam. Mugisha, on the other hand, encouraged him not to give up on Pam. He told him that, although he did not have, as Makula well knew, any experience with women, he had heard over and over that a man needed to be patient to get a good woman. Makula was exactly that.

A month before his final examinations, Makula returned home to Kasaka to see his mother and to check on the farm. His mother was well, his sister seemed to be healthy, and the farm was thriving. Kabejja was very excited about seeing her son, especially now that he was about to graduate. This was going to be a first for Kasaka, and she told Makula that the whole village and, indeed, some people from the surrounding villages were already preparing for the big celebration party.

Makula told his mother that he had found a girl whom he was interested in.

"What do you mean 'interested in'?" Kabejja asked, eager to know the details.

"Mother, I have found a girl who I think I would like to marry," Makula replied.

"Very good! Tell me more," Kabejja said. "Where is she from?"

"She is from Kampala," Makula replied. "She will soon complete her studies, just like me."

"That is good, but do you think a kid from Kampala could cope with our rural lifestyle?" Kabejja asked.

"I didn't say that if I married her we would live here," Makula said.

Kabejja told him, "I know, but when you marry someone, you become part of their family because you marry into their family. Believe me when I say that 'you marry into a family.' When I married your father, I was very young. I came alone to join his large family, and at first everybody seemed to love and care about me. However, when you turned five and your father decided to move away for work, everybody turned against me. I stayed in the marriage only because I loved my husband and because I had to stay here for your sake, to raise you."

Makula became very emotional after hearing Kabejja's story. "Sorry my son," Kabejja apologized. "It's not about me now. We should be celebrating your new love. I am only concerned that she may not be able to cope with our lifestyle."

"No problem. She would cope," Makula assured her. "She already knows about my humble background. In fact, I have already visited her home and met her parents."

"What?" Kabejja exclaimed.

"She told me that she couldn't marry me without the consent of her parents. She therefore organized everything, and I went to see her parents," Makula said.

"Alone?" Kabejja asked.

"No," Makula replied. "I went with her. I met her mother, her father, and her brother. They are very welcoming people, something that is rare among rich people."

"They are rich?" Kabejja asked warily.

"Yes. They are very rich." Makula told her. "Their big and beautiful home left me speechless. Their living room is almost as large as our house."

"What?" Kabejja said, incredulous.

"But that was not the real highlight of the visit," Makula said. "The highlight was the barrage of questions that I had to answer from each of her parents."

"You talked to her mother too?" Kabejja asked in disbelief.

"Yes," Makula replied. "She too questioned me."

"What? I couldn't question a future son-in-law, let alone sit to address him more than necessary. That is contrary to our culture," Kabejja said.

"Mother," Makula said, "these are educated people and times have changed."

"You are right my son. Times have changed, but culture is culture," Kabejja said stubbornly.

***

When he returned to the university, Makula felt energized and ready to write his final examinations. His farm was doing well, and all the plans were in place to open the farm market as soon as he returned to Kasaka. After arriving on campus, Makula took a shower and then enjoyed a cup of tea and a slice of bread. Before going out, he pinned a stapled note to the door asking Mugisha to pick up dinner for the two of them from the dining room as he would be late in returning from the library. When Mugisha arrived, he saw Makula's note on the door. When he went into their room, he saw another stapled note on the floor by the door, addressed to Makula. He put Makula's note on the table next to the window, read the note meant for him, and went straight to the dining room to fetch their dinner. When he returned, he served himself a bit of rice and meat and then went to Ahmed Jingo's room next door to watch the evening news.

Makula was very hungry when he finally got back from the library. He put his books on a chair, washed his hands, and quickly served himself some food. After he had eaten, he rested on his bed, and then got up to wash the dishes before going to see Jingo to say hello. Makula opened the window to get some fresh air and saw the note addressed to him lying on the table. He immediately recognized Pam's handwriting. However, just as he reached for the note, the wind picked it up and blew it out the window.

Makula rushed out of the room as if the hall of residence were on fire. As he reached the bottom flight of stairs, he met Chris Luku, but Makula did not stop to speak. In his frantic rush, he missed the last step and fell flat on his face just by the entrance. A small group of students saw him fall and began to laugh. One of the girls asked him if he was all right, but Makula ignored them all as he rushed outside to look on the ground for his note. It was beginning to get dark, so he had some trouble locating it. The cashier at the hall canteen saw him searching and asked him if everything was okay. Makula did not answer. And then he finally saw the note lying on the lawn. He picked it up, scurried into the dim light of the canteen, pulled it open, and read:

> *Hi, Mak.*
> *The answer is "Yes." What is the question?*
> *Love, Pam.*

Makula ran back upstairs to his room, shouting, "It's a Yes! Thank goodness! I am the luckiest man!"

The cashier at the canteen had watched Makula run back up the stairs. He wondered what all the joy was about.

Makula found Mugisha seated on his bed with a bottle of beer in his hand. They chatted excitedly for a little while, and then Makula went downstairs to share the good news with Luku.

CHAPTER ELEVEN
Kampala, Uganda, June 1987

Makula's last weeks at the university were good ones. Things were going well with Pam; they had agreed to get married within a year of leaving university. And his farming venture showed signs of developing into a booming business in the near future.

Makula and Pam wrote their final examinations and left the university. Pam took a holiday for two weeks in London, England, while Makula returned to Kasaka to work on his farm. He had already hired three men to help prepare for the busy planting season and had also cleared an acre of land to build stalls. Here, Othieno's wife Auma, and three other women would sell the produce from the farm. Makula's two cousins Makko and Lukka, who had left Kampala and returned to live in Kasaka, also began working on the farm.

A rumour started in Kasaka that Makula might not have been studying at the university all this time. People in Kasaka and the surrounding villages wondered why a university graduate would "stoop so low" as to work on a farm. When Othieno heard this rumour, he told some of the villagers, "What Makula is doing is setting an excellent example for all the young people in this area. You study to get knowledge to carry on with your life, not necessarily to get a job. You can study, and then use the knowledge to set up your business and employ yourself and others, and I am sure that these are Makula's intentions."

Some said they would wait and see while others believed Othieno because, as one of the educated few in the village, he was a leader of public opinion. Others laughed at the idea. "The hand hoe is a very dangerous implement," Luyima's father said. "As you thrust it into the earth, it thrusts you into poverty. I wouldn't want to see our educated young man waste away in this village. There is no future in this primitive farming."

After a month in Kasaka, Makula returned to Kampala both to see Pam and to check on the results of his examinations. Makula was pleased to learn that he had passed all his courses and was ready to graduate. Mugisha had remained at the university to complete a fourth short term, so when Makula arrived, he went to the hall canteen and began chatting with the cashier as he waited for Mugisha to come back to the residence. When he did, he was delighted to see Makula.

That evening, Makula went to a public telephone and called Pam, who was very glad to hear from him. She agreed to come to the university and meet him. When she arrived, she told Makula that he did not look healthy because he had lost some weight. "Are you overworking yourself, my dear?" she asked.

"Who wouldn't work hard to prepare for a marriage to a queen?" Makula replied.

"Thanks, but come on, don't be funny. Why don't you leave that rural area and come to live here in the city?" Pam asked.

Makula told her, "I will when we start our home. For now, I will stay in that rural area to set up my projects."

"Good for you. But I'll be glad when you're back here," Pam said.

As they talked, Makula had his arm around Pam's waist. When he drew her close, she pulled herself free of his embrace. She said, "Listen, Mak, I wouldn't want to hurt your feelings, but I can't do anything with you. Do you understand?"

"I understand what you mean and respect you for that," Makula replied, "but that's not my intention. I just can't help touching you because it's been so long."

"All right," Pam said. "But I have some news for you. My father says that you need to write a letter to him declaring your intentions. You must also state the date on which you will be formally introduced to my family."

Makula frowned. "Oh. Do we need to go through all that?"

"Well, what would you like to do instead?" Pam asked. "My parents may be modern but they value our culture a lot. We need to prepare for the traditional ceremony where my paternal aunt will formally introduce you to my entire family. After that, if you are accepted, we will wed."

"If I am accepted?" Makula said, incredulous. "You already said yes!"

"Whatever," Pam responded. "It is a necessary formality. If you want, I could find out if my father is available tomorrow to discuss all the details with you. Believe me, he can't wait for the big day."

With a wide smile, Makula said, "I am glad to hear that."

He and Pam had dinner together and then she took a taxi home.

The following morning, Pam came back to the university to see Makula. She told him that her father wanted her to visit Makula's home and meet with his parents, just as he had met hers. After that, Makula and Pam could hold the formal introduction ceremony. Makula was not exactly thrilled at this idea. "Pam, I don't think it would be a good idea for you to visit my parents at this time," he said.

"Why not, my dear?" Pam asked, rather surprised by Makula's response.

Makula tried to explain. "My parents' house is still incomplete. I am still working hard to give it some finishing touches. I wouldn't…"

"No, Makula, I am not visiting to see your parents' house. I am going to meet them and to see your home and to get to know you better. I would actually go whether there was a house or not," Pam said.

"Are you determined to do this?" Makula asked.

"Yes, why wouldn't I?" Pam replied. "You know I love you. I don't care whether your home is poor or not."

When he heard that, Makula pulled Pam close to him. "I love you too, darling," he said, and kissed her on the forehead. "So when would you like to visit?"

"Patrick would like to come with me, and the only time he can do it is next weekend," Pam told him. "He is returning to London the following week."

"That's rather soon, but I am very excited about your visit," Makula said.

"We can come next Saturday, then," Pam said, "if it is okay with you."

"That is okay. Fortunately my father is home for the rest of the month. So yes," Makula told her, "come next Saturday."

When Makula returned to Kasaka, he told his mother about Pam's plan to visit the following Saturday. Kabejja was pleased to hear the news. "I will let your father know as soon as he returns this evening. This is exciting. We need to prepare for a big party."

"Mother, I don't think Pam would like a big party," Makula cautioned her. "I think she would like to join us for a small meal inside the house, with just a few people around."

"Well, she will be the visitor, and we will be the hosts," Kabejja argued. "All the arrangements will be up to us."

When Filipo returned, Kabejja told him about their future daughter-in-law's upcoming visit. Happy with this news, Filipo asked Makula what kind of arrangements were necessary. Makula said that a simple meal for the family and a few friends would suffice. Filipo agreed, since this was only her first visit, but Kabejja wanted a big party. "We can invite all our relatives; this is a great honour for us," she said. Makula, however, insisted that the event be small and intimate so that Pam could get to know his family and close friends.

Makula was anxious about Pam's visit. He woke up early the following morning, and along with Othieno and two of the farm workers, he cleaned the little compound, plastered the outside of the house with cement and sand, painted it, and cleared out all of the bush close to his parents' house. Filipo invited Othieno and his wife Auma to join them for lunch to meet Pam and her brother.

The following Saturday, Makula left early to go to Kayunga where he had arranged to meet Pam and Patrick at eleven o'clock. As he walked the three kilometres to the bus stop that morning, he recalled walking the same path many years before when he was still a student at Kasaka Primary School. He delighted in how far he had come—from the little village school to graduating from Makerere University.

Makula, Pam, and Patrick arrived back in Kasaka around noon. Many of the village children followed the visitors' car, as it was a novelty for them, to Makula's parents' home. Kabejja welcomed the visitors with shouts of joy, and Pam relaxed. Patrick was also pleased to see that, although these folks were obviously poor, they seemed happy. He also noticed how different the Musokes' house was from the rest of the houses in the village. It was larger and its plaster and sky-blue paint were fresh and bright.

Kabejja was awestruck by Pam's beauty and was all smiles as she hugged and greeted her. Filipo, however, kept his distance and greeted the visitor from where he was seated. It was not proper for a father-in-law to shake the hand of a daughter in-law or touch her in any way. Patrick sat on a wooden chair next to Filipo and they quickly started a conversation as if they were old friends. Lameka arrived shortly after. He too sat on a wooden chair next to his brother and joined the conversation. Both Filipo and Lameka were impressed with Patrick's intelligence and good manners.

Makula was worried that Pam would not sit on the mat prepared for her but he was both relieved and happy to see that she did so comfortably. Pam gave a beautiful dress to Makula's sister, three-year-old Manjeri, which made the little girl happy. Kabejja put it on her immediately, and Manjeri eagerly sat next to Pam. "She is so cute!" Pam said as she touched Manjeri's hair. Kabejja served the guests a cup of tea and ears of roasted corn. Patrick remarked that he had not eaten such tasty corn in a long time.

When they had finished their tea, Kabejja invited Pam outside to have a woman-to-woman talk. She started telling Pam about her only son, how he had been born amid extreme poverty, how her parents had sent her away from the family home, and how they had coped with the hard life that followed. This topic made Pam feel a little uncomfortable. She attempted to change it, but Kabejja continued with her story.

Pam was saved from her discomfort by the arrival of Othieno and Auma. When they arrived, Makula was chatting with Filipo, Lameka, and Patrick. Othieno complimented Makula on having chosen such a beautiful fiancée. After he had shaken hands with both Pam and Patrick, Othieno sat on the chair that Makula had vacated for him. When he found out that Patrick lived in England, Othieno asked him all about London—its history, its monuments, its geography—and the way of life for its residents. Meanwhile, Filipo and Lameka discussed Makula's upcoming graduation. Patrick answered so many of Othieno's questions that he was relieved when Kabejja announced that lunch was ready to be served.

At two o'clock, Kabejja and Auma served the visitors matooke, sweet potatoes, and smoked beef, along with banana juice. Patrick told them that, although he had visited several European cities and enjoyed various types of dishes, he always missed the simplicity of this kind of food, prepared with the most natural ingredients. Pam too enjoyed the lunch, although she did not talk much—her mother had warned her against it.

Before leaving with her brother to return to Kampala, Pam told Makula that she would like Manjeri to live with them in their home when they get married. Makula too thought this was a good idea as they could offer her a much better life than the one she had in Kasaka. However, he knew his mother might object. He told Pam that he would try to convince her that it would indeed be the best thing for Manjeri.

After the visitors had left, Kabejja told Makula that she was glad he had insisted on having only a small party for Pam and Patrick. She was happy to have had time to speak with Pam and told Makula how much she liked her. Makula was glad to hear that.

***

A few months later, the people of Kasaka joined Filipo Musoke's family to prepare for the first graduation ceremony ever of one of "their" children. In fact, Filipo became a celebrity in the area for having fathered his brilliant son. Filipo left the preparations for the big party to his brother Lameka, who began doing so early. To set an example for all those who were to pledge food items, Lameka promised to slaughter a bull. Others promised to bring matooke, sweet potatoes, chickens, a goat, and some beer.

Makula received an official invitation to the graduation ceremony for both him and his parents. Filipo asked Makula's former headmaster Mr. Kasule to allow them to spend the night in his house in Kayunga as it would be impossible for them to travel to the university from Kasaka in one day and arrive on time for the ceremony. Mr. Kasule made arrangements with his sister in Kampala, who let Makula and his parents spend the night at her home. Meanwhile, in Kasaka, preparations were in top gear. Twenty people got up very early on the day of Makula's graduation party to start cooking. More than 250 guests were expected at the biggest party that had ever been organized in Kasaka. The whole village was in a festive mood. A huge shed with a roof of tree leaves was erected in front of Makula's parents' house, and celebratory banana trees decorated with wild flowers were erected for about half a kilometre along the path that led to Filipo's and Lameka's homes. The shed was decorated with flowers and balloons, and local drummers were hired from Kayunga to entertain the guests. Luyima had also arranged for one of his friends to play disco music. Kasaka braced itself for the big event.

The graduation ceremony was very colourful. Makula's parents, especially his mother, were very proud of their son.

After the ceremony, the happy parents and the graduates took pictures. Some of those that had cars got in them and drove away. Makula and his parents walked slowly down the hill and off the university campus. At the busy road outside the university's main gate, some parents were buying bouquets of flowers for their graduating children. Having kept some change in her handbag, Kabejja, on impulse, decided to buy flowers for her son. Without alerting either her husband or her son, she started across the road to reach the flower vendors and was hit by a speeding car. All that Makula and his father saw were her shoes flying into the air. In shock at what had happened, Filipo and Makula panicked as a girl yelled, "A woman has been killed!"

Makula ran to offer aid to his mother who was lying on the road, unconscious. He started crying as he reached her and ripped off his graduation gown to place under her head. Two other graduates came to help him. They said that they had just completed medical school, and asked Makula to step aside as they took care of Kabejja. Filipo stopped a car that was travelling in the opposite direction, and he and the two young doctors carefully lifted Kabejja inside. Then the car sped off with all of them to nearby Mulago Hospital. Makula could only look on helplessly.

Makula returned to the university to look for Pam. He spent almost an hour looking for her among the crowd but was unable to find her. He had wanted to let her know about the accident and to see whether her father could assist them. Unable to find Pam, Makula walked to Mulago Hospital. There, he found his worried father sitting on the floor next to an empty bed.

In Kasaka, the celebratory mood did not last as the villagers waited for the graduate and his parents in vain. They waited impatiently for any sign but no one came. Many of those who had come to celebrate Makula's graduation went to the neighbouring village of Nanziba to attend Senfuka's party. They could no longer wait; the music from Senfuka's party was very loud.

Makula's first headmaster, Mr. Kasaato, sat quietly on a bench. He continued to pull out a written draft of his speech from his shirt pocket to add new ideas. He was eager to tell those attending the graduation party how he first met Makula and how the young man had boldly persuaded him to allow him to enroll in Kasaka Primary School.

Makula's former teacher Miss Namata was also present. Lameka had left her name off of the list of speakers because he thought there would be too many, but she had insisted on speaking at "her son's" graduation party. She was prepared to tell the audience that her tough disciplinary actions, including caning, had given Makula a firm foundation and contributed a great deal to his academic success.

When Senfuka arrived at his parents' home at around five o'clock, he shared the bad news of Kabejja's accident. He told the gathering that Makula's mother had been hit by a car and was in a serious condition in Mulago Hospital. "These poor people don't know the city," Senfuka muttered in disgust. "I wonder why they thought they could walk around all by themselves." A few people from neighbouring Kasaka overheard him and were shocked at his words. Several villagers rushed back to Kasaka to tell everyone what had happened.

Lameka let the party begin despite the bad news. There were fewer people to participate than there had been earlier in the day, and they ate in total silence. Lameka suggested that those who wanted more food take it home with them, and the celebration was over.

Makula arrived in Kasaka at around three o'clock the following day, tired and hungry. He had not eaten in over twenty-four hours. When he arrived at his parents' home, many people were gathered there, waiting for news. Lameka asked everyone to keep quiet. Then he asked Makula to tell them what had happened. Makula did so and ended by saying that there was hope for his mother's recovery as the doctors had said that her condition was serious but not life-threatening. He added that both he and his father had been so relieved that she had miraculously survived and to hear that only her left leg was broken. Kabejja spent three months in hospital before returning to Kasaka.

***

The day of Makula's formal introduction to Pam's family was a memorable one for both him and his family. Although it was customary for a man to bring presents to his fiancée's family, the Sempakas had asked Makula not to bring much. Because he and Pam were young and just starting out in life, it would be better for them to save for their future together than to spend money on presents.

Makula organized a group of seven men, including his cousins Makko and Lukka, and four women to accompany him to the home of the Sempakas. Pam had purchased suitable clothing for everyone in the group as she did not want to be embarrassed if they turned up poorly dressed. Mugisha told Makula that this was a sign of a controlling woman, but Makula disagreed. Makula's party hired a fourteen-passenger van to drive them early to a salon in Kayunga where the men would have their hair cut and the women, their makeup applied.

The Sempakas did not need to do much to prepare for the introduction. Their mansion was always immaculate and the lawn well trimmed. They invited a few friends to attend the ceremony. They also contracted with a hotel to cater the event.

Makula and his party arrived as expected at a quarter to two. Although Pam had instructed them, through Makula, not to act shy, for most of them this was the first time they had seen such a beautiful compound. When they stepped out of the van to be greeted, the women lowered their eyes as Pam's cousin Esther pinned carnations to their clothing. The men looked up at the tiled roof of the house, mesmerized.

When they were welcomed into the house, Makula's spokesman Luyima faced tough questions from the hosts' spokesman, who pretended not to know who the suitor's party were and why they had come: "Who are you? What do you want? Where are you from? We were not expecting any visitors; are you lost?"

Luyima was not a man to be intimidated, though. He spoke loudly and humorously and made the traditional, drama-laden ceremony fun for all who were present. And after a few minutes of haggling, Makula's party were allowed to sit down. They were then asked to state the reason for their visit.

Luyima said that Pam's aunt, her father's sister, had told them that her niece was ready to get married and that he was representing the young man who intended to marry her. After they had argued and haggled for a while, Luyima presented the hosts' spokesman with a symbolic gift that represented the dowry. The spokesman said that Makula and Pam would wed in a church, and that Makula was formally allowed to marry Pam. Luyima said that the wedding would take place in three months.

The visitors were then served a sumptuous meal that delighted everyone in Makula's party. After dinner, they thanked their hosts for their hospitality and returned to Kasaka.

***

In order to prepare for the wedding, Pam and her cousin Esther drew up the wedding budget, which Makula thought to be too extravagant. However, Pam told him not to worry as her family would pay for the bulk of what they needed. Two months prior to their wedding, Pam and Makula were meeting weekly to plan for it. Many of their former schoolmates who were now working in various offices in Kampala were also invited to these meetings, which were held to raise money from the friends of the bride and groom to supplement the contribution from their families. Makula in particular appreciated this custom, as his family lacked the means to support him. There was a lot of drama as Makula's former schoolmates competed with one another to see who would contribute the largest amount of money. Some used these meetings as a venue to show off their newly acquired wealth.

To honour the people of Kasaka, Makula decided to let his parents invite family and friends to the wedding. Filipo and Kabejja invited almost everyone they knew to attend the big feast. After all, this was "their son" who was going to wed and, for many, this was their first church wedding and also their first time visiting Kampala. Everyone wanted to look their best for the occasion. Those who did not have clothes befitting the event borrowed from those who had more clothing. Some borrowed outfits from friends or family members who lived farther away. The preparations for the big day took months, and whoever stepped foot in Kasaka was greeted with news of the upcoming wedding.

At around eight o'clock on the morning of the wedding, the bus came to Kasaka to take Makula's family, friends, and relatives to the cathedral. Although the bus was meant to hold only sixty people, eighty-five turned up for the journey to Kampala. Makula's cousin Lukka, who was in charge of the transportation, was surprised to see some young faces that he did not recognize. However, he did not want to spoil the mood, so he let these young men and women board the bus. The journey to Kampala was very exciting as many in the group looked out the windows and waved vigorously to whoever they met on the highway.

At the wedding, Makula's guests outnumbered Pam's and this was very obvious as each of these groups sat in opposite pews in the cathedral. The ceremony was very colourful. Pam looked stunning in her white wedding dress as she walked gracefully down the aisle hand-in-hand with her father. The matron and the maids of honour, including Makula's sister, Manjeri, followed the bride and her father. Makula waited patiently, handsome in a grey suit, for his bride to arrive at his side. After Makula and his bride had exchanged their vows, there was much shouting and cheering in the church. Later, numerous photographs were taken. Makula's guests were so excited by the chance to be in a photo that they stole the show from Pam's guests. They struck funny poses on the steps outside the cathedral, under the trees, and in the parking lot. Two young men even got their photograph taken as they dangled from a short tree near the church. Makula was a little embarrassed by this, but being the groom, he could not speak to anyone about it.

The reception was held that afternoon at the Nile Hotel, with over three hundred guests in attendance. There was a lot of merrymaking while everyone enjoyed a sumptuous meal. While they dined, Afrigo Band played live music. Many more friends and members of the Sempaka family attended the wedding reception. Their obvious wealth intimidated many of Makula's guests and, unlike at the cathedral, they were reserved at the reception. They sat quietly in their seats as they watched the bridal entourage cut the cake and walk to and fro in the ballroom greeting their guests.

Makula's family had chosen his Uncle Lameka to speak on their behalf. "Radio Uganda" spoke into the microphone as he highlighted Makula's strengths, his ability to rise from a boy in a small village to a man who shone in the nation's prestigious university, and of how he had brought honour to his parents, and indeed to all the people of Kasaka, by marrying a wife. Lameka continued, "And to my daughter-in-law, I have this to say. In the past, we would be telling you to obey your husband, to be submissive in all ways, and to welcome members of his family with a smile. Have many children, and all those sorts of things. But, no, that is not what I am going to tell you today. You and Makula are equal partners in this marriage: love one another, respect one another, and be there for each other. If you do this, you will succeed in marriage."

There was applause and cheers from those present as Lameka continued to speak. "This is a young man who went to Musasa High School barefooted." The people laughed a lot at this. "However, this did not stop him from pursuing his dream of getting a good education. As they say, good things come to those who wait. Now his patience has paid off. On top of that success in education, he has got a wonderful wife."

The people shouted and applauded once again. Lameka concluded his speech by saying, "Love and communicate clearly and affectionately to each other. If you do that, you will enjoy a long and happy marriage."

Dr. Sempaka spoke on behalf of his family. He praised his daughter for her exemplary behaviour and thanked her for honouring them by waiting to complete her education before thinking of getting married. "Let me thank you and your husband for honouring us. Many of you know that, these days, young people feel that they can do whatever they wish, wherever, whenever. Many have ended up eloping and many families have lost their children to epidemics, fuelled by indecent behaviour." As he concluded his speech, Dr. Sempaka asked the bride and the groom to walk to where he, his wife, and two of Pam's maternal uncles were seated.

Pam and Makula slowly made their way through their guests, who were delighted with Pam's smile and her beauty. When they reached the table where the Sempakas were seated, Mrs. Sempaka handed a large envelope to the bride and the groom and asked them to please open it. Inside was a photograph of a beautiful two-storey house along with an original land title. This was their wedding present from the Sempakas. In their joy, Pam and Makula held up the picture of the house to show their guests. Such a gift was common in Pam's family, but Makula's family and guests clapped and shouted, for such a generous gift was unheard of.

CHAPTER TWELVE
Paris, France, July 1988

Makula and Pam had planned a two-week honeymoon in Paris, France. When they arrived at Charles de Gaulle Airport, they took a taxi to the hotel where they had booked a room. The receptionist received them warmly. "Hello, welcome to the Palais Legrand. My name is Jean-Marc. Do you have a reservation?" he asked.

"Yes, we do," Pam said, as she stood at the counter beside her husband.

Jean-Marc chatted with them as he checked on their reservation. "So, is this your first time visiting Paris?"

"No, it is the second time for me but the first for my husband," Pam replied.

"Nice. Welcome to the City of Light. I think you will enjoy your visit here. So, are you here for business, a meeting…?" Jean-Marc asked.

"We are here for our honeymoon," Makula said.

"Great! You chose a good destination. Welcome to Paris." Jean-Marc handed the key to Pam and announced, "Room 522."

Makula followed Pam to the elevator. He hadn't gone far when he remembered their suitcase and returned to pick it up. Jean-Marc told him not to worry—someone would bring it up to the room for them in a moment. He gestured to Makula to come closer and said, "You got yourself a gorgeous wife, you lucky man."

"Thank you," Makula said, smiling.

"Remember," said Jean-Marc, "I am here at your service. When you have had your rest, let me know. I will give you a list of all the beautiful places to visit in Paris."

Makula thanked Jean-Marc for his kindness and then turned to join Pam at the elevator. Jean-Marc called him back to the reception desk, winked at him, and said, "Hey, man, enjoy your honeymoon."

Makula laughed and said, "Sure, I will," and went to join his wife.

The newlywed couple enjoyed a blissful time at the hotel. In the afternoon, Pam swam in the swimming pool while Makula watched.

On the second day of their honeymoon, as they strolled along the breathtaking Avenue des Champs-Elysées, Makula said to his wife, "Thank you, darling, for bringing me where I've never been before."

"You are welcome, honey. Do you like it here?" Pam asked.

"Oh, yes. I'm having a wonderful time," Makula answered.

"I'm glad you like it," Pam said.

"Why don't we stay here?" Makula asked.

"What do you mean? You don't want the honeymoon to end?" Pam asked.

"Who would want a honeymoon to end? But that's not what I'm talking about," Makula replied. "I have always been fascinated by life overseas, in a developed country."

"You are on your honeymoon. I guess that should be different from real life in any country, be it developed or underdeveloped. As an economist, though, you should be more realistic," Pam said.

"I know that. But still, I would love to live here," Makula said.

"Yes, everything looks picture-perfect—people sipping coffee in sidewalk cafés, beautiful summer weather. But that's not how life is every day. Remember that many of these people are tourists who have to return to their real lives."

"I guess you are right," Makula agreed. "But all the same, I would love to live overseas."

***

When they returned from their two-week honeymoon, Makula and his bride went straight to their new home in Kampala. Pam's cousin Linda was there to welcome them.

"Mak, you remember Linda, don't you?" Pam asked. "You met her at my parents' home when you first came to meet them."

"Yes, of course. I am glad to see you again, Linda," Makula said.

"And you too, Makula," Linda replied.

"By the way, Mak, Linda will be staying with us while she attends school. She has two years to complete before entering university," Pam added.

"Nice," Makula said, a little surprised that he was only now hearing this news.

After leaving their suitcases in the living room, the couple started a tour of the house. Makula was a little overwhelmed by the newly furnished home. He had never switched on a TV, he did not know how to operate an electric stove, and he did not know what the toaster was for. However, he kept his awe and anxiety to himself. After telling Linda about the wonderful time they had had on their honeymoon, Pam announced to Makula and Linda that she was going to take a shower.

"There is one part of the house that you have not seen," Linda said.

"Oh, what's that?" Pam asked.

"The garage," Linda said.

"Whatever," Pam said, as she turned to go up the stairs.

"You have to see the garage," Linda insisted.

"Okay, if you say so," Pam said as she and Makula followed Linda to the garage and opened the door. Inside, there was a refurbished Datsun Sunny, a present from the Sempakas to Pam. She jumped with joy as Linda handed her the keys and asked both Makula and Linda to get into the car to go for a test drive. Makula enjoyed the short drive in the neighbourhood, and, as he was still unemployed, Pam suggested that he start driving lessons that week. He had his first lesson two days later.

At home, Pam took control and did not consult with him much as she carried on with the chores. Makula was glad that his wife had taken charge, just as his mother had managed their small home well for years when his father was away at work. Because Pam was not accustomed to doing a lot of housework, she told her husband that she needed a helper. Even though Pam's cousin Linda was also living in their home, Pam said that she needed a "house girl" to help with the housework.

"I don't like the term 'house girl,'" Makula told her. "It is demeaning. Why don't you use 'domestic servant,' 'maid,' or something of the sort?"

"Well, everyone calls them 'house girls.' I didn't invent the term," Pam explained.

"But why do you need a helper when Linda is here? Manjeri too will be joining us," Makula said.

"Oh, yes, that is terrific," Pam said. "Was it difficult to convince your mother to let her come live with us?"

"Surprisingly, no. Even she could see the advantages for Manjeri. She only warned me not to spoil her. Anyway, since both Linda and Manjeri will be living here, we won't need a helper," Makula said.

"You can't really count on Linda—she is lazy," Pam replied.

Makula laughed a little and then said, "There are many young girls in my village who would be happy to come to work here. However, because they have never lived in a home like this one, you would need to train them."

"I wouldn't mind training one or two girls," Pam responded. "But I've heard people say that when these village girls get to learn the city and the way things work here, they don't want to be told what to do anymore…"

"What do you mean?" Makula asked.

"Well, they become bigheaded and stop listening to their boss's instructions. In other words, they want to take over the home," Pam replied.

"Oh. How so?" Makula asked.

Pam, who was now employed in a bank, said, "One of my co-workers actually had to send her house girl away because the girl started making advances toward her husband."

"What?" Makula exclaimed. "I hope you are not thinking that I would ever get involved in something like that!"

"No, honey," Pam assured him. "I am just telling you a true story. Seriously, though, I need help. I hate coming home from work and having to go straight to the kitchen."

"I understand that, darling," Makula said. "Will you get along with a girl from a rural area?"

"Why wouldn't I?" Pam asked.

"You can be very strict and particular, you know," Makula teased her.

"For your information, two 'rural people' helped raise me and my brother!" Pam said.

"Oh! Who?" Makula asked.

"Do you remember Mr. and Mrs. Kamoga, the couple you met when you came to visit my parents' home for the first time? They have been my parents' domestic servants for close to twenty years," Pam added. "They are actually Linda's parents."

"What? But you always refer to Linda as your cousin," Makula said, puzzled.

"What should I have called her?" Pam asked. "She was born into our home and her parents helped raise us. They are now like our relatives."

Pam was pleased when Lukka brought Manjeri from Kasaka to live with them. "She is so cute," she said.

***

Two months after marrying Pam, Makula had an interview with Star Hardware Limited. The company manufactured hand hoes and other farming implements, such as leaf rakes, machetes, and watering cans. He was hired as a marketing manager, responsible for innovation and corporate accounts, and led a department of twenty employees at the company's head office and close to fifty in the district offices. With the position came a new company-owned pickup truck. Because he was a new driver, Pam did not trust Makula to drive her car, especially on long journeys outside the city. When he got the company pickup, Makula was glad that he now had his own vehicle and could drive wherever he wanted to go.

Makula felt good about his success. He liked the atmosphere at his new workplace and enjoyed working in a spacious office that he shared only with his secretary. A few months into his new job, Makula introduced some innovations to the company that made his bosses proud. Star Hardware began to manufacture mattresses and metal beds that sold well countrywide. And by the end of the following year, the company had expanded and hired more employees.

The newlyweds enjoyed a blissful life, and Pam often told her husband how happy she was that she had chosen him. There was one thing that she did not like about him, though. Makula could not give up doing household chores, and she thought these were beneath him. When she returned home from her job at the bank each day, she would find him washing dishes or mopping the floor and once again raise the issue of their finding a house girl.

> Pam argued, "Darling, if we don't get a house girl, I will have to do all the housework myself—I hate to see my man mopping the floor. We can't rely on Linda; I know how busy she is with school. Seriously, what would my girlfriends think if they saw you doing that kind of work?"

> "Of course, honey, I understand what you mean, but I don't see a problem with a man washing dishes or mopping the floor in his own home. Isn't it another way of showing you that I care about you?" Makula asked.

> "True, but it is not one that impresses me," Pam told him.

When Pam talked to her boss, Josephine, about wanting to hire a house girl, she strongly advised against it. Pam realized that, just like a co-worker with whom she had discussed the idea, Josephine had had a bad experience. "I hired a girl to work at my home last year," she told Pam. "Whenever I was at home, she would act like any humble girl. She did all of the work around the house and took good care of the children. However, when I wasn't there, she showed her true colours. My neighbour told me that as soon as I had left the house to go to work, the girl would put on one of my good dresses and walk around the neighbourhood to show it off. At first I did not believe it. But then one day I arrived home earlier than expected and caught the girl chatting away with a young man. She sat on the sofa with her legs crossed as if to say 'I own this place.' And she was wearing a beautiful pink outfit of mine. I fired her then and there." Even though she understood that there were risks, Pam wanted to try her luck with hiring a house girl. She certainly didn't want to do all of the housework herself. And Makula finally agreed to hire a girl from Kasaka to help Pam.

Makula loved his new home, but just as he had felt that his freedom was restricted when he had attended Kayunga Primary School years before, he also felt so now. In Kasaka, being at home meant going outside to reach the kitchen; and if you needed to go to the toilet, you had to walk twenty metres to the latrine. Although he did not miss the outdoor latrine, he longed for the exterior kitchen where all the food could be cooked on a wood fire. Makula's favourite dish was matooke and smoked beef cooked on a wood fire—matooke did not taste the same when cooked on an electric stove.

Makula broached the subject with Pam. "Sweetheart, why don't we build a little kitchen in the backyard? I really miss cooking with a wood fire."

"Are you crazy?" Pam asked him. "The city council would evict us immediately! Such kitchens are not allowed in this area. I guess you will have to ask your mum to bring you some of that food from Kasaka whenever you feel like eating it," Pam said, laughing as she pictured a kitchen spitting smoke out in their backyard.

Makula was eager to show off his pickup truck to everyone in Kasaka. When he and Pam went there to visit, the villagers gathered to admire it and to congratulate "their" son for his achievement. Othieno asked Makula if they could go for a ride, and he and two of his sons sat in the bed of the pickup. Joyous and triumphant, as if the truck belonged to them, they waved to everyone they saw.

While there, Pam asked her mother-in-law whether she could help them find a house girl. Pam thought she could employ one of Makula's many cousins, but Kabejja didn't like that idea. She said that she would talk with the parents of Namugga, who was one of the well-behaved young girls in the neighbourhood, about whether Pam could take her as a house girl. After speaking with Namugga's parents, Kabejja returned with fifteen-year-old Namugga and introduced her to Pam. Makula remembered seeing her when she had been much younger. With her parents' approval, immediate arrangements were made for Namugga to go to Kampala with Pam and Makula.

Namugga began working in their house, and, just as Kabejja had said, she was a very well-behaved girl. She was also hard-working. However, she was also shy and afraid of the many things in the house that were unfamiliar to her. She was fearful of the sound of the refrigerator and of standing near or cooking with the electric stove. She was suspicious of what she saw on TV. In fact, she didn't want to touch anything electrical. When Pam asked her why, Namugga told her that her mother had warned her about "electricity shocks." Overhearing this, both Linda and Manjeri laughed at Namugga. Namugga's first month of working as their "house girl" was therefore a difficult one. Makula, however, encouraged her by telling her that most of these things had been new to him as well when he and Pam had first moved into the house.

After Makula and Pam had been married for a few months, members of Makula's extended family began to visit, uninvited and on a regular basis. First to come was Makula's cousin Lukka, who visited at least twice a week to store fruits and vegetables destined for sale in the market, in their garage. Pam hated Lukka because he talked a lot. He also annoyed her because whenever he came he would sit on the sofa, remove his shoes, and put his feet up on the coffee table. Pam found his hole-filled socks disgusting. Three other cousins of Makula who were looking for work in Kampala were also frequent visitors. Pam complained to her cousin Esther, "I love my husband so much, but I really can't stand his army of relatives. They are driving me nuts."

When Kabejja found out that these cousins were visiting "her children's" house, she thoroughly scolded them. "I don't want you to become a burden to my children," she told them. "Let them enjoy their home."

"But Aunt," Lukka explained, "we go to Makula's house because he is the only relative we have in Kampala."

Kabejja said, "You worked in Kampala long before Makula and Pam moved into their home. Why don't you stay with the many friends you made over the years?"

When Makula and Pam's son Richard was born two years into their marriage, the number of visitors to the home increased and included uncles, aunties, and other members of Makula's extended family. Among those who came was Makula's cousin Toofa. After a brief chat, Makula took Toofa on a tour of the house, which Toofa admired. He said, "I now believe the saying 'Good things come to those who wait.' Who knew that you would end up this successful and rich?"

"I am not rich," Makula responded.

"You are to me," Toofa said.

As they talked, Namugga called them to the table for the evening meal. She first served a salad and glasses of juice, followed by a dish of pasta. Toofa, who ate a lot of the pasta, expected another dish to arrive but none did. Later, alone in the guestroom where he was to sleep, Toofa found himself still hungry.

He called Makula and asked him to join him outside—he had something confidential to tell him. Makula wondered what this could be since they had talked for over two hours that evening. Once outside the house, Toofa, embarrassed, told Makula that he wanted more food. Makula was not surprised but wondered how to help him. "There is some bread. If you want, Namugga could serve you a cup of tea or coffee and bread."

"No. That won't help," Toofa said. "You know me—I do a lot of manual labour, so I need more food. Is there anything to eat like sweet potatoes or cassava?"

"No," Makula said.

"Is there a market nearby?" Toofa asked. Makula told him there was and drove Toofa there where he enjoyed some deep-fried fish, deep-fried cassava, and a cup of hot milk. Upon his return to Kasaka, Toofa told his wife that Makula's home was very beautiful but that there was no food.

Makula's friend Ben Kasede, who he had not seen in close to a year, also came to visit. Makula hugged Kasede and shook his hand as he welcomed him into the house. Although Makula had greeted him with joy, Kasede seemed preoccupied and unhappy. Makula asked his friend to sit down on the sofa and served him a glass of juice. He sat down beside Kasede and asked, "So, how are you doing, my friend?"

"I know you will be disappointed to hear this. But I am not doing well," Kasede said.

"Why not? What is the problem?" Makula asked.

"I am almost unemployed," Kasede told him. "You know, one morning when I arrived at the market, I noticed some commotion. When I reached my stall, I noticed that mine and the three neighbouring ones had been wiped clean. As we talk now, I have very little stock left.

"My wife is not doing any better either. You know she lost a brother and went away for a month to attend to his affairs. Since she overstayed, she was let go by the school where she had been teaching. To make matters worse, her brother had two children. So guess who is taking care of those orphans? My wife and I are. Yet, as you know, we have two children of our own."

"I am so sorry to hear all this, Ben," Makula responded.

"That's all right, my friend," Kasede said. "You know, in life, there are people who seem to have an unfair share of problems. Unfortunately, I am one of those people."

"Don't worry, Ben. I will see what I can do for you," Makula said as he stood up to hug his friend.

"Thanks for caring so much about me. I didn't come to give you a list of my problems but, to be honest, any help would be appreciated. Thanks again," Kasede said.

He was grateful to leave with two plastic bags full of groceries and a few thousand shillings with which to restock his stall.

***

In her years of working for Makula and Pam, Namugga had learned a lot. Although she was strict with Namugga when it came to the standard of cleanliness of her home, Pam was kind and treated her house girl well. Namugga took good care of their son Richard and kept the home spotless. Whenever she returned home from work, Pam would always be surprised and pleased to see how much work Namugga had done during the day. And although Makula's relatives visited in droves every other weekend, Namugga seemed to take good care of them.

When Makula's relatives came to visit, Pam would greet them, pick up her son, and then go to visit her parents' home. She would not return until it was time to go to bed. At first, this behaviour bothered Makula, who felt that a wife should stay at home to entertain visitors, even if they were "annoying villagers." However, when he realized that her leaving reduced the number of quarrels he and his wife had, Makula was content to let her leave while he and Namugga took care of the guests.

One day, while alone in the house, Namugga answered the telephone for the first time. The caller laughed and hung up. Namugga had recognized Pam's cousin Esther's voice. When Pam returned from work, Namugga told her about the incident. Pam wondered why Esther would call and not leave her a message.

A few days later, Pam and Esther met for coffee and a chat. When Pam asked Esther whether it had been she who had called, Esther, laughing loudly, admitted it.

"Why are you laughing?" Pam asked, perplexed.

Esther said, "When I called, your girl picked up the phone and yelled, 'Speaking!'" Pam laughed too but said she was glad that Namugga now had the courage to pick up the phone. "At first, whenever the phone rang, she would simply walk away and go to the kitchen."

Makula continued to work at Star Hardware, and every two weeks he went to Kasaka to check on the development of the growing farming business. Othieno was managing it well, and they had hired more employees. Makula also asked Othieno to build more stalls and expand the market area. In a few months, the residents started building more mud houses to accommodate new settlers who paid rent. Soon, the area was buzzing with activity. Truck drivers transporting fish from the lake stopped to buy food in what came to be known as "Makula's market." Makula was very proud. He began dreaming of seeing this village grow into a town. His relatives were also very happy as many of them were now employed either on the farm or in the market. The only one who did not work there was Toofa, who had found himself a job in the hospital in Kayunga just when the farming business had started booming.

Whenever he went to Kasaka to inspect the farm and the market, Makula was pleased to be introduced to new people, some of whom were looking for work. Makula would direct them to Othieno, who always found them something to do. This annoyed Luyima, who felt sidelined and found it strange that Makula seemed to enjoy having control over the people of Kasaka. Senjo, who had never really recovered from his remorse at stealing the matooke, grew less involved in the business and spent most of his time working for some new settlers in exchange for banana beer.

When Makula realized that the people now had some money to spend, his company, Star Hardware, started selling them beds and mattresses it had manufactured. The company offered credit to a few people who could not afford to pay for their beds or mattresses in full. Makula didn't know that this would cause him problems in the near future.

Chapter Thirteen
Kampala, Uganda, March 1992

Simeon Senfuka had been nicknamed the "Fish Farmer" because he had promised to turn the university's "wasted" swimming pool into a fish pond. As if to prove to the people who had booed this idea that he had an enterprising mind, Senfuka had developed a very lucrative farming business in Sanda, twenty-five kilometres from Kampala. Senfuka, with his new degree in agriculture, decided not to look for a job. Instead, he took advantage of a new scheme offered by the East African Bank of Commerce that provided credit to farming businesses. Unlike Makula, who continued to run his farm in Kasaka, Senfuka rented 300 acres of land in Sanda and took advantage of the village's proximity to the city to develop his business. He grew cabbages, tomatoes, green peppers, spinach, green beans, and many similar vegetables. Consequently, the small company he had started while he was still a student had grown within three years into a booming business that employed twenty clerical staff and about one hundred others that toiled on the farm. Senfuka had named his company Food Basket Limited. It supplied fresh produce to a number of corporate customers in Kampala, and he had plans to start exporting fresh produce in the near future. Food Basket's head office was housed in a building that belonged to James Kabenge.

Like the people of Kasaka who were employed in Makula's business in Kasaka, Senfuka employed many of the villagers from his native Nanziba on his farm. They stayed in Sanda to work and returned home on the occasional weekend to see their families. The two villages of Kasaka and Nanziba competed to be the most prosperous.

Makula's friend Ben Kasede got a job at Food Basket Limited as a cleaner and "office messenger." Makula was worried, however, that his friendship with Kasede could cost the latter his job—Senfuka continued to dislike Makula.

At the peak of Makula's success in farming, a long, dry season began, and Kasaka, which usually received a lot of rain, was hit by a severe drought. Many crops on Makula's farm failed. Makula understood the risks of depending solely on rain to water his crops but he could do nothing about the drought. The farm was too large for him to hire people to water the crops. And even some wells went dry.

Because of the drought, Makula's farming business could not compete with Senfuka's Food Basket, which utilized, thanks to credit provided by the bank, modern irrigation technology and had a more reliable source of water from a nearby river. Senfuka was well aware of this and whenever he met anyone from Kasaka, he would say, "Tell your boss to stop wasting his time on that unprofitable business. Let him come to me; I will employ him." When he heard about this, Makula said, "If he wants, let him come to me. I will employ him."

The enmity between the two men grew although they never met in person. Makula knew that the bad feeling between his family and Senfuka's was not new, but he did not feel he could do anything about it. Kabejja tried hard to convince her son to find a solution, but Makula refused, claiming that Senfuka was too arrogant. Kabejja argued, "He may be arrogant but have you even tried to talk to him about an amicable way to settle your differences? Who knows, perhaps he will welcome the idea, so we can settle this once and for all. Everyone in both villages would be so happy if we could get along." Makula told her that he did not want to pretend to look for a solution to a problem that he had not created. And Kabejja gave up. For a while.

One Saturday morning, Kasede came to Makula's home and told him that he had some shocking news. Makula thought that his friend had lost his job at Food Basket. But Kasede told Makula that he had seen Tom Kabenge talking to Senfuka as they walked to the elevator at the offices of Food Basket. Because Kasede had been sweeping the hallway, he had been able to overhear bits of their conversation. Apparently Kabenge was telling Senfuka that Makula had snatched his girlfriend and that he intended to make Makula very sorry for that. "Is it true that Pam was Kabenge's girlfriend?" Kasede asked.

"Not really," Makula answered. "What did Senfuka say? Did you hear anything?"

"No. Not much," Kasede replied. "As they got closer, I think they may have noticed that I was listening, so they lowered their voices. Kabenge looked right at me, but I don't think he recognized me. He looked suspicious, though."

Three weeks later, Tom Kabenge's brother, John, wrote an article in his newspaper, *The Daily Messenger*, in which he accused Makula of selling beds and mattresses on credit to poor rural people through Star Hardware. "Of what use is a good bed to a man who is not sure how and from where he will get the next meal for his family?" he wrote. Makula wrote a letter to the newspaper explaining the company's position but it was never published. In the letter, Makula had explained that Star Hardware wanted to make decent beds available to people everywhere on affordable terms. He had also said that food production in the area had risen and therefore people did indeed know where their next meal was coming from. In comments published by *The Daily Messenger*, some customers in Kampala said that they would boycott Star Hardware's products if the company did not stop selling "useless" beds and mattresses to their poor relatives on credit. Considering that it had been John Kabenge who had written the newspaper article that questioned Star Hardware's actions, Makula and Pam had no doubt that Tom Kabenge was trying to get Makula fired from his job.

Pam advised Makula to organize a press conference to clear up the matter for Star Hardware. Makula therefore wrote to various newspapers to let them know that he would be holding a press conference on Monday afternoon. Many news reporters and journalists turned up, and Makula found himself in the hot seat. However, he answered many questions convincingly and clarified the truth of the situation. The only person who was hard to silence was John Kabenge, who insisted that Makula had not verified the financial ability of the people to whom he had extended credit, to pay back the loans. Kabenge also said, "It is obvious that there was a conflict of interest for you in this deal. Not only do you own the farm and the market where these people work but you also work for the company that purports to be helping them by selling them these beds and mattresses."

Makula did his best to answer all the questions and most of the journalists seemed convinced by his sincere responses. However, he was angry with John Kabenge, who continued to claim that Star Hardware was "gouging its gullible rural customers."

Makula was left wondering whether he would lose his job. He returned home that evening tired, angry, and hungry. He was eager to tell Pam how the conference had gone and to hear her opinion. When he opened the door, though, he was greeted by his cousins Makko and Lukka. They immediately told him that their father Lameka was very sick and asked Makula to go to Kasaka to bring him to hospital for treatment. Makula simply couldn't deal with this news or with his cousins' request and lost his temper. "And who says that I am here to entertain such nonsense?" he yelled at them. "If you realized that he was very sick, why didn't you find some form of transport to bring him to hospital? Did you have to come here for me now when you could have done something there and then?"

Makko started to explain. "But…"

"No!" Makula interrupted. "Don't tell me anything. Be reasonable. Do you expect me to go to Kasaka right now to pick up the old man because you failed to do what you were supposed to do?"

"Sorry for disturbing your peace, Makula. Good night," Lukka said as he and Makko stood up to leave.

"Good night," Makula said, closing the door behind them. He didn't know where they would spend the night, nor did he care.

The two brothers walked away from the house in silence. Then Makko asked Lukka, "What really happened with Makula this evening? I have never seen him in such a mood. I have never seen that side of him until now."

"It's money," Lukka told him. "Now that he has money, he thinks that he is on top of the world. I wish him good luck with his money."

Inside the house, Makula sat down in the sofa to wait for his temper to cool down. Manjeri, who had heard him shouting, came in to see him. She was surprised that her two cousins had already left, as they usually stayed for hours whenever they visited. Makula asked her where Pam was, and Manjeri told him that she was not yet home.

When Pam arrived soon after, Makula told her how the press conference had gone that afternoon. She congratulated him on having done a good job. She said, "Of course, we know why John treated you that way, but that will not stop you from doing the good job that you are doing for the people. I am very proud of you." Makula felt much better after talking with Pam. He took a warm bath and enjoyed his dinner with his wife.

When they were in bed, Makula told Pam that his cousins Makko and Lukka had come to tell him that their father was very sick. "What? You are only telling me this now? I thought you cared about your uncle! You should have told me this right away," Pam said. Makula was surprised to hear this from Pam, who had never seemed to care about his relatives. She asked him, "What condition is he in now? Where is he?"

"He is in Kasaka," he told her. "They had come to ask me to bring him to the hospital."

"And what did you tell them?" Pam asked.

"Listen, Pam," Makula explained. "I had had a bad afternoon and I was not in a good mood. I yelled at them and they left immediately."

Pam then said, "You yelled at them and sent them away just like that? Are you crazy? Did you give them some money to help?"

"No," Makula admitted. "I just sent them away."

"What? Your beloved uncle is very sick and that's how you chose to help?" Exasperated, Pam turned away from him and readied herself for sleep.

Makula felt very remorseful. He loved his Uncle Lameka very much and he had been wrong to treat his cousins that way. He wanted to go that very night to Kasaka but when he told Pam his plan, she asked him to wait till morning.

Makula could not sleep. He imagined how his cousins had felt and was certain that they would let his uncle, and his father, know how he had treated them. He remembered his uncle's sense of humour and his love for Makula. This almost made him cry. He set off for Kasaka at five o'clock and was at Lameka's doorstep by seven.

Lameka was suffering from high blood pressure but was not as ill as his sons had claimed. All the same, he was very glad to see his nephew. He told Makula that he was feeling better and perhaps no longer needed to go to the hospital. Makula insisted he do so, though, and soon he was driving his uncle and one of his wives to Mulago Hospital. Although Kayunga Hospital was closer, especially for his family to visit with him, Makula knew he would receive better treatment at the hospital in Kampala. Lameka was admitted and remained there for two weeks until he had recovered.

The following evening, a rested Makula welcomed another visitor. Ben Kasede had come to see him, but he did not bring good news. Kasede had been fired from his job as a cleaner and messenger at Food Basket Limited. Makula was sorry to hear this, and although he did not share his thoughts, he knew that Kasede had lost his job simply because he was Makula's friend. Makula assured him that he would find him another job "in a matter of days," and Kasede soon left, relieved. When he told Pam what had happened to Kasede, she said, "Poor man. He is just a victim of circumstances."

Two days later, early in the morning, Makula rushed Pam to the hospital. Mere minutes later, she delivered their daughter. They named her Dawn.

When he had returned to work, Makula happened to look out his office window and see James Kabenge, who had recently retired from his long service at the East African Bank of Commerce, and his son Tom walking into the building. He wondered what they wanted, but because some of his fellow managers knew about his bad relationship with Tom Kabenge, he did not feel comfortable asking any of them. Their visit to Star Hardware really bothered Makula, but he did not tell Pam about it. A couple of months later he finally learned the reason for the Kabenges' visit when the managing director of his company said to him, "When the company gets into the hands of its new owners, I think it will perform even better. They are both men of experience, and Mr. James Kabenge is an excellent manager."

"What are you talking about?" Makula asked excitedly.

"Aren't you aware that the Kabenges are buying this company? It might be theirs within the next year or so," the director responded. "I sent out a memo about this to all the managers last evening. Haven't you checked your mailbox?"

Makula did not answer. He knew that he would not even last a week once the Kabenges had taken over Star Hardware. And he certainly did not want to work for a company that belonged to them.

When he got home, he could not keep the news to himself. He told Pam that the Kabenges were set to acquire Star Hardware Limited.

Pam knew what she needed to do.

CHAPTER FOURTEEN
Toronto, Canada, June 1993

Makula and his family arrived in Toronto late in the spring. They were very tired from the twenty-four-hour journey but were also happy to be in their new country, Canada. Chris Luku and his wife Peggy picked them up at the airport. On the drive back to Luku's house, Makula and Luku talked excitedly as they had a lot to catch up on.

"Who else among our acquaintances lives here?"
Makula asked Luku.

"Pius Bitaro. Do you remember him?" Luku asked.

"Yes, I remember Bitaro very well," Makula replied. "I knew that he came to Canada to do his master's degree in law but I didn't know he had stayed here. What does he do now?"

"He is a stay-at-home dad," Luku informed him.

"What does that mean?" Makula asked.

"Well, he stays at home to take care of his two daughters," Luku said. "It's his wife who is employed."

Curious, Makula asked, "What does she do that would convince the brilliant lawyer that it is okay for him to stay at home?"

"She and her father own a construction company. They build

high-end homes," Luku replied. "You know, that's the kind of life that Bitaro always dreamed of, a beautiful home, a quiet life, luxurious vacations. He's got all that."

"You know Bitaro and I never really got along well. I found him too snobbish and pretentious," Makula said.

"I think he has changed. But what hasn't changed is his short temper," Luku said. "As you know, Nicholas Wabudi, Tom Kabenge's former classmate, also lives here in Toronto."

"Yes, I knew that Wabudi lived here. We have written a few letters to each other. But I didn't know that Bitaro lived here as well," Makula said.

Makula and his family had arranged to stay with the Lukus for two weeks in their two-bedroom apartment while they searched for a place of their own. Luku suggested that they stay until either Makula or Pam found a job before looking for an apartment. Makula thought that this was a good idea, but Pam wanted to find one right away or even look into buying a house since they could afford a down payment. However, Luku cautioned them that things were not as they seemed. "Mak," he said, "I hope you know that in order to get Canadian experience, you need to find any kind of job, even one far below your qualifications."

"Yes, I know that," Makula replied.

"In other words," Luku continued, "don't expect to get your managerial position in marketing right away. That may be possible later on, but for now, we need to find you a job to help you settle here."

"So where should I begin?" Makula asked anxiously.

"We will go to the job search centre," Luku said. "They will help you to write or rewrite your résumé and…"

"What is a résumé?" Makula asked.

"A CV," Luku told him. "It's called a résumé here."

***

Luku's apartment was a hub of activity. Friends were always stopping by, especially on the weekends, to drink, to eat, and to talk. On Makula's and his family's first evening in Toronto, Luku's friend Tunda came to see the newcomers. "Brother, welcome. I hope you like it here," he said to Makula.

"I hope so too," said Makula, who was feeling very disoriented. "How long have you lived here?"

"Twenty years," Tunda said.

"Twenty years? That's a long time. What brought you here?" Makula asked.

"Do you really want to know? Well, my story is a very long one. It might be best if I told it another day because now you need to rest," Tunda said, sipping his beer. To Makula's surprise, Tunda leaned back on the couch and was snoring within the next few minutes. He slept there for an hour and Makula wondered why he had been so tired. Peggy told him that Tunda was very fond of two things: working and drinking. She said that it was either one of the two or a combination of both that had caused his fatigue.

The following day, Nicholas Wabudi came to see the newcomers. He was happy to see Makula again for the first time since university. Wabudi had left Makerere University one year before Makula and had come to Toronto soon after. After exchanging pleasantries with Makula and Pam and "high-fiving" Makula's son Richard, he said, "I'm curious as to why you guys decided to come here instead of staying in the warm climate at home." This shocked Pam. Why would Wabudi ask such a question when he himself had not stayed home?

"Nick, that's not the right way to welcome people," Luku said. "Don't you realize it would be better to make them feel comfortable here? They are going to need lots of support, not discouraging statements, buddy."

Although Makula had talked with Pam about Wabudi, Pam was only now meeting him. Later that evening, she told Makula that she had not been impressed by his comments. Makula said that Wabudi was, on the one hand, a good and helpful man; on the other, he never seemed to think before he spoke.

When they had been in Toronto for a week, Pam started looking for an apartment. Like Makula and Pam, Luku and Peggy had two children, and Luku suggested that they try to find a place nearby so they could help each other out and not spend a lot on child care. Pam reluctantly agreed to look in Luku's downtown neighbourhood, even though she found it rather noisy. She would have preferred to live in a quieter area away from the downtown core. Makula, however, felt differently. "This looks like a good neighbourhood to me," he said, as he and Pam searched the area for a place to live.

"Listen, Mak," Pam said. "I couldn't say this in front of Chris. You know that Peggy is a good friend of mine, but I can't stand living with her, not even for two weeks. Never again. I had enough of her at the university."

Makula knew that Pam had been Tom Kabenge's first choice as a girlfriend and that Kabenge had ended up with Peggy after Pam had married Makula. He wondered whether Pam's comment had anything to do with Peggy's and Pam's involvement with Tom Kabenge back at university, but he shrugged the thought aside. Just thinking of Kabenge depressed him—he had caused Makula a lot of misery.

When they had found a two-bedroom apartment about four kilometres from the Lukus, Pam insisted they move in right away. Luku offered to give them some used furniture—a sofa and a mattress that he had picked up from the curb one garbage collection day—but Pam politely declined. Instead, she asked him where the new furniture stores were located. Luku said that he could take them around to the stores the following weekend, but since they needed it so urgently, they would have to go by themselves. "Just make sure you don't let the salesmen talk you into applying for a store credit card," he warned.

"Why would I buy furniture on credit? I have enough cash to pay for it," Pam replied.

"Good. Go ahead and pay with cash. That is always the best choice," Luku said.

As he sat in their empty tenth-floor apartment pondering what to do next, Makula felt sad. He had never lived in so confining a space. He wished he could go out to dig in a garden or pick fruits in some shrub like he used to do in Kasaka, but there was no such thing in sight. All he could see out of the window was a sea of cars. He remembered his first day in Kampala and wondered now at how overwhelmed he had been. He knew he should be grateful. On the day that they had arrived, Luku had told him, "You are lucky you arrived in good weather, and there was someone to receive you at the airport. I came in the middle of the winter with only a little jacket on my back and, boy, was it cold. On top of that, I didn't know where to go."

Richard and Dawn stayed with Peggy while Pam and Makula went out shopping for furniture. When they arrived at the store, Pam enjoyed looking at the different makes of couches that were on display.

She seemed to be happy with their new life, but Makula was hurting inside. He was so homesick that he fantasized about boarding a plane to return to Uganda. When they had chosen and then paid for a sofa and a loveseat, including the delivery fee, Makula assumed they would be relaxing on them within hours. Both he and Pam were shocked to learn that the furniture would not be delivered until Wednesday, four days away. Neither of them looked forward to sitting on the floor or on their bed, the only furniture in the apartment, for the next few days.

Luku had advised them to buy a computer as they would need one to write cover letters while applying for jobs. A used computer would do. However, Pam wanted a new one. They found one that would suit their needs, and after they had paid for it with cash, Makula asked the salesman whether they could take possession of it now.

"What do you mean?" the salesman asked in a surprised tone.

"When we went to buy furniture we were told that it will be delivered on Wednesday so I was wondering whether the computer would also need to be delivered later," Makula explained.

"It's your computer," the friendly young salesman told him. "I guess you are taking it with you now."

"Do you install?" Makula asked.

"I beg your pardon? I don't know what you mean," the salesman said.

"Can you send somebody to our home to install the comput-er for us?" Makula persisted. A technician had installed all the new computers at Star Hardware in Kampala. "What? It's the first time that anyone has asked me that. You don't need any expertise to install your computer. Just take it home and plug it in. It's that easy. Bye, now," the salesman said, as he turned to the next customer.

***

After four months in Canada, neither Pam nor Makula had been able to find a job. Pam was not worried; she had been told that it could take a long time. And in the meantime, she knew that she could call on her father whenever she needed money and he would send her what she needed. When she called Dr. Sempaka to tell him about her difficulties, he said encouragingly, "Hang in there, my girl. I know you will succeed."

Mrs. Sempaka, however, thought differently. She advised Pam and Makula to return to Kampala since they still had not found work. Pam refused to consider this advice, but Makula, who was now very homesick, longed to return home. Luku had advised Makula to take any type of job so he would at least have an income while he continued his job search, but Pam was against this. "How can my husband work in a factory or in a store? I can't let this happen," she said.

Since he could no longer bear to sit around and do nothing, Makula defied Pam. He asked Luku to direct him to an agency that placed people in temporary positions, and he went there to fill out an application. That very afternoon, Makula got a temporary job as a shipper in a furniture warehouse. The manager told him that he could work as a shipper in the evening, go home to sleep at night, and concentrate on his job search during the day. "You know, searching for a job is a job in itself," said the friendly manager. "I came to this country myself seven years ago, so I know what you are going through." Unfortunately, Makula could not start work that afternoon because he did not own a pair of safety shoes. The manager described what these were and told him where he could purchase a used pair. Pam grudgingly let Makula go to the warehouse the following day to begin work because she realized that he had become unhappy and restless at home.

The following day, Makula's first shift at the warehouse went smoothly. He was given a long list of items and a scanner that he used to check stock in the aisles of the large warehouse. Makula found the work easy and felt that he could do this job until he found an appropriate position. At the end of his shift, his supervisor, who happened to be going to the same area, gave him a ride home.

However, on the second afternoon, Makula was told to unload a fifty-three-foot truck with another employee named Winston. Makula could not understand Winston's instructions and therefore did not follow them correctly. Winston had a problem understanding Makula too because of his accent. Even worse, Winston found that Makula worked too slowly. He grew frustrated with him and yelled, "Hey man, you don't do no work in a warehouse before?"

"No, I haven't," Makula responded anxiously.

"Yeah, I can see that, but you are gonna have to work faster. I don't give a damn whether you don't do no work in a damn warehouse before. What the…?" Winston said, as Makula simply stared at him in disbelief. He was a man with considerable experience in marketing and he was being yelled at like he was a young boy. Losing patience, Winston yelled, "Grab the damn palette man, put on the bloody boxes, and off we go! We don't have all evening to do this, you know what I mean?"

Makula loaded box after box onto the skids as Winston hauled them off the truck with the forklift and placed them in the warehouse. Makula felt very tired and thirsty, and wondered when they would finish emptying the truck. He continued working, slowing down occasionally to rest, until someone yelled, "Break!" Makula sighed with relief and asked Winston how long the break would be.

"The supervisor didn't tell you? It's ten minutes. See ya later," Winston said, as he opened the back door and lit a cigarette.

Makula drank thirstily from the water cooler and then went to lie down on the couch in the lunch room. Two minutes later, he had dozed off.

He woke up to Winston's yelling. "Ten minutes is ten minutes, man! You think the boss gonna pay you his dollars for sleeping right here? Nope. You know what I mean?" Winston shook his head and chuckled. "We gonna empty the damn truck. Ten feet to go."

Makula put two other skids on the truck's floor and started pulling at the boxes. Winston yelled, "You gonna need a dolly for those. That's small size coffee table, you gonna toss them directly on the dolly. That works faster." Makula stared at Winston. He did not know what a dolly was. He was saved from embarrassment, however, when Winston said, "I am gonna grab a dolly. Back in a sec." Winston returned with the dolly. As Makula placed the boxes one by one on the truck's floor, Winston started wheeling them into the warehouse. By nine o'clock they had emptied the truck. Makula, exhausted, knew that there were still two hours left in his shift. He wished he could just go home.

"Grab a broom, we gonna sweep the warehouse," Winston told him. "It's not good to leave it messy for the evening. You know what I mean?" So Makula picked up a broom and began to sweep. "No!" Winston yelled. "You gonna sweep without putting no sweeping compound on the damn floor? You not gonna make us sweep with all that dust?"

The shift finally ended. When they left the warehouse, Winston said, "See ya tomorrow. Drive safe," and rushed to the parking lot, started his car, and sped away.

Makula walked to the street, unsure of where to board the bus for home. However, before long, he saw a bus bearing the same route number as the one he had taken to get to the warehouse. He got on the bus, paid his fare, and collapsed on one of the seats. The bus trip continued for about twenty minutes, stopping a number of times to pick up a few passengers. Makula actually slept for about five minutes. When he realized that the trip was taking longer than it had when he had come to work, he asked the driver, "Is this the right bus to the subway station?"

"No," the driver replied. "Actually yes, except that you should have crossed the road and caught the bus going in the other direction."

"Oh, my goodness," Makula said, angry with himself for not having asked when he had first boarded the bus.

"Sit tight," the driver told him. "I will be turning around at the end of the route and heading back to the subway."

Makula did not arrive home until one o'clock in the morning. Despite the late hour, Pam was waiting up for him. "How was your shift, dear?" she asked.

"It went smoothly. I am very tired, though, as it involves some lifting," Makula said. He did not want her to know exactly how much lifting was involved for fear that she might dissuade him from continuing with the job.

Makula arrived for work the following afternoon worried that he would again be working with Winston. However, he was pleasantly surprised when the supervisor introduced him to a friendly young man, Drew, and told him that they would be working together for that shift.

"Hi, Mak," Drew said, as he shook Makula's hand. "This afternoon we will be delivering some furniture to customers' homes," Drew said as he pointed to a truck parked close to the warehouse. Makula followed Drew, who handed him a list and explained that they would use the list to organize the orders before they set off.

"So you worked with Winston yesterday," Drew said.

"Yes," Makula said.

"Did he give you griefs?" Drew asked.

"I beg your pardon?" Makula replied.

"I don't know how you found him," Drew said, "but he is actually a good man, though he swears a lot."

Makula agreed. "I noticed that."

"Have you done this kind of work before?" Drew asked.

"No," Makula said. "How long have you worked here?"

Drew told him, "A couple of years now, but I'm thinking of quitting. This job sucks."

Makula and Drew brought out the pieces of furniture one by one from the warehouse using a dolly and placed them near the truck. There were mattresses, sofas, coffee tables, book shelves, wine tables, and a dining table. Drew checked the list to ensure that all the items were accounted for and then he and Makula started loading it. After watching Makula for a minute, Drew said, "Hey, watch out. You are lifting the furniture the wrong way. That can cause damage to your back. You need to bend your legs as you lift." Drew showed Makula how to lift the heavy furniture safely. "Remember to think about your safety first," Drew said. When they had finished loading the furniture, Drew looked at the map to find out where they needed to go to deliver the first item and off they went.

Because he was already feeling tired, Makula was grateful to be resting while Drew drove to the various clients' homes. As they delivered the furniture to various houses and apartments, Makula worried that someone who knew him, a former schoolmate, for example, might see him and know that he was doing this manual work for a living.

Makula delivered furniture for the next two weeks and was continually exhausted. He complained that his body ached all over. Pam suggested that he quit the job, but he continued working. One morning, however, after an evening shift in which he had unloaded yet another truck with Winston, Makula found it difficult to get out of bed. He picked up the phone and called the furniture company to inform them that he was quitting.

"That's all right," the manager said. "I could see it coming. Your pay will be deposited into your bank account, and we will mail your T4 slip to you next year. Bye, now, and good luck."

**

Some of Makula's relatives and friends in Kasaka were very disappointed in him because they had neither heard from him nor received any of the financial assistance that they had expected.

"We have relatives overseas, but they are of no use to us," complained Makula's cousin Toofa, who had just lost his job as a casual labourer at the hospital in Kayunga.

"When people go abroad, they forget their old friends. After all we went through together, how can Makula forget me, of all people?" Lukka asked, sipping from a bottle of gin.

"One mistake we usually make is to think that people become rich as soon as they board a plane to go overseas. Makula didn't have a job ready for him in Canada, and he only left recently. Perhaps he is still trying to settle down," Othieno said in Makula's defence.

**

After quitting his job, Makula stayed at home the rest of the week and continued to mail out copies of his résumé to various companies. When Luku called him at the end of the week to ask how his job was going, Makula told him that he had quit. "Hey buddy, don't keep stuff to yourself," Luku advised. "You've got to let us know what's going on so we can see how to help. You can't network when you don't tell people what's going on with your job situation."

Luku asked his friend Tunda whether he could help Makula figure out what his next steps should be. Luku and Tunda went to visit Makula, and Tunda told Makula not to worry as many newcomers go through a series of difficulties before they are able to settle down. "Brother, don't worry," he said. "A breakthrough will come at a time when you least expect it."

"Thanks for encouraging me," Makula said. "I really need it."

"And don't think that you are suffering, because you are not. I suffered a lot, but now I have settled down," Tunda said.

"You promised to tell me your story. How did you come to be here?" Makula asked.

Tunda asked Makula for a beer before he started telling his story. Luku, who had heard Tunda's story many times, excused himself and went to the kitchen to talk with Pam.

Tunda began, "One afternoon, exactly twenty years ago, I left home with no particular destination in mind. I walked for about twenty minutes and ended up at the port in my city. For the previous three years, I had wanted to go to Europe, but I didn't have the money or the necessary papers. When I arrived at the port, I stood near one ship that carried a lot of goods and appeared ready to set off. I didn't know exactly what I was doing, but I stood near the ship for a while. Then one of the workers saw me and came over. He asked, 'What do you think you are doing?'

"I said, 'I would like to leave.'

"He asked me, 'Where do you want to go?'

"I replied, 'I would like to go to Europe.' The man did not answer me; he just walked away. However, he returned after a few minutes and asked me to come with him. We went into a room in a nearby building where he gave me overalls like he was wearing and told me, 'Here, wear this. Then follow me.'

"I didn't really know whether I wanted to go with him or not, but I wore the overalls and followed the man onto the ship. Once there, disguised as one of the workers, I realized that there were many other young people on board in my situation. Anyway, we travelled on the sea for about two weeks. I cried most of the time as I missed my mother and also worried about her a lot as she did not know where I was. We finally saw land at a distance, and the man who had helped me onto the ship asked me, 'You know how to swim?' I told him I did. He said, 'You will swim to that land over there. That is Europe. Get off and run to the left as soon as the ship docks and start swimming.'"

"What?" Makula said.

"Yes. I was shocked. I asked him how he expected me to survive in a place where I did not know anyone. He said that it was none of his business, and he vanished. I got off the ship, ran to the left, and swam. There were many of us, but I don't know how many made it to shore. Three young men and I walked throughout the night but separated as soon as it was daylight for fear of being caught. I ended up in a big city where I did not know anyone and did not understand a word of the language. I suspected that I was in Spain, Italy, or even Portugal, but I was not sure."

Pam came in and asked Makula and Tunda to come to the dining table for lunch. Tunda said that he would summarize his story to shorten it.

"I had removed the overalls and walked aimlessly on the city's streets. I was extremely hungry and thirsty, so I approached the first guy I saw who was working in his small grocery store. I communicated to him using hand gestures. I think he had already seen people in a similar situation to mine. He gave me water, food, some clothes, and a room at the back of his store in which to rest. I slept like a log and couldn't tell where I was or what time it was when he woke me up.

"Anyway, he watched me suspiciously for a week until I had gained his confidence. I helped him in his grocery store for close to six months. Believe me, it took me more than a week to even figure out that I was in Spain. Finally, I got a chance to come to Canada as a refugee. That in itself is another long story," Tunda said as they joined the others for lunch.

After lunch Luku invited Makula to his apartment to meet with a group of his friends, insisting that it would be a perfect opportunity for networking.

"By the way, starting this week, we will be having pizza night at home every Friday," Luku said to both Makula and Pam. "If you guys want, you could come over, or we could alternate and have pizza at your place once in a while."

This is how Luku introduced Makula to the culinary pleasures of Toronto and turned him into an avid lover of fast food.

CHAPTER FIFTEEN
Toronto, Canada, December 1993

Makula, Pam, and their children went to Luku's apartment for the first "pizza night." There were about ten other people there, eating and drinking. There was a lot of noise in the living room as the men talked about everything from jobs to hockey. There was also pizza and soda pop, and Richard ate three slices of what was to become his new favourite food.

A man named Bala seemed interested in talking with Makula when he found out that he was a newcomer looking for a job. Bala was the brother of Tunda, who was conspicuously absent that evening. When Makula told Bala that he was looking for a position in marketing, Bala told him that it was very fortunate that Makula had come to the party that evening. He pulled a business card out of his pocket and handed it to Makula, who saw that he was the president of SimpliCity, a company located in Calgary. Before Makula could ask what kind of business it was, Bala explained that his company provided various services to wealthy individuals who did not have the time or did not wish to do them themselves. These services ranged from home cleaning to grocery shopping, to taking kids to doctors' appointments. Makula remarked that this seemed to be a good line of business—the potential for growth seemed limitless so long as the clientele remained prosperous. And Bala told Makula that he was willing to hire him to sell his company's services if he were willing to relocate in Calgary.

"That would be a very good opportunity for me and my family," Makula said, and he signalled to Pam, who was in the kitchen talking to Peggy, to join them.

"Yes, this would be a perfect opportunity for you as a newcomer, and if all goes well, you could also invest in the business and become a partner," Bala said.

Arriving at Makula's side, Pam overheard the last comment and was immediately interested in the conversation. Makula introduced her to Bala, and the three of them discussed the business in detail. Bala said that there were many potential clients, and all he lacked was a good marketing professional to take the business to a new level. "Right now I have eleven employees who are temping for me," Bala told them. "I would need your assistance in finding more clients, which would not be difficult as the company is already known in the city and beyond."

Makula did not know what "temping" meant but did not ask for fear of appearing to be unfamiliar with business terminology. He felt pressured to accept the job offer immediately, and quietly told Pam that they should first talk to Luku and Wabudi about the opportunity. Pam disagreed. "No, Mak, you know how negative Wabudi is. He will dissuade you. Let's not pass up this opportunity. And he certainly didn't impress me when he asked why we came to Canada." Makula did not know what to say to this.

Bala stood back as Makula and Pam discussed the offer. Makula told Pam that he thought it would be wise to talk with those who knew Bala before making a decision, but Pam insisted that he accept the job right away.

Bala and Makula finally agreed that Makula would move to Calgary the following week, and his family would follow him there after he had found a place for them to live. Makula wanted to stay and talk to Luku about this decision, but, on Pam's insistence, Makula and his family quickly thanked their hosts and took a cab back to their apartment.

Makula called Luku early in the following week and left him a voice message to let him know that he would be travelling "out of town" for a while to look for employment.

It was winter when Makula arrived in Calgary, and the temperature in the city with the wind chill was -30°C. When he stepped outside at the airport, he wondered whether it had been a good decision to move to a new city during the cold season. Although he had experienced the Toronto winter during the previous few weeks, the cold seemed more severe in Calgary. Makula remembered Mr. T.B.'s geography lessons from Musasa High School and immediately understood why lakes froze over. It was so cold that he touched the tip of his nose to see if he could feel it.

Bala picked Makula up at the airport and welcomed him to Calgary. They then drove to the building where Bala's office was located. There was another rented room upstairs in the same building where Makula would live. Bala told him that he owned a house in another area of the city. They went into the office, which was only one room furnished with a table, two chairs, and a computer. Bala showed Makula a newly printed company directory that contained about twenty companies and individuals to whom the company provided services and a few other potential customers. There was also a long list of telephone contacts. Makula's job would involve calling potential customers or visiting houses door-to-door to sell them various services.

Makula spent most of the night awake as he missed his family. He finally called Pam at two o'clock in the morning to tell her about his first impression. Pam answered and said, "Thanks for calling. I couldn't sleep, and I was thinking about you. Is everything okay?"

"The situation is very different from what I expected, honey," he replied.

"Why? What's wrong?" Pam asked.

"Bala has only a tiny and poorly furnished office and a directory. And that is pretty much all there is," Makula said.

"And where are you spending the night?" Pam asked.
"In a hotel?"

"No, he rented a room for me upstairs from his office. That's where I am." Makula said, "The bed is so small and squeaky. This is so stressful."

"Don't lose hope yet," Pam said. "Your first impression might be wrong."

In the morning, as Bala and Makula were walking to Bala's car to tour the city, Makula slipped on the icy walkway and fell flat onto the pavement. "You've got to be careful walking on the ice," Bala cautioned. "Are you okay? Are you injured?"

"No, I am all right," Makula replied.

"Let me see your boots," Bala said. He looked at the bottom of

Makula's right boot and said, "It's those boots that made you fall. They have a smooth sole. You need boots that won't let you slip on ice. Also, be careful about wet, dark areas on the sidewalks; they are usually slippery."

By the time they reached the parking lot at the back of the building, Makula was shivering. Bala took Makula around the city, and showed him the various areas where potential clients lived. They toured the city for most of the morning. Then they went to a store where Makula bought a warm winter coat and some heavy boots. He wore the new coat over the one he had on and changed into his new boots. He felt warmer immediately. They also stopped at a grocery store to buy food for Makula. When they returned "home," Makula put the food into the refrigerator in his room. Bala then told him that he would be away in Chicago for a week and that Makula could start work the following day.

The following morning, Makula took the directory and started "cold calling" potential customers. He left voice messages for most of them, as they did not answer. During the two hours that he spent on the phone, he was able to speak to only four people, three of whom politely declined his services. The fourth person, an old woman, rebuked him for disturbing her sleep to "talk nonsense."

Bala had told him, "You should try various means to reach potential customers. Remember, it's not easy to earn dollars; you've got to work hard to earn a living here." So that afternoon, Makula decided to go out to solicit potential customers. He wore his two winter coats, two pairs of socks, his boots, gloves, a hat, and a scarf. He put about two dozen flyers in his bag, then picked up a map of the city. He tried to remember the two major streets in the neighbourhood that Bala had showed him, took a guess, and went on his way.

At the first two houses he stopped, Makula rang the door bell but there was no answer. He stuck a flyer in each doorway. He stopped at three more houses where the owners politely declined his services. By the time he reached the end of the street, Makula's hands and feet were numb, and he longed for a warm fireplace. At the last house on the street, an elderly man opened the door. Makula felt a little excited because the man showed interest in his flyer. He invited the shivering Makula inside and told him that it was not wise to do door-to-door business on such a cold day. He gave Makula a cup of hot chocolate to drink before Makula embarked on the half hour's walk back to his room.

Makula continued calling potential customers for the remainder of the week but no one wanted to contract for their services. He was further disappointed when, on the morning that he was supposed to return, Bala called him and told him that he would be spending another week in Chicago.

Later that morning, two women who appeared to be mother and daughter visited the office. The older woman asked, "Could we please speak to Bala?"

"Bala is not here," Makula told her. "He's in Chicago and won't be back until next week."

"He's in Chicago? Are you sure about that?" she asked. "I thought I saw him in town this morning. Anyway, please let him know when he returns that we want our money."

"What is your name? What kind of service did you do for us?" Makula asked, trying to look officious as he moved some folders about on the desk.

"My name is Claudette, and this is my daughter, Karine. We cleaned two houses two weeks ago, but he has not paid us. Yet we know that the clients pay in advance for this work," she replied.

Makula was momentarily tempted to ask the two women whether Bala's business was legitimate. However, he had already aligned himself with Bala by saying "us" when he had asked the women what work they had done. "I am sorry to hear that you have not been paid. I'll let him know that you came by. I'm sure he will call you back," Makula said.

"I hope so," the older woman said, and they turned to leave.

It was now clear to Makula that he would not be able to market Bala's business with any success. He thought of calling Pam to let her know that Bala might be less than a good employer but he decided not to. Instead he picked up a newspaper to look for a job that he could do temporarily until Bala returned, as he needed to earn enough money to pay his airfare back to Toronto. He called about a position with a garbage collection company whose office was located only two blocks from where he was staying. He had an interview that very afternoon and got the job.

The following morning, Makula got up very early to get ready for work. It was so cold outside that both his mouthwash and aftershave, stored on the sill of the bathroom window, were frozen. The window itself was completely frosted over. When he stepped outside, he was greeted by the frigid temperature. He thought about calling the garbage collection company and telling them that he couldn't take the job but he decided against it. He walked slowly on the icy sidewalks, being careful not to fall, and by the time he arrived at the company's office, the garbage trucks had already been started to warm them up for the long day.

A driver greeted Makula, led him to their truck, and off they went. He told Makula that he would be training him for the first couple of days. When they reached the first stop, the driver said, "Jump out as soon as the truck stops because time is of the essence in this business. However, don't forget, your safety is first." Makula jumped out of the truck and stood on the sidewalk next to the garbage cans. His hands were already beginning to feel numb. He remembered Luku mentioning something called "frostbite" and he wondered if that was what he was suffering from. The driver showed him how to haul the garbage can onto the truck and pour the garbage in before placing the can back on the sidewalk. He demonstrated this process with two cans and then watched Makula as he emptied the remaining cans. "It's quite an easy job once you learn it," the driver told him. "It's challenging at the beginning, but it's not hard. You'll get used to it," the driver said as he walked back to jump into the truck.

"I don't want to learn this job," Makula thought as he ran to jump inside the already-moving truck. "I only want to earn enough money to pay for my ticket to get home."

By the time they had collected the garbage from the first street, Makula's feet and hands were numb. "It's so cold out there," he told the driver.

"True, it's cold, but it could be colder. Do you know what winter is? This is only the beginning," the driver said.

Makula explained, "This is my first winter…"

"I can see that. Do you think you can do this job?" the driver asked.

"No, I don't think so," Makula replied.

"All right," the driver said. "I'll drop you off at your home. I think you started in the wrong season."

That evening, while Makula lay on the little bed wondering what to do, the phone rang. Bala told him that he still had not been able to complete his business and that he would likely stay an extra day in Chicago.

As soon as the call ended, Makula dialled Pam and asked her to buy him a ticket home to Toronto.

***

When Makula and his family had arrived in Canada, Richard was three and Dawn was nine months old. For Makula, the real challenges of parenthood did not begin until he returned from his failed mission in Calgary. Pam began a course in Early Childhood Education at Central College the following week, and Makula was alone to take care of the two children. Peggy was now working as a supply teacher, and with her unpredictable schedule, she was only able to take care of both her own children and his on the days she was not teaching. He and Pam had therefore registered their two children in a daycare centre. The first three weeks were quite easy. Since Makula was unemployed, he had plenty of time to dress the children, feed them, and then take them to the daycare centre. He would then return home to prepare and mail out his résumés.

Luku, who was displeased with Makula for having gone to work for Bala without consulting him, advised Makula to look for a job in a retail store. "I worked in a retail store for about two years. I didn't earn much but I could pay my bills," he said. "As a newcomer you don't want to waste time working for a struggling business like Bala's. Bala is a good man, but his ideas are all over the place. He needs to zero in on one business that he can run well. Right now, one day he is cleaning peoples' houses; the next day, he is taking kids to soccer games. It is too much to handle effectively."

Makula went to several retail stores to fill in job applications. He got the impression that the stores did not look as attractive when he went there to apply for a job as when he went there to shop. He spent three weeks filling in applications and only one store told him that they would get back to him in a "couple of days."

Pam thought that his method of searching for a job was inefficient. "Isn't it a waste of your time having to board the bus every day to fill out applications?" she asked him. "Why don't you stay at home and simply call the stores where you want to apply for a job and ask if they are hiring?"

Makula did not respond as he did not wish to argue, and as he dressed to once again go out searching, he felt frustrated at not finding the job that he so desperately needed. Then the phone rang, and Fashoniz asked him to come in for an interview whenever he had time that week. Makula told them that he was available for an interview immediately. The manager on the other end of the line asked him to hold as he checked to see whether anyone was available to interview him that morning.

Makula was delighted to hear that someone was.

Makula was hired to work in the warehouse section of Fashoniz. When he told Pam about his new job that afternoon, she was happy but not excited about it. "I hope you are not planning to do that kind of work for long," she said. "I would like you to look for a real job."

"I was not planning on doing the job for long, but I have to do it. Who knows, it might lead to another opportunity," Makula responded. Pam did not comment any further.

The following morning, after he had taken his children to the daycare centre, Makula took a bus, then the subway, and then another bus and arrived at the store's entrance early. When the assistant manager came, he was pleased to see the new employee already there. Makula's orientation began. He was shown a video that urged all employees to be honest and to avoid stealing from the store. He was then taken to the warehouse behind the store where he was introduced to Joe Chen, a young man who Makula thought was probably no older than nineteen. Chen was cheerful and welcoming, and Makula was soon impressed by his physical strength and speed. Chen showed him how to arrange shirts according to size. He also demonstrated how to install anti-theft devices on the clothing, how to put size tags on the hangers, and how to haul the racks onto the store's shopping floor. Although this job would require him to work quickly, Makula was convinced he could do it.

Makula was assigned to a huge pile of shirts while Chen dealt with a pile of jeans. Shortly after, two other young men came into the warehouse. They introduced themselves to Makula and started working right away. For a while, the four men worked in silence. Chen would move to Makula's pile every five to ten minutes to show him how to work "faster and smarter." He told him, "You can accomplish more when you put all the materials you need within your reach. That way you reduce the trips you make to and from the materials bin. You got it?"

"Yes, I get it. Thank you," Makula said, still missing his position as marketing manager in Kampala. He remembered going into the "field" where he would spend long afternoons eating and discussing business with new clients or with those whose contracts were due for signing.

After working for three hours, the four men took a ten-minute break in the lunch room. "So, Makula, I've been trying to figure out your accent. Where are you from?" Chen asked.

"By the way, you can call me Mak. I am from Uganda," Makula replied.

"What was that?" Chen asked.

"Uganda," Makula repeated.

"Uganda? Is that a country?" Chen asked. "I've never heard of it before."

"Uganda is a beautiful country in East Africa. That's where my wife and I come from," Makula told him.

"Great. You are married?" Chen asked.

"Yes, I am married," Makula said. "And you? Are you married?"

"No, all three of us are students. We go to college and work here part-time. It's great working here. I'm sure you will like it," Chen said.

The break ended, and they continued their conversation as they returned to the warehouse. "And how is your commute. Do you drive?" Chen asked Makula.

"No, I don't drive," Makula replied. "I took a bus, then the subway, and then another bus to get here."

"Oh, that's a long commute," Chen said. "It would be better to drive. I live nearer here than you, but I drive."

"I kind of like it on the subway. I read a newspaper on the way but it was not a good idea. I almost missed the station where I was to get off," Makula told him.

"Oh, you like public transport. I have not used it much, and I actually hate it," Chen said. "But I guess you used buses back in Uganda…"

Makula said, "No, I used to drive to work."

"Wow, you drove to work in Africa?" Chen said, surprised.

"Yes, I drove to work," Makula said.

Makula found the young men interesting, and when he eavesdropped on their conversations, he realized that they used a lot of slang that he did not understand.

Child care became harder when Makula got a job in Fashoniz. He occasionally worked afternoons, but on the days that he worked the morning shift, he had to wake up early, take a shower, and then wake up the children. Three-year-old Richard would cry, which would usually wake up Dawn who would start to cry too. "Can you kids shut up?" Makula would yell as he rushed to brush Richard's teeth and get him dressed. He then had to wash Dawn, change her diaper, and get her dressed.

One night he told Pam, "I think it would be better if I skipped giving them breakfast. That would save some time."

"No, we can't take the children to daycare without giving them breakfast," Pam said. "Remember at the daycare they have their snack at nine o'clock. You can't let them go without eating from seven-thirty to nine." By the third week, Makula had mastered the morning routine.

One morning, after the children were already in their snowsuits and winter coats and they were ready to leave, Richard started crying. "What's wrong with you?" Makula asked.

"I want to poo," Richard answered.

"What? Why now? Can't you hold it?" Makula yelled, though he knew the three-year-old needed to go to the washroom immediately. Dawn looked at him, scared by her father's tone. Makula undressed the boy, removing the layers of clothing one after the other. He then rushed him to the washroom and returned to secure his daughter in the stroller. Through the window, Makula could see that it was snowing heavily outside.

When they were finally outside the apartment building, Richard said, "My hands are cold." Makula realized that he had forgotten to put Richard's mittens back on. He cursed, and then they all turned around to go back upstairs to their tenth-floor apartment to get the mittens. Once they were again back outside, he noticed that one more person had joined the three that had been waiting for the bus. As he neared the bus stop, he heard one of the women complaining, "I have been waiting for the bus for the last fifteen minutes. I wonder whether they know that people have to work even when it's snowing." Makula remembered living in Kasaka and having to wait at least an hour for the bus to Kayunga in order to return to school. If he missed it, he would have to wait until the following day to travel.

Rather than waiting for the bus, Makula decided to walk the eight hundred metres to the daycare centre. He asked Richard to hold on to the stroller as he pushed. The three-year-old boy fell twice on the snowy sidewalk as his father rushed; he did not want to be late for work.

However, Makula did arrive late. The manager, Tamara, saw him clocking in at twenty minutes after nine. "Mak, may I ask why you are so late?"

"I have some problems," Makula replied apologetically. "Sometimes I can't make it here on time."

"Everybody has problems, but work is work," Tamara told him. "Don't let it happen again."

Makula continued working for Fashioniz and gained some knowledge about clothing and shoes, especially men's clothing. Whenever they were not busy in the warehouse, he would be asked to "help out" in the fitting rooms. Makula met many customers and got to know some of the regular ones on a first-name basis.

There were a few things that Makula did not like about his job at Fashoniz. First, he found it difficult to stand for long periods of time. Second, he didn't like having to always appear to be doing something even when he had nothing to do—you did not want to be seen idling around when you were being paid for each hour that you spent at the store. Third, he hated being searched by the security guard at the end of each shift. Although he understood that the security guard had to ensure that no employee went out of the store with stolen merchandise, he thought the searches were intrusive.

Makula worked at the store five days a week and occasionally on weekends. He found working on weekends difficult as that was when the store was busiest. One of the employees' tasks was to clean up the store and rearrange the merchandise for the next day. One Saturday evening, as Makula cleaned up the men's winter clothing aisle after a busy day, Tamara came over to talk to him. "Mak, I'm sorry they did this to you," she said.

"What are you talking about?" Makula asked.

"When people go shopping they sometimes act crazy. Look at all that clothing strewn on the floor," Tamara said as she began picking up the winter coats and scarves.

Makula almost said, "This is my job and I am supposed to do it. Why are you sympathizing with me?" but he kept it to himself. Tamara continued picking up merchandise from the floor and placing it back on the hangers as she talked on her walkie-talkie. Makula realized that the managers worked even harder than he and the other employees. "I don't think I would like to be a manager here," he thought to himself.

Six months after Makula started working at Fashoniz, Pam's parents came to visit. Pam's mother did not like their apartment. She decided to extend her stay in Toronto until "her children" had bought a house. Dr. Sempaka said that it would be better for the "children" to wait until they got better jobs before buying a house, but his wife disagreed. Pam's mother gave them enough money for a down payment on a house, and promised to "chip in" whenever necessary.

Pam felt better about herself after they had moved into their new house. Makula was worried about the expenses that came with owning a home, but Pam assured him that her parents would help them whenever there was a need.

A few weeks after the Sempakas had visited, Pam told Makula that it seemed that he had stopped searching for a better job. "Mak, I don't want you to get comfortable in that retail job. You have to continue to look for a real job," she said.

"Darling, I am still looking for a job," Makula assured her, "but you know it is not easy to get one just like that."

"But how can you search for a job when you are working there all the time?" she asked. Makula had no answer.

***

Mr. Craig Lewis was one of the regular customers whom Makula got acquainted with at the clothing store. One afternoon Mr. Lewis came to buy a shirt, and when he went to try it on in the fitting room, he found Makula working there. Makula said that the shirt looked very nice and convinced him to buy a pair of pants, a tie, and socks that "matched and looked very trendy" together. Mr. Lewis left the store with two shirts, a pair of shoes, a pair of pants, and a tie. About a month later Mr. Lewis returned to the store. When he saw Makula, he said, "The store is certainly lucky to have you. You are an excellent salesperson."

After looking around to make sure he wouldn't be overheard, Makula said, "Thank you, Mr. Lewis, but I don't think I would like to continue using my skills here. I would like to move on."

"What would you like to do?" Mr. Lewis asked.

"I would like to find a job in my field, but so far it's been hard," Makula replied.

"And what's your field of work?" Mr. Lewis asked.

Makula told him, "I have a degree in economics and a lot of experience in marketing."

"You didn't need to tell me that; I could see that already. Well, you are talking to the right guy. I have lots of useful contacts," Mr. Lewis said as he pulled his business card out of his wallet and handed it to Makula. "Give me a call," he said as he walked away. Makula glanced at the business card, which read "Craig Lewis – Life Coach," and then put it away in his pocket.

Makula called Mr. Lewis the following morning. Mr. Lewis told him that they could meet to discuss Makula's prospects when Makula was free. Makula told Mr. Lewis that he was off work the following day, and Mr. Lewis suggested that they meet in the afternoon. On the evening after Makula met with Mr. Lewis, Makula and Pam hosted the weekly pizza night. When he told Luku about Mr. Lewis, Luku said, "See what I told you? Talk to people, that's what networking is all about."

Mr. Lewis helped Makula to obtain a position as a salesperson in an outlet of Master Communications, a telephone company. Both Makula and Pam were glad that Makula had found the kind of work that he loved to do, and Makula felt better about himself wearing formal casual clothing to work. He recalled all the manual labour he had done in his years in Kasaka, and realized that he had changed. He loved white-collar work and could never again be happy breaking his back to earn a living.

Soon after Makula landed his new job, Pam completed her course in Early Child Education and began work as an assistant in a daycare centre. She found it hard to cope with looking after the children, working full-time, and doing housework. She often said that she wished her former house girl, Namugga, were there to help her. And even though Pam complained to him that the sink was always full of unwashed dishes, Makula did not do any housework.

On his first day at his new job, Makula arrived at Master Communications at half past eight, where his boss, twenty-seven-year-old Kimberley, was there to greet him. "Hello, Mak. Welcome aboard! This is a busy place, but I know you will like it here. Everyone is friendly, and the job is pretty easy. All you need to do is make as many sales as possible," she said as she led him to his work station. "Have a seat here, and I will be with you in a bit."

When Kimberley returned, she gave Makula a quick orientation tour, asked him whether he had any questions, and then introduced him to another employee, Kyle, with whom he would work for the day. His encounter with his young new boss made Makula feel very old.

Kyle said, "Kim must have told you that the job is pretty simple and that's true. Unlike in our call centres, where you have to call people to sell them services, here the customers or potential customers come to you. In many cases they already know what they want. Your job, therefore, is to advise them on the best products to buy. That's not all, though. You have to try to sell them other products and services and that's where being a good salesperson comes in. Another thing customers want is to be treated with the utmost politeness. That is the major focus of our customer service here. Avoid using rude and impersonal phrases like 'Next' to let customers know you are ready to serve them. As people wait in line, take a moment to acknowledge them even while you are serving another customer. You could say something like 'Ma'am or Sir, I will be with you in a moment,' and when you are done, say 'Can I serve the next person in line?' Or address the customer directly by saying 'I will serve you next.'"

Makula observed Kyle complete a few transactions and then told him that he was "good to go." Kimberley therefore observed him that afternoon while he dealt with four customers. When the fourth customer had left, and there was a short lull, she told Makula that she was impressed with the way he had handled the transactions and commended him for how courteous he had been with the customers. "Good job, Mak. Way to go," Kimberley said, giving Makula a "high five." Makula was grateful for his manager's comments and felt a great sense of camaraderie with everyone at Master Communications.

The following day, Pam informed Makula that she had heard that the Kabenges had sold Star Hardware, the company where Makula had begun his career, and had renovated the building to house Fiducia, a bank in which James Kabenge and his son Tom were the major shareholders.

After a few weeks at his job, Makula noticed that the atmosphere at home was less tense and he felt more comfortable dealing with his long list of bills.

During his second year of working for Master Communications, Makula applied and was admitted to a Masters in Business Administration course at the University of Toronto. Two evenings a week, he would attend a four-hour class right after work. The course was so intense that Makula found it necessary to get up at 3:30 a.m. and go to the basement of his house either to do his assignments or review his notes. The basement was a bit cool, which kept him alert, and he found it to be an ideal place to study. These early morning study sessions reminded him of the mornings at Kayunga Primary School when he and his classmates would dip their feet in plastic basins half full of cold water to keep themselves awake. They had called these study periods "winter sessions." However, now that he knew what a real winter was like, Makula laughed at whomever had coined the phrase.

Because of his classes and early-morning study sessions, Makula was so sleep-deprived that he frequently dozed on the subway, missing his stop either to or from work.

On the occasional weekend, Makula would meet with his buddies Luku and Wabudi for a "boys' night out." Their favourite meeting places were fast-food restaurants where they would eat burgers and French fries before heading to the movies. Makula enjoyed such nights because they gave him a break from the monotony of his life.

***

From the age of ten, Makula's sister, Manjeri, had felt that her name sounded old-fashioned. This was confirmed for her when she learned that she had been named after her maternal grandmother. In her final year of primary school, Manjeri therefore changed her name to "Angela." When the students filled out the application forms for secondary schools, Manjeri used her new name without telling her parents. When she had completed her Primary Leaving Examinations, Makula wrote her a letter to ask her to spend the holiday with her parents in Kasaka, but Angela refused. She wrote back saying that the conditions in Kasaka were too harsh for her. Makula understood. He did not push any further.

Angela stayed in Kampala with Linda in the apartment the Sempakas had rented for her close to the university where she studied. When the results of the examinations were released, Angela found out that she had done very well. She wrote to Makula to tell him so, and three weeks later, Angela was admitted to Buweela High School, the school of her dreams. Buweela High School, like Musasa High School where Makula had completed his secondary education, was prestigious. It was a girls'-only boarding school whose students were the daughters of mainly rich parents. Unlike Makula, who had studied on a very tight budget at Musasa, Angela had a "rich brother abroad" who could pay for her education without any difficulty.

Angela prepared a long list of items that she would need to go to Bu-weela. Linda called Makula, and read the list to him over the phone. Makula thought the number of items was excessive. When he showed the list to Pam, however, she supported Angela. "The girl is right. She needs to have everything in order to concentrate on her studies. Can you imagine what a pain it would be if you had to go to school without having everything you needed?"

"That was the case for me…" Makula reminded her.

"That was then, Mak," Pam said. "Besides, you didn't have a rich brother overseas."

"I guess you are right," Makula replied. "I actually think that all she needs is three hundred bucks. I will wire the money to Linda."

***

One visitation Sunday, when Angela was close to completing the last term of her Senior 1 year, an unexpected visitor arrived at the school—her mother, Kabejja. Angela had been expecting a visit from Linda. And when she saw her mother arriving, she went and hid. Angela was ashamed of how old and shabbily dressed her mother was; she did not want her friends to see how different she and her mother were.

Kabejja carried a handwoven bag on her head that was full of cooked food, including cassava, sweet potatoes, and yams. Many of the girls stared at her as she entered through the gate and wondered what she was doing there. Kabejja asked several of the students whether she could see her daughter but no one seemed interested in helping her. She finally found the teacher on duty, who asked for her daughter's name and class.

Kabejja gave her daughter's first name, Manjeri, and her maiden name, which, in Baganda culture, was her daughter's last name. "My daughter is Manjeri Nabasirye. She is in Senior 1," she replied.

The teacher checked the Senior 1 roll call lists. "I don't have anybody with that name. Are you sure she is in this school?" the teacher asked.

"Yes, I am sure," answered Kabejja who, frustrated, was now beginning to lose her temper.

The teacher said, "Many of the students use their fathers' last names. What is her father's last name?"

"Musoke," Kabejja replied.

The teacher checked the list again and found an Angela Musoke. The teacher found Angela and, against Angela's will, insisted that she meet with her visitor. As soon as Angela appeared, Kabejja yelled out, "Yes! That is my daughter!"

When Angela came up to her, Kabejja said, "Since when did you become Angela? Your name is Manjeri. Why should I have to go through all this trouble to find you?" And at the end of the visit, she was saddened to realize that her daughter had not been pleased to see her. She blamed Makula, who had spoiled his sister from the time she was born. Kabejja wished for a long face-to-face conversation with her son to give him a piece of her mind.

CHAPTER SIXTEEN
Toronto, Canada, September 1999

"Mak, you seem to be getting comfortable in that sales job. I don't think, though, that it's the kind of job you should do your whole life," Pam told Makula one Sunday morning. "You should either strive to move up to a better position in Master Communications or look for another job."

"I would like to move up, but my promotion is not within my control," Makula replied defensively.

"You can work harder. You can try every means to get noticed," Pam said. "But now that you have your MBA, why don't you simply try to find work elsewhere?"

Such discussions about Makula's failure to be promoted or to find other work often caused serious arguments between Makula and Pam. Whenever Pam accused him of not trying hard enough to "reach his full potential," Makula would tell her that she had not done so either. She worked in a daycare centre, yet she had considerable experience in banking.

Pam's certainty that Makula should try harder to look for another job led her to contact their friend, life coach Craig Lewis, who had arranged for Makula's employment at Master Communications. Makula was surprised when Mr. Lewis agreed with Pam. "It's true that you have a position that you love at Master Communications. How long have you worked for them?" Mr. Lewis asked.

"About five years," Makula replied.

"Do you want to work for them in the same position and earn the same salary for the rest of your life?" Mr. Lewis asked.

"No, I wouldn't want to work for them my whole life," Makula said.

"Well, then, you have the power to change that. There is a good company that I know that is searching for a vice president," Mr. Lewis said, pointing to a brief description of the position on his laptop computer.

"Vice president?" Makula said. "Wouldn't that be too high a position for a man of my calibre to even consider applying?"

"And what calibre are you? You have lots of experience in sales and marketing, and you have an MBA. That's all you need. Remember, when you think like you do now, you are standing in the way of your own success. You've got to tell yourself 'I can do it,' then get up and go for it," Mr. Lewis said encouragingly.

At Pam's insistence, Makula sent a résumé to Prime Realty Inc. in application for the position. When the company acknowledged receipt of his application, Mr. Lewis worked with Makula for two hours every day for a whole week to prepare him for a probable job interview. He also offered to serve as a professional reference for Makula.

At that week's pizza night, Makula told his friends Luku and Wabudi that he had applied for the position of vice president at Prime Realty Inc. While Luku proposed a toast to celebrate Makula's ambition, Wabudi just laughed it off. "Makula, that's a good thing you did, but do you actually think you can get such a job?" he asked.

Makula responded, "I didn't think so either, but the coach said that I could…"

"Yeah, I knew it—it's your 'coach' once again. Why do you waste your time with him? Are you paying him for that advice?" Wabudi asked derisively.

"Yes," Makula replied.

"Why do you waste your money, Mak? It's rich people and celebrities that need life coaches. Next you will be telling us that you want to hire a publicist because celebrities hire publicists. Tell me what you don't know that you need a coach to tell you. You worked hard on your own to get yourself out of that small village back home, and you are smart enough to know that you don't need a coach to tell you what to do," Wabudi said persuasively. "Come on, be realistic."

But a month after he had applied for the position, Makula was surprised to receive a phone call from Prime Realty Inc. A woman who introduced herself as Lori asked him whether he was still interested in the position. When he said that he was, she asked him if he had a few minutes to complete a preliminary interview over the phone. When he answered in the affirmative, she began asking him questions.

Makula was asked about his experience, and whether he had researched Prime Realty Inc. When he told her that he knew about the company, he was asked a few questions about it. Lori told him that he had answered the questions to her satisfaction and then asked whether they could contact his current employer. Makula wanted to say "no," but he remembered Mr. Lewis's advice: if this question came up, say "yes," and let the interviewer decide what to do next. He therefore said that they could contact his current employer and gave Lori, Kimberley's telephone number at Master Communications. Lori said that she would be in touch with Makula in a couple of weeks.

A week later, Lori called and left him a voicemail message. She hoped to meet with him in two days' time for an interview.

On the morning of the interview, Makula woke up very early, carefully groomed himself, and dressed in a grey suit that Pam had laid out on the bed. As he opened the door to leave, Pam kissed him and reminded him to switch his phone to "silent" mode before going into the interview. Makula decided to do it now because he knew that he might forget later. He knew Pam could be controlling but had to acknowledge that this trait was sometimes helpful to him as he tended to forget things.

Makula arrived in downtown Toronto at a half past eight, even though his interview was not scheduled until ten, and parked his car in a private parking lot. He paid to park for the whole day, not knowing how long the interview process might take. He went into a café that was directly across the street from the offices of Prime Realty Inc. He ordered a coffee and a muffin, and then sat looking out the window at the goings-on at Prime Realty. He ate the muffin, but he hardly touched his coffee—he didn't want to have to interrupt his interview to go to the washroom. He watched everyone who entered the building, gauging how nice they seemed in case they were on his interview panel. One middle-aged woman in particular caught his attention. He thought she looked mean. He would be in trouble if she were on it. He also saw two men go into the office together and was convinced that one of them was Andrew Philips, the president. He found out later that he was right.

At a quarter to ten Makula entered the office and walked up to the receptionist. The mean-looking lady he had seen earlier was on the phone behind the reception desk. As soon as she placed the receiver down, she looked up at him and asked, "Can I help you?"

"Hello," he said. My name is Makula. I am here…"

"For the interview," she said, smiling as she interrupted him. "She is not mean, after all," Makula thought.

"I'm Lori. We spoke on the telephone. Welcome, Makula," she said, still smiling.

Makula stretched out his hand to give her a firm handshake, and replied, "Nice to meet you, Lori. How are you?" He felt proud of his gesture, and thought that if Mr. Lewis were watching, he would be pleased to see that his time in preparing Makula for the interview had paid off. Without his coaching, Makula would never have offered to shake Lori's hand.

"I am very well, thank you," Lori said. "Please have a seat in the boardroom. It's the first room down the hallway to your right." She pointed to the right of the reception area. "I will be with you in a bit."

Makula went into the boardroom and stood there briefly, wondering where he should sit. He chose a chair in the middle of the large table, placed a copy of his résumé on the table, then sat down. Lori soon walked into the room carrying a file that appeared to contain some literature and a pen. Makula was reminded of the national examinations he had written years before in Uganda.

She sat down across from him and gave him the material. "Please read through this; it contains key information about the company. I know you already have a good grasp of it but it does no harm to have it in front of you in print. Would you like some coffee or tea?" she asked.

"No, thank you. That's very kind of you to ask," Makula replied.

"The washroom is right down the hallway," she said and then checked her watch. "The team will be here to meet you in about ten minutes. Good luck."

"Thank you," Makula said.

When Lori left the room, Makula started perusing the material she had left for him. Ten minutes later, two very well dressed women, much younger than he, came into the room. Each had brought a cup of coffee and a file folder.

"Hello, I'm Jen, accounting analyst" one woman said as she shook Makula's hand.

"I am glad to meet you, Jen," he said. "I am Makula."

"Hello, Makula. I'm Rhoda, team leader of sales for Prime Realty," the other woman said as she too shook Makula's hand.

"I am glad to meet you, Rhoda," Makula replied.

"Thanks for coming this morning. Our colleague Ted will be with us shortly. Isn't the weather amazing?" Jen said.

"Oh, yes, it is amazing," Makula said, trying to hide his nervousness. He thought about how weird it would be in Kasaka to refer to a cloudy day as "amazing."

"It's so mild for this time of the year. I went for a jog this morning, and I really enjoyed it," Rhoda said.

At that moment, Ted walked into the room. He was the younger of the two men Makula had seen walking into the building together earlier that morning. He too had a cup of coffee. "So, you must be Makula. Hi, I'm Ted, the manager of human resources," he said as he offered his hand to Makula.

Makula stood up to shake it, and said, "Hello, I am glad to meet you, Ted. I am Makula."

"Oh, haven't these mean ladies offered you tea or coffee, Makula?" Ted said jokingly.

"Sorry about that. Jen started chatting about the weather as soon as we sat down. We forgot to ask," Rhoda told Ted.

"Lori offered me coffee, but I am fine," Makula said.

"All right, then," Ted said as he sat in the chair at the head of the table. It was obvious that he would be leading the interview.

"So, what makes Makula, Makula?" he asked.

"Sorry, I didn't understand that question," Makula said.

Ted rephrased it. "What makes you stand out from the crowd? What makes you special? For example, if we had three other candidates here to choose from, how would you differ from them?"

"I am driven, passionate, and enthusiastic. Those are the three words that best describe me. I also have outstanding organizational skills, skills that are crucial to a strong company like Prime Realty. I…" Makula paused.

"You are applying for the position of vice president. What kind of experience do you have?" Rhoda asked as Ted began taking notes.

"I started my career in marketing twelve years ago in Uganda," Makula said as he briefly made eye contact with each of the three interviewers. "I worked as the marketing manager for a medium -sized company that manufactured and sold hardware, which included, among other things metal beds, mattresses, and hand hoes. I managed a department of twenty employees at the head office and about fifty more in the regional offices."

"Good," Ted said.

"What was your major role?" Jen asked.

Makula replied, "My major role was product innovation and working with my assistant to ensure the smooth operation of the distribution channels for all the merchandise that my company manufactured. In addition…"

"Sounds like you had many lines of business," Rhoda interrupted. "Did you oversee the distribution of all merchandise or was that the responsibility of your sales department?"

"Yes, as the marketing manager, although I was not directly in charge of sales, my responsibilities covered all merchandise," Makula said, hoping that he was sounding sufficiently professional.

"What was the major highlight of your first two years in that position?" Ted asked.

Makula answered, "The major highlight was that, under my administration, the company's sales went up by 35 percent in the first two years. And…"

"Wow, great," Ted said.

"Similarly, the company, which had been known only for the

manufacture of hand hoes, became a household name in all rural areas within my first year," Makula said.

"How was that?" Rhoda asked.

"As I said, the company had been known mainly as a manufacturer of hand hoes. But when I started there, I introduced and promoted the sale of beds and mattresses. For the rural population, these were essential items that had never before been marketed on a large scale," Makula said.

"Can you talk to us about your Canadian experience?" Ted asked.

"In Canada, I have worked in various positions. I worked in a retail store that sold clothing, but I have worked the longest time in my current job. I do sales for Master Communications and I earned my MBA while working there," Makula replied.

Makula answered many other questions until Ted said, "I guess we are done, unless either of you ladies has more questions."

"No, I'm good," Rhoda said.

"I'm good too," Jen said. "I hope you didn't find the process too uncomfortable, Makula."

"Oh, not at all. Thank you for the interview," Makula said.

They thanked him for coming in for the interview and then Jen said, "I will see you out." The man who Makula had seen earlier with Ted was at the reception desk. Jen introduced them, saying, "Hi, Andrew. Meet Makula. We just had a good interview. Makula, meet Andrew. He's the president."

"Nice to see you, Makula," Andrew said. "I hope we will see you again."

After the interview Makula went back home and told Pam that everything seemed to have gone well.

Makula was pleasantly surprised when, two weeks later, Lori called him back for a second interview. When he arrived for the interview, Makula sat nervously in the boardroom, wondering if he would be interviewed by the same people. He did not have to wait long to find out. Ted and Andrew walked into the room, and unlike in his first interview, they did not begin with small talk. Under pressure to make a good impression, Makula regained his composure.

"Makula, this will be a continuation of the first interview. In other words, we are not going to begin a new interview but build on to what was covered in the first one," Andrew said, smiling.

"This is a likeable guy," Makula thought.

"You know that good marketing personnel should be passionate not only about their product but also their clientele. What are you passionate about?" Ted asked.

"I am a person who, unfortunately, was born in the midst of extreme poverty. Having endured it, both at home and in school, and after finally becoming successful, I am very passionate about seeing that many others are helped out of poverty," Makula replied.

"And you can do all this through your professional work?" Ted asked.

"Yes. I was born in a small village, and when I completed my degree in economics, I started commercial farming on a larger scale than had been done before in the area. In addition, I started a market where the produce from the farm was sold locally. Through my position at Star Hardware, I also provided assistance to the rural farmers to enable them to acquire items such as beds and mattresses," Makula said.

Ted was skeptical. "It sounds like charity to me."

"No, it was not charity work per se. I arranged small loans through a bank that these farmers paid back over time," Makula explained.

Ted asked, "How would you help your clients or potential clients at Prime Realty?"

"As vice president, I would institute programs that would make the clients happy that they chose Prime Realty rather than a competitor," Makula answered.

"Please give a specific example," Andrew said, jotting down notes.

"I would create an after-sales program that would enable us to stay in touch with our clients for at least one year after they had purchased their homes through Prime Realty. This would help us to create a relationship that would go beyond merely keeping a record of our clients' names. We could do this through something as simple as a social event, like a barbecue," Makula told him.

"I noticed on your résumé that you are now working in telecommunications. Do you have any experience in real estate?" Andrew asked.

"I don't have experience in selling real estate. However, I am a fast learner, and given the fact that I am an immigrant and there is a relatively large and young immigrant population here in the Greater Toronto Area, I think I would be a good candidate to market real estate to them," Makula said.

"Do you own your home?" Ted asked.

"Yes," Makula answered.

"How long have you lived here in Toronto?" Andrew asked.

"Six years," Makula said.

"And you have family here?" Ted asked.

"Yes. My wife and two children live here with me. A third child is on the way," Makula said.

"Why do you want to leave your current place of employment?" Andrew asked.

"My current employment is good, and the people are great, but now that I have new experience and qualifications, I feel it's time to explore new opportunities," Makula said.

"What is your major weakness?" Ted asked.

"That is a tough question," Makula said as he gazed up at the ceiling. "It is always hard to critique oneself. Let me see." He thought for a few seconds. "I think, when I am absorbed with my professional work, I quite often neglect my family. But this is a weakness I am aware of, and I am striving to lessen its impact."

"As you know, Prime Realty is looking for a new vision for its future. As vice president, one of your major roles would be to innovate. If you were hired, what would you do to make Prime Realty more successful?" Andrew asked.

"I know that in the past Prime Realty operated a franchise system and that it stopped doing so because it was not cost-effective. I would revive the franchise system," Makula said. Both Andrew and Ted listened closely.

"In order to do that, I would shoot seasonal TV ads for a year. I have noticed that real estate companies rarely advertise on TV, yet as a leader in this business, Prime Realty could invest in such ads to target wealthy potential clients," Makula said.

Andrew noted this point, and Makula saw Ted nod his head a little in approval.

"These ads would draw more clients to the company. Franchisees could take care of these new clients and lift the burden off the company's shoulders," Makula said. "Finally, in the short term, I would provide complimentary home staging to our sellers…"

"How would you do that without reducing the profit margin?" Ted asked.

Makula explained. "I would invest in easy-to-move high-end furniture and hire a couple of excellent interior designers. This would entail an initial large investment but it would pay off in the long run. Houses would sell in less time and homeowners who wanted to sell would choose us instead of our competitors."

"Wouldn't it be better to leave such business details to the franchisees?" Andrew asked.

"You are right," Makula answered. "But as I said, I would do this only in the short term. After the franchises are operational, the franchisees would be responsible for home staging as part of their standard operation. Still, I believe that it would make Prime Realty stand out from the competition."

Makula answered many other questions and was finally asked if he had some of his own. He remembered Mr. Craig Lewis's advice, "Don't bring up the subject of salary unless you are specifically asked about it." He therefore did not ask but was a little anxious about it. Ted, however, eased his anxiety by asking, "By the way, what would you expect in terms of remuneration?" Makula stated an amount that Mr. Lewis had helped him to establish after consulting with others in similar executive positions. He was happy when Ted informed him that the position at Prime Realty would pay more than he had expected.

"It's been a pleasure talking to you, Makula. You are one of six candidates that we have interviewed for this position. We will get in touch with you within ten business days to let you know our decision. Thanks again for coming in," Ted said, shaking his hand. Andrew also shook Makula's hand and chatted with him as they left the boardroom.

Two weeks later, Makula was seated in the boardroom with Lori, going over the job description for the position. Makula was glad that he had not seen the detailed job description before he had applied; if he had, he would probably have been too intimidated to do so. Lori then led him to the president's office, where Andrew Philips congratulated him on his being appointed as vice president of Prime Realty Inc. and informed him that he could start work in two weeks' time. Rhoda and Ted also came in to congratulate Makula. Rhoda admitted that it felt strange to have interviewed Makula, who was now her new boss and to whom she would report directly.

Pam seemed happier than Makula was with the news that he had now been hired in a senior position with Prime Realty. She told Makula she had always felt that he was suited for work in a top executive position.

"Why did you feel that way?" Makula asked.

"I just felt it. I don't know why, but I always felt it," she replied.

Makula's buddies came to his house the following day for their weekly pizza night, and when Pam told them that Makula had been hired as vice president of Prime Realty Inc., Wabudi was very impressed. He said, "Maybe those life coaches work after all. Can you give me your coach's contact info?"

***

There was a lot of joy in Pam and Makula's home that month as their third child was born. They named him Daniel.

The first thing that Pam wanted to buy after Makula had landed his executive position was a car "befitting a vice president." Makula therefore bought an SUV, a brand new BMW. Pam also wanted a bigger and better home "befitting a vice president," and her next project was renovating and selling their current home. With the help of Prime Realty's agents, the house sold in just one week. He and Pam then bought a bigger, newer, and far more impressive house in Toronto. Pam bought new furniture, new draperies, and new appliances for the kitchen and turned her new house into what Peggy called a "model home." And to show whoever came into the house that she was in charge, she placed a decorative pot on the coffee table inscribed with the statement, "If Mama ain't happy, ain't nobody happy."

Makula was shocked to learn that, although Prime Realty had arranged for the financing on his BMW, his boss, Andrew, did not own a car. Andrew told him that since his children had grown, he no longer needed one and he now took the subway to work. Makula therefore felt somewhat embarrassed by his extravagant purchase and wondered whether this was the time to start saying no to his wife. While Makula increased his efforts to boost his company's performance, Pam increased the frequency of her shopping sprees.

Working for Prime Realty was vastly different from his experience at Star Hardware in Kampala. Although both his position and salary were higher, Makula noticed that there were far fewer perks. As marketing manager at Star Hardware, Makula had had a secretary and a reserved parking spot. Every day at 10 a.m. the "tea girl" had brought him tea and a doughnut. She had also brought him his lunch. The "office mes-senger" had taken Makula's car to be washed once a week and had his shoes polished down the street whenever Makula asked him to. None of these conveniences were offered at Prime Realty. As vice president, Makula packed his own lunch, usually a sandwich. He did not have a secretary, although the administrative assistant, Lori, helped to schedule his appointments. Nor did he have a reserved parking spot; he parked his BMW in the paid parking lot next to the building just like every-body else. In fact, when he had first started working there, Makula had hesitated when Andrew had asked him if he wanted to go "grab some pizza" at the pizzeria down the street from their office. After he was more comfortable there and had become good friends with Andrew, he realized that it was okay for the vice president to "go grab some pizza."

Makula introduced some innovations to the company. The people who bought their houses through Prime Realty Inc. were now contacted ev-ery six months for two years to see whether they were happy with their homes. In addition, he and his team organized an annual barbecue in the summer, known as "Prime Realty's Ops." Clients and potential clients who attended the event would meet to talk about home renovations, furnishings, and even employment opportunities. The annual barbecue became a successful networking event that greatly boosted Prime Realty's sales and earned large bonuses for Makula and for Rhoda's sales team. Makula worked so hard that he became one of the most recognizable faces of Prime Realty.

At home, Pam hired a couple, a Mr. and Mrs. Johnson, to do the house-work. They cleaned the house, took out the garbage, arranged the shelves, did the laundry, and bought the groceries. Pam's only responsibilities were to take the children to school and to cook meals for her family. The Johnsons did the rest.

One morning, Pam told Makula that it was a shame that they had not taken a vacation since their honeymoon. She suggested that now they could afford one, perhaps it was time they did. Makula told her that they could take a vacation the following year as he was still very busy, but Pam disagreed. Thus, only six months after he first started working at Prime Realty, Makula and his family spent two weeks in Cancun, Mexico. The family had a good time on the beach and enjoyed the food, drinks, and music. While they were still in Cancun, Pam planned their next holiday. "This is awesome," she said. "I think next year we will take the children to Disneyland or go on a Caribbean cruise."

> "That would be great, but I feel kind of guilty," Makula said. "Instead of spending thousands of dollars on our vacations, I could be helping out my cousins with their kids, who have many needs and no means."

> "Whatever," Pam said. "You've got to live your life. There will always be somebody somewhere who needs your assistance. Besides, you are already helping them."

From then on, Pam arranged an annual vacation for the family. And Makula began sending money to Kasaka at least once a month to support several "worthy causes" that included weddings, medication, education, and other expenses.

Makula's business trips involved travel within Canada and to the United States. Whenever she was free, Pam accompanied him. Her most memorable trip was to San Diego where Makula met with a group of franchisees. Pam enjoyed it, and spent thousands of dollars on clothing for the entire family.

CHAPTER SEVENTEEN
Toronto, Canada, May 2001

"Honey, could you please give the children their breakfast?" Pam asked, grabbing her car keys from the bedside table.

"No, Pam, I won't," Makula replied. "Don't tell me that an eleven-year-old can't pour cereal in a bowl, add milk, grab a spoon, and sit down to eat." Makula then covered his head with the duvet. "It's my first vacation day in months; I want to sleep in."

"Please help them. You know if you don't prepare the breakfast for them, they will go to school hungry," Pam said. "Actually, take the kids to school. You can come back to sleep afterward."

"They can walk to school," Makula said. "I don't think the weather is bad out there."

"Please, Mak! Please! Get up! Otherwise they will be late for school," Pam pleaded before leaving the room.

Makula duly got up and went downstairs and saw that the children had prepared their own breakfast but had not finished eating. He told them to finish up in five minutes or they would have to walk to school.

"You are so rude, Dad," Dawn said. "I can't finish my breakfast in just five minutes."

In class that morning, Richard's Grade 6 teacher, Miss Roberts, called him up to her desk. "Richard, you are not doing your homework consistently and your agenda is not signed. I guess I will need to have a word with your parents." She then wrote a note in Richard's agenda asking to meet with Makula and Pam.

Makula went to meet with Richard's teacher the following morning before he went to work. Miss Roberts said to him, "I have noticed on several occasions that Richard's agenda is not signed. Do you actually check his homework?"

"Yes, we do. His mum checks his work regularly," Makula said. "But I guess that now that he is in Grade 6, he is old enough to do his work unsupervised." He almost added that when he had been in primary school, he hadn't needed a reminder to do his homework. If he didn't do his homework, he would be caned.

"That may be true, but you know these kids. They need constant reminders. I will continue to do my part at this end but you must do yours at home. He will surely improve. He is not a bad kid," Miss Roberts said.

One week later, Pam, who never trusted Makula to accurately relay what anyone had said, went to meet with Richard's teacher. Miss Roberts told her that Richard often yawned in class early in the day, which indicated either that he was not getting enough sleep or that he hadn't had breakfast. Pam, grateful for the report, said, "Thanks for letting me know. I guess it may be due to the fact that he does not eat his breakfast. I try to prepare everything before I leave, but he is a picky eater. The only thing that he likes to eat is pizza, but I can't let him have pizza for breakfast."

"Oh, I know," Miss Roberts said. "I have the same problem with my son. What I do is prepare all kinds of food so that he will have a variety to choose from."

"I try to do that, but since I am rarely at home when the kids have breakfast, I never know what they eat," Pam told her. "My husband doesn't seem to care that much."

That evening Pam asked Makula about the children's breakfast habits. He told her that he did not know what Richard and Dawn ate as he had to focus on little Daniel.

"I knew it," Pam said accusingly. "And I know your usual excuse: 'It's hard for a man who by the age of five climbed trees to get fruit to eat to understand why an eleven-year-old would skip breakfast when both the fridge and the table are packed with food.'"

Defending himself, Makula told her, "This morning, Rick said that he wanted yogourt, so I told him to grab some from the fridge. He said that he didn't want chocolate, he wanted either strawberry or vanilla. Can you imagine that? Refusing to eat just because you want a different flavour?"

"Yes," Pam conceded, "our kids are lucky; they have the privilege of choice. But why didn't you just go to the convenience store to buy him the strawberry or vanilla yogourt?"

"Honey," Makula said, "you know how expensive the convenience store is. Actually I think that if we stopped buying from that store, Idriss would have to shut it down. We could save so much money if you wrote your grocery lists beforehand and bought everything from the bigger stores rather than my having to shop for items at the convenience store."

As the children grew, Makula noticed that they often behaved in the same way he had when he was young, even though his circumstances had been very different. He was surprised to note that, like himself at the age of eleven, Richard did not like to bathe. He would open the shower and let the water flow for about three minutes, then run to his bedroom with a towel wrapped around his waist.

"Rick, that was quick. Did you really shower?" Pam would ask.

"Yes, Mum. I did," he would answer.

Whenever Makula checked, he found that the boy had only wet his hair; the rest of his body would be completely dry. Makula would laugh and send him back to wash himself properly.

One evening Makula went in to Richard's bedroom to see if he had showered. He found that he had not and reported it to Pam. "Once again, only his hair was wet," Makula said.

"Of course you know what to check to make sure," Pam replied. "Didn't your mother say that you had never liked to bathe?"

"That's true," Makula admitted, "but my circumstances were different. I didn't have hot water running in a cozy bathroom."

Pam laughed and said, "Well, now you know. The apple doesn't fall far from the tree."

The following day, during lunch, Makula complained to Andrew about the difficulty of raising children in culture so different from the one in which he had been brought up. "The kids don't listen; whatever you tell them to do, they ask what for. They don't seem to learn anything. They don't want to work. All they want to do is play video games, watch TV, and eat," he said.

"But don't you think your father also found it hard to raise you?" Andrew asked.

"I don't think so," Makula said, not mentioning that his father had been away working for most of his childhood. "In any case, I feared my father so much that I did whatever he asked me to do right away. There was no room for debate."

"Did he spank you?" Andrew asked.

"Never. I guess I was so obedient that he didn't need to spank me," Makula replied. "Let me give you an example of what I am talking about. Yesterday, I asked my son to go make his bed, but he refused to do it. When I asked him why he would not make his bed, he simply told me that he did not want to. Can you imagine that?"

"Times change, of course," Andrew said. "When I was young, I couldn't tell my dad that I didn't want to do what he told me to do. I just had to do it. That's not the case with kids these days."

"After my son refused to make his bed, I asked my daughter to go make hers. She answered, 'I don't wanna,' and continued watching television," Makula said.

Andrew recommended a parenting seminar to Makula. When he mentioned it to Pam, she thought it was a good idea. Makula did not think that parenting could be taught, but Pam, tired of the arguments between Makula and the kids, insisted that they attend.

At the parenting seminar, the female instructor gave the participants five minutes to write down two things they could change in the way they dealt with their children. Makula stared blankly at the ceiling, trying to come up with two things, while the five minutes quickly elapsed. Each of the other parents began sharing at least two things they could change, but Makula was still finding the exercise very difficult. Although he knew that there were some behaviours he would have wanted his own father to change, he was firm in his belief that a parent's judgment should never be questioned.

As his turn to speak drew closer, Pam saw that he had written nothing and whispered to him, "'You have to be less harsh,' and 'You should learn to negotiate.'" Makula shared these with the group but was unable to convincingly explain what he meant.

"Okay, let's put it another way," the instructor said. "Makula, if there was one thing that you would have wanted your father to change in his behaviour toward you, what would it have been?"

"I would have wanted him to change how he made me feel," Makula answered.

"Can you elaborate on that?" the instructor asked. "How did he make you feel?"

"The way he talked to me made me fear him," Makula said.

"And what impact did that have on you?" she asked.

"I think I feared him so much that I couldn't ask him questions about many important things," Makula responded. "I therefore missed out on learning things from him."

"Okay," she said. "And are there things that you admire about the way your father raised you that you would like to emulate?"

"Ah, let me see," Makula said, with his eyes affixed to the ceiling.

"Take your time," the instructor said.

"Well, whenever he was home when I was in my teens, I think my father took the time to talk to me about certain important things in life. As for me, most of the time I'm focused on doing my work on my computer, and my kids spend their time watching television or playing video games. I think I would like to talk to them more," Makula said.

"Good for you," the instructor said to Makula. "You've finally got something to work on." When it was Pam's turn to speak, she said that she needed to work on finding a balance between being her children's mother and being their friend.

On the drive home after the seminar, Pam asked Makula whether he felt that it had been useful. Makula refused to share his opinion with her, fearing an argument. Pam said that it had been a waste of their time if he would not tell her his opinion of it. He did not respond.

***

As Christmas neared, all of Toronto reflected a festive mood. Many streets and homes were decorated with Christmas lights, and Christmas music played on all the radio stations and in the shopping malls.

Makula had taken his kids to the annual Santa Claus Parade in late November. Many parents braved the cold to ensure that their children did not miss the big event. The younger children shouted with excitement as the decorated floats passed by. Some of the mascots threw candy or candy canes, while those on foot handed out balloons. Three hours after it began and hundreds of floats later, Santa finally appeared. Both the children and the adults cheered as Santa shouted, 'Ho, ho, ho!' and waved to the crowd.

With only one week left before Christmas, Pam asked Makula, "Will you come with me to do some shopping? We could have lunch in the food court afterward."

"No," Makula replied. "I hate being in the malls at this time of year. I hate having to wait for a parking spot and then having to wait in line to pay for the stuff."

That afternoon, Makula put up strings of coloured lights on the exterior of the house while Pam, Peggy, and the kids decorated a huge Christmas tree in the family room. Makula had not finished outside before the afternoon grew dark, but the children urged him to turn on the lights. The effect was amazingly beautiful.

The following morning, Makula finished the outdoor decorations by placing a huge snowman next to the main entrance to their house. Richard told his dad that he had created a wonderful "winter wonderland."

On Christmas Eve, Peggy and her two children came over to spend the day and night at Pam and Makula's home. The children were very excited, and tossed balloons into the air. Pam baked a cake and its aroma spread throughout the house. Peggy helped Pam to prepare dinner. They cooked chicken, beef, peas, and rice for the adults, and lasagna for the children. Luku arrived before sunset and started the barbecue in the backyard. Pam's brother, Patrick, who was visiting from England along with his six-year-old daughter, asked Luku how he planned to barbecue chicken in the cold. Laughing, Luku said, "I love my barbecue, so the cold can't stop me from enjoying it. Come to my place any time—you'll be sure to enjoy my barbecue!"

Before she went to bed, Dawn put a glass of milk and two plated cookies by the chimney for Santa to enjoy after he had delivered their presents in the middle of the night.

The children woke up early on Christmas Day and ran to the Christmas tree to open their presents. They were very happy with Santa because he had brought them so many toys—video games, dolls, remote-controlled trucks, colouring books, disposable cameras, and many other things.

"Santa is awesome," Dawn said. "He brought everything that I wanted. Cool."

The younger children played with their toys the whole morning, and it was hard to get them to take a break to eat their lunch. That evening, Makula and Luku took the children to see a movie while Patrick, Pam, and Peggy stayed home to chat. Makula was shocked to overhear Richard say that he was bored with the holidays, especially when New Year's Day was still so far off.

Pam went shopping every day for the next week to take advantage of the "Boxing Week" sales. She bought many items of clothing that she placed in a pile on the couch; the Johnsons would put them away in the closets when they returned from their holidays later that week. Makula cautioned, "Honey, I think you are spending way too much money on clothes."

"Not really, Mak," Pam replied. "Most of these clothes are 70 or 80 percent off. The discounts are too big to resist."

CHAPTER EIGHTEEN
Toronto, Canada, January 2002

Makula's old friend Paul Mugisha travelled from Kampala to Toronto to pay him a visit. The two friends were delighted to see each other after so many years. Mugisha was glad to know that, like him, his friend was doing well. Pam and the children also enjoyed having him there. Mugisha said that Daniel resembled Makula, and Dawn resembled Pam, but he could not tell who Richard resembled. Richard wanted Mugisha to come to his bedroom to play some Nintendo games, but his father said that the visitor needed some rest.

After he had given him a tour of their beautiful house, Makula asked Mugisha to sit down, and they chatted as they drank some beer. They discussed Makula's job and the cost of living, then began talking about the "good old days," beginning with their years at Kayunga Primary School. "Have you met with any of our former schoolmates from Kayunga?" Makula asked.

"Yes," Mugisha replied. "Do you remember Bukirwa?"

"Yes, I remember Bukirwa very well. You and she were the academic giants in our class," Makula said.

"Just last month I met her in the market in Kayunga. She owns a makeshift restaurant there. I felt bad as I saw this very clever woman struggling to make ends meet," Mugisha said.

"That's very sad," Makula said. "She could have become a doctor or a lawyer or something else had she not dropped out due to her pregnancy."

"Hey, wait a minute. I have more interesting news. I treated Pili Pili a few months ago at the clinic!" Mugisha said.

"Pili Pili?" Makula exclaimed.

"Yes, just imagine!" Mugisha said. "Someone brought him to the clinic for treatment. He was glad to hear that his former student was now a doctor at the clinic."

"That's amazing, Paul," Makula said. "And how was he?"

"Well, he is old and seemed to be in a state of depression," Mugisha said. "The poor guy; I asked him to return for further treatment the following month but he never did. So, I don't know how he is now but it was evident that he was living in poverty."

"By the way, did anyone find out who it was that beat him up so badly after our examinations?" Makula asked.

"I think everybody in Kayunga knew," Mugisha replied.

"What do you mean, 'Everybody knew'?" Makula asked.

"Do you remember Constable Ogwang?" Mugisha asked.

"No," Makula told him. "The name sounds familiar, but I don't remember him."

"Constable Ogwang used to come to the school every month to give us a talk on road safety. I think he did that for a year," Mugisha said. "He also dated my older sister for a while."

"Oh yes," Makula said. "Now I remember him."

"Constable Ogwang came to the clinic one afternoon," Mugisha said. "He had brought his granddaughter for immunization. When the nurse was done with them, and he was ready to go, he asked her whether he could talk to me. She knew that I would be happy to talk to an old acquaintance, so she showed him in to my office. And do you know the first thing he said to me?"

"No," Makula said. "What was it?"

"He said, 'Doctor, are you still as stubborn as you were during those school days in Kayunga?'" Mugisha replied.

"Uh oh," Makula said. "That doesn't sound like a good beginning."

"I told him that I had never been stubborn," Mugisha said. "So he said, 'You were very stubborn. You were one of the group of five boys and two girls who beat up that teacher, Mr. Mubiru. Pili Pili. Yes, Pili Pili. You used to call him Pili Pili.'"

"Oh, no. And what was your response?" Makula asked.

"Well, I was left speechless. I could not deny the fact. I knew that they had all the details, given that he knew the exact number of students who had participated in the beating," Mugisha told him.

"There were seven of you in total?" Makula asked, laughing.

"I don't remember exactly, but we were about seven," Mugisha said. "Seven or eight."

Pam, who had been listening while she set the table for dinner, asked, "Why would you guys beat up your teacher? That's strange."

"It was in revenge for the spankings he had given us during those years," Makula said.

"He used to spank you? Why would he do that?" Pam asked.

"You rich city kids never got beatings in school. You never got to know the kind of hell that we poor kids had to go through," Mugisha said, laughing.

"Well, I heard that many students were beaten in their primary schools but I never understood the reason. Why would that happen?" Pam asked.

"Well, a teacher would find any flimsy reason to cane you. It could be something as simple as a student failing to get a passing mark or failing to complete homework. Some of us were beaten even for speaking our mother tongue," Mugisha said, emphasizing "some of us" in clear reference to Makula.

As they ate dinner, they talked about Musasa High School.

Mugisha said, "We had an Old Boys' reunion last month. I remember I e-mailed you about it just a few weeks before it took place."

"Yes, I remember that e-mail. How did the reunion go?" Makula asked.

"It went very well. Many of the boys were there…"

"You mean many of the 'men.' We are not 'boys' anymore."

"Well, yes. Many 'old' boys were there…"

"Was the reunion held at the school?"

"No, at the Namala Hotel."

"I don't know that hotel. Where is it?"

"It is about a kilometre and a half from the school. I thought you knew it."

"No. I last visited the school many years ago."

"Do you remember Namala, the woman who used to run the school canteen?"

"Yes, I remember her very well. She is dead now, isn't she?"

"Yes. Her sons built that hotel and named it after her."

"Those boys had the means to build a hotel?"

"Oh, yes, they are both very rich."

"Where did they get the money? If I remember correctly, those boys never went to school."

"Well, as you know, they owned a lot of land that they inherited from their late mother. That area is not rural anymore. They sold just a small portion of it to get a start, and as they say, the rest is history."

"Wow. Didn't Mr. T.B. predict those boys' success years ago? I remember we just laughed it off when he said that they had the potential to become wealthy."

"Speaking of Mr. T.B., he was also at the reunion, and he asked about you."

"What? He remembered me?"

"Yes he did. It seems teachers never forget their outstanding students."

"Thank you for the compliment, but I don't think I was out-standing in any way."

"Apparently you were. Why else would Mr. T.B. remember you?"

"And how is he doing?"

"He is still strong. You know that he is now an important man. He is the headmaster of Buweela High School."

"That's great. Good for him. So, what was on the agenda of the Old Boys' reunion?"

"Many things were discussed, but the main item was the ground-breaking ceremony that was held for the new school library that we had all pledged to build for the school. Mr. Atiku was present to cut the tape, as the library will be named after him."

"Oh, that's nice. How is he now? Isn't he quite old?"

"Surprisingly, although he is old, he seems to be as strong as ever. I remember when he used to chase us with a stick whenever the bell rang. His address at the reunion made us laugh, you know, with his dry humour. It was such a joy to listen to him. We really missed those good old days, especially when we went on to tour the dormitories. Camp Hope is still as good as new."

"Tell me more about Namala's sons. I am very interested in hearing about their success story."

"They are very rich. Actually they made a point of being at both the opening and closing ceremonies of the reunion, with their spokesman and their lawyer, both of whom are Old Boys of the school."

"Oh. Who are they?"

"John and Tom Kabenge, respectively."

Makula did not comment. "How is Luku doing?" Mugisha asked, changing the topic from the Kabenges.

"He's doing fine. You should be able to see him this weekend."

At that moment, Makula's telephone rang. When he saw who was calling, he said, "It's Chris."

"Hey, Mak, how are you doing? Is the doctor already in town?" Luku asked.

"Yes he is," Makula answered.

"How is he doing?"

"He is right here. Would you like to speak to him?"

"Yes."

Makula handed the phone to Mugisha. "Hey, Paul, how are you doing man? Long time no see," Luku said.

"Hello, Chris. I am doing well. I can't wait to see you. How are you?" Mugisha asked.

"I'm good, man. No complaints, doc," Luku replied. "How is your family doing?"

"The children are well. My daughter is eight and my son is two. Everyone is all right," Mugisha replied.

"Great. What explains that age difference? Eight and two," Luku asked, laughing.

"You know my wife is a doctor too. Between the clinics, conferences, and trips, I guess we are too busy to concentrate on anything else," Mugisha said.

"I will come to see you tomorrow after you've had a good rest," Luku said.

"Thanks, Chris. I'll look forward to it," Mugisha said.

"I know Nicholas will also be happy to see you," Luku told him.

"Nicholas who?" Mugisha asked.

"Nicholas Wabudi," Luku replied.

"Nicholas lives here too? I didn't know that. I've been wondering for years where on earth that guy ended up," Mugisha said.

"Well, he lives here in Toronto. I'll see if he is free to come with me tomorrow. We will have a blast," Luku said.

When he ended the call with Luku, Mugisha said to Makula, "I didn't know Nicholas lived here."

"Oh yeah, he lives here. He is a chemist, and he is doing well," Makula said.

"Great. I would like to see him. That's one guy I didn't expect to ever meet again," Mugisha said.

"He's been here longer than any of us. When Chris came to live in Toronto, Nicholas was already here. I think it was during Chris's first week that he was lucky enough to meet someone who knew Nicholas. One afternoon, during the winter, he was standing in the lobby of the shelter where he was living temporarily, and probably, as a newcomer, looking worried and lost. A guy called Tunda, who, by the way, has been Chris's friend ever since, had come to the shelter to deliver the mail. He saw

Chris and said, 'Brother, you look worried. What's the problem?' And during that conversation, Chris mentioned that he was from Uganda. Tunda told him that he knew another Ugandan. He wrote down the man's name and telephone number, and that's how Chris found out that Nicholas lived here. They met that very afternoon, and life became easier for both of them as they now had each other for company," Makula said.

"Wow, that's a great story. Who else lives here?" Mugisha asked.

"Pius Bitaro also lives here," Makula said.

"Oh, I remember Bitaro. What does he do?"

"He is a lawyer, but I really don't know exactly what he does. When we arrived here, he was staying at home to look after his children while his wife worked. Later, he returned to his practice but I rarely see him, even though we live in the same city."

"Will I be able to see him?"

"Not when you are my visitor. Remember the old enmity? He called me a snitch way back in Musasa, and he is still not speaking to me."

"That's childish. I wouldn't have expected him to still be hanging on to that unfounded grudge."

"I see him once in a while at the meetings of the African Society. He's the chairman and founder."

"Yes, I've heard about the African Society. What is it about? I mean, what is its purpose?"

"The African Society is a think tank that tackles the socio-economic challenges faced by Africans here in Canada. Not only that, it also taps into the opportunities available."

"That sounds like a useful organization…"

"Oh, yes, it is. It's in its infancy but it has already proven its usefulness."

The following evening, Luku and Wabudi came to Makula's home to see Mugisha. The four friends were very excited to see each other again.

Luku told Mugisha that he was living the Canadian dream, and that life was very good for him. Luku wondered why Mugisha himself didn't consider moving to Canada. Mugisha told him that he had never considered living abroad and he did not think that his wife would support the idea. Wabudi told Mugisha that the first few years in Canada had been very challenging for him, but that he was now happy working as a chemist.

The four men then turned the visit into an Old Boys' reunion. They talked about their days in Musasa High School, then recalled their adventures in Makerere University.

They were interrupted by a call from Luku's wife, Peggy, who asked him to pick her up from the subway about twenty minutes away. Luku excused himself, and said that he would be back. When Luku left, Mugisha said, "I wonder whether Chris is still investing in Uganda."

"Did he tell you that he has investments in Uganda?" Wabudi asked.

"Yes, he mentions it in every e-mail I receive from him," Mugisha replied.

"What kind of investments does he claim to have?" Wabudi asked.

"Houses, land, and others," Mugisha told him.

"When I first arrived here, he also told me that he had considerable investments in Uganda," Makula said.

"If you think that that guy has changed, you are in for a big shock," Wabudi said.

Pam was disgusted with Wabudi. She hated men who gossiped, and Wabudi was known for his love of it.

"I was surprised to learn that Chris and Peggy are married. How did those two end up together?" Mugisha asked.

Wabudi leaned closer to Makula and Mugisha and said, "Tom Kabenge took Peggy on a vacation to an island in the Caribbean slightly more than a decade ago. After they had had a good time together, he vanished, leaving her stranded at the hotel."

Pam, seated next to her husband, grew uncomfortable at the mention of Kabenge.

"Mum, Dad, can someone help me? The TV isn't working," Dawn called out from the family room.

"I will be with you in a sec," Pam called back, and then excused herself and left the room.

"So, what happened next? What did Peggy do?" Mugisha asked.

"I think Peggy was too embarrassed to return home," Wabudi said. "She got in touch with Chris, who, as you know, had been interested in her for years. To him, this event was a blessing. I don't know how he pulled it off, but anyway, to make a long story short, he managed to convince her to come to Toronto. They are now happily married, and they have two children. It really changed his life. Remember that he had abandoned his study of medicine at Makerere University and immigrated to Canada as a way of dealing with Peggy's rejection of him."

"What does he do now? I've never had the courage to ask him. You know how, back home, we are told never to ask our people who live overseas what they do for money," Mugisha said. Makula and Wabudi laughed.

"He went back to school here to study education. He is now a teacher," Wabudi replied.

CHAPTER NINETEEN
Kampala, Uganda, December 2002

Makula and his family were finally able to return to Uganda to visit their families. He and Pam were very excited about seeing Uganda after their long absence. Their children, however, were even more excited as they did not know what to expect. They had heard a lot about the country and its people from their parents but now they would have the opportunity to see everything for themselves.

Dr. Sempaka and his wife came to the airport to greet the family after their long flight. They were delighted to see their daughter and son-in-law but even more so to see their grandchildren. They all hugged each other, and Pam and her mother even shed some tears of joy.

They were driven to the Sempakas' home where they would stay while in Uganda. As they drove through Kampala, the children were surprised to see so many people walking about. "Why are there so many people here?" Richard asked.

"This is a city. The people are buying stuff. Some are going to the taxi park," Pam explained.

"What is a taxi park?" Richard asked.

"Why are there so many people on that truck?" Dawn asked.

"That truck is a means of transport. I guess those people are going to a soccer match or something," Pam told her.

"Be prepared to answer a lot more questions," Mrs. Sempaka said. "This is only the beginning."

"These kids ask too many questions sometimes," Pam said.

"It's good when they ask questions. That's how they learn," Dr. Sempaka said. "That's exactly how you were, Pam, when you were little. I remember the first time we took you to Kampala. You were five. You asked about three questions a minute."

Makula was quiet, remembering the first time that he had been to Kampala on his way to Musasa High School. And he recalled being conned of his money during his second visit to the city. He vaguely remembered the man who had approached him that morning. He wondered whether he was still alive and whether he was still a thief.

Pam was glad to be back in her childhood home, which looked as beautiful and immaculate as it always had. The first thing she did was go to her old bedroom. Dawn followed her mother and was surprised to see both her own picture and a picture of her mother at eight years of age pinned to the wall. The resemblance between them was very striking.

They all had lunch and then the visitors took a nap. An hour later, Linda and Angela arrived and woke them up. Angela hugged them all, and Dawn and Daniel took turns sitting on their aunt's lap as she told them stories about life in Kampala. Makula called his cousin Makko that evening and told him that they would be in Kasaka in two days' time. He also called his friend Kasede to let him know that he was in Kampala, and Kasede came over right away. In fact, Kasede rarely left Makula's side for the duration of his visit.

On the third day of their visit, Makula and his family went to visit his parents in Kasaka. He was looking forward to seeing his mother and father. Pam was surprised when Makula pulled over at a roadside market about thirty kilometres from Kayunga. As soon as the car had stopped, the food vendors came rushing over. Makula lowered his window and looked at what was for sale. The vendors were offering roasted plantains, roasted chicken pinned onto long sticks, roasted cassava, and fresh ripe bananas.

"We can't eat this kind of food, darling," Pam said. "What about the hygiene standards?"

"No, the food is safe. I ate it whenever I passed by here, and I never fell ill," Makula said.

"No, I'm not letting my kids eat this kind of food. It will make them sick," Pam said.

"Mum, can I have some chicken? It looks yummy," Richard said.

"No," Pam replied. In the end, everyone ate some bananas.

After Kayunga, Makula drove at a slow speed so as not to stir up the dust. The children started asking, "Are we there yet?"

When they arrived in Kasaka, Makula pulled over to the side of the road. The place where the market that he helped build once stood was now covered by bush. It made him feel bad. The big billboard that a beverage company had erected was still there, faded in the overgrown grass. It bore the message "Amazing Things Happen Here." Pam read the sign and laughed. "What amazing things could possibly happen in this bush?" she asked. Makula did not find the comment funny. He did not respond.

As they continued the drive toward Makula's parents' home, they glimpsed a beautiful, huge red-tiled house on top of the hill in Nanziba. A huge solar panel was also visible on the roof. Makula said that he was certain that it was Senfuka's house. He said that he had heard that Senfuka had built one of the most beautiful houses in the county.

When they stopped in the front yard of his parents' home, many people came over, shouting with joy to meet them. Daniel was lifted off his feet and into the air as soon as he set foot on the ground. As many as five people surrounded Makula in a group hug as Pam watched in amusement. Kabejja held Pam's hand as Filipo reached out to hug his son. There were a lot of cheers as even more people came to meet the visitors. The mood was very festive.

When the shouting and cheering had died down, they made their way toward the house. Pam looked around to see where Daniel was, but before she could call for him, he came running up to them, screaming, "Fire! Fire! Can someone call 911?"

"What is the matter? What is he talking about?" Kabejja asked.

"Where is the fire, Dan?" Pam asked.

"Over there, Mum. Fire! Call 911!" Daniel said, pointing to the fire in the outdoor kitchen. Richard and Dawn just stood there speechless, looking at the flames. Makula laughed out loud and said, "There's no problem! That's the fire that grandma uses to cook. Do you see the big black pan on the fireplace? That is the food."

Daniel did not seem to be entirely convinced that it was safe, but he said nothing more. He walked around outside the house with three of the young children. He saw two goats tied up with rope, but he was not sure what they were. He asked the other children, but they did not answer him. They looked at each other until one of them said, "It seems this kid can't speak Luganda. I don't understand a thing he is saying." The children laughed, but Daniel was not bothered. He just continued wandering in the yard and went a little ways into the coffee plantation.

***

Kabejja sat down on a mat and made each of her grandchildren sit on her lap. She was disappointed and saddened to find that they could not speak Luganda—they could not even understand a question as simple as "What is your name?" Each of the three children turned to their mother to translate for them.

"You both speak Luganda, you both live with these children, why don't you teach them the language?" she asked Pam and Makula.

Pam let her husband answer. "Mother, we talked to the children in Luganda when they were young. But once they were in daycare, we only had a couple of hours in the evening with them before it was time to put them to bed. They soon forgot what little Luganda they had learned. So you see, the situation was a little more complicated than you think."

"Namugga was available. You could have taken her with you to take care of these children. Why didn't you do that?" Kabejja asked.

Makula's friend Othieno, who was seated on a wooden chair next to Makula, interjected, "I don't think it would have been easy to take Namugga to Canada. She would have needed a visa to go there, and they are not easy to get. However, young people have always been dreaming of living overseas. If visas were not required for one to travel, believe me, you would see all of Kasaka going to Toronto to join Makula."

At that moment, more shouts and cheers were heard from the front yard as Angela and her boyfriend parked by the house. Makula noticed that neither of his parents seemed happy to see their daughter and wondered why. Several villagers, some of whom Makula did not know, hugged Angela while the young children clustered around her boyfriend. Makula went outside to meet them while Pam stayed in the house with her in-laws.

Once inside, Angela's boyfriend was given a chair to sit on, but Angela was given a mat. Pam looked on in amusement as Angela, uncomfortable, shifted and changed her position every couple of minutes.

Makula and Pam started conversing with Angela and her boyfriend. As he listened to Angela speak Luganda interspersed with English, Makula wondered why his mother had made such a fuss. His children, who had been raised in Canada, could not speak Luganda, but their aunt, who had lived all her life in Kampala, did not speak the language fluently either.

Makula went out to his car and took two large suitcases full of clothes for members of his extended family out of the trunk. He also handed Filipo a plastic bag that contained a pair of shoes. Filipo expressed pleasure with the shoes but commented discreetly to his wife that their style was too youthful. Kabejja told Filipo that he should stop being old-fashioned and learn to embrace modernity.

Kabejja took charge of the two suitcases and said she would need time to sort through the clothes to ensure that everybody got something. Makula told them that he had two more suitcases to deliver to them before he returned to Toronto. Othieno clapped happily, knowing that there would be something for him in the suitcases.

Makula went back outside of the already crowded house to meet Toofa's, Makko's, and Lukka's children. Each of the men introduced their children one by one to him, but Makula did not retain any of their names except for Lukka's older son Lawrence for whom he paid tuition fees at a college. Makula also asked his cousins about Lameka, whom he had missed among those who had welcomed him and his family. When he learned that the old man was sick and had not left his house for four days, Makula went directly to see his uncle.

He found Lameka lying on a little mattress in a dark corner of his living room. "My dear Makula," he said. "Don't interpret my not coming to welcome you as a sign that I no longer care about you. I am ailing."

"No, no, Uncle. I understand why you didn't come out. You are sick," Makula replied.

Lameka tried to sit up to hug Makula, but he was too weak to do so. Makula urged him not to bother trying, and knelt down and took a firm grip of the old man's hand.

"Sit on the chair, my dear," Lameka said. "I am glad you have come because I have some important things to tell you." Makula sat on a little wooden chair and began chatting with his uncle.

Lameka asked him about his family and had many questions about his life in Canada. "Do you live in a big city?" Lameka asked. "Are there any forests in Canada, or is it cities everywhere? What kind of food do you eat?"

Lameka said that he would like to meet Makula's family after they had had their conversation. Then he asked Makula to help him sit up, and he began telling him the "important things" he had to say. "Every family has a history," he said. "Our family has a history too. Unfortunately, there is a sad chapter in it." Makula listened attentively. "This village is not our birthplace. We moved here when I was twelve …"

"Oh," Makula said, surprised, as he had never been told this.

Lameka told him, "We hail from the present district of Mukono. My father moved here when he was asked to help establish a church in this area. This was long before your father was born. At that time, my father had three children; I was the oldest, and I had two sisters. Those two died long ago but, of course, you know their children. Your father was the only one who was born here in Kasaka."

"That's good to know. Thank you," Makula said.

"Like you when you decided to go abroad," Lameka continued, "my father left everything behind in Mukono to come to settle here. I know that many of our relatives there are still alive, but we lost all contact with them when we moved. You know in those days communication was not as easy as it is now. These days when you want to talk to someone, all you need to do is dial their telephone number. That was not the case then."

Makula pulled his chair closer. "However, my father, Makula, your namesake, had a young brother, his only brother, Laban," Lameka said. "Unfortunately the two never got along well and that explains in part why we never made contact with that part of our family. My uncle was a very difficult man. We heard that soon after we left, he started dealing in coffee. Later, he became very rich and had many children whom he was able to send to good schools. One of those children is James Kabenge…"

"James Kabenge?" Makula exclaimed.

"Yes, James Kabenge," his uncle answered.

"The banker?" Makula asked in disbelief.

"Yes. The last time I heard about him he was working in a bank," Lameka said. "You seem so surprised. Do you know him?"

"Yes. Well, not really, but I know two of his sons, with whom I went to school," Makula said.

"That's right. James Kabenge is my cousin and your father's cousin. He was my uncle's first child. He was born two years before we left Mukono. I carried him around a lot when he was a baby," Lameka said.

"What? I can't believe we had such a rich uncle and endured poverty for that long," Makula said, his face stricken with disbelief. He wanted to tell Lameka that one of James Kabenge's sons had bullied him at school and that he and the son had almost fought over his wife, but he kept it to himself. He wanted to spare his uncle the details.

"Mr. Kabenge is a close friend of my father-in-law. He was actually invited to my wedding; unfortunately he got an urgent meeting overseas and could not attend. Had he attended the wedding, somebody would have introduced him to our family," Makula said.

"Kabenge is an important man. Who could have introduced him to us rural folk?" Lameka said.

"I am so very surprised to learn that Mr. James Kabenge is my first cousin once removed," Makula said. "I am stunned."

"Now listen, Makula. I have a mission for you," Lameka said. Makula listened attentively. "Since you are now an important person, it will be easy for you to do this for us. Please get in touch with James and his family. We would like to meet them."

When he returned to his father's house, the mood of the others was still joyous but Makula was quiet. Pam, seeing this, asked him if everything was all right. "Did your uncle say something that upset you?" she asked.

"No. Not really," he answered. Pam knew that Makula treated many things, even important ones, lightly but did not ask any more about it.

After lunch, Makula talked briefly to his sister Angela about her bachelor of commerce course that she had just started at Makerere University, after which she and her boyfriend left to return to Kampala. Dawn went outside to see the "cool stuff" that Daniel had told her about. As they walked around, they stopped to watch a herd of animals passing along the path in front of their grandparents' house. They watched the many animals, more than twenty, approach. "Mum, Dad, come see some rhinos!" Dawn shouted. "And they have long horns! Cool!"

Makula came out and stood with his children in front of the house. "Those are not rhinos, my dear. Those are long-horned cattle. See that boy walking behind them? He is called a herdsman. He is taking them to pasture. My cousins and I used to do that when I was about his age."

"So this is really the house you grew up in, eh, Dad?" Richard asked.

"Yes, this is the house where I grew up. I loved it here, and I still love it," Makula said.

"But it looks kind of weird," Richard said.

"That's not nice, Rick. You should apologize to your dad," said Pam, who was now standing behind her husband.

"Sorry, Dad," Richard said.

"That's all right," Makula said.

Just then Toofa came over to Makula and asked if he could talk to him alone. Makula excused himself. "Man, just the other day I was thinking about your long journey that started right here in Kasaka," Toofa said. "You went to Kayunga, then you went to Kampala, you became successful there, and now you are a big man in Canada. I wonder where you will be heading next."

"To the moon, I guess," Makula said. They both laughed.

"Othieno told me that you are now the boss of the company that builds and sells houses in Canada. Is that true?" Toofa asked.

"What?" Makula asked.

"Anyway, let me tell you why I called you aside. Look, I have so many children now. You've already seen some of them, but I have eight of them. That guy right there is the acting last born," he said laughing while he pointed to a two-year-old boy walking alone in the backyard. "I know that money is tight, but I wonder whether you can continue helping me with these children for a few more years. You know, things are really tough for me right now," Toofa said.

Makula almost laughed. Things had always been tough for Toofa.

"Toofa, you know that I love and care for you, but right now

I can't promise anything. I would definitely like to continue helping you, and I'll try to find a way to do that. When I go back, I will devise a plan. Then I will get in touch with you," Makula said.

"Thanks, my brother. I knew you would agree to help me. You have always been kind to me," Toofa said as he hugged Makula.

Makula then took his family to meet his uncle at his house. Lameka was half asleep but woke up as soon as the visitors arrived. "Come on, young people, don't be shy. Come hug me," he told the children. "You are my flesh and blood." The children held his hands as Pam sat down on a mat. Lameka commented on the children and thanked Pam for taking good care of them.

"Me too, Uncle. I take care of them," Makula said.

"No doubt you do so, but a mother is always the one to be thanked. No father can do better than a mother," he said. Makula chose not to argue with him.

As they left the room, Lameka asked Makula to stay behind.

"Your older son is the spitting image of my Uncle Laban, James Kabenge's father. I wish I had my uncle's picture here to show you. You could see what I am talking about," Lameka said. Although he never doubted that Richard was his son, Makula now knew why the boy resembled Tom Kabenge—Tom too must closely resemble his grandfather.

As he thought about the fact that he was a close relative of the Kabenges, Makula remembered how his mother had come to Musasa High School to see him and how James Kabenge had given her a ride all the way back to Kampala. "This is a small, small world," he thought. He was sure that his mother did not know this detail of his family's history; she would certainly have told him about it years before. However, the fact that he now knew that Tom was his relative did not lessen the resentment he felt toward Kabenge.

Back in the front yard of his parents' home, Makula talked with his old friend Othieno. Othieno was with his eighteen-year-old daughter Anna, who had been admitted to the Catholic University of Health Sciences. Othieno introduced his daughter to Makula, who recognized her from when she was younger. "My daughter has been admitted to university to study medicine, but you know my situation, Makula," Othieno said.

"I can't afford to pay the tuition."

"How much will it cost per year?" Makula asked.

Instead of answering, Othieno sent his daughter home to get her admission letter for Makula to see. Since Othieno's home was not far, the girl returned in minutes.

Makula ascertained that it would cost only about two thousand US dollars per year to pay for the girl's education, so he pledged to help. Othieno was so grateful that he almost knelt down before Makula to thank him. Makula told him that it was his turn to pay Othieno back for his kindness. "I remember that afternoon so vividly, like it was just yesterday," he said. "Despite the fact that you had a fever, you not only donated your matooke to get money to pay my examination fees, you also pushed that bicycle for kilometres and stopped that pickup truck full of fish to get me to Kayunga. I wish I could meet that truck driver again. I remember him so well. When we arrived in Kayunga, he summoned all his fellow fish traders and announced out loud, 'This young man needs money to pay his examination fees. Will someone pay for these two bunches of matooke so he gets the money?' One man paid even a little more than I needed, and I was on the bus headed back to school within twenty minutes."

Othieno told Makula that he was very glad that he had returned to visit and thanked him for having committed himself to the development of Kasaka. He told Makula that Simeon Senfuka's company, Food Basket Limited, had grown so much that it now exported fruits and fish to Europe and that Senfuka's driver had told him that Senfuka was now worth three million US dollars.

After his conversation with Othieno, Makula went inside and announced that it was time he and his family returned to Kampala. Disappointed, Kabejja told him that she had prepared enough food for both lunch and dinner. Makula explained that they could not spend the night in Kasaka because they had not made arrangements to sleep over, especially for the children. "What kind of arrangements would you need to make?" Kabejja asked. "You lived here for years, and you did not die. They wouldn't die either if they spent one night here."

Makula did not answer but saw Pam send him a warning look.

Filipo said that if Makula and his family were returning to Kampala, they should leave before sunset as the dark made the road dangerous for driving. However, before Makula and his family left, Othieno insisted on making a speech in the front yard. Many people had once again gathered to see the visitors off, including a few people from the neighbouring village of Nanziba. Othieno saw this as a perfect opportunity to show off "their" son who lived overseas, along with his beautiful family. He said, "Makula, we would like to thank you and your wife for being such good children. We would also like to thank you for all the assistance that you've given us all these years. Your parents, my friend Filipo and your mother, Kabejja, would like you to know that they are very proud of you. We hope that you will return to see us before you go back to Canada." Filipo nodded in approval, although he had not asked Othieno to speak on his behalf.

Makula also took a few moments to publicly address his folks. "My wife, the kids, and I are also very glad to see you. We are very happy to see that everybody, except for our beloved Uncle Lameka, is in good health. I promise that I will return to see you before we return to Canada." After that brief speech, Makula and his family hugged several people before finally getting into the car to leave.

On the drive back to Kampala, Dawn asked her father, "Dad, why doesn't your dad have a cool house like Mum's dad?"

"My dad's house is cool too," Makula answered.

"No. It's too small and yucky," Dawn said.

"Dawn, that's not nice. Say sorry to Daddy," Pam said.

"Sorry, Dad," Dawn said.

News reached Senfuka that Makula had visited Kasaka. As he sipped a beer on the balcony of his house atop the hill overlooking Kasaka, Senfuka said, "What did he bring to his poor people? I wonder why that fellow doesn't humble himself, return home, and come to me for help. How does he expect to develop his little village when he is thousands of kilometres away?"

"Makula actually seemed to be well off," said a man who had heard Makula's speech before his family left to return to Kampala. "I even heard him say that the money that Ugandans who work abroad remit to the country is now its number one source of income, even surpassing coffee."

"How much of that money is his? Here is an example of a man pretending to be what he is not. I am sick and tired of pretenders," Senfuka said dismissively.

***

Before he returned to Toronto, Makula and his friend Kasede paid a second visit to his family in Kasaka. After being personally greeted by more than seventy people, his father asked him to pick up a wooden chair and follow him outside. They sat under a mango tree that stood close to the front yard. Makula enjoyed the gentle breeze and the smell of the fresh mangoes.

"Do you remember planting this mango tree?" Filipo asked.

"Yes, I do. I planted it during the holidays when I was waiting for the results of my Primary 7 examinations. It's all grown and big now," Makula replied.

"There are people who believe that when you plant a fruit tree and it bears fruit, whenever a person picks and eats a fruit from it, your blessings multiply. And this tree has borne a lot of mangoes this season; the children have been picking basketfuls since last month," Filipo said.

"Does that explain the bountiful year I've had?" Makula asked. Both he and his father laughed.

Makula told his father that he wanted to construct a new house for the family in Kasaka. Filipo was so overjoyed that he called his wife out to tell her the news. They both hugged their son while the rest of the family looked on, wondering why Makula's parents were so happy with him.

Makula, Kasede, and Filipo then walked around Filipo's land for an hour to choose the spot where the house would be constructed. Makula wanted to build on a spot that was closer to his Uncle Lameka's house. Here, he said, the new house would have a good view of the main road. However, construction on that site would involve cutting down a few of Filipo's coffee trees. Filipo resisted, wanting to choose another spot, but Kabejja convinced him to accept it. What she didn't know was that Makula had chosen that spot for a personal reason. Travellers on the main road could compare his house to Senfuka's as they would be able to see both houses on top of their hills, one in Kasaka and the other in Nanziba. The distance between them would be less than five minutes if travelling by car.

***

Having seen Senfuka's house in Nanziba, Makula decided to construct an even larger one in Kasaka. And he knew just who to entrust with the project. After he had returned to Toronto and received a loan from his bank, he called his friend Ben Kasede and asked him to oversee the construction. Work on the house began three months after Makula's visit to Kasaka.

Makula and Kasede agreed that whenever Kasede needed to talk to Makula, he would "beep" him. In other words, Kasede would call Makula, let the phone ring two or three times, then hang up. Makula would then call him back. This arrangement would work well for them because Makula would be the one to pay for the call.

Kasede moved to Kasaka where Makko helped him to construct a little house that he and the builders would live in for the duration of the project. He hired builders from Kampala who stayed in Kasaka to expedite the work. Kasede diligently supervised the builders and paid them their weekly wages every Friday evening. Eight more people were hired from Kasaka, including Makula's cousins Makko and Lukka and their friend Luyima, to help the builders. They brought the bricks, delivered water to the site in twenty-litre cans, mixed the concrete, and helped dig the foundation. These workers were required to be at the site by seven o'clock in the morning and they were also the last to leave in the evening, after ensuring that everything was in order.

Each week, Kasede would spend Thursday night in an inn in Kayunga after withdrawing money from the bank account that had been opened to pay for the construction of the new house. On payday, Friday, Kasede would return to Kasaka with a bag full of cash in the company of an armed guard. He treated the money like a lioness protects her cubs. He sat on a chair and laid out a list of the people to be paid in front of him on a little table. He would then pay the builders, who had to sign next to their name before he handed them wads of cash. And then, before he paid any of the local helpers, Kasede would ask each of them to give him a verbal summary of the work that they had done during the week. This annoyed the men—it was humiliating to have to give a report to someone who had been observing their every move.

> Lukka said, "That man is overzealous. You would think that the house belonged to him. Actually, Makula is to blame for all this. How come he didn't trust us to oversee the construction when we are like brothers to him?"

This comment made its way back to Kasede, who told the local workers, "Makula works very hard to earn his dollars. We too have to work equally hard if we are to make any money here. Whoever feels that he can't do this is free to leave."

In ten months, the builders had erected a six-bedroom two-storey house. By the end of the year, they had roofed it with red tiles. Kasede took pictures of the construction at its various stages, which Angela e-mailed to Makula, along with scanned copies of the expenses.

Unfortunately, the bank account was empty before the house was completed. There were no windows or doors installed, and there were only concrete floors. When Makula called, his father told him that a little more money would be needed to install both the front and back door and a window on one room. His parents would then be willing to move into the house. Makula told Filipo that he did not want them living in a house that was not finished. Filipo said, "I am ready to live in the house as it is. After all, many people die these days before they get a chance to enjoy their houses." But Makula rejected that idea.

When Makula called Kasede to tell him that the construction would be suspended until further notice, Kasede almost cried. "Makula, you know me well, and you know that I don't tell lies. The period that I spent working for you on your house has been the best time of my life. There has been peace at home because we had some money, and my wife and the children are happy. Is there a chance that we will resume construction soon?"

"Ben, I have no money left for now, so I can't promise anything," Makula said.

Kasede decided to remain in Kasaka despite the fact that he had no more work there. He rarely returned home to see his family although he sent them money whenever Makula sent him some to "keep him going."

"Why did he start construction on the house when he knew he didn't have the money to complete it?" asked Senfuka, who was aware that Makula's house, when completed, would be far more beautiful than his. "Why build such a big house anyway? His family is small, just his father and mother—do they need all that space? I'm sick and tired of pretenders."

CHAPTER TWENTY
Toronto, Canada, January 2005

Makula often received e-mails from Uganda that reminded him that he was the source of hope for many. He even received a message from Bukirwa: "Hello, Makula. How are you? How is life over there abroad? Do you remember me? I am Bukirwa Phoebe. We were classmates in Kayunga Primary School. Now I am here in Kayunga but things are not going well. Can you send me two million shillings? I want to start a business selling charcoal. Please help. I will wait for your answer. Bye."

Makula wondered how Bukirwa had found his e-mail address. Yet he was happy to note how globalization had helped transform the world—a food vendor in Kayunga could, within seconds, communicate with an executive in Toronto. He told Pam about the e-mail, hoping that she too would find this fascinating. But Pam reacted angrily. "I hope you are not planning to send money to that woman," she said.

"I thought it would be good to send her at least a hundred bucks to help her charcoal business take off," Makula argued.

"You went to school with hundreds of people over the years, and I don't think all of them are well off. How much would it cost you if you gave a hundred bucks to each of them? Are you a billionaire or something?" Pam asked. So Makula abandoned the idea of sending money to Bukirwa.

The following day, Makula received a message from a Mr. Sebina. The name was familiar but he could not immediately place him. It did not take him long, though, to remember that Mr. Sebina had been one of his teachers at Kayunga Primary School. And then to recall Mr. Sebina's love of alcohol. Makula laughed, remembering the hot afternoons when Mr. Sebina would stand behind his students to peer over their shoulders, his breath reeking of alcohol, as they laboured to read in Luganda. Makula was glad to know that Mr. Sebina was still alive.

In his message, Mr. Sebina asked Makula to send him some money to buy iron sheets to roof a school that he was building near Kayunga. Makula replied, saying that he was very happy to hear from Mr. Sebina and asking for his telephone number.

Mr. Sebina responded, and when Makula called him, Mr. Sebina said that he was glad to know that "his son" lived overseas and told him that he was building a school whose focus would be on teaching Luganda.

"That's a very good idea, Mr. Sebina," said Makula, who strongly advocated the teaching of local Ugandan languages. "I am glad to know that you are still working hard for the development of our language."

"Thanks for the encouragement, my son," Mr. Sebina said. "I am glad to know that I have the support of a learned man. People here don't understand the value of our languages. When I first announced that I was planning to build a school to promote the teaching of Luganda, people laughed at me and called me crazy. But now that the building is going up, the naysayers have started to take an interest. Who knows, the school might someday grow to become a university."

"Great. Good idea. How much money would you need to roof that building?" Makula asked, knowing that he could not do much to help Mr. Sebina.

"Any amount, my son," Mr. Sebina replied. "Any amount would help. I won't ask for much because I know that you have a lot of other responsibilities over there in Canada." Makula promised to send two hundred dollars. Mr. Sebina was so grateful that Makula had to interrupt his unending thanks to end the call.

Makula called his friend Kasede and asked him, when he had time, to go to Kayunga to have a look at Mr. Sebina's school project. He gave him Mr. Sebina's phone number. "Call him to let him know you will be coming to see the school. Oh, actually, why don't I just send the money to you? You could take it to him and assess his needs at the same time. Afterward, we could get an organization to help," Makula said.

"Don't worry. I will go to inspect the school, then I will give you a report. You can send the money after that," Kasede replied. Kasede thought that it would be better if Makula spent that money on his house or even gave it to him as he was now broke, instead of giving it to a former teacher who would no longer even recognize him.

Kasede, who had been visiting his family in Kampala when Makula called, did not call Mr. Sebina to let him know that he would be coming to inspect the school. He convinced a bus driver whom he knew to take him to and from Kayunga, promising that "his brother" in Canada would pay the bus fare later that month. Kasede arrived in Kayunga at seven o'clock in the morning, and called Mr. Sebina to ask for directions to the "school."

Right after his visit to the school, Kasede "beeped" Makula and was disappointed when Makula did not call back right away. He "beeped" him two more times in the next half hour but there was no response. He waited for about fifteen minutes and then "beeped" him a third time, although this time Makula's phone did not ring. Instead he heard a recording that stated that the customer he was calling was not available. He then returned to Kampala where he arrived at noon.

In Toronto, Pam was awakened from a deep sleep and wondered why the phone, placed on her nightstand, was ringing incessantly. Makula never wanted to answer it early in the morning as the calls were almost always from his relatives, asking for money. When Pam saw the familiar international number, she disconnected the phone. Later that morning, Pam said, "Mak, can you please ask your people to stop 'beeping' us in the wee hours of the night?"

When Makula finally called Kasede at noon, Kasede told him that he had been disappointed to see what Makula's former teacher had referred to as a school. "In fact," he said, "the old man was drunk when I called him. He didn't seem to be ready to receive me, but when I insisted, he grudgingly agreed."

"In what condition was the building?" Makula asked.

"I don't think you can call it a building," Kasede said. "It's one incomplete room in a swampy area next to his house. Actually, while I was there, I overheard two young men talking about how the crazy man had brought another crazy one to see the 'school.' They were clearly referring to me."

"Is that so?" Makula asked.

"Yes. I felt humiliated. Don't waste your money. And by the way, don't forget to send me some. I still owe the fare for the trip to the bus driver, who is a friend of mine," Kasede said.

Makula felt pity for Mr. Sebina. After ending his conversation with Kasede, he drove to the nearest Western Union. And in the next half hour, he was telephoning Mr. Sebina to give him the details of the money transfer.

***

That weekend, the third annual conference of the African Society was held in Toronto, and about five hundred delegates came from various cities across Canada. In the afternoon, the delegates attended small discussion groups to explore various topics. Makula, Luku, and Wabudi found themselves in the same group, whose topic involved finding ways through which to facilitate the entry into the job market of professionals and other skilled workers of African origin in Canada.

Makula's group started by choosing a moderator, a position that Wabudi immediately volunteered for. Luku wanted to suggest that someone else take the role, but he did not want to have to explain why. When the deliberations began, no sooner had Wabudi introduced the topic than he abandoned it. Instead, he began a debate about whether the people in Africa were better off economically than those Africans who lived and worked in the diaspora—a favourite subject of his.

"I know many boys with whom I went to high school or university, they are now doing well as businessmen, lawyers, or doctors, and they own beautiful homes," Wabudi said. "Makula and Chris, you remember your friend Ahmed Jingo. He tried to work in the UK, but things did not work out. He moved to the US, but he was deported after only two years. That was a good thing for him because, as we speak, he is one of the richest businessmen in his hometown of Masaka."

Luku lost patience with Wabudi. "Nick, I have told you many times before that if you want to return home, nobody would stop you from doing so. Stop wasting our time. That's not the topic of our discussion."

"Chris, I know that it's not the topic of our discussion, but I agree with Nicholas. So why not take a few minutes to listen to his opinions? Maybe they will be eye-openers for us," said Bala, whose home-cleaning business was finally beginning to thrive in Vancouver and who hoped to start similar businesses in at least two cities in West Africa. The argument continued until one woman threatened to walk out if the moderator did not bring the debate back to the planned topic.

Makula stayed out of it. He sat quietly and thought about Mr. Sebina. He wondered what he looked like now. He believed Mr. Sebina's school was a good idea. He then imagined a big school that he could construct in Kasaka. He thought, "If I built that school, all the children of Kasaka would be educated there. They wouldn't need to go elsewhere to get an education."

Makula's daydreaming was interrupted by a man who had been quiet since joining the discussion group and who Makula had never met before. "Ladies and gentlemen, my name is Melchizedek," he said. "I moved here from Africa close to four months ago, but I am frustrated. Although I have been e-mailing a minimum of ten job applications per day since I arrived here in Toronto, I have not received even one offer for an interview."

"Listen, Melchizedek, that's why we are having this debate," Wabudi said, even though he had led the discussion away from its intended topic.

"I know, but I am a man with excellent qualifications and considerable experience. Why is it taking this long for me to get a job?" Melchizedek said, his voice rising with frustration.

"True, Melch. Can I call you Melch?" Luku asked.

"Call me whatever you like," Melchizedek said.

"You may have qualifications and experience, but given the current state of the world economy, there's no place you can go and expect to get your highly paid professional job in four months," Luku said. "You would need…"

"I don't think this discussion is going to help me in any way," Melchizedek said, before getting up and walking out of the room.

The other participants looked on in dismay as he closed the door behind him. The discussion continued but Wabudi was unable to control Luku and Bala, whose arguments seemed to be turning into personal attacks. The woman who had earlier threatened to walk out of the meeting said, "I would like to thank you, Mr. Wabudi, for having volunteered to lead us, but I don't think you can control the participants. It would be a shame if we came out of this meeting without anything to report at the plenary session. I'm therefore left with no choice but to take over from you," as she picked up her handbag and walked toward the front of the room.

The rest of the participants clapped. Wabudi grabbed his jacket and found another chair. "My name is Prima," she said, introducing herself. "I'm originally from Malawi, but now I work as a pharmacist in Calgary where I own and operate my own pharmacy. I would be glad to lead this discussion."

The participants clapped again. Under Prima's leadership, by the end of the hour, the participants had listed "five realistic and workable action items" intended to help professionals and other skilled workers of African origin in Canada enter the job market.

As they left the room to go to the plenary session, Makula was not surprised when the chairman and founder of the African Society, Pius Bitaro, who had come to the doorway to check on their progress, shook hands and exchanged pleasantries with everybody except him.

CHAPTER TWENTY-ONE
Toronto, Canada, May 2006

Makula's son Richard was looking forward to turning sixteen. He had already planned a big "birthday bash" to celebrate the occasion, complete with limousines, a well-decorated hall, and plenty of food. Three days before his birthday, he asked his mother, "Mum, can I move out when I am sixteen?"

"What do you mean?" Pam asked.

"Can I, like, get my own apartment when I'm sixteen?" he asked.

"Yes, you can," Pam replied, "but only on the condition that you don't take any of the things from here that we bought for you."

"Whatever," he said.

The following day, Makula hugged Richard, who had insisted that his parents not attend the party, then went to work. He did not know that Pam had purchased a big birthday gift for Richard. However, when Richard came downstairs on the morning of his birthday, he received the keys to a car, a new Infiniti G35. Not wanting to spoil his son's day, Makula waited until he returned home to confront Pam about her decision to buy a car for a sixteen-year-old. Pam argued that her son deserved it because his parents could afford it. Makula thought that this money could have been put to better use, such as finishing the family house in Kasaka or helping the many members of his family whom he knew needed his assistance. However, he did not bother even mentioning this to Pam—he knew that she would not listen.

Before long, Pam too regretted purchasing the car for Richard. Not only did she have to pay even more money to insure him as a young driver, but Richard also returned home late, especially on the weekends, when Pam would spend entire evenings worrying about his whereabouts. In addition, Dawn said that she too expected to get her own new car when she turned sixteen.

One evening, Makula asked Richard, who was rarely at home, why he never bothered to do any housework. "Do you think this home is a hotel where you eat, drink, sleep, then walk away?" Makula asked.

"I did some work. Like, I cleaned the house and stuff and loaded the dishwasher," Richard argued.

"Loading the dishwasher is not work," Makula said.

"Come on, Dad. It's work to me. What do you consider to be work?" Richard asked.

"Taking cattle to graze, fetching water…" Makula replied.

"But we don't have cattle. And the last time I checked, we had running water in the house," Richard said.

"I gave those as examples of what people elsewhere call work. You don't help shovel the snow in winter, or cut the grass in the summer…" Makula continued.

"At times it gets too cold or too hot out there, but I always want to help," Richard said, defending himself.

"Let me tell you, son. Doing chores at home is not 'helping.' You do so as your contribution to the family," Makula said.

Later that evening, Makula watched his son in disbelief. The young man was seated on the couch watching TV, surfing the Internet on his laptop, and texting on his cellphone, all at the same time. His Xbox was also within reach.

"Rick, you are so distracted. Why don't you do one thing, finish it, and then start the next?" Makula asked.

"Dad, I have a lot to do. That's why I have to multi-task," Richard explained.

"But do you give any of them the attention they deserve? For example, do you understand the discussion that's on the television right now?" Makula asked.

"Oh, yeah, I do. They are talking about the hardships in the world economy and stuff," Richard said.

"Well, good luck," Makula said dismissively.

The following morning, Richard washed the dishes and then mowed the lawn. Makula was glad to see that Richard seemed to have listened to him and was now doing some of the housework. However, as soon as he had finished cutting the grass, Richard showered. And like he did every Saturday since getting his car, he drove away to a fun-filled day with his buddies.

Richard sped along the street at seventy kilometres per hour, although he knew that the posted speed limit was fifty. He stopped at an intersection and waited for the light to turn green. Although the wait was only a minute long, it seemed like an eternity to Richard. "This is taking forever. Come on," he muttered to himself.

When the light turned green, he sped ahead but reduced his speed to that of the car ahead of him. When he got the chance, he passed the car and again sped up. He had driven less than two hundred metres when he saw a parked police cruiser mounted with a radar gun.

Richard slowed down, but it was too late. The cruiser pulled out, with its lights flashing and siren wailing, signalling to Richard to pull over. The cop came up to his window and asked to see his driver's license. When he saw it, the cop said, "Hey, buddy, don't you know that you can't drive alone with this licence?"

"No, I didn't know that," Richard said.

"Didn't you read the literature that came with the licence? Don't you remember what you were told when it was issued?" the cop asked, disbelieving.

Richard pleaded ignorance. "Yes, I did, but I guess I didn't see that or…"

"Can I see your insurance?" the cop asked.

Richard handed the insurance card to the cop, who saw that it was in order. He handed the card back to Richard and then told him he had been clocked by the radar gun as travelling at seventy-two kilometres per hour. Richard agreed that he had been going too fast. The cop issued him a ticket for speeding and for driving a car alone without the proper licence. He then told him to call a fully licensed driver to come to take the car away.

Makula grumbled to Pam as they drove to pick up Richard and his car. He told her it was becoming too expensive for the family to pay for gas and insurance for three cars, and that Richard's car was unnecessary. Pam did not respond.

When they spotted the cruiser and Richard's car, Pam pulled up behind her son. She opened her door to get out but the cop motioned to her to stay put. He came to her window and told her that she should never have allowed her son to drive a car alone before he was fully qualified to do so. She said that she was sorry. Before the cop left, he greeted Makula. And Makula recognized him—it was his former workmate from Fashoniz, Joe Chen.

"Hey, Joe. What's up, man?" he asked.

"Hey, Mak, how are you doing?" Chen said as Makula got out of the car to talk to him.

"Long time no see," Makula said, as he hugged Chen.

"I am glad to see you, Mak. How are you?" Chen asked.

"I'm good, man," Makula replied. "I didn't know that you had wanted to become a police officer. I thought you wanted to become an immigration officer."

"Oh, yeah, I wanted to become a police officer, and I worked my butt off to become one. Listen, Mak, we can't talk for long now because I'm working," Chen said, so Makula handed him his business card. "By the way, I'm getting married next month."

"Who is the lucky lady?" Makula asked.

"You know her," Chen said.

"I know her?" Makula asked.

"Yes," Chen told him. "I am getting married to Tamara."

"Tamara? I didn't know there was anything between you two," Makula said.

"I'm happy, man. She's awesome," Chen said.

"Yeah, she is a wonderful young woman," Makula agreed. "She was the best manager at the store. By the way, is she still working at Fashoniz?"

"Yeah, she is still working there, but now she is at the head office," Chen replied. "I'll give you a call, Mak, at the end of my shift."

***

Two years later, Prime Realty's business began to gradually decline. Sales of homes started going down, especially in the US. Makula and his workmates tried to think of new ways to boost sales, but the situation did not improve. Management therefore started laying off some workers, beginning with the company's US offices. The figures that came from the finance department were not good, but Andrew assured his teams that they would be able to weather the seemingly temporary storm. However, the news in the various media regarding the economy was not good, especially for real estate companies.

Prime Realty endured a second year of declining sales, and one Thursday morning, at their weekly meeting, Makula was surprised to see that none of the other staff members were in the boardroom. He sat quietly as he perused the disappointing sales figures. Andrew came in to the boardroom and said, "Mak, I hate to be the one to break this news to you, but as you can see from the figures, sales have dropped drastically. Unfortunately, it's been decided that the company must undergo restructuring. This has inevitably led to the phasing out of some positions, and, unfortunately, they have decided to eliminate yours. I'm so sorry about this."

"I do understand, Andrew, but what exactly does this mean for me?" Makula asked.

"You are basically losing your job," Andrew said. "You will be leaving at the end of the month. Ted resigned this morning; that's why he is not here. Jen is also looking for another job. She too has been let go. Like I said, it's tough for me to be the one to break this news to you but things are bad, as you can see."

When he returned home that evening, Makula did not have the courage to break the news to Pam. She, however, noticed that something was bothering him. She asked him why he looked so troubled. And he finally told her that he would soon be without a job.

Outside of the family, Makula told only his friend Ben Kasede about his job loss. Kasede had been waiting for three weeks for some money from Makula to open a small grocery store. When Makula called, Kasede picked up the phone after only the second ring. "Hello, Mak," Kasede said. "I am glad to hear your voice. How are you doing?"

"Ben, things are not all right," Makula told him.
"I'm out of work."

"What do you mean?" Kasede asked.

"I am unemployed; I lost my job," Makula repeated.

Kasede was so saddened by the news that he could no longer speak. "My friend," he said, sobbing, "call me back tomorrow after I've regained my composure."

Makula's life became difficult after he lost his position at Prime Realty. He received a substantial amount in severance pay but he had no other source of income. However, the bills did not stop coming, and within six months, most of the money that he had received had been spent. Makula woke up every morning hoping to get a phone call from Prime Realty asking him to come back to work, but as the days went by, it became clear to him that this might never happen.

"Don't lose hope," Pam told him supportively. "With your experience and contacts, you will get another job with comparable pay."

"Thanks for encouraging me, honey. I really need that now," he replied.

One Friday evening, as he had been doing each day since he lost his job, Makula spent hours on his computer searching for new positions he could apply for. He wondered why he had not been contacted for any interviews, especially as he had applied for over one hundred jobs. Pam suggested that he go to bed as she knew he was no longer sleeping well, but Makula could not leave the computer to stop his search.

When he finally fell asleep that night, Makula had a dream. In the dream, he was the president of a printing company, and he was in a boardroom with three executives, celebrating the successful completion of a big job that they had been working on.

In the middle of the dream, Makula's cellphone, on his nightstand, rang and woke him up. He was saddened to realize that he had only been dreaming of success. When he answered, a man that he had trouble identifying told him that he and Makula had been classmates at Kayunga Primary School. Makula remembered his name, but he could not remember exactly who the person was. The man said that he had been laid off from his job in Kampala and asked Makula to lend him ten thousand

US dollars to start a business. Makula politely told the caller that he was not in a position to help him, but the man insisted, saying that if Makula could not raise ten thousand dollars, he could do with five thousand. He said that he was sure that he would be able to pay back the whole amount within a year, and added that Makula was the only person who could help him. When he realized that the man was not willing to leave him alone, Makula hung up and switched off the phone.

The level of energy in Pam and Makula's household dropped. The family gym was no longer used. The treadmill now served as a place to dry clothes. Both Makula and Pam gained weight as they had given up exercising.

"Rick, I am sorry to tell you this, but we will have to sell your car," Pam told her son one morning.

"But why, Mum? I need the car," Richard answered.

"Yes, I know that you need the car, but you have no job," Pam said. "I don't have any money anymore to pay for your gas. You can always borrow my car whenever you need it."

"Okay, Mum. Do you have a buyer already?" Richard asked.

"No," Pam replied, "but there are some websites where used cars are advertised, and I think we will be able to sell yours quickly since it is still in good condition."

Pam was relieved that Richard had not argued with her about having to give up his car. She hoped that when he no longer had a car, he would return home earlier in the evenings, and she would no longer have to worry about where he was. She was wrong.

One afternoon as he lay on the couch, Makula was surprised to receive a phone call from his friend Paul Mugisha. Makula had not told him about losing his position as vice president of Prime Realty. Even so, Mugisha told Makula that, since he had lost his job in Toronto and could not find another one, he could return to Kampala. Mugisha was confident that he could use his contacts to find Makula an executive position there. "There are many people here who can help get you a job," Mugisha said. "Simeon Senfuka, for example, owns a number of successful businesses, and I'm sure that he would be very glad to let you manage one of them."

"Paul, I can never work for Senfuka. I don't think you know the history between Senfuka and me, but I could never work for that guy," Makula said.

"But I still think we could find you a job within a month if you came here," Mugisha insisted.

"That would be great, but I guess I would have to make the move alone. There's no way Pam would let the family move back to Uganda, at least not now," Makula told him.

"I know that, but that's the beautiful thing about our generation—families can now discuss their future. It is no longer up to the father to decide alone without consulting the family. Talk it over with Pam and the kids and try to find a compromise. I will wait for your response," Mugisha said.

"Paul, this may sound strange to you," Makula said, "but I don't feel that I would fit in Kampala either. I have a great urge to return to Kasaka. I really miss that place and…"

"What?" Mugisha exclaimed, interrupting. "Are you crazy? Do you know what you are talking about?"

"Yes, I know what I am talking about and that is honestly what I want to do right now," Makula said.

"How would you do it?" Mugisha asked. "If you can't convince Pam to return to Kampala where she grew up, how are you ever going to convince her to live in Kasaka?"

"That's the hard part," Makula admitted. "She wouldn't even entertain the idea. I guess she would start looking for a divorce lawyer if I decided to move to there."

"I would support her on that one. Are you crazy?" Mugisha asked.

"By the way, Paul, how did you find out that I had lost my job?" Makula asked.

"Ben called me as soon as you informed him about it," Mugisha confessed. "He was crying and complaining about his misfortune in life. He said that he knew he would be okay only if you were doing well. I met with him to console him, but I don't think it helped a lot. I am not as close to him as you are."

As soon as Makula had ended his conversation with Mugisha, the telephone rang once again. It was his mother.

"Makula, call me back now," Kabejja said.

Makula called his mother, but the telephone rang twice and then he heard the recorded message, "The customer you are calling cannot be reached at the moment. Please leave a message." He tried several times to reach her over the next couple of hours but got the same message. When she finally answered, Kabejja told Makula that the phone battery's charge had been too low to complete her call to him. She had then sent a child to Senfuka's house to charge the phone. However, the boy had taken a long time to return. "I don't know why he took so long because he rode a bicycle. You used to walk and returned promptly from such places, but not these children of today. You send him to the market to buy paraffin, and he will return after two hours without the paraffin, saying that he has forgotten to buy it. You then wonder why he went there in the first place. Toofa is having a lot of trouble with his children, and I don't know…"

"Mother," Makula said, "that's not the reason why you called. You seemed to have an urgent matter to talk to me about."

"Yes, it is about your sister, Manjeri," Kabejja said.

"Angela," Makula corrected her.

"No, Manjeri. She will always be Manjeri to me. That is the name I gave her," Kabejja said.

"Yes, Mother. What's wrong with Manjeri?" Makula asked as he glanced at a photograph hanging on the wall that had been taken of Manjeri on his wedding day.

"Manjeri has caused me a lot of misery, especially in my old age…" Kabejja began.

"You are not old, Mother," Makula said.

"I am not young, either. Manjeri has refused to get married, yet she is getting old. I am furious about this," Kabejja said.

"Mother, Manjeri is not old," Makula replied. "She's only twenty-eight."

"You think that she is not old. Do you know what I was doing when I was her age?" Kabejja asked.

"I think she should complete her course before she thinks about getting married," Makula said, as he debated whether to remind his mother that she herself had not had the chance to stay in school beyond the age of fourteen. Manjeri was fortunate to be studying economic policy planning at Makerere University, a course for which Makula was paying.

"That's the other problem," Kabejja continued. "Why didn't she get married instead of wasting your money by taking another course? You paid a lot of money when she first went to the university. Don't you realize you have spoiled that girl?"

"Mother," Makula explained, "she told me that she was unable to find a job with the qualifications she had, so she decided to go back to university to improve her chances."

"She is wasting time," Kabejja insisted. "She should get married and have children."

"Mother, there is nothing to stop her from doing so now if she found a good man to marry," Makula said.

"That is the other problem," Kabejja said. "The young man that she is dating is also studying at the university…"

"Is that the young man I met when we came to visit?" Makula asked.

"No, now she has another one. I don't know what happened to the one you met," Kabejja answered.

"So what's wrong with this one?" Makula asked.

"He is unemployed and lousy and…" Kabejja replied.

Makula interrupted her. "What do you mean when you say that he is lousy?"

"She showed me his picture. He is good-looking, but his hair is in braids. Can you imagine that? What kind of man braids his hair? What kind of parents would let their son braid his hair? To which office would he go to ask for a job?" Kabejja asked.

"Mother, it's true. You are old. Those things don't matter anymore. Young people are now free to choose who they want to marry. I am afraid to say that if that is the man she has chosen, you will not convince her to change her mind," Makula said.

"True, I wouldn't be able to convince her, and I know she inherited that stubbornness from me, but I would not let him set foot here. Actually," she confessed, "I had a better plan for her but she would not listen."

"What plan was that, Mother?" Makula asked.

"I wanted you to bring her to Canada to live with you. You could find her a job and, if possible, she could get a more sensible man to marry over there," Kabejja said.

"Mother, unfortunately I lost my job months ago," Makula told her. "I am still trying hard to find a new one, but so far, I haven't been lucky."

"That is so bad, Makula, but it is not the end of the world. Don't lose hope, my son. You have always triumphed in hard situations. I know you will triumph even in your present circumstances," Kabejja said sadly.

"The other thing, Mother, is that I don't think it would be a good idea for Father and you to have both your children so far away from you," Makula said.

"I agree with you, that wouldn't be good for us, but of what use is she here?" Kabejja asked. "She does not want to identify with us. She thinks that we are old-fashioned. We don't seem to fit in her world. The only person who seems to be close to her is Linda. I am very grateful for what Linda has done for Manjeri over the years. She almost raised her, but Manjeri should not forget that we are her parents. I hate the way she dresses, and I hate the way she talks. I hate the fact that she cannot hold a sensible conversation in Luganda. She speaks in a terrible way, switching from Luganda to English and back again. When she talks, she leaves you confused and only guessing what she means…"

"Mother, I've got to go. We shall talk later," Makula said.

"Where do you have to go? You are not working at the moment. Let's discuss your sister's future, because I am having sleepless nights about her," Kabejja said.

"Mother, why don't I talk to her, then get back to you in a week or so?" Makula suggested.

"That would be fine, but I think a week would be too long," Kabejja told him. "We need to find a quick solution to her situation. And I am not willing to change my position about her boyfriend. I don't want that man. Neither does your father. We will wait for your phone call."

"All right, Mother. I will call you soon. Have a good day," Makula said.

"Send my greetings to my daughter-in-law. Have the children learned any more Luganda?" Kabejja asked.

"Mother, I will call you soon. Have a good day," Makula replied.

The following morning, Makula called his sister to discuss their mother's concerns. "Hello, Mak," Angela said when she answered. "I am glad to hear your voice. I was actually thinking of sending you an e-mail. I need some money to buy some new clothes, and my rent is due."

"Manjeri, my dear…" Makula began.

"It's Angela," she insisted.

"Sorry, Angela. I don't have a job yet," Makula said. "I don't think I will be able to send you any money."

"Oh!" Angela said. "I didn't know that you were no longer working."

"That's not what I wanted to talk to you about," Makula said. "I called you to discuss Mother's concerns."

"Concerns? What kind of concerns?" Angela asked.

"You know she is now old. You know how anxious mothers get about their daughters when it comes to things like marriage, family…" Makula explained.

"Whatever," Angela said. "When she saw my boyfriend's photo, she was, like, I don't want that kind of man and stuff. Like, she wanted to tell me who to date. Then I was like, whatever. Suck it up, old girl."

"What do you mean?" Makula asked in a serious tone.

"Mum can't choose a boyfriend for me. It's none of her business. Can we, like, talk about something else?" Angela said.

Makula knew that he could not tell his sister how to live her life, but he also knew that his mother was waiting for an answer. "If you are serious about your boyfriend, why don't you get married?"

"Mak, when you call Mum, tell her to leave me alone," Angela said firmly. "I will get married when I am ready."

"Thanks for giving me a straightforward answer. That's exactly what I will tell her," Makula said.

CHAPTER TWENTY-TWO

Toronto, Canada, December 2011

When she realized that Makula had distanced himself from his friends because he thought he no longer belonged in their group, Pam asked Craig Lewis to help. Mr. Lewis, who rarely saw Makula, was surprised to learn that Makula had been without a "proper" job for two years without telling him.

Mr. Lewis scolded Makula. "I thought I told you that you need to talk to people, at least to those you trust, if you are to solve any problem at all. Why didn't you tell me that you had lost your job?"

"I'm sorry that I didn't let you know," Makula apologized. "I think I have simply been too preoccupied with my circumstances. But I do need your help."

"So, my friend, where would you like to begin? What's the situation that you need help with?" Mr. Lewis asked.

"I have not regained my inner peace since I lost my job. I feel lost," Makula said.

"What are you doing currently?" Mr. Lewis asked.

"I returned to a sales associate position," Makula told him. "I work in an electronics store, but the job pays so little that I don't feel gainfully employed."

"Have you tried to look for another job that would be more financially rewarding?" Mr. Lewis asked.

"Yes. I don't know how many résumés I e-mail out each week," Makula replied.

"Losing a job is bad, for sure. However, it's not the real problem. The real problem is what you do about it and what kind of attitude you develop toward it. I have noticed that you seem to have lost all hope because you defined yourself by your job. But guess what? Although our jobs are important, they are not the most important thing in our lives. Other things are far more precious— like your wonderful family who cares for you and loves you. You really do have a lot to be thankful for," Mr. Lewis said.

"That's true," Makula replied. "But things were very different when I could adequately provide for my family, when I could afford the home where we live, and when life made sense. Right now, all that is gone."

"You have just raised an important issue," Mr. Lewis said. "What are you doing in a home that you can no longer afford?"

"Well, we thought that the situation might turn around, but I guess we were wrong. Right now we are in a huge financial mess, and I don't know how to get us out of it," Makula said.

"I have a friend who is a financial adviser," Mr. Lewis told him. "His name is Pietro Monterissi. I will ask him to advise you regarding your financial situation if you would like…"

"Oh, yes, great! We would love that! I think we need professional help in that area. Things have gotten out of control," Makula said. He knew Pietro Monterissi from his TV program, *Take Care of the Cents.*

"For now I will talk to you and your wife to see what we can do to ease the situation. Believe me, there's hope; there's always hope. You'll get back on your feet again," Mr. Lewis said encouragingly.

"I would also like you to talk to our son Richard," Makula said. "I think that, young as he is, his life is already a mess. I have tried to talk some sense into him but nothing seems to work."

"That's all right. I'll set up an appointment with him. What are your concerns about him?" Mr. Lewis asked.

"We paid his college tuition in full, including his boarding costs, but I don't think he completed his course," Makula said. "When I ask him about his diploma, all he tells me is that he still has some courses to complete before he graduates. I have heard that same story for six months now."

"What did he study at college?" Mr. Lewis asked.

"Something to do with film production or directing. I'm not sure. I wanted him to take a course in law, engineering, or medicine at university, but he disappointed me," Makula said.

"Yeah, I get it. And what did Richard want to do?"
Mr. Lewis asked.

"Well," Makula replied, "he studied what he wanted."

"That's right, and that is good. It would not have been a good idea for him to study what you wanted him to. Kids nowadays make their own choices," Mr. Lewis said. "Can we focus on your case for now?"

"Yes, please," Makula replied.

"Makula, you know what? I'm partly to blame for your situation," Mr. Lewis said.

"What do you mean?" Makula asked.

"When you got the job as vice president at Prime Realty, I didn't follow up with you," Mr. Lewis explained. "So when you got that position, you thought you had attained your ultimate goal. It therefore became a comfort zone and you remained there. But remember, when you start something and it works out fine, at that very point, it's obsolete."

"Wow," Makula said.

"Unfortunately," Mr. Lewis said, "you focused all of your energy on your job and forgot the things that mattered most."

Mr. Lewis advised Makula to continue working in the electronics store and promised to talk with some of his friends who could help. "But I must say," he added, "when you are no longer young, it gets harder to get a new job."

***

That month, the African Society was in the news due to a scandal involving its founder. Its members and the public were shocked to learn that the chairman and founder of the Society, Pius Bitaro, had been arrested for assaulting his daughter. The tabloid that broke the story reported that the eighteen-year-old girl had called police after her father had slapped her twice in their luxury home. The tabloid claimed to have interviewed the girl and reported that when the father had asked his daughter for a glass of water, she had dangled it close to his nose and let go of it before he had "grabbed it." The water had spilled all over his face, prompting the furious father to slap her.

"I'm not surprised that the police were called to Bitaro's home. I think that man has serious anger issues that he needs help to resolve," Makula said during his first "boys' night out" since losing his job.

"He is stupid," Luku said. "He has always been so. I don't know why they didn't lock him up for such unbecoming behaviour."

The following morning, the secretary of the African Society posted a topic for discussion on the Society's online forum: "Following the recent arrest of our chairman, what are your views on how we should raise our children to become respectful people without trampling on their rights?"

After lunch, Makula, who contributed regularly to the forum, found several interesting posts:

"Asif2k7—I found that story quite ridiculous. As a lawyer, Mr. Bitaro should know better. Who on earth assaults their daughter simply because of a little disrespectful act?"

"GrammarBoy—This was really an unfortunate event and I don't want any of you uninformed posters to misunderstand me. I don't condone Mr. Bitaro's actions. However, children must suffer the consequences of their actions and they should be taught this at an early age. Just recently my fifteen-year-old son called me 'backward' simply because I was eating millet. He said, "Dad, you are so backward. How can you eat that kind of stuff?' Like Mr. Bitaro, I wanted to slap him, but I did not. However, I was really hurt. When my son called me 'backward,' I realized that there were two classes of people in our family. On the one hand, us—the backward parents who pay for everything, like housing, hydro, food, cellphones, transportation, and all those other things. Then, on the other hand, the kids—the sophisticated know-it-all types. This is so hurtful."

When Richard went into the family room to watch TV, he saw that his father was not there and looked at what web page he had accessed on his still-open laptop. He was shocked to see that his father had been reading posts to the forum of the African Society and that the topic was the arrest of Pius Bitaro for having assaulted his daughter. His heart sank. He was secretly dating Bitaro's daughter and he was terrified that his father, who disliked Bitaro, might find out. He sat down and began to read the various posts.

One particular post, which seemed to have all the facts, almost made him faint. It read: "All of you uninformed posters should note that the story of the alleged disrespect by his daughter is simply a cover-up. Mr. Bitaro assaulted that girl simply because she had gone out with a certain young man against his will. The tabloids have more information, and they are likely to release it over the next few days."

As he scrolled down, Richard heard his father's footsteps on the stairs and quickly stood up. "Dad, were you still using your computer?" he asked nervously. "You left it on."

"No, I'm done," Makula answered. Richard put on his earphones and went out to the backyard, still trembling, while Makula shut down his laptop and closed it.

Soon after, the doorbell rang, and Makula went to answer it. A young woman he did not know asked to see Richard. Makula showed her into the living room and then called Richard inside. When Richard saw the young woman, he said nervously, "What are you doing here?" Richard wished that his father would go away and let them talk in private, but Makula did not budge.

"Aren't you going to introduce your visitor?" asked Makula, who was curious to note that she looked somewhat familiar.

"My name is Peace," the young woman told him.

"Oh, I see," Makula said. "Are you a Ugandan?"

"I guess I am. My dad is a Ugandan," she replied.

"What's your father's name?" Makula asked.

"He's Pius Bitaro," she said.

"This must be the newsmaker," Makula thought as he headed upstairs.

As soon as Makula was gone, Richard led his visitor outside. "You shouldn't have come here so soon after the incident. It seems that the newspapers know the real reason why your dad slapped you, and they might be looking for still more news. I read about it on the forum of the so-called African Society, and my dad knows about it too," Richard said.

"Whatever," Peace answered. "I just wanted to be with you."

"Let's take it slow for now," Richard said. "I know your dad has had a grudge against my dad since their school days in Uganda."

"Whatever," Peace answered.

In their bedroom, Makula told Pam that he was shocked to learn that Richard knew Pius Bitaro's daughter.

"Who is Pius Bitaro's daughter?" Pam asked.

"Her name is Peace," Makula replied. "She is downstairs right now talking with Richard."

"Oh, I've met Peace," Pam said. "She is the best behaved of all Rick's girlfriends. They only started dating recently."

"So you have met her before?" Makula asked.

"Yes," Pam answered. "But I didn't know she was Bitaro's daughter. Actually I've never asked her last name, and Rick never told me that she is a Ugandan."

"Her resemblance to her dad is so striking…" Makula said.

"I've heard a lot about Bitaro, but I've never met him," Pam added.

"What? I wasn't aware that you had never met Bitaro," Makula said. "Anyway, Bitaro is so anti-social that we never met his kids. Isn't that a shame? And I think her dad slapped her for going out with Rick, not for being disrespectful."

"What?" Pam exclaimed. "Why do you think so?"

"Read the postings on the forum of the African Society. One of these days, that boy will give me a heart attack," Makula said, as he lay down on the bed.

When he returned home late that night, Richard found his mother waiting up for him. As soon as he came in, she said, "Rick, it would be very unfortunate if you didn't finish college when you have all the facilities that you need to do so."

"I am trying to finish, Mum. Give me some time," he replied.

"Your father is hurting," Pam told him. "You know that he

worked hard and succeeded despite the poverty and hardships he faced. And here is his son, to whom he has provided everything, failing to have a career in life."

"Come on, Mum," Richard said. "I am only twenty-one."

"You are right, Rick," Pam said. "At twenty-one many of our generation didn't know what we wanted to do with our lives, but I think our parents could see that we had a clear sense of direction…"

Richard put on his earphones. "Don't you do that when I'm talking to you! Who do you think I am?" Pam yelled.

"Mum, I am working hard on my script," Richard told her. "Actually, my script is ready, and the production crew is ready. All we need now is one hundred grand to produce the movie."

"But do you have a plan B just in case this doesn't work out?" Pam asked.

"I'm sure it will work out," Richard said. "All we need now is the money."

"How sure are you that it will work out?" Pam asked.

"I'm hoping that Dad will find the money," Richard said. "I'm also hoping to try out for some minor league soccer teams in Europe. I could go to Spain, Germany, Italy, or some other place. I haven't run out of options. Uncle Patrick is ready to take me in in England."

"You think you have not run out of options? To me you don't seem to have any real ones," Pam said bitterly.

"Come on, Mum," Richard said. "I hate negative energy."

With sarcasm, Pam said, "Good luck with your options."

"Whatever," Richard said, walking away.

***

On Pam's insistence, Richard met with Craig Lewis the following month. When they met, Mr. Lewis asked, "Richard, how are you doing?"

"I'm good, I guess," Richard replied.

"You are not sure?"

"I'm fine."

"Good. Your father asked me to talk to you. How do you feel about that?"

"I guess it's a good idea because, right now, honestly, I feel lost."

"And why is that, if I may ask?"

"I feel like I am an underachiever, and honestly, my parents are disappointed in me. I would like to do better. I would like them to feel proud of me."

"Good. Do you know your strengths?"

"Yes, I know some of them."

"Can you name a few of them?"

"Yes, like…"

"What are you passionate about?"

"Pardon?"

"I mean, what would you like to do with your talents?"

"I would like to play professional soccer or become an actor."

"Let's take acting, for example. What steps have you taken to ensure success in your future career?"

"I took the course at college."

"And that's it?"

"Yes. For now."

"You know what, Richard? You are a tall, charming young man. Actually, research has shown that you tall guys have a better shot at opportunities in life than those of us who are shorter. I want you to use that charm not to woo girls but to exploit the opportunities that come your way," Mr. Lewis said.

"Wow," Richard replied.

"Listen, Richard. You've probably heard this before, but let me tell you, it's only in the dictionary that 'success' comes before 'work.' I would like you to get off your butt and start working for success. If you want to become an actor, then get in touch with some successful actors, and look for ways to network," Mr. Lewis told him.

"But how would I do that?" Richard asked.

"Have you ever been to the Toronto International Film Festival?" Mr. Lewis asked.

"No," Richard replied.

"Goodness. And you are aspiring to become an actor? Go there, try to meet the directors, get the celebs to sign autographs, and while they are it, tell them how much you admire them and that you too would like to become an actor. Who knows, your breakthrough could come that way. I'm just stretching my imagination here, but you never know," Mr. Lewis said.

"I think I would like to go away to Europe to try out for some soccer clubs, or volunteer in Africa," Richard said.

"Great. Volunteering in Africa would give you an opportunity to try to fit into your father's shoes. It would give you a glimpse of what he may have gone through and, who knows, that might give you the spark that you need to jumpstart your career," Mr. Lewis replied.

"I think I can do that," Richard said.

"Great," Mr. Lewis said. "I will give you a moment to write down a concrete action plan that I will present to your father when we meet next."

When Mr. Lewis returned, he asked to see Richard's action plan. "You know what, Mr. Lewis?" Richard said. "I've decided to go to Africa to do volunteer work for six months."

"Great! Good for you!" Mr. Lewis said, as he "high-fived" Richard.

***

Makula was afraid to contact the financial advisor Pietro Monterissi. He was so ashamed of his financial situation that he did not want anyone else to look at the actual figures. One afternoon, though, as he was taking a nap on the couch, Makula's cellphone rang.

"Hello, Makula?" a man inquired.

"Yes, speaking," Makula replied.

"Hello," the man said. "My name is Pietro Monterissi. Craig Lewis told me that you needed my help with your finances."

"Yes, that is true. Would you be willing to help?" Makula asked.

"Yes, that's why I called," Mr. Monterissi replied. "Listen, this is what I would like you to do. Gather all your bills, your bank statements, and your family budget. You have a budget, right? Bring those with you to my office. I would like to meet with you and your wife."

When Makula and Pam went to his office for the first session, the financial adviser was very frank in his analysis of the family's finances and was especially tough on Pam. "Pamela, there are more credit cards in your purse than there are letters in your last name and that's sad," he said.

"It's true that things got out of my control," she replied.

"I'll advise you what to do in the final analysis, but for now, I recommend that you get rid of all your credit cards while we look for ways to tackle your debt," Mr. Monterissi said.

The following month, there was tension during the second consultation session when Mr. Monterissi asked Makula how his situation had changed so drastically in only two years.

"I think my wife spent far more than we were making and…" Makula began.

"Excuse me," Pam retorted. "How much money did you send to your friends and relatives back home? Do you even have a clue how much it was?"

The couple argued for a minute or two until Mr. Monterissi intervened. "Our goal is not to determine who did what—it is to show you the precarious situation you are in. You are sinking in debt, and we've got to find ways of digging you out of there pretty quickly. I'm sorry to say that your situation is so bad that I don't know whether we can salvage it."

The couple remained silent, but it was obvious that Pam was boiling with anger.

"Makula, you are only working part-time at the electronics store. And Pamela, you are not making much from your job at the daycare centre. Since you don't have enough income, how are you paying for your basic needs?" Mr. Monterissi asked.

"My parents send us the rent from our house in Uganda. They also help us out once in a while. My brother also sends me money every two months," Pam answered.

"Oh, I see," Mr. Monterissi said. "You are a spoiled princess, Pamela. But guess what? You are destroying your inheritance.

What will happen if your parents can't bankroll you anymore?"

The couple remained silent.

"My only hope for you was to try to tap into the equity in your home," Mr. Monterissi continued. "But, alas, when I cross-checked, I found out that you have already refinanced your mortgage twice. You have acted as if your home is a bank machine. You take out money whenever you want to finance your lavish lifestyle."

Pam lost her temper and got up to leave the room. Makula stopped her and asked her to sit down. She sat back down but said nothing for the rest of the session.

At their next meeting, Mr. Monterissi asked them to watch two episodes of *Take Care of the Cents* to learn more about how other couples had dealt with similar situations, and to jot down what lessons they had learned.

During the final session, two weeks later, the mood was calmer. Makula and Pam were prepared to hear whatever solutions Mr. Monterissi proposed. He gave them a long list of things they needed to do in the short-, medium-, and long-term. "You need to carry out the measures in the short-term category ASAP, beginning today," he told them. "As for the long-term measures, the timeline will be up to you to determine."

The proposals looked workable on paper, and Makula remarked that they were "user-friendly." Both Pam and Mr. Monterissi laughed. Makula and Pam felt a little better when they realized that there was hope. However, Mr. Monterissi concluded the consultation on a sombre note, warning them that they might be facing foreclosure on their home. This saddened them, especially Pam, who did not want to lose her "model home."

***

In Kasaka, a group of villagers, mainly Makula's relatives, met on the verandah of Makula's incomplete house to discuss how to move forward. They were divided into three groups.

One group, led by Lukka and Luyima, thought that since Makula had failed to lead them, now was the time to contact Senfuka. All they needed was to go to him to get jobs.

The second group, which included Makko and Toofa, thought that Makula might have been experiencing temporary problems and wanted to give him time.

The third group was led by Othieno, who thought that Makula had a life of his own to lead and did not owe the people of Kasaka anything. "We are fortunate that Makula showed us the way," he said. "Now that we know that we can set up some income-generating activities in this village, I think it's time we organized ourselves and got to work."

"That's right, Othieno. We can start our own businesses, work for ourselves, and take care of our own business. We don't need to go to Senfuka," Makko said.

Senjo, one of Makula's former partners in the farming venture, asked angrily, "Makko, what do you know about business?"

"Senjo," Makko replied, "don't ask me what I know about business. When Makula helped you by finding you something to do, what did you do to thank him for his gesture? You stole his matooke. Shame on you."

Furious, Senjo got up and pushed Makko. Makko hit him hard on the cheek with his fist and a fierce exchange of blows ensued. Othieno broke up the fight and criticized the two men for behaving so badly in front of the children who were watching, horrified.

As he brokered peace between Makko and Senjo, Othieno felt a bit of shame. Years earlier, he had told Makko that Senjo had been the person who had stolen the matooke. He had thought that Makko would keep this a secret, but now Makko had told everyone. Othieno knew that Makula himself had never told a soul; he could see it from the expression on Luyima's face. Despite the fact that he had been a partner in the business, Luyima had not known that it was Senjo who had stolen their produce.

Kabejja, who had been in the outdoor kitchen when all this took place, came over to the verandah when she heard the commotion. Makko and Senjo were still hurling insults at each other, but when they saw her, they stopped yelling and acted as if nothing had happened. It was obvious, however, that there had been a fight, as Makko's lower lip was bleeding. "What's going on?" she demanded of them. "Is this about Makula? Why don't you people stop relying on handouts from Makula and start planning for your future and that of your children? I don't know whether you are aware of it, but for your information, Makula can no longer send money to you. I think it would be wiser for you to take control of your own lives now."

"Thanks for saying that," Othieno said, lighting a cigarette.

"That's the same thing I've been telling these young men. They are setting a very bad example for the children."

"If you don't take control of your lives now and stop thinking that Makula will take care of you, we will see more fights; this is only the beginning," Kabejja warned them before returning to her kitchen.

The next day, Lukka told Makula about Makko and Senjo's fighting. After his conversation with Makula, Lukka told Luyima that he had been shocked by Makula's reaction to the news. "How did he react?" Luyima asked.

"He was shocked by the fact that they had fought, but he seemed happy to know that people were waiting for him to give them money or jobs. He seems obsessed with this village," Lukka answered.

"Is that news to you?" Luyima asked. "I have known that for years."

Othieno organized a small group who still thought that they could help to develop the village. They cleared the bush from the area where the market had once stood. They planned to erect houses or cottages of varying sizes for rent to tourists.

"If we worked hard, Makula could find us some financial assistance for this project," Othieno said.

When Senfuka heard of Othieno's plans, he said, "Why are they wasting their time? What tourist will come to that little village? What is there to see anyway?"

When Makula called to talk to his father, Othieno, who was a frequent visitor to Filipo's home, told him about the proposed project. Othieno said that they were planning to build a tourist resort in Kasaka, and that they would need Makula's assistance to fund the project. "Someone told Senfuka about our project and, as usual, he commented negatively about it, saying that no tourist would ever come to Kasaka," Othieno said.

"That's interesting," Makula said. "Is my father involved in this project?"

"Yes, he is involved," Othieno replied.

"I thought he was, because I can see his ideas written all over it. But I agree with Senfuka; no tourist would ever come to Kasaka. What is there to see? Do you think people will spend their money to come to look at landscapes for days on end? I don't think so. Perhaps you could build a game park and stock it with wild animals, but I think that would be too costly. Why don't you come up with some other ideas?" Makula asked.

Convinced that Senfuka would hire them, Lukka and Luyima decided to go to his house in Nanziba. "I will take whatever job there is because, right now, I have no choice," Luyima said.

"You are right," Lukka replied as the two rode along on their bicycles. "We will take whatever jobs are available. Sometimes I wonder why I left Kampala to return to Kasaka. Many of the guys I used to work with at the market are now rich. Some have as many as two or three houses. I don't know why I ever listened to Makula. If I had not, I would be a rich man now." Luyima almost laughed aloud at Lukka's comments.

When they arrived at Senfuka's house, which was surrounded by a high brick fence, they knocked the padlock hard against the metallic gate. They could see the gatekeeper in the front yard, but he seemed to be ignoring them. They waited for about five minutes until Senfuka's younger brother heard the noise. When he came to the gate, he showed them the bell they were to ring the next time they came and apologized for their having had to wait to be let in. He then asked the gatekeeper to open the gate for them. They saw Senfuka's SUV, a new Toyota Lexus, parked in front of his huge, beautiful house. They could hear voices coming from inside the house and they knew right away that many people had come to meet with "the boss."

Senfuka's brother took them to a room at the back of the house. They emerged three hours later, thanked the gatekeeper, then rode their bicycles back to Kasaka.

When they arrived, Kabejja was waiting for them. She was eager to find out what had happened because she strongly believed that the two families needed to reconcile. "So, were you able to talk to Senfuka?" she asked Lukka.

"Yes, Aunt, we talked with Senfuka," Lukka answered.

"Was he nice to you? How did the discussions go?" Kabejja asked.

"He was a little aloof, but I think, all in all, the discussions went well. I think there is hope that he will hire some of us," Lukka said.

"Who is hiring whom?" Luyima said in a surprised tone.

"Senfuka will hire us," Lukka said, winking at Luyima to let him know that he was not to tell Kabejja the whole story.

Luyima would not let Lukka lie to Kabejja. He picked up a little stool and sat right in front of the outdoor kitchen where she was preparing dinner. "Kabejja," he began, "the truth is that Senfuka was very hostile to us. When we arrived, he came and greeted us curtly, then asked a woman to serve us lunch. It was a very delicious meal that we enjoyed a lot…"

"That was kind of him," Kabejja said. "At least he respected our culture. One should never let one's visitors go without eating."

"After lunch, we sat there for two hours without seeing anybody," Luyima continued. "Finally, Senfuka came and spoke to us from the staircase in a somewhat stubborn manner. He asked who we were, as if he did not know us, and before we could respond, he asked what we wanted. Then he walked away before we could tell him. I couldn't believe it. That man is stupid. I will never go to his house again."

CHAPTER TWENTY-THREE
Toronto, Canada, January 2012

"Dad, I've thought of doing something that I know you'll like," Richard said to Makula one Sunday afternoon as they relaxed in the family room.

"And what's that, Rick?" Makula asked.

"I would like to do some volunteer work in Africa," Richard replied.

"Nice idea, Rick. That would be great. Do you know what kind of work you would like to do and where you would like to go in Africa?" Makula asked.

"I thought of working on a small project, like helping to build a classroom block at your former elementary school," Richard told him.

"I like what I'm hearing," Makula said.

Later that afternoon, when Richard told his mother about his plan, Pam said, "That's out of the question dear. You can't go to that place. I don't know whether you fully understand what you would be getting yourself into."

"No, don't discourage him," Makula said. "Why shouldn't he do it? Millions of people do similar volunteer work in Africa and elsewhere."

"Listen, honey. You and I know what Rick can do and what he can't. I don't think volunteering in Kasaka is one of the things he can do—even for one day," Pam said.

When they both finally realized that Richard was determined to do volunteer work in Kasaka, Makula and Pam gave him their full support. Makula gave him advice on how to deal with the people—on what to say, and what not to say. Pam took him to a clinic for his necessary vaccinations and cautioned him against staying out late at night.

Richard boarded the plane in tears upon leaving his parents. Makula's tears, though, were those of joy—his son "was beginning to wake up." Pam's tears were those of uncertainty about the wisdom of her son's adventure. At Entebbe airport in Uganda, Richard was surprised to see his grandparents, Pam's parents, waiting for him. He was happy to see them but told them that he had not expected them to meet him; he had planned to make his way to Kasaka on his own. Dr. Sempaka said that, because of the jetlag, it would be best if Richard stayed with them in Kampala for at least two days before going to Kasaka. Richard agreed. While in Kampala, he purchased a new bicycle, as his father had suggested, to allow him to get around in the village. And two days later, Dr. Sempaka had his driver take him to Kasaka where he would stay with his grandparents, Filipo and Kabejja.

Richard inadvertently changed the relationship between the two villages of Kasaka and Nanziba soon after his arrival. He and a group of volunteers organized by Othieno were preparing to dig the foundation for a new block of classrooms at Kasaka Primary School. As they began to measure out the area where the building was to be erected, Othieno remarked that the spot was uneven. Richard asked if they could perhaps get a tractor to level the ground. The headmaster, Mr. Sekitto, told him that Senfuka owned a tractor but that everyone in the area was afraid to approach him, especially to ask such a favour.

"Just give me the address—I'll go talk to him," Richard said.

Othieno, his interpreter, pointed to the beautiful house on top of a hill and said, "You see that house? That's where you can get a tractor. The owner of that house is a rich man, but that is his second home. He may not be there now because he lives in Kampala. However, he knows your father." Although a decade had passed, Richard vaguely remembered his father pointing out this house when the family had visited Kasaka.

"Great. I'll go talk to him if he's there. See you in a bit," Richard said, and then jumped on his bicycle and pedalled away.

"Does that young man think that just because he speaks good English he will be able to convince Senfuka to give him his tractor?" Lukka asked.

Richard returned about an hour later and met with Othieno. He told him that he had met with Senfuka who had agreed to let him use his tractor to level the ground for the foundation. Othieno could hardly believe it but he did not share his initial doubts with Richard.

The next day, the volunteers looked on as Senfuka's tractor, driven by one of his employees, arrived at the site. And from then on, Richard borrowed various necessary items from Senfuka for use at the construction site. Even more startling to the local volunteers was seeing Senfuka himself arrive one morning in one of his trucks to deliver a donation of ten bags of cement and two sacks of rice. And then Senfuka, who never talked to anyone in Kasaka, stood by the construction site and talked with Richard for nearly an hour.

When told about Senfuka's generosity, Kabejja was pleased. "This is what we needed all along," she said. "It took someone from the younger generation to bring these families together."

In the weeks that followed, Senfuka himself was surprised by the actions of Rachel, his eighteen-year-old daughter. Rachel, who never wanted to leave Kampala to stay at their home in Nanziba, was suddenly eager to join the group of volunteers who were constructing the block of classrooms in Kasaka. Senfuka didn't know that she had met Richard.

***

After obtaining her master's degree in economic policy planning at Makerere University, Angela accepted a part-time position at Fiducia, James Kabenge's bank.

During her first week of work, Makula called Angela. They talked about the course she had just completed, and Angela thanked him for having paid for it. She told Makula that Richard and the other volunteers had done a good job on the construction of the classroom block at Kasaka Primary School. Angela also mentioned her part-time job at Fiducia.

"Fiducia? Isn't that James Kabenge's bank?" Makula asked.

"Yes," Angela replied.

"Does he work there?" Makula asked.

"Yes, he does. He is the managing director," Angela said.

"If you get a chance to meet him, you can tell him that you are related to him," Makula said.

"Related to him?" Angela said, laughing. "How am I, like, related to him?"

"He is our first cousin once removed. Uncle Lameka told me that when I visited Kasaka, but I have never mentioned it to anyone," Makula said.

"Why not?" Angela asked.

"I didn't think it was a big deal," Makula answered.

"But are you, like, sure that he is our relative?" Angela asked.

"Yes, Mr. Kabenge's father, Laban, was our grandfather Makula's only brother," Makula said.

"Interesting. Yeah, no problem. If I get a chance to meet him, I will tell him that we are, like, kind of related," Angela said.

Makula laughed at her "kind of related" comment before he ended the call.

Angela did not have to wait long to meet Mr. James Kabenge. The following day, her supervisor, Maria, the head of the bank's international division, said that she wanted to introduce her to Mr. Kabenge and asked Angela to follow her to his office.

Angela hesitated because she was a little afraid of being introduced to such an important man. Angela said, "I was just planning to head over to the university. I have some books to return to the library."

"It won't take long, Angela," Maria said. "I know it may be slightly intimidating to meet the managing director, but he is a very kind man. Besides, it's always good to meet people like him; he might offer to serve as a professional reference for you."

When they knocked on his office door, Mr. Kabenge ushered them in but told them that he would have to leave soon to attend to an urgent matter. "This won't take long, Mr. Kabenge. I just wanted to introduce Angela to you. She is assisting me on a part-time basis. This is her third day," the supervisor said.

After she had introduced Angela to Mr. Kabenge, Maria excused herself. She knew that, despite Mr. Kabenge's saying that he had to attend to an urgent matter, the conversation with Angela was likely to be long. He enjoyed conversation and was known for assisting young professionals.

"So, Angela, tell me more about yourself," Mr. Kabenge said.

"My name is Angela Musoke. I have just completed my masters in economic policy planning." Angela paused and then said, "I was born in Kasaka in Bugerere County. You and my father are actually first cousins."

"I beg your pardon?" Mr. Kabenge said.

"My brother told me that you are Filipo Musoke's cousin. He is my father and lives in Kasaka," Angela said.

"Is that so?" Mr. Kabenge said in wonder. "I know that my father had a brother, the late Makula Musoke. So your father is his son? Tell me more."

"My father is Filipo Musoke and my mother is Kabejja," Angela said. "I also have a brother, my elder brother, Makula, who lives in Toronto."

"Oh, that is great. Your brother Makula was named after my uncle? I am so glad to have met you, Angela," Mr. Kabenge said.

Knowing that Mr. Kabenge was Dr. Sempaka's friend, Angela added, "My brother is married to Dr. Sempaka's daughter."

"Yes, I know that Pamela lives in Toronto. What I didn't know was that she is married to a relative of mine," Mr. Kabenge said.

"Yes, Pam is my sister-in-law," Angela said.

"Oh, this is a small world. Listen, Angela, I have to leave now. Why don't you drop by again sometime next week to tell me more? I will be meeting with Dr. Sempaka this evening, and I will mention our conversation to him," Mr. Kabenge said as he and Angela left his office.

That evening, while James Kabenge visited with his friend Dr. Sempaka, Richard, who was also visiting, came into the living room to greet his grandfather's friend. Dr. Sempaka introduced the young man to James Kabenge as his grandson. Mr. Kabenge looked closely at the young man and told him that he was glad to meet him.

When Richard had left the room, Mr. Kabenge said, "I met a young woman this afternoon in my office, an assistant who told me that she is Pamela's sister-in-law."

"Are you referring to Angela?" Dr. Sempaka asked.

"Yes, Angela. What is even more interesting is that she told me she is related to me," Mr. Kabenge replied.

"How so?" Dr. Sempaka asked.

"She told me that her and Makula's grandfather, who, by the way, was also named Makula, was my father Laban's brother," Mr. Kabenge said.

"Are you sure about it?" Dr. Sempaka asked.

"I think so. My uncle moved with his family from Mukono when I was still very young. My father lost contact with him because, as I was told, the two brothers never got along well. It is said that my uncle was a very difficult man. But I must confess that I feel I have failed in my responsibility as Laban's first-born son to reconcile our two families," Mr. Kabenge said. "What struck me just now is how much this young man, your grandson Richard, like my son Tom, resembles my late father."

"Thank you for solving my own puzzlement. I too noticed that my grandson resembles your son Tom. I was therefore perturbed, knowing the history between Tom and my daughter," Dr. Sempaka said, chuckling.

"I am glad that today I have found this part of my family," Mr. Kabenge said. "I would like to meet my relatives in Kasaka."

"I have never visited Makula's family, but Richard could take you to meet them. He has been living in Kasaka for the last three months," Dr. Sempaka told him.

Doctor Sempaka called Richard back into the living room. After once again greeting his grandfather's visitor, Richard was surprised at how intently Mr. Kabenge looked at him and by the bear hug he received. His grandfather then told him that the gentleman was related to his father's family and asked Richard to take Mr. Kabenge to Kasaka to meet Richard's paternal grandparents.

When Mr. Kabenge returned from Kasaka two days later, he called his son John to tell him about finding his long lost family. However, John's wife told him that John was out of the country to attend a conference and then meet with business associates. When he called his son Tom's home, Mr. Kabenge got the same answer from Tom's wife.

CHAPTER TWENTY-FOUR
Toronto, Canada, May 2012

"Somebody has been 'beeping' me since early this morning, but I cannot be bothered calling them back," Makula said to Pam as he got out of bed.

"Who else would it be other than your usual 'beepers,'" Pam said.

"And who are those?" Makula asked.

"Either your friend Kasede or your spoiled sister, Angela," Pam said.

"Well, I will not call back. If it's Angela, I will send her an e-mail," Makula said. Makula checked his cellphone and saw that indeed it had been Angela who had been "beeping" him.

Downstairs, Makula switched on his computer to read his e-mail. The first message was from Angela. Makula expected her usual request for money. Instead, Angela had written to let him know that Uncle Lameka had passed away the day before. Makula began to weep. Pam came over to ask him why he was crying. When he told her that his uncle had passed away, she too wept a little. He gathered himself together to reply to Angela's e-mail, thanking her for informing him. A few minutes later Makula received a phone call from Lukka, who was weeping sadly over the loss of his father. He told Makula that the family needed money from him before they could proceed with the burial arrangements.

After ending the call, Makula could only sit with a blank look on his face. He had no money to send for his uncle's burial. He picked up the phone and called a few of his friends in Toronto for help. When he spoke with Luku, Makula was greatly relieved when Luku said that he would help him "make some arrangements." Later that evening, Luku and Wabudi gave him three hundred dollars to send to Lukka.

During the vigil for Lameka that night in Kasaka, some inebriated men from Nanziba insulted and tormented Makula's family. "Now that Lameka is dead, I can't wait to see what kind of chaos is going to take place here. He was the glue in this family, but now he is gone," one man yelled.

"You are so proud of your rich brother who lives overseas. Where is he now? Why isn't he here? But you don't need us. He can come and take care of everything. You don't need our help," another said.

Toofa wanted to chase the men away but he was warned against it. Some people suspected that Senfuka may have sent the men to purposely disrupt the vigil.

***

In Toronto, after Luku and Wabudi had left, Makula grieved for his uncle. "I miss him so much, Pam," he wept. "I wish I could have gone to pay my last respects."

"I'm sorry for your loss, darling," Pam said. "Time heals, you know. You will recover after some time has passed."

"I feel bad when I remember that evening when my cousins came to ask me to take my uncle to hospital, and I was rude to them. I wish I could undo those events," Makula said through his tears.

"Don't feel sorry about that," Pam said. "Your cousins understood the pressure you were under in your life at that time."

"I hope so," Makula said, wiping the tears from his face.

Angela called and told Makula that she was in Kasaka. "Manjeri, my dear…" Makula began.

"It's Angela," she insisted.

"Sorry," Makula said. "Angela, my dear, tell me what you were doing when you received the news of the passing of our beloved uncle."

"It was kind of shocking. Like, I had just started my lunch and then I got a text message from Lukka saying that Uncle Lameka had died," Angela told him.

"It was a shock to me too when I read your message," Makula said.

"So my boyfriend and I went to the village, and it was true; like, he was dead," Angela said. "Last night, there were, like, so many people at the vigil."

"Is that so?" Makula said.

"There were, like, three hundred people there," Angela told him.

"What? How many people?" Makula asked.

"Like, three hundred," Angela repeated. "As in three zero zero."

"Wow," Makula said.

"And people were, like, 'Radio Uganda' is now off the air," Angela said sadly. "And there were some guys from Nanziba who were drunk. They became a problem. Like, they insulted Dad throughout the night and stuff. It was so embarrassing; my boyfriend wanted us to drive back to Kampala."

"Did anyone know who they were?" Makula asked.

"It's kind of weird, but, like, everyone was saying that that man Senfuka had hired them to harass the family. And…"

Their connection was interrupted and they were cut off.

"Who were you talking to?" Pam asked when he was off the phone.

"Manjeri—sorry—Angela," Makula replied.

"What did she say?" Pam asked.

"I didn't understand most of what she said. You know these young people," Makula replied, not wanting to bore her with the details.

***

After the funeral for Uncle Lameka, some members of his family wondered why Senfuka had come to the service. They said that it looked as if he had come only to mock them. "He stood there looking indifferent and disinterested, with his hands folded close to his chest," Makko said.

"How could you even see how he looked? I wonder why he wore those dark sunglasses on a cloudy day such as this," Lukka said angrily.

As they discussed Senfuka and the chaos that "his people" had allegedly caused at the vigil, Makko's telephone rang. It was Makula. Makko stepped away from the crowd and talked at length with Makula. He told him that the family needed him in Kasaka as there were many issues to be dealt with, especially that of land. Before he ended the call, Makula noticed that Makko, who normally expressed his gratitude, hadn't thanked him for the money he had contributed. He therefore mentioned the three hundred dollars that he had sent to Lukka to help with the cost of the funeral. Makko was surprised. He told Makula that Lukka had not said anything about the money and that their "new" rich relative, James Kabenge, had paid for the entire funeral, including the big reception for the mourners.

After speaking to Makula, Makko, furious, went straight to Lukka. He said, "Lukka, tell me here and now before everyone what you did with the money that Makula sent."

"What are you talking about?" Lukka replied, as he got up and left the group. Several young men tried to follow him, but Othieno stopped them. From Lukka's reaction, it was obvious to Othieno that Lukka had received the money. Othieno led the two brothers to the back of Makula's unfinished house, where Lukka admitted that he had received money from Makula. He also vowed that he had not spent any of it. Othieno told them to avoid a fight over the money, Lukka was to hand it over to their Uncle Filipo, and that Lukka was not to return to his home that evening until he had done so.

The following week, for the first time, Senfuka went to Filipo and Kabejja's home to visit with them. He told them that he was there to express his condolences to Filipo for the loss of his beloved elder brother. Both Filipo and Kabejja were glad to see Senfuka. Kabejja told Senfuka that Makula would be happy to know that he had paid a visit to his parents and that she was sure that Makula would pay a similar visit to Senfuka's parents the next time he visited Kasaka.

"I too am glad for having had this opportunity to come here to see you," Senfuka said.

Filipo took Senfuka on a tour of the new, incomplete house that Makula had begun constructing but had abandoned due to a lack of money. He told Senfuka that they hoped to move in within a year's time. Senfuka said that the house was very beautiful and asked Filipo to let him know if they needed any assistance to complete it. Filipo didn't hesitate to ask for his help.

While Filipo and Senfuka toured the new house, Kabejja wondered why so many of the people of Kasaka thought Senfuka was a bad person. She had found him to be soft-spoken, respectful, and a good listener.

Senfuka's car was parked in their front yard. And while Senfuka chatted with Makula's parents and toured the new house, his driver, Batte, spoke in a muted voice with Othieno and Kasede. "I find your boss to be a changed man," Othieno said. "Who would have imagined even a month ago that Senfuka would come here to pay a visit to Makula's parents?"

"I will tell you a secret," Batte said. "Senfuka has not changed in any way. If anything, he's worse. He is up to something here. You know very well, Othieno, that I am not just his driver; I am also his relative, but I don't like the way he treats me. If I had another job to go to, I would quit this one. There are times when that man leaves me in the car thirsty and hungry while he enjoys lunch with his business partners or girlfriends, when he knows full well that I haven't eaten a thing since morning. And that is not all…"

Batte stopped speaking when Senfuka came into the yard. Filipo, right behind him, was wearing a big smile. Given that Filipo had been very stressed for most of the week, both Kasede and Othieno wondered why he was so happy now.

Batte rushed to open the back door of the car for Senfuka, then started the car. As they drove away, Filipo said to Batte, "See you later." Kasede and Othieno wondered what Filipo had meant by this but they did not have the courage to ask.

After Senfuka had left, Othieno talked briefly to Filipo and then went home. Kasede returned to the small dwelling, built to house himself and the builders while they constructed Makula's house, in which he still lived. He changed his shirt, and then went to the late Lameka's house to drink.

About an hour later, Senfuka's driver, Batte, returned along with another man. As soon as the car pulled into the front yard, Filipo came out of his house to welcome them. The man that had come with Batte measured the front door, the back door, the two windows in the living room, and the two windows in one of the six bedrooms, noting each measurement on a piece of paper. When he had finished, he shook hands with Filipo, and then he and Batte left.

Kabejja told Filipo that she was pleased that Senfuka had come to pay them a visit and surprised that, contrary to reports, he seemed to be a good man. Filipo said that he too was surprised to find that Senfuka was both respectful and generous. He told Kabejja that Senfuka had invited him to lunch at his home in Nanziba and that he was looking forward to it.

When Kasede returned home just before sunset, Kabejja called him aside and said, "Ben, I have good news. That gentleman who was here earlier is Senfuka, Makula's friend." Kasede discreetly rolled his eyes at this. Having worked in the head office of Senfuka's company, Food Basket Limited, for a few months, he knew that Makula and Senfuka were anything but friends. "Mr. Senfuka has generously donated the main door to the house, the back door, and four windows. We will be able to move into that house as early as next month," Kabejja told him. She was unaware that Kasede knew Senfuka well and did not suspect that Senfuka had ulterior motives.

Kabejja was therefore shocked by Kasede's reaction. He seemed very annoyed and walked away without responding. Kasede went into his house, picked up his phone, and then went into the backyard to make a call.

"Are you sure about this, Ben?" Makula asked when Kasede told him about Senfuka's donation.

"Yes, I'm sure," Kasede said. "Senfuka came, toured the house with your father, then left. Othieno and I wondered why your father seemed to be so very happy all of a sudden. Your mother just told me that Senfuka has donated two doors and four windows."

Makula was angry that his arch-enemy and long-time rival had donated materials for his unfinished house. He told Kasede that he would get back to him.

Two days after Senfuka's visit to his home, Filipo rode his bicycle to Senfuka's house in Nanziba. He felt important and respected when Senfuka received him in his large living room. After they had lunched together, Senfuka told Filipo that he wished to buy some of his land on which to dig fish ponds. Filipo explained that he could not immediately respond to Senfuka's proposal. He told him that he would first have to consult with his son, Makula. Senfuka did not know that his driver Batte had overheard the entire conversation—that he was eavesdropping in the next room. That evening, Batte told Othieno that he had information to "pass on" to Makula.

A few days later, as she was preparing to go to the field to bring her two goats home from pasture, Kabejja saw Linda's car pull into the front yard. And no sooner had the car stopped than Makula emerged and started walking toward the house. Kabejja, excited and happy with his unexpected visit, greeted Makula with a wide smile and open arms to hug him. Makula, however, seemed very annoyed and greeted her coldly. Othieno, who had seen Makula go by his house in the car, saved Kabejja from this embarrassing moment by stepping forward to greet Makula. As someone who knew the history of Makula and Senfuka's relationship, Othieno understood Makula's anger. Not long after, Filipo came home, and Makula, who had calmed down a little, agreed to sit with both his parents and Othieno as Othieno warned them about dealing with Senfuka.

"Senfuka's driver told me that Senfuka is up to something. It wouldn't be wise to let him install the doors and windows in the new house," Othieno said.

"And where did he get the idea that I need his assistance?" Makula asked angrily.

Filipo was not convinced that Senfuka had bad intentions, but he did not voice his doubts. He thought that Senfuka was only being a "good son" of the area and that he was trying to mend his relationship with Filipo's family. Othieno, meanwhile, suggested that Makula meet with Batte, who had told him that he had more information, and gave Makula Batte's phone number.

Makula spent a week in Kasaka as he waited for the right opportunity to talk with Senfuka's driver. He also wanted to meet Senfuka to "blast" him for attempting to encroach on his property, but Othieno advised against it, saying that Senfuka was notorious for humiliating people.

Over the weekend, Makula finally met with Batte, who told him that Senfuka was obsessed with buying Filipo's land. "Senfuka thinks that I don't understand English," he told Makula. "So, whenever he has some secret deals to discuss, he does so in English. One day he sat in the back seat with a man I had never seen before. When I saw this, I knew right away that this was a very important matter because Senfuka never shares the back seat with anyone, not even his wife. The man showed him papers that he claimed were from the 1950s. The papers showed that there was a high possibility that there is gold underneath your father's land, where your farm market once stood."

"And Senfuka believed that crap?" Makula asked.

"When Senfuka said that he doubted that there was gold there," Batte continued, "the man added that it was only a possibility. If there were no gold, Senfuka would not lose a thing because land does not lose value. He told him that if the land were not useful to Senfuka, it would be useful to his grandchildren or great grandchildren."

"Son of a… Sorry for swearing," Makula said. "Did Senfuka pay for that information?"

"No, he did not pay then and there but he must have paid later," Batte replied. "However, Senfuka has spoken to your father about purchasing some of his land but he didn't tell him the truth about why he wants to buy it. He told Filipo that he wants the land for its proximity to the swamp because it would be easy for him to dig fish ponds. You know Senfuka makes a lot of money from exporting fish."

"He will never get an inch of that land as long as I live," Makula said, as he handed fifty thousand shillings to Senfuka's driver.

The following day, Makula toured his former school in Kasaka with his son Richard. He was very impressed with the work that the group of volunteers had done, mostly with Senfuka's assistance. And it was this assistance from Senfuka that annoyed Makula. He told Richard that what he had done was good enough and that they should return together to Toronto. Richard, though, said that he had to honour his commitment to stay for six months, and Makula did not insist.

Before he left Kasaka, Makula met with Othieno on the land that Senfuka coveted. He saw that Othieno and Filipo had cleared part of the land, which he thought they were going to use to resume farming. After all, he had told Othieno that Kasaka would never attract tourists and assumed that Othieno had abandoned the plan for building a tourist resort. He complimented Othieno on their efforts and asked what they were going to plant.

But Othieno had not given up on his plan. "We are not clearing the land for farming, Makula," Othieno said. "Remember that tourist resort that I told you about? We are hoping that we can find an investor to construct it. The investor would lease the land for fifty years, so we would make money now through rent, and your grandchildren would repossess the resort after the fifty years had passed."

"That's a crazy idea; investments don't operate like that. Mr. Othieno, you are a grown man. I can't believe you are counting your chickens before they hatch," Makula said.

***

When he returned from his journey overseas, and after learning that his father had called twice to talk to him, John Kabenge went to visit his father. After their initial greeting, James Kabenge told John that he had met with long lost members of their family whose descendants had settled in Kasaka. "When I went to meet them in Kasaka, they were happy to see me," Mr. Kabenge told his son. "I spent the whole day with them, and we had lunch together. The only sad note was that my eldest cousin, Lameka, was very sick. I actually took him to Mulago Hospital, where he died just three weeks ago. But my younger cousin, Filipo, who is Makula's father, is alive and well."

John was shocked to learn that Makula Musoke was his second cousin and felt remorse for the way that both he and his brother Tom had treated Makula over the years. And after learning that Makula was a relative, John did not stay long with his father; he hurried to contact his editor to remove a photograph from that week's edition of his tabloid, *Informed Pages*. "Make sure that the picture doesn't go to print," he told his editor, a former classmate who also knew Makula. "I'm withdrawing both it and the story."

"It's too late, boss," the editor said.

"What do you mean it's too late?" John asked.

"The paper is already on the streets," the editor informed him.

"All right, then," John said. "But pull it from the online edition right away."

When Paul Mugisha saw Makula's photo in the print edition, he called John Kabenge to rebuke him for having used his friend's picture in such a humiliating way. "Just how far will you guys go to humiliate Makula? Why don't you leave him alone?" Mugisha asked.

"Paul, I'm really sorry about this whole thing," Kabenge said. Even though he had initially authorized its publication, he continued, "In fact, as we speak, I have assigned two guys to investigate by whom, when and where this picture was taken."

"You may be sorry, but the damage has already been done. There is nothing you can do to salvage Makula's reputation. I think you went too far this time. This must stop," Mugisha said.

"Paul, please forgive me," Kabenge pleaded. "And by the way, I don't have Makula's phone number. Could you give it to me? I would like to apologize to him personally, because I know he has probably already seen the story on the Internet. I also have something very important to tell him. And, if you speak to him before I do, please send my apologies," Kabenge said.

***

When he returned to Toronto from Kasaka, Makula spent a few days at home thinking about his financial difficulties and the enormous problems that were likely to befall his extended family with the death of his Uncle Lameka. He then met with Craig Lewis, who advised him to begin to physically drop off job applications at companies where he wanted to apply since his e-mail applications had not yielded any interviews. Makula put copies of his résumé and cover letter in envelopes, and each morning of the following week, he took the subway to various offices in Toronto and dropped them off. Whoever saw him going out every morning so well dressed might have thought that he had found a new job.

By Friday of that week, Makula had no money left, and Pam gave him forty dollars to get him through the next couple of days. And after dropping off his résumé at several companies, he felt hungry and had an urge for one of his favourite burgers. He headed to Burger King, where he overheard three women discussing the story in the *Toronto Star* about Pietro Monterissi's bankruptcy.

While he enjoyed his burger, his friend Wabudi had called him to tell him that John Kabenge had published a demeaning picture of Makula at work in his tabloid, *Informed Pages*. Given the events of the day, Makula was glad to have dinner with his friends Luku and Wabudi at a new restaurant, Uncle Lee's, on his first "boys' night out" of the year. After dinner, he left early, leaving his two friends to continue with their evening.

On the subway, Makula gave up his seat to an elderly woman and looked out at the platform. He saw that he had been so lost in thought that he had missed his stop. He squeezed himself through the closing doors and crossed the station to take the northbound train home.

CHAPTER TWENTY-FIVE
Toronto, Canada, June 2012

"Honey, I have two pieces of news. One is ironic, the other is annoying," Makula said to Pam as he arrived home that evening.

"Why don't you tell me the ironic news first?" Pam asked.

"This afternoon as I waited in line to order my lunch at Burger King, I saw three women who had a copy of the *Toronto Star* spread out on their table. They were talking and laughing about Pietro Monterissi…" Makula answered.

"Why? What about Monterissi?" Pam asked.

"Well, he filed for bankruptcy. The story is in today's *Toronto Star*," Makula said.

"What? Our financial adviser filed for bankruptcy?" Pam asked.

"Yes," Makula confirmed. "And can you believe he gave us advice when he had financial problems similar to ours?"

"There must be a good reason for him filing for bankruptcy. That's sad. He is such a good man," Pam said. "Our copy of the *Toronto Star* is on the dining table, but I haven't yet read it. Go look for the story."

Makula opened the newspaper and didn't search long before he saw the headline: "Financial guru files for bankruptcy." He called Pam into the dining room and read the story aloud. According to it, the famous financial adviser and beloved TV personality had filed for bankruptcy after going through a nasty divorce from his wife of twenty-five years.

"That explains it. Poor guy. I feel so sorry for him," Pam said, heading back to the kitchen.

"Honey, come here," Makula said. "Remember I told you that I had two pieces of news?"

"Oh, yeah," Pam said as she again sat down. "What's the other news?"

Makula pulled his iPhone out of his pocket and said, "There is a very annoying article in a tabloid called *Informed Pages*. It is owned by John Kabenge. It is printed in Kampala but there's also an online version."

Makula browsed informedpages.com for the offensive article and handed his iPhone to Pam. When she saw the title of the article, "African professionals in the diaspora. Is it always worth it?" she asked, "What's this about?"

"Scroll down. You will see the picture," Makula told her.

"What is this?" Pam asked. "Is this you?"

"Yes. Kabenge chose a photograph of me to illustrate the story about people who are not clever enough to keep their well-paid jobs in Africa; those who opt to do menial jobs in the developed world," Makula said.

"He is so pathetic," Pam said, as she handed the iPhone back to Makula and walked away.

"Aren't you interested in reading the story?" Makula asked.

"No, I'm not interested in it," Pam replied.

That night, Makula did not sleep at all. He spent most of the night on his computer searching for job openings and sending résumés. He didn't care if the recipients saw that he was e-mailing them at two o'clock in the morning. He sent at least twenty of them for jobs ranging from entry-level customer service to executive positions.

The following morning, Makula received an e-mail from Senfuka, who, on his most recent visit to Kasaka, had been told that Makula was penniless and without a job. Senfuka had deliberately copied Chris Luku on the e-mail just to annoy Makula. In the message, he said that he was sorry for Makula's loss of his uncle. He then went on to say that he knew that Makula was going through a tough time financially and that he was willing to help. "My brother, Makula," he wrote. "If you want, I can hire you to manage any one of my companies. You can choose which one, and I will pay you the same amount of money that you were making before you were sacked, laid off, retrenched, or whatever."

Makula lost his temper when he read Senfuka's e-mail and he decided to write to Luku to explain what was going on. "Hey, Chris, I guess you received that lunatic's e-mail. Even though I no longer have money and can't afford to pay my mortgage anymore, I can't work for him. On the other hand, though, I don't feel comfortable here. I feel like a fish out of water. If I had a way, I would return to Kasaka where I belong." He clicked "Reply all."

Senfuka wrote back immediately. "Yes, my brother Makula, I may be a lunatic, but this is exactly what I am talking about. Work for me and your entire mortgage will be paid off, all at once if you want. "

Makula shut off his computer. His cellphone rang. It was Luku. "Mak, I just read your e-mail. What's the matter with you?" Luku asked.

"Chris, I still don't know how I am going to manage without a proper job," Makula replied.

"All I can advise is for you to continue being patient. Things will work out one way or the other. Don't worry."

"I'm trying not to worry, but I think I'm running out of patience. If I don't find a better job within a month, we will lose this house. Our situation is that bad."

"Have you considered downsizing? I think that would be your best choice, given the present circumstances."

"Yes, I have considered it, but Pam doesn't support the idea. She thinks that we should wait for a little while because the situation still might improve. I think she is more optimistic than I am."

"What about that idea of returning to Kasaka?"

"Listen, Chris. I never intended to leave the village in the first place. I only left because I married Pam and living in Kasaka was unthinkable. I really miss it. I wish I could go back there."

"Mak, I have another call. I'll call you back later."

"All right, Chris. Talk to you soon."

Makula put his cellphone on the dining room table and went upstairs to shower. After his shower, he lay down on the bed, and since he had been awake the entire night, he soon fell asleep. Later, his cellphone rang but he could not hear it. He was in a deep sleep.

Meanwhile, Pam, who was getting ready to go out later that morning, stopped to read a text message she had received. In the message, Tom Kabenge told her that he was visiting Toronto. She wondered how he had gotten her cellphone number. She chose a flattering outfit and applied her makeup. She then asked Dawn to let her father know that she would be meeting her friend Peggy later that afternoon for a "girls' night out."

As she was getting into her car, her cellphone rang. It was Tom Kabenge. He told her that he was staying at the Prince Silvan Hotel in downtown Toronto, and Pam decided to meet with him. She drove downtown and found a parking spot on a nearby street. She inserted her credit card into the parking ticket meter, but her payment was declined. Her credit card payment was declined. She tried three other credit cards but they too were all declined. Frustrated, she went back to her car and poured the contents of her handbag onto the seat. She counted out four dollars in change, enough to park for half an hour. She put the money in the meter, put the ticket on the dashboard, and walked briskly to the hotel.

She told the person at the reception desk that she was there to see one of their guests, named Tom Kabenge, and asked her to please telephone his room and let him know she was there.

"A lady is here to see you," the receptionist said when Kabenge picked up the phone.

"Who is it?" Kabenge asked.

"What's your name?" the receptionist asked Pam.

"It's Pam," Pam replied.

"Pam," the receptionist said to Kabenge over the phone.

"Here you go," the receptionist said, handing the phone to Pam.

"Pam, darling, can you come upstairs? It's room 625,"
Kabenge said.

***

Makula woke up some three hours later and went downstairs. He checked his cellphone and saw that he had a new voice message. When he entered his password and began to listen, he realized that what he was hearing was a conversation between Luku and his wife, Peggy. Luku must have accidentally dialled Makula and not realized that the call had gone through.

"Just because Pam was in the hotel lobby with Kabenge doesn't mean she did anything naughty with him," Luku said.

"I don't think so, either. Besides, Pam is a very upright person; she wouldn't do anything that would jeopardize her marriage," Peggy said.

"I just wonder why she went to the hotel to see Kabenge in the first place. We all know how cunning that man is. And of all people, Pam knows that," Luku said.

Makula could not bear to listen to the rest of the conversation. He threw his cellphone to the floor in a rage.

When Pam left the hotel and walked toward her car, she spotted a yellow parking ticket tucked under her windshield wiper. She knew she was at least an hour past the time she had paid for, and was annoyed to read that the fine was forty dollars. When she started the car, she saw the "Low Fuel" light come on. It had appeared while she had still been kilometres from the hotel and she was surprised to find the car had even started. She drove to the nearest gas station, one block south of the hotel, and put in twenty dollars' worth of gas. When she went inside to pay, she gave the attendant each of her three debit cards but all were rejected for not having sufficient funds. She noticed that a queue was forming behind her, and she asked the attendant to cancel her transaction and take care of the other customers. She had one more debit card to try that she hoped would rescue her. She stood there, uncomfortable, as the last man in the queue ogled her. "If I were a 'bad girl,'" she thought to herself, "I would ask this fellow to pay for my gas." When the clerk had dealt with all the other customers, Pam presented her last debit card. But it too was rejected. She told the clerk that she would be back and walked away from the gas station, leaving her car in the lot.

Pam thought of calling her friend Peggy to help her out, but she was too embarrassed by her situation. She decided to call Bashir, a cab driver whom she had known for years.

The phone rang once, and someone said, "55.3 Express FM."

"Hello," Pam said and started to apologize for having dialled the wrong number.

The radio disc jockey said, "Hello, you are a very lucky caller! All you have to do is answer question number ten for your chance to win five hundred dollars in cash and a pair of tickets to the *Black Eyed Peas* concert. The previous caller Tasha did the heavy lifting for you. What's your name?"

"Hello, my name is Pam," Pam said, wondering if she would be able to answer the question.

"Hello, Pam. Here is the final question. Are you ready?"

"Yes I am," she answered, giggling.

"You have ten seconds. Okay, here it is. 'The former president of which country was portrayed in the movie *The Last King of Scotland*?'"

"Uganda!" Pam yelled. "That's where I'm from!"

"Is that so? Well, congratulations, Pam! You have just won yourself five hundred dollars in cash and a pair of tickets to the *Black Eyed Peas* concert! Are you a fan of the *Black Eyed Peas*?"

"Yes, I am."

"That's great. Thanks for calling 55.3 Express FM. Please stay on the line," said the disc jockey as he went to a commercial break.

"Congratulations, Pam. You can pick up your winnings at our station."

"Could you please give me directions?" Pam asked.

"We are located right across from the Prince Silvan Hotel in the tall, dark brown building. You can't miss it. We're on the fourth floor."

"Thank you very much," Pam said.

"And hey, Pam, before I let you go," the disc jockey said, "we need to agree on a password that will allow you to claim your winnings. What word would you like to use?"

"Let's use 'Dawn'; D-A-W-N," she said, spelling it out for him. "It's my daughter's name."

"All right, Pam. When will we see you at the station?" he asked.

"I will come right away. I'm actually in the neighbourhood," Pam told him.

"Okay. Come over in about half an hour, at the end of the show. See you in a bit," he said.

***

After leaving the radio station with her winnings, Pam picked up her car and drove home to share her exciting news. However, as soon as she walked through the front door, Makula, who had been waiting for her, yelled, "Where have you been?"

"Why are you talking to me like that?" she asked.

"I want you to answer my question. Where have you been?" Makula demanded.

Pam was shocked. She had never seen Makula so angry. She put her handbag down and stood facing him.

"Listen, honey…" she began.

"Answer my question, or you will suffer the consequences," he said.

"Why don't you calm down, and tell me what's wrong?" she asked.

"Mum, Dad, can you guys turn down the volume? I am trying to watch some TV," Dawn said, closing the door to the family room.

Having heard his mother's voice, Daniel came into the living room to hug her. And at that moment the doorbell rang. "I'll get it," Makula spat out as he walked to the door and opened it. Two teenage boys stood in the doorway. "Good afternoon sir. We are raising some funds…"

"Get lost!" Makula yelled as he slammed the door. The boys stood there for a moment, terrified, before leaving.

Makula picked up his car keys from the table in the living room and left. He drove away in a rage.

Furious and lost in thought, he almost drove through a red light. He headed straight to his favourite fast-food restaurant, the Burger King. He sat down for a minute, and then called his friend Luku.

"Chris, I need to talk to you now," Makula said. "Can we meet?"

"We just talked this morning. Are you all right?" Luku asked, puzzled.

"No, I am not all right. I would like to talk to you. It's urgent," Makula replied.

"Where are you?" Luku asked.

"I am at the Burger King," Makula answered.

"Okay. I will be there in half an hour," Luku said and ended the call.

One of the workers at the restaurant, who recognized Makula as a regular customer, stopped mopping the floor and came over to the table where Makula was seated. "Hey, what's up, buddy?" he said.

"Nothing much, man," Makula said without looking up. Seeing that Makula was not in his usual cheerful mood, the worker walked away and returned to his mopping.

When Luku arrived at the Burger King, he saw Makula seated at a table next to the window. He looked pensive, and Luku wondered what the trouble was. He walked over to Makula and tapped him on the shoulder, and Makula jumped, his body tight with worry and anger.

"What's the matter, Mak?" Luku asked. "What's wrong?"

"Is there anything you would like to tell me, Chris?" Makula asked.

"I thought you called to tell me something," Luku replied. "Would you like to have something to eat?"

"No, I'm fine. I won't be eating," Makula told him. Luku now knew for certain that Makula was truly upset; he had never seen Makula not want to eat at the Burger King. Luku told Makula that he wanted to get some food before they talked further and got up to order a Double Whopper, medium fries, and pop. He came back with his tray and sat across from Makula.

"Mak, you look terrible. What's the matter?" Luku asked before biting into his burger.

"I thought you could tell me what's wrong," Makula answered.

"Tell you what's wrong? Come on," Luku said.

"Do you know anything new about Kabenge and Pam?" Makula asked.

"What are you talking about?" Luku asked, as his heart began to race. He placed his burger back on the tray.

"Listen to this," Makula said and played the recording of Luku and Peggy's conversation on his phone.

Luku listened for a few seconds, and then said, "Oh, Mak, I had no idea that my phone was on. I can't believe this. I'm so sorry…"

"No, it's not your fault," Makula said. "It is best that I know. I shouldn't have trusted Pam. It's all my fault."

"Listen, Mak," Luku said. "Why shouldn't she speak with an acquaintance in a hotel lobby?"

"Chris, you and I know that Tom is more than just an acquaintance to Pam…" Makula said.

"True, but did you ask Pam why she met with Tom?" Luku asked.

"No, I didn't," Makula answered.

"If I were you, the first thing I would do would be to get the details from Pam about her meeting," Luku said.

"I guess you are right," Makula said, embarrassed. "Should I call her?"

"No. Calm down, go home, and wait for the right time to speak with her. It is never good to jump to conclusions before you know the facts," Luku said.

"Thanks so much, Chris. I feel much better now," Makula said. He had demanded to know where Pam had been and she had not told him, but he realized that his tone must have shocked and frightened her.

"Would you like to eat now?" Luku asked.

"Yes, I'll have a Double Whopper," Makula answered.

Luku pulled out a twenty dollar bill from his pocket and handed it to Makula who went up to the counter to order his food. "How did you find out that Pam went to meet Kabenge?" Makula asked as he placed his tray on the table and sat down.

"My neighbour told us…" Luku said.

"What? Your neighbour?" Makula exclaimed.

"Yes," Luku continued. "My neighbour Assumpta is a good friend of ours, and she knows Pam well since Pam is often at our home. So our neighbour had just ended her shift at the Prince Silvan Hotel when she saw Pam seated on a couch in the lobby talking to a man. She quite innocently mentioned it to us. But then last night, after you had left the restaurant to go home, Tom Kabenge called Nick to tell him that he was in town and staying at the Prince Silvan."

"That makes sense now," Makula said.

"Sorry, but Peggy got too nosy. When our neighbour told us that she had seen Pam in the hotel lobby, she asked her, though not in a manner that would raise her suspicions, to describe the man whom Pam had been talking with because we already knew that Kabenge was staying there. Because of her description, we knew it was him. But, see, this is exactly what I was saying to you about this new technology—my cellphone let me down. You got to hear a conversation that you were not meant to hear. I'm so sorry, Mak, for the mishap," Luku said.

"Don't worry, Chris. I have to apologize to Pam and then try to find out what happened," Makula said.

"Don't you trust her?" Luku asked.

"I trust her 110 percent," Makula said. "My anger was caused by my hatred for Tom, not my lack of trust in Pam."

"Trust is what matters," Luku responded. "And you know what? Nick found out that the woman in that picture with you in *Informed Pages* is Kabenge's mistress."

"Which woman?" Makula asked.

"The customer you were helping. You know, last evening, that picture may have been the talk of all the Old Boys of Musasa who are now in North America," Luku replied.

"That son of a…" Makula caught himself swearing. "Who does Tom think he is?"

***

When he returned home, Makula found Pam seated in front of the dressing mirror fixing her hair. He tried to hand her a bouquet of roses, but she told him to put it on the bed. When he realized that she was not in the mood to talk to him, he went downstairs and asked his son Daniel to join him in the backyard.

Half an hour later, Makula went back to the bedroom and apologized to Pam. She told him that she was ready to tell him the whole story and that there was nothing to be upset about. "The only thing I am sorry for is having gone to that hotel," she said. "Actually, if you had been awake, I would have told you that I had received a text message from Tom. I only went there to tell him that he and his brother John should just leave us alone." Hearing her say this made Makula feel good.

"So when I got to the hotel," Pam continued, "he asked me to go to his room, but I refused. I told him, 'No, I can't come to your room. Remember that I'm a married woman.' So he said that he had an important 'family' matter to share with me. When we spoke in the lobby, though, we ended up arguing about that story and the picture in John's tabloid for close to thirty minutes. He tried hard to excuse John, saying that he may not have seen the picture before it was printed. I told him that I hoped that that was going to be the last time that either of them disturbed our peace. And before he could tell me what the 'family matter' was, his cellphone rang. He told me that it was an important call from Pius Bitaro. I waited for nearly fifteen minutes while he talked on his phone, and then I noticed that I looked like someone who had nothing better to do. I just walked away. He didn't even have the courtesy to stop me. That guy is a jerk."

"You know what?" Makula said. "I think he wanted to tell you that he is my cousin."

"What? What do you mean?" Pam asked.

"Yes, we are second cousins. I don't know whether that is the correct term or not, but our grandfathers were brothers. My family found out only recently when Rick took James Kabenge to visit them just a few weeks before Uncle Lameka died," Makula told her.

"What?" Pam asked again. At that moment, Pam's cellphone rang. It was Peggy. Pam told Makula she would take the call and that they would continue their "very interesting" conversation about the Kabenges afterward. The conversation was a long one as Peggy apologized for having gossiped about Pam. When Makula noticed that Pam was losing her temper with Peggy, he left the room. He decided to take his usual "me time" walk that Mr. Lewis had recommended to him.

Makula walked around his neighbourhood and wondered whether any of the other homeowners faced foreclosure as he did. "You never know what is happening behind closed doors. You are not alone," Mr. Monterissi had told them during one of their consultations. Makula then went into the convenience store, and after greeting Idriss, placed his lottery ticket in the checker. He jumped with joy when he saw that he had won seventy-five thousand dollars. But wanting to be sure, he checked the figure again and realized that there were three more zeroes. His heart skipped. And for a split second he thought he was in a dream. He tried to compose himself, but he couldn't. He called Idriss over, who confirmed that he had indeed won seventy-five million dollars.

Pam was sweeping the deck in the backyard when she saw Makula running toward her with his hands in the air. She could see that he was very excited, but she had no idea why. When he reached her, he lifted her off her feet like he had done so many times early in their marriage. He then kissed her all over her face before he let her back down onto the deck.

"What's going on?" she asked, perplexed.

"I won the lotto! I hit the LottoMax jackpot!" he shouted.

Pam was very surprised because she hadn't known that Makula purchased lottery tickets. She thought that this was simply a joke that Makula was playing on her. And for a moment, she even thought that her husband was going berserk. "I didn't know you played the lottery, Mak," Pam said. "I wonder what else you do that I am not aware of. Are you really sure you won?"

"Yes, I won seventy-five million dollars! Here's a printout that Idriss gave me. You can go talk to him if you don't believe me," Makula said as he handed the printout to Pam.

"Wow, I can't believe this! Is this real? Am I dreaming?" Pam said as she scrutinized the little printout that bore the figure "$75,000,000."

"No, you are not dreaming! It's true. It's real life. Monterissi doesn't have to be bankrupt anymore. He's just got himself a job!" Makula said, jumping up and down with joy.

"I have never seen such a big jackpot announced here…" Pam said.

"Yeah, this is gonna be the biggest jackpot ever in Ontario, or even in Canada," Makula said as he did a few push-ups on the deck.

"Calm down," Pam said. "Go inside to cool down a bit." Pam followed Makula as he went into the family room. "Calm down.

Go take a nap. Then we can see what steps to take next. This is awesome!" Pam said as she too began jumping up and down excitedly, just like a child.

"Let me make two phone calls home before I take a nap," Makula said. "This is unbelievable."

The phone on the other end rang for a while before Richard answered. "Pick up buddy, pick up," Makula said. When his son answered, Makula told him, "Rick, I'm now in a position to help you to pursue your dreams. I hope you are going to be serious this time. Get on the plane and come back home now."

"Cool. That's nice to hear, Dad," Richard said. "Have you found another job that…"

"No. I now have all the money we need," Makula replied.

"Wait a minute. Where did you get the money from?" Richard asked.

"I won the lotto!" Makula exclaimed.

"What?" Richard asked, disbelieving.

"Yes, I won the lotto! I hit the jackpot and not just any jackpot; I won many millions of dollars!" Makula said excitedly.

"What? Oh my gosh. What? I can't believe this!" Richard said.

"Get on the plane. I guess you have a return ticket," Makula said, and ended the call.

He then made another. The phone rang twice, and then Kasede answered. "Ben, I won a big jackpot! We will be completing that house soon!" Makula said.

"What?" Kasede asked.

"Yes, I won the lotto! I won many millions of dollars! I am now richer than Senfuka, James Kabenge, Tom Kabenge, and John Kabenge combined!" Makula told him.

"What? Oh my goodness. What? I can't believe it!" Kasede said.